**THIS IS HIGH-TENSION
ADULT MATERIAL.**
Captain Blood maintains a level of such uncompromising frankness that, according to Mario Puzo, "it will set the standard for action fiction of the new decade."

Michael Blodgett's razor-sharp insights and acute sense of the macabre have created an anti-hero whose repressed rage causes him to walk the fine line between good and evil.

CAPTAIN BLOOD

Michael Blodgett
CAPTAIN BLOOD

Harmony Books/New York

Copyright © 1979 by Michael Blodgett; All rights reserved. No part of this book may be reproduced or transmitted in any form or by any means, electronic or mechanical, including photocopying, recording, or by any information storage and retrieval system, without permission in writing from the publisher.

Published by Harmony Books, a division of Crown Publishers, Inc., One Park Avenue, New York, New York 10016 and simultaneously in Canada by General Publishing Company Limited.

HARMONY BOOKS and colophon are trademarks of Crown Publishers, Inc.

Manufactured in the United States of America

Grateful acknowledgment to Open End Music for permission to reprint "Good Enough", © 1975 by Hall Music/Mojahanna Music, Divs. of Open End Music. All rights reserved; and to Queen Music, Ltd. for permission to reprint "We Are The Champions" by Freddy Mercury, © 1977 by Queen Music Ltd., controlled by Beechwood Music Corp. in the USA and Canada. All rights reserved.

This book was first published in hardcover by the Stonehill Publishing Company, New York.

Library of Congress Cataloging in Publication Data

Blodgett, Michael.
 Captain blood.

 I. Title.
PS3552.L6355C3 1982   813'.54   81-20157
ISBN 0-517-546698   AACR2

10 9 8 7 6 5 4 3 2 1

First Harmony Books Edition 1982

Contents

I

II

III

Doctor Blood saw his beautiful naked boy.
He asked where he came from.
    He said, "I come from God."
    "Where did you leave Him?"
    "In virtuous hearts."
    "Where are you going?"
    "To God."
    "Where do you find Him?"
    "Where I part with all creatures."
    "Who are you?"
    "A king."
    "Where is your kingdom?"
    "In my heart."
    "Take care that no one divide it with you!"
    "I shall."
Then he led him to the street.
    "Will you let the errors, crimes and injustices pass?"
    "Then I should be no king."
    And he disappeared. For it was God Himself—
Who was having a bit of fun.

I

Mrs. Pearlstein

Dreams never frightened him and he understood that this was a dream. The sobbing would come and go, and somehow that part seemed real. The rest of it was an exaggerated reaffirmation of what he knew to be the truth in this country today: elderly people, wandering the dark streets alone, homeless, with their empty palms turned upward, their hollow eyes filling you with guilt. At least it filled Captain Blood with guilt. He was impressed with their plight: to be old in America and have to scrounge pennies to live. Work all your life and save so that when your muscles give out and your joints get sore you can relax in some sort of peace—not in the U.S.A.

The old woman wailed again. He felt the ground rolling forward beneath him, and while suppressing a chill of vertigo, he looked down to find himself backing off of the earth.

"Rapists," Captain screamed, reeling and then gliding away, banging against his own disjointed appendages. He fell into a black hole, thinking that it wouldn't matter if there were plenty to go around or if the old geezers had it comfortable, but no, ram it to them, make them sweat, our mothers and fathers.

He turned over into an oblique cut of radiation that exploded brightly into his eyes and warmed the skin on his forehead. Then he felt hot, so he kicked the rest of the covers off and started coming up to reality.

Captain opened his eyes into the morning sun. He blinked against the light and sat up out of it. Stretching, he spoke over a yawn. "Jesus, what a way to wake up, like God himself was peeing in the window."

The walls of the little apartment were splashed with brilliant yellow, and the worn chocolate brown carpet was the color of saffron where the rays of the sun lighted. Nude, Captain went to the open window and inhaled. Not a cloud. It was the kind of day when nothing can go wrong. A day made in heaven for special people, he thought, scratching his light brown pubic hair and shivering. It was a day when a higher power takes charge, and your bladder.

On the way to the toilet, Captain slowed in front of the long hall mirror and gave himself an admiring stare. He thought that he looked clean and strong. His flushed penis hung heavily and looked thick, so he twisted the itching foreskin back and forth. He slapped his penis against his thigh. He guessed that it looked beautiful. Men and women were often jealous of his good looks, but that wasn't enough for him. Captain stared at his private area and wanted to be appreciated for having a big cock.

He wanted people to see him and nudge each other and point. For men to say "Lucky devil" or "I hate him"; for women to make excuses or break away from their cliques to come and stand next to him at the bar, to smile nervously and let him know with their eager eyes what they wanted of him.

4

He tightened his sphincter muscle and made it sway. "It is big, isn't it?" he asked himself. It sure wasn't as big as the porno star he'd seen with the fourteen inches. The entire audience in the theater had let out a gasp when he turned around for the first time. The fellow had a penis like a baseball bat. Captain couldn't believe his eyes. He felt something like fear and envy chase each other up and down his spine and remembered the only saving grace was that the actor was white. He leaned against the door-jamb, put the other hand on his hip and assumed a casual pose. He wondered if it would look bigger if it were black.

Last night's Scotch belched past his teeth and sent him into the john wincing. He hated Scotch; it made your breath smell. He only drank it when there was nothing else around or when he was desperate. Iris had sent her maid into town to clean up Captain's apartment the day before. The fresh towels and shiny porcelain made him feel orderly. He sat down on the cool toilet seat and touched his penis again to tuck it in.

Still not completely awake, but picturing the porno star, Captain heard himself chuckle while he finished urinating. He always sat to urinate except in public places. His father, the Doctor, had said it was "best . . . most relaxing . . . live longer." Sitting there, his bowels felt pursed, and it came to him that he might be there for awhile, so he bounced up off of the toilet and out to the front door to retrieve the morning paper.

There was nothing like sitting on the toilet with the newspaper and letting everything happen with ease. He unlatched the security chain and opened the door into the darkened hall. With a clear coast he darted out, grabbed the paper and jumped back into the apartment. Before he could close the door, there came a reminiscent sound from down the hall. He stood there for a time and listened.

It was softer now, but there was no doubt that it was the same sad lament that had disturbed his sleep. Sensing the direction from which it had come and knowing the tenants in the building and their hours helped him to associate the sorrowful sound with Mrs. Pearlstein. She lived across the hall and three apartments down in a single apartment the same size as Captain's.

He tried, but it was beyond him to conjure up an exact picture of the woman's face; he'd never paid any attention. He did know, however, that she was the older lady who remembered every occasion with a childish card in his mailbox, paid her rent when it was due and never made a complaint. She was also the one who dropped the empty gin bottles down the incinerator chute to make more work for the handyman. Captain only knew this because he had overheard Mrs. Pearlstein take delivery of a fifth of Squire's gin one Saturday, and that's what kept turning up broken in the ashes. After making the connection, he mulled it over and then told himself, "So what? She's old; she can do anything she wants."

Forgetting what he was doing and after a moment's indecision, he closed the door to say, "It's not right to worry like that on a day like today. If you're going to cry, you should do it while it rains. Poor old broad."

Captain went over and threw the bed up into the wall and closed the Indian drape over it. He pulled on a pair of navy blue shorts that were hanging off the end of a barbell, adjusted the supporter and walked barefoot onto the cool kitchen linoleum. He stopped and leaned against the wooden counter top that separated the tiny kitchen from the dining room. He felt his mood begin to change. He seemed to lose his concentration during these periods, so he didn't try to think. It was what he felt that lulled him to the next place anyway. It was as though he were seeing it all sitting atop his own shoulders.

Then, as they'd gone, his feelings came rushing back, and he became so excited that he couldn't stay still. His hands moved first, pouring two fingers of vodka into a water glass on the counter in front of him. "Good morning, God," he said and drank it down. "You old coot," he shuddered, "I'm coming." The alcohol was through his stomach lining and into his bloodstream instantaneously. Feeling heady but fast he went and returned with the newspaper and put it and the bottle of vodka under one arm. He popped the refrigerator, took out a can of cold ale and slammed the door with his foot. The can went under his other arm, leaving his hands free for the decanter of brandy for Mrs. Pearlstein—Ruth, Ruthie, Ruthie Pearlstein. That was it.

He stopped and surveyed the kitchen. Changing plans, he carefully put everything down on the sink board, rinsed his face several times with cold water and dried himself with a dishtowel. He went through two cupboards before he found the pretty long-stemmed glass he was looking for, gave it a rinse and somehow managed by twisting fingers and applying pressure properly to carry both bottles, the fancy glass, his water glass, the malt liquor and the newspaper out through his door and down the hall to Mrs. Pearlstein's door.

The sad sounds had stopped. He jiggled the door with his bare foot and offhandedly called, "Ruthie, it's Captain. I've got a surprise." If he hadn't been the building manager she probably wouldn't respond, and he knew that. He used his knee to rescue a sliding glass from a pinched finger. "Come on, come on, I've got my arms full and I brought you the paper." There was no reply. "Shit," he said to himself. "She probably wants to suffer. Leave her alone." He paused and listened—nothing. Trying to look through the enameled wooden door, he squinted and tried to imagine the unhappy creature living on the other side. Doesn't she know I'm out here to help, he wondered? "Hello, Ruthie," he said in his most salutary tone. Goddamn, she's got to be interested. Has she lost all the joy of expectation, all hope. It's a beautiful day and I'm bearing gifts. Maybe she's dead. An urge to kick the door off the hinges flooded him, and he decided that that's just what he was going to do if the door didn't open in one minute; or he could go get his master key—that was it—that's what he'd do. Suddenly he felt embarrassed and presumptuous. Jesus, he thought, I guess she's got a right to cry, to be alone with her problems. I'm probably way out of line. But I can swallow her rent for a while, if money's the problem. I can help her—she could be my own grandmother, "It's right to help you," he yelled, fingers numbing. How the hell can I help her if she won't help herself? "Hope—hope is here Mrs. Pearlstein. I've brought hope. Hell, I am hope," he laughed, and then the answer choked quickly back from the other side of the door in a most unladylike fashion:

"Hope is a whore," she complained.

Captain was stunned at first, but then he smiled. Not at the comment—he thought that was bullshit—but at the way she said it. Mrs. Pearlstein was saying that she was angry and that her melancholy was abating. But then she continued by saying, "Please go away. I don't want any help. Thank you, but go," this in a tearful tone again.

God, if she's so blown out, why doesn't she give it up, go to a home? Then she wouldn't have to worry about herself, she could join the kazoo band. Now he was teasing himself, trying to keep his ire up to pursue. That's it, the senior citizens' kazoo band. If things are so tough, so lonely, that's just the place.

He felt uncomfortable even thinking about it. Never in any mind of conscience would he let her or anyone go there. Doesn't she have any children? Where are the children?

His fingers were numbing, and he couldn't imagine Mrs. Ruth Pearlstein ending up old and alone in a single apartment in West

8

Los Angeles with some small means of support and not having been through a family. He figured that they were around but probably in hiding from the sight of wrinkling skin and senility, especially if there were physical resemblances. "Chicken shits," Captain yelled at the door without thinking. Now he really wanted the door open. Why is it that when I pray for tolerance, what I get is something to tolerate? he reflected, trying not to think about his lifeless fingers. He could yell, "I'm calling your family." He had no idea who that would be, but it might work. The manager always knows secrets. Instead he yelled, "Where are your people?" Then, without waiting for a response, he let his dander fly and said in a loud but even tone, "I'll tell you what, Ruthie, if you're tired of having your own bath, if you've lost the battle for your privacy, if you're finished, I will assist you in finding an old ladies home where—"

The chain dropped, the locks popped and Mrs. Pearlstein swung the door open so hard that she pulled it onto her slippered foot. She was red faced and fuming. Her intention had undoubtedly been to open with a barrage of abusive language, but jamming her toe sent her scurrying back into her apartment. She dropped onto the bouncy cushions of an overstuffed, doilied, purple wool davenport. Her tears were of frustration. She pulled her foot out of the skimpy slipper, rubbed her toe, slammed the back of the davenport with her open hand, stopped crying, said damn twice and went back to rubbing her toe. Captain walked in and put the things that he was carrying down onto the first flat surface he came to, which happened to be the front of an open desk. The air in the room was stuffy and smelled like cigarettes. And sure enough, they were there, the photographs—lots of pictures of a couple and their child, a little girl who apparently grew up and became the one with the cap and gown. Captain opened and closed his hands for circulation. Mrs. Pearlstein didn't move or look up. He went back to the door and shut it quietly.

She looked sixty-five. Her dyed, short-cropped, spray-netted hair fit around her head like a shiny black helmet. She self-consciously adjusted her lime green robe up to cover her left knee. She held her hand there, and that was where she fixed her eyes. Holding her robe fast, she slumped back against the bolster. Captain folded his arms but stayed still. His hands went into his armpits and became wet with perspiration. He let them stay. Mrs. Pearlstein appeared pathetic and not at all like he'd imagined, not like his grandmother.

The temptation to turn and leave came. "You're better now; see you later." Or, "Here, here's some brandy. Drink it, it'll make you feel better." Or, "Call me if you need me, I've got business."

Standing there, with his hands in his armpits, he suddenly felt awkward. He realized that he was grinding his teeth and shuffling his feet and stopped. He felt self-conscious and wondered what she was thinking. He watched her and decided that Mrs. Pearlstein really did look better, quiet and consoled, dry-eyed.

"Can I help you?" he asked.

She turned her black eyes on him and started a soft smile. The uneven skin on her cheeks suggested hellious teenage years. "You already have," she said. The proof of her statement twinkled in her eyes. He felt himself blush, and it felt good.

Mrs. Pearlstein took a package of Salem cigarettes and a gold gas lighter from her robe pocket. Avoiding Captain's stare, she lit up and inhaled deeply. She held it for the effect and exhaled. It seemed to relax her. "What are you going to do with all of that liquor?" she asked, smoking again.

God, he felt sorry for people who smoked. He knew that was one habit that would kill you. Come to think of it, her color didn't look too good. He bet it was due to smoking. He retrieved the can of ale from the desk, popped the top and drank half of it off. It bit his throat but tasted good. "I brought it for you—for us—to cheer us up."

"What's the matter with you, dear?" she asked, truly concerned. She continued looking at him but leaned over and rubbed her swollen ankles. The backs of her hands and the skin over her ankles matched with brown liver spots.

Captain let his eyes fall onto his own hands. They looked tan and strong. He made fists, and blue veins raised up and wiggled around under his skin. Looking away quickly, he belched before he could stop. "I'm sorry. And I was just kidding about being in a bad place. I just said it to make you feel better."

She looked miserable and said, "I understand, dear."

"Can I open the windows?" he asked.

"Certainly. Does the smoke bother you?"

"Sort of," he replied, moving to the curtains, which he pulled open. He went to all three of the windows in the small living room and opened them one after the other. Then he went to the dining nook and did the same.

She started to apologize for the mess the apartment was in, the ironing board being out and all, but Captain said, "Now that's better, isn't it. Isn't that better?"

Mrs. Pearlstein shrugged and smoked. She placed her ashes into a precariously balanced china ashtray at her elbow on the arm of the davenport. He poured the brandy into the fancy, long-stemmed glass and held the decanter up against the light to admire its color. He sniffed at the mouth of the glass.

"Now that, my good woman, is cognac for a queen."

She sipped the brandy and agreed. He poured vodka into the water glass, swallowed some and finished the beer. His intestines sent him a signal, and he answered yes, yes, I know—just a few more minutes. She finished the brandy without taking the glass

11

from her face and said in the most sheepish tone, "May I?" He handed her the bottle. She lit another cigarette. He looked away.

"You know, Ruthie, unless you're going to tell me that you have cancer or something that we can really drink to, I'm going to tell you that you're a pretty silly girl." He could see her fall on her face sobbing, screaming, "How did you know?" He hoped that her problem wasn't health.

Mrs. Pearlstein stopped what she was doing and looked down at her thinning carpet, then directly back at him and into his eyes. "I woke you, didn't I? I'll bet I woke you. I'm truly sorry. I've been to the store and back twice. I thought—"

"Forget it," he cut her off. "It's too late to sleep anyway."

Mrs. Pearlstein tried to straighten her legs out, but her robe fell open to her upper thigh. She closed it and looked away with a blush. "It was just silly, I suppose," she said.

"Whatever it was didn't seem silly to you." He got up and went into her kitchen, which was just like his but better equipped to cook in. He opened the small refrigerator. "Talk, I'm listening." He stretched a look back over his shoulder to see her lost in thought. The inside of Mrs. Pearlstein's refrigerator smelled and looked like a delicatessen display case. He never could understand how raw fish packed with sour cream or vinegar didn't spoil. People kept it and ate at it forever. He filled his glass with ice and settled for prune juice as mix.

"When I see you, you look so young and energetic and beautiful. And when I have this brandy, it all seems so foolish—everything. I mean, I try to take care of myself and handle things, but I never quite get used to being alone. It'll be four years right after the holidays." It didn't matter, but he supposed that she meant the Jewish holidays, one or another. "Ken was such a strong man; sometimes I'm just at a loss."

Captain leaned against the doorjamb of the dining nook and

mixed his drink with a finger. He liked the way she trusted him to have the run of her apartment. "Excuse me for wandering around. I'm listening. He was your husband, right?"

"Yes, he was my husband and what a man! But—but he worked himself to death. I always told him, 'Kenny, you work too hard, honey. Take some time off,' and he'd say, 'No, no, not now, when I retire, when I retire.' Three more years and he'd have made it."

The same old story. Work your ass off and die, he thought. He shook his head. "Aside from that, was he insured?"

"The answer to that one is a long story, dear. Suffice it to say that he had a partner and partnership insurance. It was his own brother and he was a crook. He handled all of the books. Does that answer your question?"

"No," he answered. "Didn't he make arrangements for you in case this happened?"

Her answer came in a familiar high wail, a whine. "No, no, there was nothing." She jumped up as though from a hot seat, knocking the ashtray onto the floor. She looked to be holding back a fit of hysteria when she clasped her hands over her face. All that she uttered, however, was "Oh." She stood there holding her face.

"How about your children?"

Mrs. Pearlstein threw her hands down stiffly at her sides and made white-knuckled fists. "She's married and lives in Washington. And that's my problem, my business. She calls every Sunday and—"

"All right, all right, take it easy." He went to her and put his hand on her shoulder. Her lime green robe was made of synthetics, and the odor of spray net ran even with burned tobacco. "I understand now," he said placatingly, "I understand."

Her eyes had become momentarily fixed on something behind

13

him, but she broke the gaze and looked quickly up into his face. "Oh, no, heavens, that isn't what I was bothered about." She looked at his drink. "What are you drinking?" she asked.

"Prune juice and vodka."

She started to laugh and fell back down onto the davenport. He anticipated trouble with the robe, but it settled correctly. "Oh, my," she sighed. "I've learned to put Ken out of my mind and to deal with my daughter. That's not my problem. It's the stupid iron, that's all—the straw that breaks your back. Prune juice— oh, my, that's a good one." She laughed some more. Her teeth looked mostly white, straight and healthy.

"Are you hungry, dear?" she finally asked.

"No . . . no, I'm fine." He sounded impatient. "Actually the prune juice tastes good for a change." He was looking at the steam iron and ironing board.

He walked to the iron and picked it up. "What's the matter with the iron? It looks new."

"It is." She came and presented him with a cold opened bottle of Giant Brazilian Green Olives. "The seeds are still in them and they are very very special. I'm going to have one of my special before-lunch martinis—up, with a drop of sherry instead of vermouth. I have some Squire's gin and two pretty, old-fashioned, cut-crystal glasses in the freezer. Not that I don't appreciate you bringing the brandy. It made me feel much better, but I think that you're what made me feel better. Please let me make you one of my martinis. I can't afford to do it regularly, but this is special today. You didn't come to visit me just because you manage the building, did you? Because you felt it was your duty? Oh, don't answer that. I'm sorry, I don't want to know. Do you like gin?"

"Yes, yes, I do, and one of your special martinis sounds good. But how about the iron?"

Mrs. Pearlstein didn't pay any attention. She was flitting

around as though she had a new beau and everything was suddenly special. She headed for the kitchen.

"When a man wants a drink he should have one I always say. One dry Squire's gin martini coming up."

"Goddammit, Ruthie, will you tell me why the new steam iron makes you cry?" He wanted to scream, "I've got things to do . . .," but didn't.

"For almost two months now I haven't had an iron that works. Mine broke down again, and the man who runs the electric shop on the corner says it's finally had it. So I've been watching the ads real good and finally I found a steam iron at Bloom's for eighteen dollars and seventy-nine cents, which seemed about the right price."

She brought the iced glasses out, dropped the olives in, gave the mixer a final stir and poured the martinis. Captain's mouth was watering so he didn't wait to taste. The sherry smoothed the sharp edge of the gin so that it went into his system without a sting. The iced gin made him warm immediately. Who gives a shit about the weather, he laughed to himself.

"Ruthie, this is the best. Where did you . . ."?

Mrs. Pearlstein raised her finger as if to scold him. She sipped, closed her eyes and swooned. Savoring, she slowly took in and let out her breath and went to sit down and smoke. "Kenny brought the secret back from France after the war. He called it our drink. I love the taste. Once you get used to it you'll never mix vermouth with gin again."

Mrs. Pearlstein put her cigarette out and got up as though she'd forgotten something. She opened the largest closet in the apartment, and dirty clothes bundled out onto the living room floor. She sighed and made a kicking gesture toward them. "I don't have an iron and I can't afford the cleaners. Where does that leave me? With this mess."

15

Captain looked at the iron on the board. Mrs. Pearlstein shook her head. "Broken. The darn thing is broken." She turned around and scooped and pushed the clothes back into the closet and tried to force the door, but it wouldn't shut. She finally let it fall open again and started to cry.

"Just don't kick the door again," he said, laughing and making light. He came to her and hesitated. Her head hung. He looked at the back of her neck. The skin was white and smooth, not old looking. There were two not unattractive cowlicks on either side of her neck just below her scalp. Her hair was black and fine against her pale skin. You've had your mouth on worse, he thought. He put one arm around her and hugged her. It was easy. Her bones felt soft and fragile.

He forced the closet door closed with his other hand until it clicked shut. He escorted Mrs. Pearlstein to the straight-backed antique chair in front of her desk and turned it around with his bare foot to accommodate her. He couldn't bring himself to touch her hair but rubbed her lower neck and shoulders while he sat her down. Reaching his hand, she squeezed it.

"Sit tight," he said. He brought back a handful of toilet paper from the bathroom, and she blew her nose and wiped her eyes.

"Don't I have any kleenex?"

"It's all the same," he said, putting her drink into her hands. He went to the iron, picked it up and examined it. "What's the matter with it?" he asked.

"It won't heat up. It's plugged in and it stays cold. I plugged it into another socket too—where the radio is—and it doesn't matter, it won't heat up. It's broken." She put her forehead on the heel of her hand and sighed.

"Well, take it back."

"I did. I took the bus all the way back down to Bloom's the second time, and they wouldn't take it back. They said it was my fault that it was broken."

"Is it?"

"No, it never turned on once for me. It never did work." Her voice began to crack again with frustration.

"Hey, Ruthie, drink your drink will you and let me take a look at this thing."

He wiggled the cord where it entered the iron. Stooping, he did the same thing where it was plugged into the wall. He played with the on switch and put the flat of his hand on the bottom of the iron. Nothing. Cold. He held it there and smiled at Mrs. Pearlstein, whose expression showed that she wanted it to work very much. She was hoping.

"Why did you say that about hope when I was banging on your door?"

"Kenny used to say that," she said, moving into the kitchen.

"Why?" Captain asked.

"Well, Kenny, he would catch me dreaming or telling Sarah made-up stories when she was a little girl, bless her heart." Mrs. Pearlstein came from the kitchen, filled both of their glasses, took out her cigarettes and lighter and stood over the spilled ashtray. After a moment she let the mess lay and sat down to use a new ashtray made of green marble. He liked her for that.

She sipped and smoked. "I used to tell her that she could be a ballet dancer if she wanted to be badly enough. She loved to dance, but Ken would say that we've worked hard for everything we've got, not dreamt about it. Hope will sell to anybody who will pay the price, he'd say. I guess he was right," she said, sighing.

Captain snapped at the side of the iron, "What was the price? What did it cost to get hope to put out, if you know what I mean? Do you understand what I'm asking?"

Mrs. Pearlstein dropped the olive pit into her ashtray and chomped away while she talked. "Yes, I understand. The price was to fall on your face from dreaming for things instead of

17

working for them. End up pretending you've got it instead of having it. That's right, you know.''

"What bullshit," Captain said, feeling contempt for the man Mrs. Pearlstein had married. He supposed him to have been the kind of dogged old guy who stuck to the old ways at the risk of his family's health. The kind of man who insists on a strict orthodox home life for his young, while they find modern literature in their schools and bebop on the streets. The culture doesn't budge and father won't, so the children remain unable to adjust until they develop ulcers on their colons and end up defecating into bags that hang from their sides. Of all the things he could have left his woman to remember, an attitude of anticipation, things that would uplift her spirit; but no, he left her to be practical and remember that hope is a whore. Captain wondered what kind of a man would envision expectation taking money for the deed. The asshole is better off dead, he thought.

Mrs. Pearlstein said, "Oh," in an intimidated way and changed the subject. She could see the iron sitting on his leg but asked the question anyway. "Will it work?"

"No, you're right, it's no good. Where is Sarah, Ruthie? Where is your daughter?"

Mrs. Pearlstein looked past him and became sad-faced. Then she was able to change her thought, smile thinly and meet his stare. "She's not well, dear. She has problems."

With a crack from his startled knees, Captain stood and replaced the iron on the ironing board. He stood still for a moment thinking; then he stretched and yawned. "I feel good. The gin makes everything all right," he said, smiling.

"Isn't everything all right with you, dear?"

"Oh, sure, I didn't mean it like that. It just helps to insulate me from my chores. I'll bet my answering service is holding twenty calls for me. I've got my phone turned off. If it's not one thing, it's another around this place."

"Do you like running the building?"

"No—Yes—Well—I don't like the thought of it; forty units is quite a responsibility. I'm not crazy about responsibility, but I don't do much. I mean, I decide what has to be done and farm it out, and I've got a handyman. It's something to do, though. It keeps my mind off of other things, other problems, that work themselves out if I stay out of the way." Captain sighed and continued. "Yes, I guess when it comes right down to it, I like to know that I have something to do and that I can't play all of the time. It helps me to feel that I've done something constructive. It helps me to sleep at night."

"Could you afford to play all of the time, dear?" she asked.

He was tempted to tell her about the trust fund: the ten thousand dollars a year, two hundred dollars each week left to him by his father, the check that arrived like clockwork on the first of every month from his uncle's law firm in Rochester, Minnesota. Not a fortune, but Doctor Blood hadn't wanted it to be. He had said it in the will. Ten thousand dollars a year to my beautiful son, Captain, so that the necessities of life should never be a problem. Captain almost told her that he didn't need to work. Then he thought that it would probably make her jealous.

"Would you, dear, if you could?"

"What?"

"Play all of the time."

"Yes, sure. But I'd have to watch out that I didn't become a drunk."

"Yes, I know. You've got to listen to the policeman up there."

"The policeman—up where?" he asked.

"Up here." Mrs. Pearlstein pointed to her forehead. "Up here, in your mind."

Shit, Captain thought, who would want a cop in your head.

Mrs. Pearlstein continued. "You've got to have him there

always. You can't forget him—or else." Captain almost asked, or else what? but Mrs. Pearlstein seemed so sure of the answer that it made him feel uneasy. Captain didn't want to hear and let the subject drop. "Who turned your phone off?" she finally asked.

"I did. I do it when I don't want to be bothered by the ring. But my answering service still picks it up. I'll bet I've got twenty calls sitting there."

"Speaking of the building, captain—I don't mean to bother you with this, but you know there's no hall light on the way down to the garages and—"

"I don't want to hear about that right now, Ruth. Any complaints you write down and put in my mail box, you know that."

"I'm sorry," she said. "I just thought—"

"That's all right." He finished his drink and smacked his lips. "Let's see about this damned iron." He went over, picked it up and looking at the bottom, spit on it. Unaffected, the spittle ran down the stainless steel and dripped off onto the pad of the ironing board. Nothing. He touched it all over, trying it first one way and then another. Holding it in his hand he said, "It's broken, any fool can see that. It just doesn't work."

"I know, but they won't take it back."

"What do you mean they won't take it back? They have to take it back if it never worked."

"I went all the way back in the bus with my receipt and everything, even spoke to the owner of the store, and what a frightening person he is. He said that they were all checked out when he bought them and that I must have done it, because it worked when it left the store." Reenacting fear and then disgusted, she finished her drink and headed for the kitchen.

"Wait a minute, Ruth. Did they test it down there?"

"No, they never took it out of the box."

20

"That doesn't seem right," he yelled after her. "What kind of place is it—Bloom's?"

"It doesn't say very much for me, I guess—my taste, my judgment—but I suppose you'd say it was a clip joint." Captain heard the oven open and tin foil stir.

"What frightened you about the owner? Did you say that the owner frightened you?"

Mrs. Pearlstein closed the oven and came to the doorway to stare at him in a serious mood. "Oh, cripes, Cappy, he was just frightening, that's all. Big and dark and hairy. He yelled at me." She looked down, embarrassed. "Made me cry."

"You're kidding. Was he the owner or just the manager?"

"Oh, no, he's the owner, all right. He's the owner. He's Mister Bloom. His name is Reno, Reno Bloom, and he's the owner." Mrs. Pearlstein began acting nervous. Perspiration showed on her upper lip and forehead. "He's the one who said it to me. He was so stern, and I cried. I suppose that it sounds silly but—"

"No, I understand and don't cry again. Some people are like that. It's no big deal. Do you have any idea what time it is, Ruthie?"

"I just looked in the kitchen—11:20."

"All right. It's a gorgeous day out, right?"

"Right."

"And we feel pretty good ourselves, right?"

"Right," she said hesitantly.

"Okay. This is what is going to happen, Ruthie. I want you to throw on some clothes, while I do the same. I'll get my car, put the top down, meet you in front, and we'll go get the iron problem handled. And we'll get some sun along the way. Now how does that sound?"

Mrs. Pearlstein put her hand up to the cheek of her surprised face. She stood still and stared into his eyes. "No, no, I couldn't let you. Oh, no. And besides, Mister Bloom, he said—"

"Never mind what Reno Bloom said. I can be pretty frightening myself. Forget him. Well, what do you say?"

Mrs. Pearlstein had become contemplative. "I am very much taken, Captain," she said, "but I'm not too proud to say yes. Yes dear, that sounds just—well—nothing could sound better."

"That's good. And if you're a good girl, I might consider stopping along the way to introduce you to a bartender friend of mine."

Preoccupied, Mrs. Pearlstein ran into the bathroom, opened the glass shower door and turned on the shower. Over the splash she questioned, "How long do I have?"

"Fifteen minutes to meet me in front."

Hurrying, she said, "Turn the oven down." She shut the hall door in his face. He set the oven on low, straightened out a few things in the kitchen, looked both ways out of habit, took a slug of warm Squire's gin from the square, dark green bottle, shivered it down and gobbled another Brazilian olive. As he left, he yelled in the direction of the running shower, admonishing Mrs. Pearlstein to hurry. She probably couldn't hear, but it served to spur him.

Captain used his foot to slide a ten-pound barbell plate in front of his door to hold it wide. He stood in the opening, perspiring. Shit, he thought. I feel good. It's the gin and helping somebody who needs help. It's the gin for sure, he thought.

A summer breeze smelling of freshly mown grass rushed through his apartment and past him into the darkened hall. It swathed his wet open pores and cooled him. He pushed against the doorjamb with the backs of both hands and closed his eyes. Breathing deeply, he let go with his hands and rubbed his fingertips over his abdomen. The skin felt smooth and clean. Flexing his stomach muscles, he touched them. He breathed the sweet air deeply again. He felt strong and confident, second to none.

The apartment was the same as Mrs. Pearlstein's, with one important distinction. Unlike her apartment windows that opened to look across at another building, Captain's windows looked over a beautifully manicured garden that occupied the entire next lot. In a way, the garden was his pride. He loved to get out the long, soft, green rubber—not nylon—hose with the strong bronze adjustable nozzle and soak the hedges, trees and flowers until they hung heavily in the sun.

Captain brushed his teeth and swallowed the rinse. Rubbing his chin, he examined the faint trace of beard and decided to pass on a shave. He acclimated himself to the water by a warm soaking and then turned the shower to cold and kept it there. "Holy shit, that'll put lead in your pencil." He never could quite get used to that.

Utilizing thick white towels from the Beverly Hills Hotel to dry himself, he used Eau Sauvage under his arms and Lubriderm lotion for his skin. The hair dryer and his hand put his shortish hair in style. Checking the hall mirror as he went, he donned white bikini briefs, tennis shorts, Adidas runners without socks and a pale blue, short-sleeved polo shirt. The shirt he tucked into the shorts, and he strapped to his wrist a thin black lizard band which held the gold Cartier watch that Iris had given him.

"I'll bet she's called five times," he said to his image. He looked out to the phone in the other room and back to the mirror. He changed the disgruntled look he had given the phone to a smile. He looked mighty fine.

He made it down the hall and into the empty four-place elevator without having to confront a single tenant. Riding to the garage seemed to take forever and he tried to think, as he often did, of any other elevator in any other three-story building that he'd ever ridden in that went so slowly.

The door slid open with a thud and poised with his finger out was Hays, the garbage man. "Hey, Cap, that broad is parked in front of the cans again. Go tell her to move it, will ya?"

Hays stood there, a sweating, six foot three, rotund black man with discolored purple gums, puffed and empty to his eye teeth. The waist of his gray work pants rolled over a dark brown leather belt that was stretched to thinness and hung out of its buckle and down in front of his fly like a shriveled, limp penis. Long too, as Captain would expect from his big black friend. His gray work shirt had the wrong name, Ronald, sewn above the pocket in white cable stitch. The sleeves were rolled up to where they wouldn't go any further over his heavily muscled forearms.

Captain put his hands on his hips. "Hays, what are you doing? Do you know what you're doing?"

Hays gaped.

"I mean, you're standing down here with your finger out when you should be out in front, grabbing one of those horny silks that walk up and down the street with their poodles. Why don't you do something constructive? Go out and grab yourself a broad and work on her real good. Bruise her up so that she'll need a doctor. Then we can bring that weirdo brother of yours a patient."

Hays made a fist and swung it at the ground. "Goddamn, Cap, don't grind me about my brother. It's no fun."

"Oh, isn't that too bad. Did I hurt your feelings? Shit, Hays, I'm just ribbing you. Sorry if I hurt your feelings. I happen to like him, that's all. I guess it's my way of asking how he is—How is he?"

"He's better, he's out, he's clean and he's still a doctor. And never mind about all of that shit man. You're just changing the subject on me. Can't you just ask the broad not to park in front of the cans on Fridays, that's all."

"Hays, my friend, come here." He put his hand on the big man's shoulder and ushered him deeper into the subterranean garage. Hays looked back over his shoulder, and Captain followed his glance toward the silhouette of the garbage truck up and out of the concrete drive on the street. The engine was running at a loud, fast idle. "Never mind," he said, turning him around. "Just come on."

They stopped in front of a green metal storeroom door set in white concrete brick. Captain felt his stomach working on the toothpaste solution he had swallowed. He figured that it must have sugar in it, probably dextrose, because, although slight, he was getting a nutritional boost.

After selecting a key, then using it, Captain swung the heavy metal door open into a cool, moist, cement room. The floor was a concrete slab. He snapped on an overhead bulb that swung loose on a long, braided electrical wire. It cast funny moving shadows along the walls and into the corners until he put another shaded reading light on that sat atop an old wooden desk. At the end of the room next to a well-supplied working bench, amidst neatly arranged storage, stood an old refrigerator with a busy concentric cooling element fixed to the top. Captain opened it. The shelves had been removed, and it was stacked full of brown bottles lying one on top of another on their sides. He removed one cold bottle and holding it up against the light for mutual admiration, said, "This, my friend, is a twelve-ounce bottle of iced Budweiser beer."

"I know, I know," Hays said, eyes open wide.

Captain shut the refrigerator and using his finger like a windshield wiper, stripped the cold sweat off of the bottle and flung it to the floor. "You see, Hays, when the Budweiser people went to cans and disposables four years ago, they still had a warehouse full of twelve-ounce, long neck, glass-bottled beer. And we know who bought a 100 cases of that beautiful aged stuff, don't we, my friend?"

Hays slapped his thigh and grinned his grin. "We sure do."

"And we know who's still got twenty-two cases left, don't we?"

Hays licked his lips and said it again, "We sure do."

"For special occasions and good people."

"Uh huh." Hays was reaching. His big hand gently pawed at the air like a hungry Yellowstone bear.

The head of the bottle went against the work bench into an opener. Captain popped it and handed it to Hays, who put it into his mouth in record time. He threw his head back and with the bottle parallel to the walls, sucked it dry. The empty bottle hung in Hays's hand, and they stared at each other, waiting. Hays's mouth was open and starting to form a smile to match Captain's vicarious grin. Hays's breath was short. Captain thought Hays's feet might leave the floor. He looked as though someone had run a tube up his rectum and filled him with helium.

Hays opened his mouth wide as though to receive a doctor's tongue depressor. He belched. Captain saw his pink palate blown forward against the roof of his throat. A grandiose bellow came. "Aaaaaaaah," enunciated like the last letter in conga— conga*aaaaaaah*.

Hays's flesh shook. The room's heavy walls contained the report and ended it, when it ended, with a thump. Then the noise of the truck.

"You know something, Hays, you've got a lot of class. Come here." Captain opened the second drawer of the desk, pulled out a liquor bottle and plunked it down on the desk top. "Here's the bottom of a bottle of bonded Old Fitz." While he talked he opened a closed drawer and took out a pair of heavy-duty tin snips. "Finish it and have another beer or two."

Hays didn't waste any time reaching for the bottle and when he did, Captain pulled out the piece of sloppy belt and cut it off. It measured by estimate at between ten inches and one foot.

"Hey, man, what'd you do that for?"

Captain didn't respond. He toyed with the leather, rubbing it on both sides. It was smooth and then rough. He dropped it to the floor and stood on it. "Don't forget to pull the door shut behind you when you leave." He twisted his soles into the piece of leather beneath him. It squirmed from the force. It seemed slippery. Probably greasy, he thought. He pulled the old chair out for Hays. "Sit if you want, be comfortable." Captain looked at his watch, kicked the extra piece of belt out into the garage and was out the door.

"Oh, and, Hays, move the goddamned cans around the car, will you. I'll owe you a couple of bucks."

By this time Hays had his feet up with a beer in one hand and the bourbon in the other. "Forget it, Cap," he said, synchronizing a friendly open-armed gesture with both bottles. "I'll handle the work. Thanks for it—and my pants too." He looked down at the proper-looking, clean-cut stub of his belt and shaking his head, laughed. Then he stopped and said quietly, "Thanks, Cap, friend—for always treating me right, for being fair."

Running, Captain kicked the leather piece out of sight under a parked car. He sprinted the forty or so yards to the last stalls in the garage, quickly unlocked the door of a cocoa brown, Jensen interceptor convertible, jumped in, started it with one try and accidentally squealed for the exit.

Braking before the ramp, he popped the transmission into park, jumped out and ran over to the tan Mustang under which the end of the belt had disappeared. A cursory examination revealed the piece lying up against the inside of a front tire. He brought it. The truck blocked the exit to the street. At the last minute, gunning it, he turned the car abruptly to the right onto the sidewalk and stopped in front of the building. Unsnapping the convertible top, he watched it fold down neatly to fit behind the rear seat. The day flooded in on him. He looked up into the sun and let it blind him. It had the immediate calming effect of what he remembered to be 200 milligrams of Thorazine, a quieting drug used in asylums. The scream of the garbage truck bothered him.

Turning off the Jensen, he went back to the truck, stood on his toes and peered into the cab. He turned the ignition key off. The big engine screamed and whined to stay with it but finally gave up with a gulp. He threw the belt tip onto the seat next to Hays's hat and a lunch box. Captain cupped his hands to his mouth and yelled into the garage, "That was me."

"I figured," was the reply.

"Remember, good friend, I trust you." Which he did. And Captain paused to consider that in a certain profound way, Hays might be his very best friend.

Captain pushed his clenched fists up into the warm sky. Stretching, he drew in a deep breath filled with the scent of his garden. He yawned. The hedges appeared full and green and from what he could see, a group of new yellow sunflowers was blooming toward the rear of the lot.

His attention was drawn to the building's antique, wrought-iron front door, which was opening. It opened onto a large brown concrete and used fire brick stoop eight steps up from the sidewalk. It appeared a stage. Hesitantly at first, like a bad guy checking to see if the coast was clear, she stepped out—clack, clack—onto the cement into the sun. The door shut behind her. She was holding the iron and staring at him. Realizing that he was gawking, he shut his mouth. They both stood there, he in disbelief, she looking like a fashion plate from some era that he didn't know or couldn't remember or didn't understand, but that pleased his eye.

"Goddammit, Ruthie, you look like a painting."

"Is that good?" she asked with reluctance.

"Yes, yes, of course it is. Come on. Be careful, but come on."

He ran to the passenger door of the Jensen, opened it and standing aside, made a sweeping gesture into the car with his arms and upper body, as though to seat royalty. "Madame," he encouraged, smiling.

Mrs. Pearlstein was wearing a turban, a soft, pink-colored, silken turban with a piece that hung down the back of her neck and fell over her shoulder. It had a jewel, a gaudy but beautiful old-fashioned green jewel, pinned prominently on the left side. Large round green earrings that looked like shooter marbles hung from her ears. Her necklace and bracelet were made from the same stones. They appeared heavy. She was wearing a dark brown dress jacket with swollen shoulders over a pink silkish blouse that ruffled at the collar and cuffs. The blouse was tucked into dark brown shorts, Bermuda length, the same color as the jacket. Her knees had knobs on them, but her bare legs looked fine as they went into dark brown wool socks that were neatly folded over at her ankles. Then the brown and white wingtip oxford golf shoes. She continued looking around with uncertainty. When she turned her head, the sun did dazzling things with her emerald turban jewel.

Captain couldn't help himself and laughed out loud before he sang, "Hey, good lookin', whatcha got cookin? How's 'bout cooking something up with me."

Hesitating, she looked down and tried to smile. "I have no good shoes . . . I . . . ."

"Ruthie, you're with me, and you look fantastic. All is well—trust me, trust me. We must trust our friends, or be alone."

She said, "You're right, dear," and—clack, clack, clickety clack—down the stairs she came to nearly jump into the waiting beige leather seat.

"God, you're as agile as a young girl, Ruthie," he said, meaning it.

"Nothing wrong with me," she smiled up at him into the sun. She was wearing makeup, eye liner, mascara and probably false eyelashes, applied with expertise.

"Your eyes look pretty, a nice light brown."

"Hazel," she said, shielding her face from the sun with her hand. She continued to look up at him.

At midnight, on the iris of her left eye, a tiny pie-shaped shadow box the color of brilliant copper shone in the sun. Captain thought that he could see through it, into her eye. Captain thought that he was able to observe the fibrous tissue that comprised the rear interior of Mrs. Pearlstein's left eyeball. Her eyes began to water and she looked away. Then she looked back with constricted pupils to smile warmly at him with her eyes and face. It embarrassed him slightly and looking away, he walked around and got into the car. He turned the key, moved the car up along the sidewalk to a reduced curb and slid it onto the street.

The Palms

The seat leather was warm. The sky was clear, blue and cloudless. It was a quiet sky. He looked at her again while he paused at the corner. She was letting out a deep breath and appeared interested in what was going on around her. If it was the floodlit day or a light makeup base he wasn't sure, but her skin looked healthy. Other than too much lipstick, she had done herself justice. Captain felt something in his hair and brushed a large leaf away.

"How do you feel?" he asked.

Mrs. Pearlstein breathed the warm breeze. "Fine. I feel just wonderful dear, just marvelous."

They both spoke at once and laughed. He deferred politely. "Go ahead."

"Did I keep you waiting? I would have been sooner but—well—I shaved my legs. I hope you didn't have to wait too long."

"No problem. Did you bring the receipt?"

"Yes, yes, I did. I brought both the sales slip and the cash register receipt."

He pushed the buttons and lowered all of the windows. He wanted to look at her legs and see if they appeared shaven but suppressed the desire. "This is a day for kings and queens, Ruthie, don't you think?"

"It's simply beautiful, dear. This is so kind of you. Are you sure that I look—?"

"You look as wonderful as the day, Ruthie, no bull, and in a couple of blocks I'm going to give us a little surprise." He pulled onto Santa Monica Boulevard, turned left, wobbled on the underlying railroad tracks for a moment and then settled into the correct lane. Santa Monica Boulevard was busy. Captain turned the rearview mirror toward Mrs. Pearlstein and handed her a kleenex from the dash. "Tone the lipstick down just a bit, Ruthie."

She looked to him and he winked assurance. She blotted her lips. "Better?"

"Much."

He turned the mirror back and waited for the display of insecurity that didn't come.

"This is a simply gorgeous car, Captain, but haven't I seen you in another one too?"

"This one is leased, Ruthie. The other one is the old police car that I have. The purple one with the silver fender. Is that the one you mean?"

"Yes," she said.

Captain noticed and was sure that she must too, the people that stared at them from car to car as they drove. "People are staring at you, Ruthie."

"At me?"

"Yep. They think you're somebody special, which you are."

32

She acted coy. "Oh, now, dear, come on, you're the one." He smiled. "Why do you have two cars, dear?" she asked, making conversation.

Captain thought about that and wasn't sure what to answer. "I just use the other one when I—when I get crazy."

"When you get crazy—What do you mean?"

He thought for a time and then pointed up the street. "That's where we're going before we do another thing, Mrs. P., right up there. See the long yellow sign that says the Palms?"

She strained to see. "I don't think I—"

"Never mind. We'll be there in a jiff." I'll bet they think I'm with a swami, he thought. He wanted in the worst way to tease her not to tell any fortunes in the bar, but he used what he imagined to be maturity and his better judgment and kept silent.

Then it came to him. "Woodhue by Fabergé," he announced, being positive now.

"Close," she said.

"Shit. Okay, tell me."

"Act IV by Fabergé."

"They're both the same," he said.

"What are?" Mrs. Pearlstein asked.

"Act IV and Woodhue—they are both made by Fabergé."

"Yes, that's true. If you'd have just said Fabergé, you would have been right."

Captain was beginning to feel restless when he pulled the polished brown convertible into the passenger loading zone in front of the Palms Bar.

"Are we here?"

"We are."

"My, that was fast." She reached into her jacket pocket and took out her Salem cigarettes and lighter. He'd forgotten.

"You've been dying for a cigarette, haven't you?"

33

"Sort of," she answered, nervously crinkling the cellophane package.

"Jesus, Ruthie, it's only a car. I could care less. No, that's not true. I mean, it is true about the car—I could give a shit—but I'm glad you didn't smoke because of the beautiful day."

Captain secured the drive train and pushed the keys under his seat behind the beige carpet."Leave the iron on the floor; I'm sure it will be all right."

"Really?"

"Yes, really. Don't worry about it, it's caused enough aggravation already. It's broken."

"Yes, but—"

"Never mind." He checked the traffic and bounded over to her side of the car. "Madame." He held her door open and reached for her hand. "Right this way, please." The sun was getting warmer. Captain was ready for a cold drink.

Mrs. Pearlstein stepped out, adjusting her clothing. Captain pushed the seats forward to shield them from the sun. He took her arm. The round green earrings bounced against her neck, and her shoes clacked along the few steps to the propped-open door.

The bar seemed unusually quiet from the street. Captain held Mrs. Pearlstein's arm as they entered so that her shoes wouldn't trip her up and until her eyes became acclimated to the cool, dark room.

"Cappy, good morning," a cheerful female voice with a thick Swedish accent came from within. "Come on straight ahead. Here are two in the middle down here."

Captain ushered Mrs. Pearlstein up to the two places that Ingrid was holding for them. The man closest to Mrs. Pearlstein's stool moved over. Captain sat her down and lit the cigarette that had magically appeared between her fingers. He stayed on his feet and squeezed up to the bar.

"Hey, big boy," Ingrid said, imitating Mae West.

Captain turned to find Ingrid leaning forward over the bar on stiffened elbows and flat palms, eyes closed, her lips puckered. She was six feet tall and commanded the reach. Her hair was bleached blonde and showed an inch of brown roots on either side of the center part down the top of her head. The white ends hung down and over her huge, harnessed bust.

Captain planted a wet kiss on Ingrid's large naturally cherry red lips and slipped his tongue in and along her strong white teeth. She opened her eyes and they looked at each other. "Nice lips," he said, wishing that they were someplace else. Ingrid reached around the back of Captain's neck, held his head and gave him a kiss for real.

"You look good enough to eat," she said, staring him in the eye.

Captain stepped back and nearly burned his hand reaching through the smoke and fire to Mrs. Pearlstein's shoulder. "Ingrid, I'd like you to meet Ruthie, my friend. Ruth, this is Ingrid."

Grinning, Ingrid reached over the bar for Mrs. Pearlstein's hand. "Glad to meet you," she said with her thick accent. "I really love your hat." She leaned closer and examined it as Mrs. Pearlstein took her hand and they shook. "I mean I really like your hat. It's gorgeous."

Mrs. Pearlstein, pleased and befriended, started into a story about her husband Ken: he made the shoes for Ziegfeld—she and Flo Ziegfeld—the hat was from the Follies and *blah*, *blah*. Captain wanted a drink. He feigned an audible yawn and patted his open mouth. Mrs. Pearlstein noticed and said, "Oh—oh, I'm sorry. Who would want to hear about that." She looked away, hurt.

Ingrid was fuming. Her hands were on her hips, her big chest was heaving. "I swear, Cappy, sometime I'm gonna—"

"Of course we want to hear your stories, Ruthie. Just let me order a drink." They were calling for Ingrid, but she didn't budge.

"Hey, Ruth, look—look at the Gestapo with her hands on her hips. It looks like you've got a friend, because she's sure as hell p.o.'d at me."

Mrs. Pearlstein turned toward Ingrid, who was letting her see whose side she was on.

"I love to hear those stories—and look at your hat. It was a time when people cared about making things that lasted—craftsmanship," Ingrid said.

"Oh, shit. Do you mind, girls?" Now they were a team. Mrs. Pearlstein had a friend and that was nice. "Don't forget the iron, Ruthie." She was blank. "The iron—Bloom's—the crybaby?" She caught on, smiled and went for yet another new smoke. He hugged her shoulder and winked at Ingrid. "Now hear this. I'm going across the street for a surprise. Ingrid will make us two strong Toms, please, with good gin, the way only she can make them. You see, Ruthie, Ingrid is the worst bartender in town, but she's got a hot-looking body and overpours. So," Ingrid was smiling, "we will leave the Tom Collins's to her. And while I'm gone, which will be two minutes, Ingrid will give you four red quarters for some music, and she will make you feel at home. Right, Ingo?"

He leaped out the door. The bright day caused him to squint. The temperature was climbing. Dodging traffic, he crossed Santa Monica Boulevard in four strides. His legs felt strong. He bounced in and out of Santa Monica Florists after having paid too much for a gardenia for Ingrid and a beautiful white camelia for Mrs. Pearlstein.

Ingrid got wise that he was taking too long to pin on the gardenia. Wise that while he was pinning, he was rubbing the tip of her nipple through her sweater with the end of his little finger, she slapped his hand, and moisture flew from the flower's petals. Mrs. Pearlstein pinned her own. They thanked him profusely and demonstrated their new friendship by finishing each other's sentences while explaining how they had settled on Charlie Rich's song, "Behind Closed Doors." Captain thought it sounded good. Mrs. Pearlstein whispered to him that the title seemed appropriate since that's how this whole thing got started. "That's where I was—get it?"

Captain toasted, "Women, who should be running the country."

"We already are, big boy," Ingrid said in a sexy tone sounding like Mae West. The three of them clicked glasses and drank.

Mrs. Pearlstein sipped, licked her lips and beamed. Ingrid took a good swallow. "This was a good idea for a warm day," she said, pleased. Captain drank his entire drink in one pull and placed the glass on the bar after an easy expulsion of breath.

"One more time, Ingo, and put two fingers of gin on the side. Same for Ruthie."

Ingrid looked at Mrs. Pearlstein, who shrugged approval. Captain's resistance was no match for the powdered sugar and gin. He felt himself mellow fast, made room and sat down to listen to Bonnie Raitt. Mrs. Pearlstein wanted to talk, but he put his finger over his lips. He matched stares with a grouper in the aquarium tank behind the bar until he gave up to close his eyes and listen.

His concentration was suddenly broken by two men a few stools up on his left at the turn in the bar, arguing about yesterday's seventh race. "Goddammit, Rick," he shouted, "there are other people in here beside you." But the moment had passed. "Assholes," he said under his breath. He picked up a water glass that carried two and a half to three inches of warm gin and swirled the contents around. Ingrid walked by and shuddered, as if she had the chills.

"I don't know how you can drink that straight, Cap," she said questioningly through a squint. He drank off half of it and chased it with the new Tom Collins.

"That'll put lead in your pencil," he said with a sigh.

"God, I would get drunk," Ingrid said.

"Have you ever seen me drunk?" Captain demanded.

"Not you—me. It would make me drunk. No, I've never seen you drunk, Cappy."

"Haven't you ever been drunk?" Mrs. Pearlstein asked.

"No, I haven't. I don't think so."

Captain watched Mrs. Pearlstein drink the top off of her new Tom Collins and nonchalantly pour the straight gin in to fill up the glass. "May I have another ice cube, please?"

Ingrid was at the end of the bar offering a smell of her gardenia to a Hollywood floozy that Captain knew and liked. He substituted for her by reaching over the bar to retrieve two ice cubes, which he plopped into Mrs. Pearlstein's drink, overfilling and spilling it. She licked the sides and asked if they hadn't better go after this one and wasn't she imposing on his day.

"You're not imposing on my day. This is our day. In fact, Mrs. P., it's your day and you're not sad anymore, are you?" Mrs. Pearlstein smiled in embarrassment and shook her head no.

"Hello, beauty," a soft female voice came from over their shoulders, cutting him off at mid-sentence.

Captain knew whose voice was in the air and whose long, thin-fingered brown hand was touching his shoulder before her sweet scent answered the question for sure.

"Hi, Sheila. What are you having?" Ingrid interjected forcefully past Captain's head.

"Nothing from the bar right now, Ingo. I've found what I

want," was the answer from behind him, in the same soft voice.

"Good luck," Ingrid said, throwing out her watered-down drink and brusquely immersing the glass over an electric washing head in yellowish antiseptic water. She drew a beer.

Captain glanced over at Mrs. Pearlstein, who was smiling at Sheila. "How do you do," came the voice. "My name is Sheila."

"Hello, dear. My name is Ruth Pearlstein." Sheila's hand stayed, so he presumed that they didn't shake.

Captain spent these few moments guarding his memory. He didn't want to think about Sheila. He was disgusted with her, with what she had done. Her smell hadn't made him remember, nor the sound of her voice, nor her touch. But then she leaned lightly over his right shoulder and released her warm moist breath into his ear.

Captain felt the shivers run through his body and his penis jerk. His memory unlocked, and he remembered another beautiful summer day not unlike this one two years before. He had been driving west on Sunset Boulevard when a new, white Cadillac convertible, the top down, had pulled up next to him. A good-looking, sun-tanned brunette was at the wheel alone. He remembered being embarrassed at the time when he had said it. It wasn't really a hustle, it was what he felt when he looked into her dark eyes. The heat of the day and her thick black hair that shimmered rusty made him say it. "I can smell you," he said, and she stared back into him for a long, self-conscious moment until horns honked behind them and she pulled away. Sheila made the next stoplight but he didn't, and she slowed and waited for him to catch up.

She licked her full lips and smiled, but neither of them spoke while they parked their cars next to each other in the cool subterranean garage. Captain watched her slide out of the seat and walk to the elevator. She wore a white silk sun dress that was hemmed above the knee, white heels and no jewelry. Her long tanned legs shimmered and seemed in a constant flux of lubrication. She threw her beautiful head back and invited him to follow with her eyes. Her black hair hung past her shoulder with little curl, and that day she had worn it parted on the left side. This division would easily find itself again after she tossed her head and it ran straight and perfect back into a natural swirling cowlick that buried itself into her rich, healthy-looking albino scalp.

Captain loved the way that she walked and held herself. She was a Jewess with strong, proud, distinguishing features.

They rode alone in the elevator, and Captain couldn't match her stare. She let up on him by looking down at his pants, at his erection.

Sheila's father was a liquor baron, and they didn't speak in his luxury suite. Sheila didn't speak but wet her lips and went to her knees in front of him for the first part of it. Then they laid each other down into the deep brown carpet and made the sounds of love. They made love on the thick carpet amongst the overstuffed furniture and even up against her father's gigantic oak desk. The air conditioning in the suite had given him a cold, and his knees had stayed burned for a long time.

When they finally spoke, she had gone first and while holding him with all of her strength she said that she needed him more than she'd ever needed any man before. She spent what seemed like hours petting his face, tracing her fingers over his brows and touching his lips. She thought that his nose was the most beautiful that she'd ever seen, and he had jokingly told her that it had been reconstructed by a doctor friend of his father's, a famous plastic surgeon from the Mayo Clinic. She was particularly fond of making love with him in front of a mirror and in the end had her entire bedroom ceiling and walls redone in one-piece, perfect reflection, specially cut mirrors.

Sitting at the Palms Bar all of these months later with her breathing down his neck, he wanted to evaporate. Shit, he thought, starting to feel blue. I don't want this reunion. It had been such a fine day. Then he caught himself and thought, the hell with that kind of thinking. Don't get down; it can be handled. It's all okay.

Sheila had told him all along that she was engaged to a doctor and had even suggested a meet, but Captain knew better. He refused often. Then one rainy evening she had called him and cajoled him to come to her at her penthouse. She seemed fearful, so he went for one drink. That didn't suit her and she begged him to stay; she even told him that she would suck his cock all night long.

He stayed for some of that and finally the house phone rang. "Send him up. Send him up," she screamed.

Captain bolted for the door, and she stopped him with a small silver automatic. After deciding that she might use it and after what seemed an interminable wait, there was a knock on the door. Sheila pulled the large double door open. And stark naked, with her full bust swinging, a gun in one hand and saliva running from the corner of her mouth, she screamed in a most hysterical fashion, "There, Jerry—there—I want one like that. I want a nose like that."

Captain's first thought was that someone had drugged him or that he had fallen off of the beam. A nose like mine, he thought. What the hell?

Doctor Jerry was a comic character who wore a vested suit and spider spectacles. The hair on the side of his head was parted and combed up over the balding top. All five foot five inches of him advanced on Captain saying, "Pardon me." He then reached out and began feeling Captain's nose. Chagrined, Doctor Jerry turned to Sheila and said, "This bone has never been broken. This nose has never been done."

41

Sheila stood aghast while Captain threw on his clothes and left, not to hear a word from her again for several months.

But Sheila had gone ahead and opted for the change anyway, and from his first glimpse of it on, it had never ceased to make his skin crawl. The self-effacing bitch.

Captain had a swallow of straight gin and didn't chase it. It made him shudder and he stood, letting Sheila's hand fall from his shoulder. Forcing an open expression, he turned to face her. He didn't speak. The dimly lit room served her features well.

He felt her stare and after a moment's hesitation to bolster his courage, he returned it. She went deep immediately, reaching for his soul. Then she licked her lips. She licked around that wonderful wet mouth, and he was able to break the stare and look at it, too. Captain loved her mouth. He was happy to see that she hadn't changed it. He had forgotten how beautiful it was. He watched it pout. Full lipped, when she spoke or threw her head back and laughed, the interior edge of her pink lip line became visible and from that point on, in and around her flashing strong white teeth to the rippled flesh in the back of her throat, it always looked wet. The base of her fat tongue and molars were bathed in what appeared to be sparkling, clear, sweet syrup. Captain would stare and want to jam in and lap at it, roll his tongue into a straw and vacuum her mouth, suck it dry once and for all.

Sheila was a smart Jew broad, as they can be, and Captain knew that Sheila knew that he was staring at the luscious hole in her face. He felt her watching for his reaction as she slowly moved her thick pink tongue along her lips. Then she threw her opened trap back to laugh at what she saw in his eyes.

"Hi, baby," she finally said, settling down. "I leave messages on your service until I'm too embarrassed to speak with them anymore. You look very well."

Captain remained silent.

42

"Could I speak with you for a moment—alone?" she asked quietly.

Something was getting through, a bridge was still up, a door open, the stimulus was coming home. His loins became excited, blood was starting into his penis. Captain thought that he could smell Sheila's vagina.

"Please, baby," she said again, both pleading and demanding in the tone of a spoiled child.

"What are ya waiting for kid?" interrupted Pepper, a balding, paunchy, homosexual police detective, eavesdropping from a few stools away. He did nothing to hide his lascivious way. "I mean, she's laying it right out there for ya boy, and she ain't no slouch." He jeered, "Look at them rags, will ya," and, noticing, "Man, how about that ring—look at that ring, will ya."

Without thinking, Captain stepped over to Pepper and easily took hold of his left ear. The music stopped to change, and some people quieted to watch. Captain crunched the ear up firmly in his right hand and began to slowly turn it backward. Pepper didn't move but sweated and continued with a smirk, speaking intimately. "That's got to be five carats, kid. Why, from what I hear about you—" He looked at Captain's crotch. "With what you've got, I'll bet—"

Suddenly, Pepper stopped and grabbed the edge of the bar. He squeezed his fat eyes closed and after holding a long breath, squealed, "God, stop, you're tearing it off."

Anyone sitting close who wanted to listen could hear the cartilage pop. Pepper threw his hands under himself and sat on them. He turned his round face up toward the ceiling, closed his eyes and shrieked a clenched, long-pitched *eeeeeeee* through his teeth. The skin at the top of his ear tore. Blood trickled down over Captain's knuckles and through Pepper's stubble. In obvious pain, Pepper seemed ecstatic.

43

Captain was aware now and imagined that he was observing Pepper as he was when he took it in the rectum and loved the ripping pain. Captain imagined Pepper with some poor busted queen who didn't want to get run in. He could hear Pepper saying, "Stick it in my ass hard, and I'll let you go. Ram me and I won't expose you." Pepper screamed again, louder than before, and Captain stopped.

"Ingrid, bring Pepper another drink here on me. And bring my friend Ruthie a quick one too, please. Someday, someone is going to tear that off, Pep." Captain backed away. Pepper's hands flew to his ear. He rubbed it.

"Bastard," Pepper mumbled, turning back into the bar. "You'll get yours."

Someone was already headed for the juke box. Captain asked for the bill to be made ready, put Sheila's purse in Mrs. Pearlstein's lap, told Mrs. Pearlstein to sit tight and escorted Sheila over to a dark corner and into the ladies room. Sheila was wearing a two-piece summer dress made of pinkish-colored silk scarves that flowed as he pulled her along. Her thick dark hair was parted in the middle and put up into pony tails that hung from the sides of her head in large pink ribbons that had been tied into bows.

Inside the ladies room Captain reached around Sheila's bare midriff with both hands and sat her up at the end of a yellow linoleum counter. This was built against a large mirror next to the sink. Two tubular fluorescent lights hummed above them. Their deep purplish hue made him look tired, as though he had bags under his eyes. He reached overhead and pulled the closest plug. The light directly above them flickered and clicked off. The remaining bulb further into the room left an eerie but comfortably realistic lavender glow.

John Denver sang in the next room. Sheila straightened up and tried to adjust herself to comfort. The silk scarves fell around her right thigh while she lifted her long leg up, bent her knee, unstrapped a Charles Jordan high heel, let it lie and put her bare foot into the sink. She allowed her left leg to hang down over the counter top, to bend at the knee and swing in the air. He noticed the blonde hair on the inside of her smooth, unblemished thigh until he realized that she was watching him from the reflection off of the mirrors in the room.

"Caught you," she said coyly.

He felt himself blush but looked into her eyes anyway. "What do you want, Sheila?"

She put her wet pink tongue out and licked her full mouth. Some of the moisture stayed on the soft down above her upper lip. She smiled. Her nose really didn't look that bad, he guessed. From the front the only giveaway was the unnatural pull on the muscles in the corners of her eyes when she changed expression; they contorted. Nothing and everything, he thought.

Raising her left leg up, she unbuckled the strap of her other shoe. She let it fall to the floor. She put her warm bare foot against the hair of his leg and rubbed it up and down with her toes. The pink silk scarves hung down over her crotch.

"Come on, Cappy, kiss me. I miss you so damned much." Her pupils dilated, her lids hung heavily.

They had left the air conditioning outside, and Captain felt flushed. The combined smell of their body odors, perspiration and summer lotions was intoxicating. For a split second his knees went weak and his head spun. His penis became completely stiff and strained against his clothing. Captain felt his scrotum draw tight. His hips twitched with his heart beat, a spasmodic jerking in the muscles of his groin that he hoped didn't show. Sheila's eyes were tearing and losing their expression. She stopped rubbing his leg and put her foot behind his bare knee. Using her foot, she pulled him to her against the counter. Her lips were slightly parted, her breath came in hoarse spurts, almost a pant. She smelled sweet, like milk and fruit and sugar. He remembered all of the good things about her as a lover; the smells, especially the smells.

The room smelled of sex.

"Feel me," she said, entranced. "Feel how hot you make me." Sheila's tanned bust heaved against the V-neck of her pink silken dress.

Captain could feel his heart beat in his temples and behind his eyes. Look at her beautiful mouth, he said to himself. The least that you could do is kiss her. Go on, participate in her deceit, go all of the way with it, tell her how it is. You're so groovy, you cute little pug-nosed thing. Here, take this—and this—wham, wham. Bullshit, he thought. His interest had been in a sabra, not a Judy.

He dropped his eyes to her upturned thigh and rested the knuckles of his open left hand on the blonde softness. He permitted himself to rub it gently. Moving quickly, she pulled his hand up under the silken scarves.

"Feel what you do to me." Her voice was trembling.

Captain resisted the pull, but it didn't matter. She wore no panties. "I put them in my purse when I saw your car," Sheila whispered, managing a faint smile.

Her inner thighs and pubic hair were wet. He looked back into her eyes; they were glazing. He slipped his fingers the final few inches to her sex. His erection had pushed under the elastic of his briefs to end up in the pocket of his tennis shorts. His inclination was to tear his shorts down, pull her to him and plunge into her, work her walls, or to take it out and pump it with his hand, end his frustration on her tanned legs. The room was filled with the smell of them—sticky, close. Perspiration stung his eye.

46

The opening to her body was hot and puckered. The flesh seemed to be flowing, melting over his hand. He moved his knuckles up and used them to ease her open.

"Oh, Jesus," she said, closing her eyes and biting her lower lip.

Turning his hand over, he pushed in and found it, the feel of a distended, pounding vein. A vessel that ended right there against the tips of his fingers.

"Jesus, God," she cried, trying first to clutch at him and then throwing her head back into the mirrored corner with a slam. "I'm—I'm—I'm on fire, baby. It's burning up. Oh shit, take it out and slide it into me. Please, Cappy, do me."

Captain flashed on dropping to his knees, resting his chin on the counter and pulling her legs around his face. That he would really enjoy. He felt the impulses go out, but it didn't happen. The front of his shorts were wet. "Sit back," he said. He quickly put his right hand between her breasts and straightened out his arm, pushing her firmly against the mirror. He held her fast, nearly pressing the air out of her. "Spread your legs," he demanded.

She lifted her right foot from the sink and moved that leg further away against the mirror. The other leg hung loose. Sheila's vaginal lips pouted too. Captain loved the feel of them.

Captain opened Sheila's sex again and began running the tips of his fingers up and down along her slippery shaft and over her clitoris. She tried to move ahead, indicating her discomfort, but at the same time rolled her eyes back into her head and started moaning with his touch. Her pulse heightened under his fingertips.

Captain held her firmly with his straightened arm and concentrated on caressing her flesh as lightly as he could without breaking contact. He thought of safe crackers with sand-papered fin-

47

gers, of flutists who warm their hands in gloves before they can play—the touch, the sensitive touch.

"Uh, uh, uh." Sheila made grunting sounds and began to thrash. Her arms flapped like broken wings. Captain observed as the seizure came. It enveloped her; she enveloped it. She worked with it and against it at once. She bucked and arched against his arm, and it took all of his strength to hold her.

Every muscle in her body seemed to become rigid. She shuddered aloud and pushed her pelvis against his fingers. She grabbed his flexed straightened arm with both of her hands and held on. Sheila shook and cried out with tears. Then she let out one wretching series of "Boo hoo hoo," and it began to pass. She twitched and jerked and after a long sigh, slumped into the corner.

Captain brought his wet left hand away and to his face. Passing his nose, he thought of the sweet pollen over his garden on those special lush days. He put his fingers into his mouth, sucking them. The taste was mellow but not flowery. It was the taste of a clean, healthy vagina: the female orgasm. A flavor that he enjoyed and respected.

Sheila sat and stared. Captain made a bunch of paper towels wet. He squeezed them out and gently wiped the perspiration from her face and the mascara from under her eyes. He made one wet again, folded it and held it against her forehead. She dropped her eyes to look at his shorts.

"Don't you want to do something about that?" She gestured toward his crotch with a limp-wristed hand. "You can't walk around like that all day."

"I'll survive," he said.

Suddenly she snatched his wrist. The brown paper towel rolled down her bosom to lie on the counter top. "Son of a bitch," she said. "You heartless son of a bitch."

48

THE PALMS

Captain looked away.

"You hate me, don't you?" she sobbed.

He didn't speak.

"Don't you?" she screamed, shaking his arm. "You won't even look into my eyes. You told me my eyes were beautiful. Liar—goddamn bullshit artist—liar."

Captain counted to three in his mind and pulled his wrist free with enough force to jar her. "Sheila, I don't hate you. And I do think that you have beautiful eyes. It's just that—"

"What?" she demanded.

Only for a microsecond did he consider telling her the truth. Shit, it would scar her for life. An honest analogy, seeing how she is, he thought. It's not your affair. It's too late, leave it.

"It's that woman at the bar, Sheila," he said in low conspiratorial tones. "She's a very special person, lives in my building. It may appear that we're playing, but we're not. I'm taking care of something for her, something very important."

It would do, for an untruth. Captain did not like to lie, and he disliked people who forced him to do it, usually to save feelings. He did realize that it served a purpose to lie, and that people did it. But that was for them. He knew the difference; he knew better, what was right. It galled him to lie.

"Yes, I can understand that, but that doesn't explain—"

"Sheila, don't lean on me. I've said what I'm going to. Besides, I have to pee."

Sheila shut up. He unzipped his shorts, got into his bikini and wrangled out his half-hard penis. Standing on his toes, he lay it on the counter up to the sink and urged his bladder. Sheila jumped off of the counter and reached for his penis. "Here, let me hold it while you go."

"All right, but let's go to the toilet; the angle is wrong here."

He moved over to the toilet with her holding on to him. She

49

acted excited, like a kid who'd been given a favorite toy to calm a fit of crying, a reward for shutting up. She was squeezing his organ with both hands, diversifying the pressure from finger to finger. She stared at it. He felt it starting to get hard again and pushed her hands away. He pulled both pairs of pants down below his knees and leaning over the toilet bowl, put his flat hands on the walls to the sides to steady himself.

Sheila was reaching. "Don't touch it, Sheila. I've really got to go and I can't concentrate.

"But look," she said, quickly touching the hole in the end of his penis with her pink-nailed pointer finger. She pulled it back, and a strand of clear discharge came away, connected to her finger. It hung there making Captain think of a white nylon hammock.

"Please, Sheila," he said, pushing her hand away. For a moment it looked as though the pre-semen might make the stretch, but it fell away, back against his leg.

Sheila clasped her hands against her bosom and appeared offended. Captain closed his eyes and relaxed with a breath. His sphincter muscle remitted, and urine poured out of him. He went and went. It was good.

"It's so pretty," she said.

Captain opened his eyes to find Sheila kneeling on the torn linoleum floor, next to the urinal, watching. She held her hands behind her back like a speed skater.

"Sheila, get up. It's probably filthy down there."

"Just let me kiss it. It's so big and pretty. And the veins—"
He reached down under her arms and lifted her to her feet.

"Oh," she said sadly.

He put himself away, tucked and closed his clothing and headed for the door. "Come on, Sheila. I'll buy you a drink."

She moved with him and stopped him in front of the mirrored

door. "Why don't you let me buy you the most beautiful house in the whole world—anywhere, name it and it's yours. You love the ocean. All right. I'll buy you a piece of it." She waited, then, "What's that old douche bag going to do for you? I've got more money. Since father died I've got more of everything than anyone you know. It's all yours, Cappy. Don't you know, it's all for you." Her countenance became especially sober. "I am serious, you know. You are all that I want. I've thought a lot about it, an awful lot. Come away with me—pick the spot."

Captain looked into her face for a long moment. "Not today, Sheila."

Turning, he started to push his shoulder into the glassed door. She stopped him, holding his upper arm. "Then, what? Is this it? Do we just walk out of here? Is that it? Am I just supposed to walk out of here and walk away?"

Captain smiled warmly.

"It's like David Bowie says, Sheila, 'Planet earth is blue and there's nothing I can do.' "

He leaned over and gently kissed the bridge of her nose. He turned his body, winked to her over his shoulder and blasted out through the door.

The circulation of air in the big room was refreshing. He tucked at his shirt and ran both hands back through his hair. "Let me finish that, Ruthie." Captain took what was left of Mrs. Pearlstein's drink from the bar in front of her. Finishing it off, he gave the empty to Ingrid, whose confab with Mrs. Pearlstein he had interrupted.

"This is a fabulous dame, Cap," Ingrid said. Then Ingrid's eyes dropped to look below Captain's waist. Fixing her hand on one hip, she spoke like Mae West. "Hey, big boy, is that a gun I see in your pocket, or are you just here to tell me that you love me?" There was laughter.

51

"Here, Ingrid, here's something else for you. Keep it safe and sound. Sheila will be right here." He gave Ingrid Sheila's purse from Mrs. Pearlstein's lap. "Be careful now," he said to Mrs. Pearlstein, picking her up off of the stool.

He lifted Mrs. Pearlstein along. Some of the patrons raised an arm or a glass and said "Goodby, have a good day," and so forth. Finally as Mrs. Pearlstein's shoes clicked and clacked onto stone, a final note from Ingrid in her most mellifluous tone: "Thank you for the flower, Cappy. I love you for it." Captain waved and they stepped into the sun.

The day was becoming a scorcher. Captain made a crooked visor with his hand and shielded his squinting eyes. Mrs. Pearlstein did the same. "Goddamn fantastic sun. Good for what ails you."

"Oh dear. There's that man again."

Pepper had pulled his unmarked Plymouth into the space in front of the Jensen. He was sitting on his trunk with his feet up on the front bumper of Captain's car. His shirt was opened down to his rumpled suit coat and tie, both of which he held folded in his lap. His shirt sleeves were rolled up. He dabbed at perspiration from his fat neck and jowls with a pale yellow handkerchief. Mrs. Pearlstein hesitated. When Pepper knew that he had their attention, he bounced on the cars and grinned. Captain urged Mrs. Pearlstein along to the Jensen.

"The seats shouldn't be too bad," he said. Holding her door, he pushed the passenger seat to the upright position. He put his hand on the seat. "Not bad at all, Ruthie. Come on in." She looked out over the hood of the Jensen. "Come on. Don't worry about him."

Captain closed the door gently, turned on his heel and headed for Pepper. Showing considerable agility, Pepper left the cars bouncing as he jumped into the air to land squarely on both feet.

He continued to hold his jacket and tie gathered up in front of him but quickly moved them aside just enough to expose the hatched wooden butt of a revolver holstered onto his belt.

"Don't get too close, kid." He wiped the top of his wet head. When he withdrew the hankie, what little hair he had stood straight up in back, making Captain think of a bedraggled cock sparrow.

Captain stopped at the curb. He tried but could not get Pepper to return his stare. Pepper seemed to look back into Captain's mouth or at his scalp or past him altogether. Captain assumed that Pepper could read the truth in a person's eyes just like anyone else but didn't want it. It would throw him off, make him question the external evidence, allow him to float out of his pugnacity long enough to learn about morality and probably die. But Captain didn't harbor any persisting indignation toward Pepper. He didn't carry those feelings around. Pepper would have gone long ago. Captain thought that Pepper was a character, an excuse for a man, a joke, a wasted life.

"What?" Captain said sternly, demanding.

"I just want you to know who your friends are, good looking. Black and white were here writing you when I came out. He put his handkerchief in his shirt's stretched-out breast pocket and after rummaging, brought a folded manila parking ticket out of his suit jacket. He held it up. "See what I mean, kid? I told them to void it, that you were a friend. Ya know what they said?"

"No, what?"

"They said that they know the car and that you park it any goddamn place you want."

Captain stepped off the curb and passed next to Pepper, who quickly pulled his stomach in and gripped his gun. "I'm going to go now, Pepper." Captain looked up and down the street and leaned against the door to clear a passing car.

"Sure, kid, sure. I'm off too. Going to go and cruise the park." He giggled. "See if I can catch me a pervert. You know how I am about sickies." He laughed and it ended with a *hee hee*. "Oh, and kid—"

Captain opened his door and jumped into the seat that Mrs. Pearlstein had made ready for him.

"Hey, kid."

Captain gave him his attention.

"You've got come on your pants." He laughed and spun around and did a little jig. He ended it with a slap to the roof of his car. He was repeating the joke to himself and enjoying it again while Captain pulled the Jensen out into traffic.

Blooms

Is he a real policeman?"
she wanted to know.

"Yes."

"Well, how can he be? I mean, he's terrible."

Captain was the one to laugh now. "Yeah—he is, isn't he. They say that he's got something on somebody big. Something to do with drugs, I've heard. I've got a hunch that in some ways he's a good cop too. He lives on the street, knows everybody, where the bodies are buried. Too bad he's such a low life."

She thought about that. "How do you feel?" he asked, handing her Iris's tortoise shell sunglasses from the dash and putting on a lightweight, gold-framed pair of his own.

"I feel fine—fabulous, actually. I'll be very careful of the glasses. I hope she won't mind."

"She won't."

Mrs. Pearlstein resumed her comfortable corner position with her arms on the seat back and door top. Curious about her habits, her tolerance, Captain was formulating a question about drinking when she said it just exactly like Kalvin used to say it, word for word, with the same intonation.

"You are a good driver, Captain." She said it proudly too, with the same emphasis on the word good.

Yes, he thought, I am a good driver and I know how to drink. Shit, I learned them both from the expert. He thought about his father. The man knew how to drink.

Mrs. Pearlstein had been trying to get Captain's attention; she gave up. Taking her hand back, she looked at the passing store windows, the people and things all hiding from the sun.

"Ruthie, I'm sorry. What is it?" She smiled, not upset. He continued, "I was going to compliment you, the way you can hold a drink, and I went off on an old thought about my father. He was quite a guy. He drank good too. Something you said or did reminded me—" Captain trailed off.

"That's all right, dear. Is he—?"

"You can smoke if you want, Ruth," he cut in.

"I know, dear, but I can wait. Is he alive, your father?"

"No. No, he's not. He got tired of—" He paused and saw the intent look on Mrs. Pearlstein's face, her interest.

"Go on, dear. Tired of what?"

Captain changed his mood. He added humor to his tone and with a casual smile said, "He just got tired, Ruthie, just tired. And one day he went into the steam room, sat in a yoga position and opened the veins in his ankles."

"He—?" She hesitated; her jaw hung off kilter.

Captain noticed that her lower face was a bit heavy, a bit unfeminine. "Yep, he killed himself. And that was almost that."

"Almost what?" she ventured.

"He knew I'd take it." Captain shouted out into the sky above him. "You old cocker you, I love you."

Mrs. Pearlstein, acting confused, asked, "He knew you'd take what?"

Captain collected himself and calmly said, "It, Ruthie. It." He acted as if she should know. She seemed puzzled. "Oh, I'm just shittin' you, Ruthie. Answer me one big question. I don't care really—just for fun, though."

"All right, but were you kidding about all of it? About your father?"

"He's dead, and I don't want to talk about that. I do want to know how many of those green Squire's bottles go out of the building in different ways other than the incinerator. Come on, fess up. You're too sophisticated a drinker to be as casual with it as you say." Teasing her, he tried to imitate her in a falsetto. "Oh I don't know, dear—I may have one. Oh, no, no, not too much now—I rarely drink—only before my meals." He laughed and slapped his leg. He passed a dog pound truck, loud with barking.

Mrs. Pearlstein's impulses were obvious and real. She was first flushed and angry, then insulted and haughty, and finally hurt. "What kind of a sneak are you that examines the trash?"

"Now wait a minute, Mrs. P. Don't get excited. Jesus, I trust you with my day, and the minute I ask you for a little inside stuff, you get uptight. The incinerator doesn't burn empty bottles of gin, that's all. The rest is just a put-on. Come on now." He tried to rub her bare leg. She jerked it over next to the other one against the door.

"I have a budget."

"I know, I know. Oh, the hell with it, forget it."

"I drink a case every month," she blurted. "Is that a sin?"

57

There was a long pause. He lost the sense of fun he'd been having and was angry at himself for prying. He turned south on Western Avenue. The area was rundown. The sky was the same, but the air was stilted, perceptibly polluted.

"All right, I'll tell you a secret. Do you want to know my secret?" she asked. They passed over the Hollywood Freeway.

Captain looked down. The traffic was moving easily. It relaxed him. Congested freeways made him sweat. "No, I don't."

"Oh, come on. I've decided it will be fun to share it with you." Captain sighed. She didn't wait for a reply. She began speaking. "I play let's pretend."

"That's a kid's game."

"Not the way I play it, it's not."

"Oh," he said.

"I used to be a makeup artist. That's how Ken met Ziggy. He came backstage every night after the show—this was New York now, remember."

"Oh," Captain said again.

"That's how Kenny came to make all of the shoes for the show, the movies too."

Captain watched in his periphery as Mrs. Pearlstein got wound up over the old days. A tingle ran through him, and he felt happy and relaxed. He didn't question it. He'd learned to wallow in it when it came.

"Well anyway, I was very good—not just a slopper like they are today—an artist. They could see every eyelash from the fifteenth row. So anyway, this is what I do: I make one of my special shakers of martinis and I go to my dressing room."

Captain ran a mental flash of her apartment. "Dressing room?" he questioned.

"In the hallway. You didn't notice my mirror?" He hadn't. "It's a large stage mirror surrounded with bright light."

58

"You mean with bulbs all around it?"

"Yes. Anyway, I scrub my face clean, take my shaker of iced martinis, my special olives, my iced glass and my makeup case, which is very professional, and I paint my face." She was proud.

"I'll bet that is fun."

"Yes. I dream and play with my thoughts, but that's not all I do."

"How about the gin?"

"What do you mean?"

"Nothing, just what part does the gin play in all of this? How does it help?"

Captain envisioned her in the small cubicle that she called her dressing room, tanked, playacting up a storm. He looked to her happy face. He lost some of the sadness that he had felt for her. She was not like he'd first imagined: a beaten old dog, downtrodden, past rescue. She's a victim, he agreed. But she hasn't lost her spirit.

"All right," she said. "I know what you mean about my martinis. And it's probably true, but I don't care. I have a good time."

"What's probably true?" he asked, wanting to hear her say it.

She laughed. "That I get prettier and look more like Hedy Lamaar with every drink, of course." She doubled up her fist and gave him a pretty good punch on the shoulder. They both laughed. "Wait till I tell you about the time I got going on my hair with the scissors. I—"

"Look," Captain interrupted, pointing up the street. Bloom's Department Store was coming up on their left.

Mrs. Pearlstein's attitude changed the second that she saw it—the long, two-story, vertical red sign on which Bloom's Discount Department Store declared itself.

Captain couldn't see Mrs. Pearlstein's eyes, but he felt her regress in the seat beside him. She seemed to have a real foreboding of the place. "You'll be all right, kid," Captain assured her, patting her knee. "Here we go."

He waited for clearance, then pulled into a three-story, concrete parking structure directly across the street from Bloom's. The ceiling shaded them and it was slightly cooler.

Anxious, he scanned the first level and found a painted yellow wedge on the floor next to a huge round cement pylon. It said "No Parking" above it. He sneaked the Jensen in alongside the circular grey stone abutment on top of the yellow diamond and stopped.

Mrs. Pearlstein carried the iron, and Captain was sure that he detected a hesitation in the reserved click-clacking of her footsteps. A truck let them pass onto the crosswalk. "I'll bet you'd rather be home in front of your mirror," he laughed, helping Mrs. Pearlstein up onto the curb.

She didn't look up, just down, and spoke quietly as though to herself. "I'd rather be anywhere else. I forgot who I was."

"Will you knock that shit off. Jesus, I'm going to get the iron for you, and we'll be out of here in five minutes. Come on, Ruthie, buck up."

The sidewalk was not crowded. Glass display windows faced the street. They featured "Close Out," "Sale," and other come-ons soliciting bargain shoppers. Beige celluloid sun shields with tattered edges hung on the inside of the glass, inhibiting any honest color appraisal of goods.

"Don't you want to know what happened when I was here this morning?" she urged.

They walked into Bloom's through two large, aluminum-framed, piate-glass doors, wedged open into the store. There were no electric frills. "Just show me where you bought it—in what department."

"In the back," she said, without looking.

The store was a large, single-story, outmoded, five-and-dime or dry goods emporium. An office was housed in milky glass in the rear at the head of a short flight of stairs. The air smelled sour. They walked. There were signs throughout, hung from the ceiling and in chrome frames atop counters. More red lettering with promises and prices.

Mrs. Pearlstein grabbed Captain's lower left arm and held it tight. She stopped. He followed the direction of her look. There, leaning against a cash register, was a sales woman, her arms crossed with one foot up on the rim of a heavy metal wastebasket.

Captain continued Mrs. Pearlstein along. He watched the saleswoman's stare become cold as she followed their approach. "That's her," Mrs. Pearlstein whispered.

When he could, he read the white plastic name tag on M. Solomon's bosom and observed that she wasn't quite fifty, had thick Slavic features and used too much silver color in her hair, which shone blue. She possessed a skin condition that blotched the lines in her face and the one elbow that he could see with irritated-looking, red and white crusted skin. Her heavily boned brow shaded her eye sockets. Her long nose met her lips. She stood there, a totem.

They were close now. Captain removed his sunglasses. He put on his most guileless expression and looked into M. Solomon's eyes. He gave her his send your soul with me and trust look, and for a short time it seemed as though she would go. She stared back from neutral territory, the DMZ; he'd brought her that far.

"Hello. My name is Captain, and this is my friend Ruthie. Are you Miss or Mrs. Solomon?" he asked, flirting.

Her mouth moved, and while opening it to speak, she suddenly bit down hard on something white, the size of a kernel of corn. It oozed out between her upper and lower set of perfectly straight, white front teeth. When it crawled down onto her lower lip, M. Solomon became aware and snapped to all at once.

M. Solomon coughed. She raised a hand to cover her mouth. It arrived late. The white glob flew from her lip and landed across the last left-hand digit of the number-three buttons on the old-fashioned brown cash register. They all stared at it.

M. Solomon firmed her chops together and without a pause said, "Never mind all that. What do you want?"

The rotten breath that accompanied the projectile and now the words smelled ungodly. She was the one now; she had Captain on the lam.

"Never mind what?" he asked, hoping for something.

"Whether I'm married or not." Her eyes said that she was ready to fight.

"I was just trying to be friendly. This iron—Give me the iron, Ruthie—Here, this iron is defective and I would like to replace it with one that works—A simple thing."

Mrs. Pearlstein was rigid.

"Listen, mister, I've already been through this with her. Twice I've spent time with her today, even listened to her cry. I sold it to her; it was in the box when it left here. Do you hear that? In the box."

Speaking of boxes, he thought, I'd like to kick you in yours.

She pointed to a counter a few yards away. "Look there," she said. A sign read "Sale—Steam Irons—Factory Seconds, $17.89—Guaranteed."

"They're all in boxes, just like I told you." She looked at Mrs. Pearlstein and spoke in a cold, even tone. "Doesn't matter that you got friends, doesn't matter that you bring him back with you, that you come back all snazzed up and bring him—doesn't matter." With that she seemed to slump, to lose her strength. "Besides," she sighed, "I only work here. Mr. Bloom's the boss. I told you that this morning. Now I've got things to do."

"Wait a minute," Captain said firmly. "We didn't mean to upset you. Where is Mr. Bloom?"

M. Solomon made a motion with her open thumb and closed hand, like a hitchhiker, back over her shoulder, toward the stairway. "Up those stairs in the office. But it won't do ya no good, you know it won't." She looked at Mrs. Pearlstein. "Forget it. Go home."

"What is Mr. Bloom's first name?" Captain inquired.

"Reno" was the answer.

"Well, pick up your phone, please, and tell Reno Bloom that there is someone to see him, and tell him that it won't take a minute."

M. Solomon looked very tired. Mrs. Pearlstein pulled on Captain's arm. "Please, dear, don't you see how difficult it is? Please, let's just go. I can do without."

He discarded Mrs. Pearlstein's arm and looked in at her through her sunglasses. "Did you break it—the truth?"

"No, no. It never worked, honestly. You can believe me of that. I just took it out of the box and—and—plugged it in and—and—nothing."

"Are you sure?"

"I swear it."

"All right, Ruthie. M. Solomon, call Reno now, please."

M. Solomon didn't resist any longer. She moved the short distance to her phone slump-shouldered.

Captain looked down at her legs when she turned away. He saw the broken, purple veins stand out through what he assumed was a cheap pair of support hose. The arches of M. Solomon's shoes were broken. An ache ran through his feet watching her shuffling walk around to the side of the counter. Jesus, he thought, what a way to have to go. He realized that he was grinding his teeth and stopped.

M. Solomon dialed one digit. Captain heard the phone ring

behind the clouded glass in the office above them at the head of the stairs.

"Talk," came the tough abrupt answer from overhead.

"That woman with the broken iron is back," from M. Solomon.

The man answered in an aggravated gruff tone. Captain couldn't distinguish the words.

"No, the one this morning that cried. She brought a friend." M. Solomon seemed exhausted. Captain figured that Reno Bloom must have inquired "Which one?" for M. Solomon to specify "The one that cried."

"That's cute," he said out loud. "The one that cried. That's real cute."

Did that mean that there were others? How many? He wondered. He started to feel uncomfortable, hot.

Reno Bloom was apparently short tempered. He slammed the phone down. It hurt M. Solomon's ear. Captain watched a large black shadow get up and move across the clouded glass windows above them. The gold stenciled office letters were fraying. The entire office shook when the door burst open at the head of the landing.

He stepped out. "Yes, what is it?" the big man demanded, glaring.

After Dr. Blood's death, the family was brave. Captain's uncles came and took over, making all of the arrangements. Nicklaus, a lawyer, handled the paper work. The insurance was satisfactory. Nothing would change for them. His mother and sister became closer, if that was possible, and Captain was sent away to finish high school at Bradock, a military academy. He hadn't minded at first. It got him away from the house. But it turned out to be a bore. One and one-half years of tedious regimen, spiced only by the ongoing investigation. The school's most offensively malicious bully had been found in the gymnasium, hanging upside down over a plastic garbage can. His ankles had been tied to the chin-up bar with a jumping rope. Castrated, the boy's upper body pressure points had been torn open. A mop and bucket stood close by. The slayer had waited to clean up his mess. The authorities were everywhere, doing everything. It was fun to watch them work. It went unsolved.

Captain stared up at Reno Bloom. The man was leering down at him. A knot began to tie itself in Captain's gut.

"Who wants me?" boomed the voice again.

Captain rolled his eyes. Mrs. Pearlstein looked like a frozen gypsy. He flicked his eyes to M. Solomon. She had turned her back on the entire thing and was resting on her stiffened arms and palms. Both of her elbows were infected. Changing her position, she scratched at the knuckles of her right hand, she dug at them, she chewed them.

"I'm a busy man. Who wants me?"

Captain dropped the iron from his right hand, his sunglasses from his left. They lay where they landed. Captain measured the stairs as he ran. He made the staircase in three strides, grabbed the railing with his left hand and drove himself up the flight to the step just below Reno.

"I do," he said on fire, but with a changing mind.

Reno had let go of the office door; it closed. The smell was strong again—fish—smoked fish, like a delicatessen. Reno put his burly left forearm in front of himself; his right hand was formed into a mitsu karate driving wedge, the thumb firmly fixed against straightened fingers. It was held taut and steady and aimed directly at Captain's heart.

Captain's gaze was held by Reno's watch. The face reflected light into Captain's eyes. He tried to read the time in spite of it. He felt a need to know the hour, but it couldn't be done. He wondered about Reno's discomfort in removing the watch, the gold expansion band being engulfed in thick black hair.

Reno turned his watch arm over and hooked his thumb into his belt before Captain could figure it. "You look like you need a baby, kid," Reno said in a sleazy tone. His right hand remained the wedge.

Captain was six feet tall. Discarding the stair that separated them, he made Reno at at least six three, probably six feet four, and about 230 pounds. Standing above him as he was, Reno appeared a giant. The sleeves of his white monogrammed shirt were rolled up, flat gold cuff links hung from the open cuffs. He wore synthetic dark blue suit pants and had on a shined pair of black lace oxfords that looked to be Navy issue.

"Goddamn, you've got big feet," Captain thought out loud.

"What'd you say? Come on kid, move on me. I thought you were gonna move on me. Nothing would be sweeter, my own store and all. When you came up the stairs, I had it all put together, 'cause I'm fast. It's my business to be fast."

Reno loosened his fingers and began to gesticulate by moving his big hairy paws like thick pinkish cleavers. He used them to cut the air, to make room for his words. He was excited. Spittle was forming in the corners of his mouth. "All you'd have to do, pal, is clench your fist. That's all, just clench it. I'm watching that free hand like a hawk. Or move that one off the rail. Go on, take it off the rail and clench it—That'll be all she wrote for you, pal."

Captain watched Reno's mouth work. It was especially ugly, the kind with short teeth and long gums. He didn't listen to the words, just observed the twist and curl of that frothing animal mouth.

Captain stepped down one step. "Sorry about this," he said placatingly.

Reno was ecstatic, on his very own stage. His ego ran around crazy in his eyes; they danced. Reno grabbed both railings and leaned his upper body toward Captain. "Yeah, yeah, I'll bet that you are sorry, poop chute. D'ya take it in the poop chute, kid?"

Reno laughed a repulsive laugh. He was perspiring freely, his toupee loosening from his forehead. It would have been a beauty of a time to take him, but Captain pushed the thought past.

"I'm only trying to do what is right, Mr. Bloom, trying to fix a broken iron for an elderly lady friend of mine. Why don't we—"

"Crappo, pal. I know what you want, and it's all crappo. You and her both need a baby."

"Need a baby? What do you mean, need a baby?"

Reno slowed down and smiled. He'd been asked to participate. There was a new sparkle in his eye. Saliva draped between his lips. "You both need to get screwed, that's what." He knew his store, how far voices traveled. He yelled it, but only the three of them heard. He stepped up to his office door and opened it.

"You're quite a guy, Mr. Bloom, and I suppose this is a tough business."

"Yeah, yeah. What's the point?" he gloated.

"I want to replace that iron."

"No way." He let the door close again. He pulled his slacks up and left his thumbs in the belt. "Now get outta here and take that old—take her with you, and consider yourself lucky, pal. I'm a black belt." He held out his huge hands. "I've killed with these and that's no shit."

"I believe you, Mr. Bloom, but leaving all that aside, if you thought in your heart that the story she told you earlier was true, would you exchange the iron— I mean, it does say guaranteed on the sign."

"Yeah, well, that's not your business. I don't know why I'm talking to you. The answer is *no*." He opened the door and stepped into his office.

"For anyone?" Captain yelled.

67

"Not even my mother," he called back. "And if you don't like it, call a cop." The door closed.

Captain watched the dark shadow move across the office and sit down. He thought he heard him laugh. Captain became aware of his trembling hands. His stomach felt queasy. He had experienced Reno Bloom, seen the beast for himself. It's little wonder Ruthie had cried, he thought. "Easy does it, friend. All will be well," he spoke quietly to himself.

"Dear—Are you all right, dear?" Mrs. Pearlstein called hesitatingly from below.

Captain exchanged whatever look he wore for one of embarrassment. He turned to see Mrs. Pearlstein at the foot of the stairs, obviously distressed. M. Solomon was leaning on her sick arms, looking out into the store, just as she'd been before. A totem, he thought, his anger rising. This he caught and trimmed immediately. He would not allow himself to take things out on M. Solomon. Captain knew what to do next; the very thought of it made him feel chipper. But, it would have to wait till later. He smiled down at Mrs. Pearlstein and skipped down the stairs two at a time. He checked his watch.

"Ruthie, I've got a surprise for you. How does an iced rum julep or two and Cantonese food in a cool dark corner at the Beachcomber sound?"

Mrs. Pearlstein seemed stunned; her jaw hung in that funny way. "The Beachcomber. But what about—?"

"You were right, that's all," he cut her off. "And it's no big deal—Come on." He picked up his dark glasses from the gray carpet and left the iron. He walked over in front of M. Solomon, whose sullen expression held no secrets. Captain withdrew a handful of paper money from his pocket and selected a fifty dollar bill.

"M. Solomon, please give me two guaranteed steam irons and

test them to make sure that they work." He put the bill under a heavy tape dispenser on the counter.

"We don't test the irons," she replied in a monotone.

"All right, just look in the boxes and make sure that they have plugs and cords. Okay?" he laughed.

M. Solomon went and returned with two cardboard boxes from under the iron display card. She brought them back and opened them. Mrs. Pearlstein stood close while Captain inspected the first iron. He approved it and put it back into the box.

"Well, now, look at this." He held the second iron in his left hand and tugged lightly on the cord with his right. The black fiberglass insulator between the cord and the iron was brittle and cracked in two, exposing a piece of copper wire.

"There, you see," Mrs. Pearlstein said. "They're junk, just junk."

M. Solomon took the iron from Captain and sat it down on the counter next to the tape dispenser. She went and selected another boxed iron. She opened it herself and applied the same test that Captain had been using.

"That one looks good," he said. "Give me my change."

M. Solomon rang $17.89 twice and added the tax.

"Here, Ruthie, take these." He handed Mrs. Pearlstein the boxes containing the two good irons.

"Thirty-seven ninety-three with tax," M. Solomon said.

"Go ahead," Captain gestured to the bill beneath the tape. He didn't like to carry change, especially pennies, so after pocketing the twelve dollars, he put the seven cents into a Muscular Dystrophy decanter next to the register. The coins dropped against hollow tin, and he smiled at Mrs. Pearlstein. "It doesn't take much figuring to guess who this money makes well, does it, Ruthie." Captain took the boxes from Mrs. Pearlstein and helped her toward the door.

69

"You don't think—?"

Captain could see the question in her eyes beneath the dark glass.

"What do you think?" he answered.

The soft leather seats were cool against their legs as they pulled back into the day. The afternoon sky was burning a bright brownish orange. They used the Jensen's sun visors driving west into Hollywood. Captain could feel Mrs. Pearlstein wanting to say, I told you so, or, He even told you off—You see, I do have a hard way to go. But he wouldn't acknowledge her feelings. She had her new iron, and time would cure the hurt. Time cured everything, he thought, except malignancy, and that could only die.

He played loud music, sang along and put his finger over his lips to shush her most of the way. She appeared warm under the sun, and he helped her off with her jacket, which she then carried on her lap. Stretching to loosen the jacket, her surprisingly large bust pushed out against her silk blouse and strained the buttons; the ruffles separated. Funny how I missed that, he thought. It must have been the robe, then the jacket. He noticed the thick bra straps, how they dug into her shoulders from the strain, the weight.

He imagined a heavy duty brassiere, specially made with an extra full cup. There were other straps too. Thin silky ones from a camisole. Her blouse was wet under the arms with perspiration, but that was no cause for aversion. Because it was there, right there under her arms that you could see the puffed flesh enter the front of the bra.

He watched her breasts jiggle and bounce. He wanted to casually undo one button and slip his hand through the ruffles and into the top of her brassiere. He would knead those big tits like they were dough, roll her nipples between his fingers until—. Mrs. Pearlstein turned his attention to her face by pantomiming

70

cigarette smoking. He blushed while he conceded, having completely forgotten the identity of his passenger. She smoked the rest of the way.

Captain stopped the music, pulled up into the shade of the Beachcomber's bamboo awning and parked next to the valet parking sign. The luncheon crowd had thinned; the automobile attendant was undoubtedly catching a bite in the kitchen.

Captain recalled his car-parking days at the famous Beefeaters Restaurant on La Cienega Boulevard and what lunch had meant to him during that time. While studying biology at UCLA, he had earned himself a twenty dollar bill every afternoon plus all he could eat. He had led a quiet existence, spending most of his time alone with his books. He stayed too thin and was poor by design. Beer and bourbon were never far away; he ate once a day, a feast. The gourmet meals that left the Beefeaters Restaurant under Captain's jacket or in his pants could have made the most particular connoisseur swoon.

One day he had just come from the kitchen with a beautifully aged New York steak in his jeans when Mrs. Julia Robins, one of his late luncheon regulars, pulled her pink Continental in. As usual, she was full of champagne and wouldn't consider leaving her car until Captain was at her door so that she could give him a view up her skirt as she alighted. This was always accompanied by some off-color remark about her impotent husband or what she liked to do in bed.

On this particular afternoon, when he opened the door of her Lincoln for her, she looked at his crotch, bleary-eyed and said, "When are you going to let me see that big piece of meat, honey?"

Nietzsche said, "Audacity is essential to greatness." That and the bonded bourbon, the timing and his just plain inability to resist temptation, prompted him to unzip his fly and fumble around in his pants for the small end of the New Yorker. Mrs. Robins' painted eyes were frozen on his action. He gorged the big fatty piece of red meat through his pants, and it filled up his fly at the base, such a gorgeous hunk of meat it was. He squeezed it hard and watched for her expression.

Mrs. Julia Robins' eyes rolled up into her head; she gulped out loud, swallowed her tongue and fell back into her pink car in a dead faint. Captain laughed at the memory.

"Now you're the one that's laughing at a secret," Mrs. Pearlstein said.

"No, Ruthie, that's not it. There are no secrets. I just feel good. I'm grateful, that's all." Smiling at her he touched her sleeve and arm. "I'm grateful for the beautiful day—my health—for you. I'm happy, Ruthie. It makes me laugh and feel like having fun."

"Even after—after that—that scene at Bloom's?"

"Especially after that. That just makes me appreciate the good things. There is too much good in life to worry about what happened. Life is true and just if you don't let other people bother you. You can't worry about them; you have no control. Just be honest with Ruthie, that's all. God wants unity. He has ways of keeping score, take my word for it."

Mrs. Pearlstein had been looking down. She looked into his face. "I'm glad I know you, Captain. You're a good person."

Henry Aldrich

It made him feel excited. It was her way of saying thank you. He accepted it. "I don't know how really good I am, Ruthie. I'm not sure I even understand what good means." He jumped out of the car, folded two singles under the windshield for the boy and opened Mrs. Pearlstein's door.

She had something on her mind.

"What is it, Ruthie?"

She paused first, then said it straight at him, like a real friend would do. "I don't want to be judged by you, Captain."

He laughed and hugged her. "Ruthie, I give up my judgment for your friendship. Come on, I'm thirsty."

Captain dropped the car keys into her coat pocket while he helped her on with it. He stood in back of her and cursed his positioning when she put her elbows together to fill the sleeves. He tried to look over her shoulder to no avail; fabric was moving.

73

She yawned. "Oh, I'm sorry."

They walked. "I know how you feel—the booze and the sun. You're probably ready for a nap."

"I can go as long as you can," she laughed.

A green Astro-turf carpet laid out in front of the place was made for her shoes. She feigned making a putt. The door was polished, wooden and heavy. "Oh, that feels good," she said, stepping into the cool dark room. Captain agreed, letting the door close in back of them.

The next instant from the darkness they were greeted with, "Yes, please—lunch for two?"

Captain felt his perspiration rapidly begin to dry, leaving his skin too cool. He was glad that Mrs. Pearlstein had worn a jacket, lightweight as it was.

"Is Brad here?" he asked into the darkness.

"Oh, you want Brad. Oh, Brad—yes, he's in the bar."

The room was empty except for a white-haired man in a rather good-looking, cream-colored suit who drank alone at the end of the bar, and Brad. Brad was behind the bar in his customary not-busy hunch, his eyes two inches from a newspaper. He was smoking.

Brad was famous, or at least Captain thought of him that way. He had been born with congenital cataracts on both eyes, a malady that cannot be corrected by surgery or improved by prescription glass. His vision was 20/20 up to one foot; thereafter it became a blur until at one mile he claimed an ability to distinguish features. In spite of his problem Brad was a beauty of a guy with a wife and daughter that he loved more than his existence. He spent every minute with his little girl, Penny, a chess master at thirteen.

He mixed a decent drink despite his not touching the stuff and smoked five to six packs of cigarettes a day, which freaked Captain out completely. Brad was a tall, thin, dark haired, close to handsome, forty-year-old authority on everything, and try as he might, Captain could never find him wrong.

The light in the bar was much better than the dining room had been and reflected a reddish hue. Standing in the shadows with Mrs. Pearlstein wouldn't be fair. Captain moved into the illumination of the room and cleared his throat. Brad reacted like a cat. Captain loved it, watching Brad's senses at work. He stared at the two of them; his nose seemed to twitch.

Captain held Mrs. Pearlstein's arm and didn't move. Brad didn't blink; he pointed like a springer spaniel. Soon he broke the trance, stood up straight with a proud smile, clapped his hands together and said, "Captain, my man. And who's that with you?"

"My name is not Captain," Captain said in a gruff, deeply southerned accent. They moved toward the bar. The smile fell off of Brad's face.

"Oh—oh, I'm sorry, I was sure that—"

"Bradley, I can't do it to you," Captain interrupted, unable to watch his friend's discomfort.

"I was right, aha. Captain, how are you?"

"A lot better now that I see you. Got any fresh juice for the rum?"

"Coming up," was Brad's reply on the way to the kitchen.

"Excuse me, dear, I'm off to the ladies room."

"Just walk slow and easy."

She headed for the bathroom carefully but with dispatch. Captain bet that she'd been holding it since the Palms. He pulled out two stools opposite Brad's paper and sat down. The man at the end of the bar wore clear glass, octagonal spectacles with gold wire bows. They made him look knowledgeable. The man saw Captain observing and raised his glass as though to toast. He

75

nodded, smiled and went back to his drink, clear liquid on the rocks without an olive.

Brad's chessboard sat next to the opened newspaper, a few pieces in place. "Can you figure it out?" Brad asked, returning behind the bar with a green plastic pitcher. Captain saw the drawing of a chessboard in the open newspaper and supposed Brad had been working that day's problem.

"No, I just noticed it now."

"Is that Iris?" Brad asked.

"No, her name is Ruth Pearlstein. She lives in my building."

"Is she a looker?"

The silver-haired man at the end of the bar watched Captain for his answer.

"She's sixty years old going on twenty, Brad. A good broad, a friend. Knows how to drink too."

"Well I put a fresh pineapple through the juicer. Smell." He held the pitcher under Captain's face. The biting acidic fumes filled Captain's nose. His eyes watered; he sneezed out loud into the room behind him.

"Wow," he said, blowing his nose on a bar napkin, "that is fresh."

"I've got mint too," Brad said, "right here in the refridg."

"What are you blabbing for then—Fix 'em up. How about you, mister? One of Brad's rum juleps on me?" he invited.

The man secured his glasses with a push up on the nose piece from his middle finger. "Kinda sweet, aren't they?"

"No, just fresh juice, two kinds of rum and plain soda. Pineapple is the sweetener. Try one, Henry. Oh, Henry, shake hands with Captain. Captain, this is Henry Aldrich. Henry, meet Captain Blood."

They were casually reaching to shake hands when Brad spoke their last names. They paused with a questioning look at each other and looked to Brad. Brad's perception of movement and instinct must have signaled him that something was wrong. He rubbed his chin with his hand and immersed himself in thought.

"My God," he said quickly. "That's the truth. I mean that's—those are your real names. How about that—I didn't think of it until right now. It seems I know you both so well, I take your names for granted."

Captain couldn't help but smile. Judging from Henry Aldrich's expression, he was amused also. Captain left his stool and shook hands with Henry.

Mrs. Pearlstein returned, and Captain introduced them. She put out her hand, Henry took it and kissed it. The old goat, Captain thought, introducing her to Brad. They sat and Brad explained the ingredients of a rum julep to Mrs. Pearlstein while he quartered a lime.

"I like your name," Captain said.

Henry Aldrich lit a Camel and blew a cloud of smoke out of the corner of his mouth. He laughed and coughed into his hand. "I like yours too. Somebody in your family like pirates?"

Getting a whiff, Mrs. Pearlstein and Brad started smoking too. Captain waved the smoke away with his hands. "My father was an Errol Flynn fan, I guess. That's how the story goes anyway—Thought he looked like him."

"Interesting. Did he?"

Captain remembered. "Yes, he did—handsome man."

"Yeah. Blood's your family name, though, is it?"

"Yep. Yours Aldrich?"

"Yeah. So your dad picked your name, huh?"

Captain nodded.

Brad started with Henry Aldrich. He put a long-stemmed rum julep in front of him, then one for Mrs. Pearlstein and Captain.

"Have you got any brothers or sisters?" Henry wanted to know.

"A sister."

"What's her name?"

"Iris," Captain answered.

"Well, that's normal enough for 'em." He laughed and lifted up the new drink to toast. "Here's to Ruth, the beachcomber of the month."

Mrs. Pearlstein blushed and said, "Oh," but they all laughed and toasted each other. Brad had rubbed the rims of the glasses with fresh lime, which caused a small crack in Captain's lip to smart. The drinks were delicious, heavy with dark rum.

Mrs. Pearlstein excused herself from the stool to take her jacket off. Captain thought she could do it while still sitting, but that wasn't what she wanted. She refused help and stepped out in back of Captain to shrug the garment. Her arms behind her, she wrestled to get out of the sleeves. She nonchalantly pushed her heavy bust out. There was no mistaking who the display was meant to arouse. Henry Aldrich was staring.

"Brad, I'm going to pull this table up close," Captain said, moving a heavy, metal-based wooden table up to within a few feet of the bar. He brought two chairs and then a third, to leave the side of the table nearest the bar open for a direct line to Brad. "Come on, Henry. Come on, Ruthie," he said, moving the chairs out to accompany them. "Any problem, Brad?"

"No problem," Brad answered. "You want a tablecloth?"

"Sure, why not do it right," and after looking at Henry Aldrich scooping up his Camels and Mrs. Pearlstein with her Salems, he said, "And a big ashtray—a big huge one."

Henry Aldrich brought Mrs. Pearlstein's drink. While he ambled over to the table, Captain and Mrs. Pearlstein had a chance to size him up. Captain tried to look at her sternly. She smiled, unashamed. She apparently liked what she saw. Henry's build appeared strong and lean under the beige suit that had been cut during another time. It was complete with a vest of the same good

78

material. He sported a tasteful gold chain that went from vest pocket to pocket across his chest. He wore a light blue shirt frayed at the collar but spotless. He tied his own bow tie, brown with small yellow flowers; the bows hung down from the knot, accentuating his jowls. The loose brown spotted skin underneath his jaw apparently took up the slack, because the skin over the rest of his face, though wrinkled, was taut. The tearing corners of his aging blue eyes were exaggerated behind his glasses, and there was his handsome, silver gray, full head of hair, the ends cut too abruptly by an amateur.

Henry clicked his glass against Mrs. Pearlstein's and nodded with it toward Captain as he'd done earlier. "Heck of a drink," he said.

"Yes, dear, it's absolutely delicious," she said, smacking her lips.

Captain swallowed two large mouthfuls. It made him feel good, but it didn't compare with their approval. And now they were looking at each other, sipping; no conversation, yet no tension. Captain could feel the relaxed feeling pass between them. It was listless but very pleasing. It made his taint tingle. (Taint rectum and it taint scrotum).

"Where do you golf?" he asked her.

The mood was broken, and Captain saw the color drain from Mrs. Pearlstein's face. "It was my idea," Captain interjected before she could answer. "I thought we'd at least be able to catch the back nine, but the day hasn't worked out that way. Do you like your name, Henry?" Captain knew the question was a bore and would have hated it if asked of him, but—

"Yes, I do. There was a time when it was famous on radio, and I guess I just got used to it—all the bull. But I'm kinda proud of myself, I guess. I've been through quite a bit in my life and survived, so I'm proud of my name. It's me."

"That's very nice," Mrs. Pearlstein said. She went to light up; Henry Aldrich lit it for her with his disposable lighter and lit one of his own.

"I mean, there's really nothing to a name. It's a label, that's all. Got nothing to do with what's in the package, on the inside, good or bad, if you see my point."

"Yes, yes, I do, and it's a good point," Captain said.

"You look like a czarina," Henry spoke to Mrs. Pearlstein.

"Is that good?" she questioned.

"It sure is. That turban is sure sharp looking. It gives you authority like a czarina. It gives you class, I guess they'd say."

Mrs. Pearlstein blushed and looked like she was going to start panting. But keeping it together she said thank you.

She became suddenly soft, vulnerable. Captain felt defensive on her behalf. He wanted to cut Henry Aldrich off, to make him stop. She's been hurt enough. Don't give her false hope. But before he could conjure up the words, he saw that it was too late. Neither of them cared about his opinion any longer; they were into each other, becoming infatuated.

Jesus, Captain thought, finishing his drink, I'm a third wheel. When he stood, Mrs. Pearlstein broke away to ask, "Are you all right, dear?"

"Yes, sure. All is well. I just need a refill."

Brad had moved the paper and the chessboard to the end of the bar. Captain sat down across from him. "Excellent drink, my friend. One more, please." Captain glanced over his shoulder. Henry Aldrich was pointing an accusing finger at Mrs. Pearlstein. She was gesturing to explain, and they both started laughing. Henry Aldrich slapped the top of the table and reached across to squeeze Mrs. Pearlstein's hand. Captain reproved himself for thinking dirty, but that didn't stop him from imagining Mrs. Pearlstein wet between her legs, readjusting to that good old feeling.

Brad put a fresh napkin down and a drink on top of it. "You okay, babe?" Brad inquired.

"Absolutely," Captain answered. "I don't drink when I'm not."

"Is that the truth?"

"Yes, acquired the habit from my dad. When business is bad or you're sad or lonely, that's when not to drink. How's your kid, Brad?"

"Penny?" Brad's eyes widened and he smiled and shook his head. "She's too much, just too much. She took the Minnesota Multiphasic I.Q. test last month, and we got the results last week. Guess what her reading level is—Go on, guess.

Brad asked the question as though it were a dare, he was so proud.

"You're sure crazy about her, aren't you?"

Brad looked at the bar boards under his feet and shuffled around in embarrassment. "Me? Oh, yeah," he said finally. "She reads at a college freshman level, Cap. How about that?"

"That's nice, Brad, but—" He drank the rum.

"But what?" Brad asked.

"But what happens when you love someone that much and something happens to them? Shit, you're finished, aren't you?"

"What do you mean, something happens to them?" Brad questioned.

"Oh, I don't know. You know, a bad heart or getting hit by a car or a disease. You know, you lose her."

Brad started to laugh. "I don't worry about that stuff, Cap. Hell, I'd go nuts. I just love her the best I can, that's all I can do. God's been good to me. He won't take her away." He lit a cigarette and blew the smoke out over his shoulder. "Man, is it dead," Brad said, walking over to the phone and dialing.

Captain started to feel the heat of the rum in his system. He turned to glimpse Mrs. Pearlstein. Henry Aldrich had moved to

81

her side of the table. He had one long arm around her, the other in the air to make a point. Captain supposed that it was all well and good, Brad's love and what was happening between Mrs. Pearlstein and Henry Aldrich. He didn't want her to come crying when Aldrich took a walk though. No, he would stay with his love for ideals. Sex with a partner wasn't the odds-on favorite with Captain. Not that he put it down, either, but he could please himself and minimize the losses.

The hottest climaxes in his life had come while he was alone. He had his ways, his special lovers, but he maintained self-preservation. Life size, they came through the mail, under a plain brown wrapper, in black and white: Evelyn West and her treasure chest and Tempest Storm—he loved them. Evelyn held her huge breasts up and squeezed the dark gray nipples at him. The pigment must have been eight inches across. The Tempest just let them hang. They were gorgeous, and her smile said that she knew it. With the family away, Captain would put a rubber sheet down to contain his untidyness; he hated a mess. This in front of the full-length hall mirror. The chandelier burned brightly, and he would make love. A small cut over their vaginas served as an entrance, while a pound of butter with a tight hole handled the action from behind. His women gave him spectacular pleasure but no lip.

He cringed and drank rum, thinking of the thermometer. He thanked God and knocked on the wooden bar that he'd given that one up when he did. The ladies had lain on the floor beneath him. They watched while he did it and never, ever, judged him. He abused himself. He liked to slip an oral thermometer into his erect penis, all the way in until it vanished. He would then flex his sphincter and the muscles of his lower torso and watch it reappear. He would find a trace of blood on the instrument, but any tissue damage was overshadowed by the immensely gratifying orgasmic sensation that he experienced.

HENRY ALDRICH

Captain had a vivid recollection of the dread day when he had stopped this practice. He had frightened himself out of it.

Exhausted, half-sitting and half-lying, nude, in an overstuffed chair in the living room, he was recovering from an extended session with the thermometer. Many times he had pushed it in and out to experience an unusually heavy orgasm during the last expulsion. The thermometer hung from his hand. He stared at it.

Captain rubbed the long thin stem of the rum julep glass. It came back to him again, the vision. Anna from Auschwitz was there and Trina from Treblinka and the bitch from Belsen: The beasts who roamed the compounds of frightened men, a herculean sadist at their side, looking for tattoos, deciding who would go down behind the horrendous pain from unspeakable tortures, deciding whose testes would be smashed. Captain was brought with other men for her wicked pleasure into her room, her theater, her lair. The place of blue-green tile from floor to ceiling. His high school shower room without the hardware, but the floor sloped to a drain. The drain was there, and voices echoed. Hoses were connected and lay rolled into corners. Liquids seeped. Naked, they were put into stocks, like cattle. They shivered and cowered. Their penises shrunk. They stood numb, prayed out. The stench of excrement and starch was there.

She walked down the line of men, disrobing, her eyes flashing between their eyes and their penises. Her helpers were in the shadows. They had their meat out, watching, pulling and pushing, beating. She began touching the victims, and they responded. She hung around Captain. She went to a table and retrieved a blade. She slit the throats of the others. They moaned and bled over themselves into the drain. The brutes ejaculated onto their leathers.

She stripped, and Captain saw the swastikas branded over the nipples of her heaving breasts. Unhealed, she picked the scabs. The crooked crosses ran red. She gritted her teeth and smiled.

83

Her clitoris was enormous and stood out like a pear from amidst her shaven vulva. It pounded purple. Captain's eyelids were gone; he had to observe. She played with him. He thought against it. He redirected his blood. Don't go there. It's my life—my soul—my man—keep soft. But it grew. She teased and it grew. She touched and stooped to lick, and it grew against his wishes until it had never been gorged so full. He looked down and wept. He was saying goodby.

She went to her table and returned with the thermometer under her tongue. She petted his organ. Her helpers abused each other with cords and the lash. They performed anal intercourse in the shade. Captain's breathing had stopped. She slid the salivated thermometer into his erection. She teased his balls and waited. She reached up into his scrotum and pushed. The thermometer reappeared from his stretched hole like a tire gauge under pressure.

She held it up and read it. Smiling, she pointed at the number for him to see. 1,000 degrees—the fluids in his body were boiling, his organ was melting. He could have told her. She slid it back in and grabbed his rigid penis with both hands, like the last two grips on a baseball bat when you're a kid and choosing.

The dead men watched. The helpers were humping. The room spun. She screamed like an animal, a banshee, a loud, piercing cry that stopped when she broke Captain's penis. She dropped it and watched excitedly. It hung there, half hard, choked with broken glass. Gray fulminated mercury filled his veins.

Then he was hard again. His penis was silver, then chrome. The skin split down the center like a ruptured sausage and spilled bubbling, thick semen onto the bitch's face. She closed her eyes and reveled in it. She licked her chops. She retrieved her blade. She put it against Captain's forehead and drew it down. He fell in half. He looked into the pieces and they were empty. He was

84

hollow, made of nothing. And that had scared him more than the priestess of pain.

The delicate thin stem of the rum julep glass cracked within his grip. The drink and broken glass splashed onto the bar. Captain watched Brad tell Marilyn to hang on, drop the phone and come running.

"Cappy, what the hell?"

The receiver hung and spun crazily in the air, around and back around. "Cap, you're soaked with sweat. What is it? And your hand, you've cut your hand." Brad grabbed him by the shoulders and shook him hard.

Not making an issue, Brad threw Captain a bar towel and stepped back to make a new drink. "Wrap that around your hand. That daydream—ahh—looked more like a day-mare." They laughed together.

The new drink was poured into a deep glass dish, a tub. It tasted strong. Brad said hello from Captain, told Marilyn that he loved her and hung up.

"How's Iris?" Brad asked, making conversation.

"Right now she's probably pissed off, wondering where I am. I should call her. But she's the same, Brad—beautiful."

"God, the last time that you were here, after you left—man, the guys at the bar went nuts about how hot-looking she is. I sure wish I could see better."

Captain thought about that. "I remember. She had her hair up, all piled up, and that top," Captain laughed, "that yellow halter top. I remember. I don't let her dress like that unless she's with me. It's even dangerous then. The next time that we're in, Brad, I'll ask her to let you have a little feel. Then you won't have to wonder about what she's got."

Brad blushed. "Oh, no. Marilyn wouldn't like that, I'm afraid."

"I mean it," Captain said. "Iris would probably let you if I asked—maybe."

"I mean it too," was the retort. "I'm a married man, you know, not that I don't appreciate the offer though." He wiped a glass.

Son of a bitch, Captain thought, he won't consider it, won't even jerk himself off a little with the thought. Not that Iris would ever consider it anyway, but shit—. Acting salty, Captain picked up his drink. "Here's to monogamy." He drank the drink dry.

"Damn it, Cap, that's just the way that it is for me. Don't hassle me."

Captain didn't speak. Inside, he admired Brad's recalcitrance. "Brad, I'm kidding."

"I know, I know you are, you crazy man you. Another?"

"Another."

So people got themselves into all sorts of problems chasing Iris, but Brad—Brad was being offered a feel and was afraid of what Marilyn might say. Captain looked at Brad. Brad was true blue. He kept it simple and was happy. "You're a good man, Brad," he said, meaning it.

"We're friends," was the reply, and that described Captain's view of their relationship perfectly. Thinking about it for a moment, Captain guessed that he trusted Brad in much the same way that he trusted Hays.

Then Reno came to his mind, and Captain was anxious to move. Mrs. Pearlstein and Henry Aldrich were finishing their second round. Captain would bring up leaving. He was weary of his list, but he ran it one more time. Once more and then, when the moment came to fill it, it would take care of itself.

A. The Dodge.
B. The new iron.
C. A 20-foot extension cord.

D. An A/C electrical converter.

E. Clothing—includes towels, gloves.

F. His Welby .455. (A big bore for a big bore.)

He laughed at that one.

Brad looked up from his paper and smiled.

"Dear," Mrs. Pearlstein called. Captain turned to see them both with comfortable expressions on their faces. "We're starving, dear. What are we going to do?"

"I'm not eating," Captain replied. "No point in blowing a twenty dollar high with a three dollar lunch."

Henry Aldrich laughed and Mrs. Pearlstein said, "Oh, now, dear."

Brad called attention to three large menus he was holding. Henry Aldrich asked Brad to hold on while he walked over to Captain. Being friendly, he put his large hand on Captain's shoulder. He explained that he and Mrs. Pearlstein were really hitting it off and had a whole bunch of things in common. The most important one at the moment being an aversion to Oriental food.

"All right, all right, I've got the picture," Captain said. Henry opened his mouth to speak, but Captain shushed him. He removed Henry's hand. "Answer me a couple of questions, Henry?"

"Anything," he volunteered openly.

"Do you have a car?"

"Yes, yes, I sure do, right in the lot outside. Dependable too."

Captain looked into Henry's eyes for a long moment. He bade Henry to follow and went to Mrs. Pearlstein. He spoke to both of them.

"Dear," Captain said. "You two have made progress."

"That's just a figure of—"

"Sure, Henry, sure."

87

"But you'll be joining us, won't you?"

"Not today, Ruthie. Now I want to ask you—Do you still want Henry here to take you home in his car and come for lunch? Have you consulted the policeman?" Captain pointed to his forehead.

She answered yes as casually as she could. There was excitement in her eyes. Why the old kootie, Captain thought, I'll bet you take him home and have him for lunch.

"Brad, put a couple of bottles of good white wine—cold—in a bag for my friends to take." Henry turned to help Mrs. Pearlstein up, but Captain caught his upper arm and turned him back around. He stared into Henry's eyes. "Henry, I expect you to do what is right—no more, no less. Is that a deal?"

"That is a deal," he said seriously. He put out his hand to shake. Captain took it. Kissing Mrs. Pearlstein on the cheek, Captain told her that he'd bring the irons and to have fun. He winked. She blushed. Captain told Brad that the bill was his. Henry protested to no avail. Captain scooped up his drink and headed for the john.

The mens room was white. It smelled of detergent and looked clean, befitting a better restaurant. The single, old-fashioned porcelain urinal was built into the wall.

Captain placed his drink next to the sweaty, stainless-steel flushing handle at chest level. After a moment and a sigh he released a heavy flow of clear urine. He watched it pour out of him and over the concave milk-colored glass walls. It swirled around the recessed bowl, which lay at the tips of his toes. It disappeared through the mesh of a raised metal drain shield that resembled an oversized thimble.

Suddenly, startled by the initial splash, a large, shiny black cockroach darted out from its hiding place beneath the urinal's protective lip. A cold chill shot through Captain's body. His sphincter muscle jolted shut, cutting the flow. Captain watched the black bug scramble crazily up and around the slippery white surface, only to slide back down again. The protruding metal sieve kept him from the sewer, while the abrupt curvature of porcelain made escape up onto the floor impossible. The creature was trapped.

Captain relaxed. The roach made another frantic run for it but glided back down. Captain's instinct was to help, to set him free. He carried that thought to its end and envisioned the insect, with its long, hairy black legs full of excrement and germs, running to spread filth and disease among men. He should die, he said to himself. And what a target.

Because of childhood abuse, Captain's urinary tract was enlarged. He didn't pee, he pissed. The bug wiggled his long antenna. "Feel this," Captain said. Using the first few spurts as tracers, Captain zeroed in and pushed. He poured it onto the black jacket with all of the pressure that he could muster, and the beetle stood fast. He held there, over a drain hole that was too small to accommodate him and reveled in the downpour. His slick tuxedo repelled it, and his long feelers flailed away in what appeared to be glory.

Captain was running out of steam. He went to the flusher. Water and air roared together, and in the midst of the swirl, the bug let go. He didn't resist, he relaxed and let the force consume itself around him. He rolled with it. After the last wash, he calmly floated up to the surface to ride the clear water down as it subsided. There he stood, fit as a fiddle, and clean.

Captain finished and washed his hands. "You deserve to live," he said aloud toward the urinal. He crunched up the paper towel and threw it into the bowl. Using his toe, he carefully pushed the rough brown paper between the porcelain lip and the raised metal drain to form a bridge. The roach sensed the aid and moved immediately toward it. Captain finished his drink, threw the ice cubes into the sink and rinsed the glass. The roach was on the towel, hurrying.

"See you around, pal. Maybe someday the shoe'll be on the other foot."

On the way to the bar Captain's stomach felt queasy. He felt pressured, anxious. "It's only a water beetle," he mumbled. "Bullshit," he retorted. "Cockroach—cock roach—cock roach—roach of cock—nocturnal ferrier of pestilence—that black devil is a killer of men and you let him pass—fool—asshole."

Captain slammed back into the mens room. The roach was scampering to freedom along the white tile floor. Captain ran at him. The wise insect increased his speed and disappeared under a white wall. Captain stood still and stared at the spot. It wasn't deep. A feeler and part of a black leg showed. They both were still. Captain said, "Oh, well," but muscled himself up onto the sink where he sat on his haunches. An Oriental man came in, his hand on his fly. Captain whispered, "Out—get out. Don't ask any questions, just get out." The Oriental looked at Captain crouched up on the sink. Captain shook his fist at him. The Oriental backed slowly out of the room. The door closed. Captain waited. He ran his list again.

A. The Dodge.
B. The iron.
C. The extension cord.
D. The converter.
E. Clothing, towels, gloves.
F. His Welby .455—a big bore for a big bore.
He smiled inside.

There was a soft knock on the mens room door. It opened a crack. "Cappy, are you in there? Are you all right?"

Captain figured that Brad could see motion, particularly with the window behind him. He moved his arms frantically, motioning Brad away. The door shut. He heard muffled conversation. They went away.

Suddenly both feelers and the head appeared, then both front legs. Captain didn't breathe, his heart pounded in his throat, his stomach was upset. Finally, with the boldness of victory, the cockroach emerged. Fearlessly he strutted two, three, seven inches into the room, a foot. Captain didn't spring. He inched his feet forward and fell, head first. He flattened his palms. Looking for the roach's face, he missed the expression, but he heard the shrill scream. He took him with his right palm. The roach popped like an expressive double bubble. Captain ran careful sensations into his hand. There was no movement beneath. He stayed kneeling for a time, all of his weight on the flat of his hand. He realized that he was grinding his teeth and stopped. After cleaning the mess, he carefully washed his hands. He inspected them. Satisfied, he dried them.

He stood before the mirror. Running his fingers through his hair, he decided that he looked handsome. His stomach was settling and he felt fine.

The Oriental was leaning on the bar waiting when Captain returned. Mrs. Pearlstein and Henry Aldrich were gone. She had left his car keys and a thank you note. The Oriental wouldn't look Captain in the eye as he hurried past into the mens room.

Brad had cleaned the table and was returning the last chair to its proper place. They were alone. "Are you all right, man?" Brad wanted to know.

"I'm fine, Brad. I'd have helped you with that, though."

"No sweat; it's my job. What'n hell were you doing perched up on the sink?

"Laying for a cockroach."

"You're kidding."

"Nope. Got him too, finally."

"Mr. Chow is afraid of you."

"Good. Is Ruthie going to be all right with Aldrich?"

"Sure, he's a harmless old fart. Nice guy, no problem, forget it. Let her be. Shit, she's three times seven. Besides I gave them two bottles of good cold California champagne—didn't have any decent white wine—I just pour from the half gallon. Do you want some food?"

"No, no food, and no more rum. It's making me tired. I do want a quick one to pick me up, though, while you get me a bill."

"How about a hot cup of coffee?" Brad asked. "Half an hour fresh."

"No, thank you, no coffee. Give me a glass of Jap beer and two fingers of that Old Grand Dad back there, the bonded stuff, in a water glass."

The beer was ice cold, and it tasted refreshing with salt. Captain held up the bourbon and looked at it against the light before he threw it down. He stopped the gag with a good swallow of beer and said, "One more." His eyes and nose watered. He paid Brad, tipped him too much and wasn't bothered by the second blast of bourbon. Captain finished the beer and met Brad at the end of the bar for their customary hug.

"Love your people for me," Captain asked.

"I do," Brad answered. "Be careful."

The G.O.B.

The restaurant's front room seemed quieter than it had been. It was dark. Captain saw a small but bright light in the direction of the front door and headed for it. He belched beer and bourbon. His nerves felt insulated. The small, shielded bulb spilled illumination over the keys of a piano. Sheet music was stacked haphazardly on top of a square, pleated, leather stool. Captain stared and became mesmerized by the texture, the shine of the ivories. He went behind to the keyboard.

Bumping the piano stool, he didn't try to stop the slide of sheet music that splashed to the floor. He sat down. Spreading his fingers to make octaves, he set his hands down easily, to stroke, not depress, the keys. A cigarette glowed not two yards from his right elbow. The voice came—mellow, easy, black.

"Go ahead, man, let's hear it."

The presence of another human being did not embarrass him. Not about to try and please some nonentity musician, he ignored the voice. Besides, his wrists were too stiff. Captain began to play "The Lost Chord." He'd played that at his recital when he was eleven. His fag teacher kept telling him, "Loosen your wrists, loosen your wrists," and that's all that Captain could ever think about, not the music but his wrists.

"The Lost Chord" was morbid. He played and sang: "A, you're adorable, B, you're so beautiful, C, you're a cutie full of charm. D, you're a darling and—" He pretended that he was Caruso, the great operatic tenor. He struck the C chord, stood and sang "Ridi Pagliacco" unaccompanied. Then he sat and resumed "A, you're adorable," and he thought of his powerful Dodge; "B, you're so beautiful"—the iron; "C, you're a cutie full of charm"—the twenty-foot extension cord. He stopped. Anxious, he bolted from the place.

Later, after an uneventful but calming drive back to the apartment, his list came together without a hitch. He added an empty plastic orange juice container now filled with ice, Old Crow and Diet Seven-Up. He tested the steam irons and they both worked.

The sound of easy music filtered from Mrs. Pearlstein's apartment. Captain left one new iron against her door in a brown paper bag.

Speed bragged about having broken every bone in his body. Captain figured that many of those bumps had been to his head. A Steve McQueen look-alike, he was a lovable guy, totally consumed by things fast. He had driven and won at Lake Elkart, mechanicked Parnellies' car two years at Indie, raced motorcycles all of his life and hang-glided into a high voltage wire and lived. His body and mind had taken it all until he shot too much methedrine underneath his tongue and died. Captain missed him. Speed had built the Dodge.

Captain was not a hot-rodder. He'd have loaned Speed the thousand unsecured, but Speed had insisted and signed over the pink. He left the Dodge with Captain and rode his Harley. The car sat in the garage for a year after Speed's death. Finally, as a commemoration, Captain drove it to the desert to blow it out, to let it go, and could it go.

The Dodge was aggressive, a brute. When Captain fell into one of his moods, when he felt like being tough, he drove it. It backed him up. It was his gang.

The sun was going into the Pacific behind him. The traffic wasn't as bad on Fountain Avenue as it might have been for the time of day. He drove carefully and didn't think about Reno. He checked the rearview and had a drink. Captain liked the way that he looked in his hat. It was his favorite, canary yellow with a stiff visor like a baseball hat. Truckers and heavy machinery operators wore them. A patch on the front said "John Deere" or "Mobil" or "STP" or "Sears." Captain's hat was made of nylon, had an adjustable strap at the rear and a button at the peak, similar to a golfer's hat. Three gold initials were sewn on the bright blue patch above the visor: G.O.B. He dreamed about the boys that had given him the hat, years before, and how they'd saved his white ass.

With his father's death, Captain's apprenticeship ceased. He understood a great deal about right and wrong and the nature of man but was left with an insatiable yearning to know about other things. He was not well traveled. During his last days at the academy, he planned a learning experience, a hitchhiking tour of the states. The year was 1965, the nation was unsettled, unsafe for a kid alone. He was a pigeon, but he had to see it on the ground, first hand, his country.

The bold print on his suitcase said "STUDENT—MIAMI." Getting rides was the name of the game, so he avoided looking bummy. He wore long underwear beneath a durable green corduroy suit and an oxford-cloth white shirt and dark tie. The first item in his suitcase was a cold-weather raincoat. In its pockets were a navy blue, knit stocking cap and warm gloves.

A typewriter salesman would have taken him to the outskirts of Chicago, a good ride. While driving through Wisconsin, however, they fell in behind another interstate car with Indiana plates. The typewriter man was good natured and assisted Captain in flagging the station wagon down. Captain rode with this new friend into Terre Haute.

A couple stopped next. They were going through to Coral Gables—what luck. The husband wanted Captain to do things to his wife while he watched and did things to whomever. The wife had hair on her face, huge thighs and giggled. It was out of the question. Angry, the husband dropped him before dawn, in Harkinsville, Kentucky. He said that it would teach him a lesson and drove away.

Harkinsville is a bleak industrial town that pours into a single-span automobile bridge on its southerly border. The Cumberland River flows beneath the bridge and is the natural division between Kentucky and Tennessee. Captain had $50 in his pocket and another $450 in his bag. His gold Rolex sport watch was hidden inside, in the toe of a sneaker. He was not armed.

The little town was asleep, and absolutely nothing moved on Route 41 going south. He waited. A dirty gray dawn began to break. Captain saw silhouettes first and then was able to make out the smokestacks and factories that surrounded him. A loud industrial whistle startled him and sounded for several minutes. He was wishing hard for a ride, a car, but nothing. The scene was eerie; it depressed him.

He could feel the local inhabitants begin to stir. They lived in shacks in the shadows. They shuffled as they made their way through the haze. Old, black and poor, they seemed to drag themselves along. He watched their eyes. They wouldn't look up, wouldn't acknowledge him. They passed by him. He didn't exist.

Captain craned his neck and looked for a white face; there were none. Then he saw them and he knew real fear. He realized why those who had passed earlier wouldn't look him in the eye. They were afraid—for him.

The others came, crowded together, mumbling jive talk—a big bunch of them. A dark clump of young, strong, black men was coming through the gray morning. They wore do-rags.

Captain beseeched the highway to produce a vehicle, but none came. When they saw Captain they stopped. They stared. A hush fell over them. The quiet tore at Captain's senses. Somewhere, perhaps in the real world, he heard Fats Domino singing "Blue Monday."

He tried to act calm while they approached. They carried tattered lunch bags and were huge together. They loomed up around him. He wanted to scream a nightmare scream, and he admitted that he was stupid. As one last honest thought, he admitted that he was dumb. He'd let those people drop him in a southern black town. They'd left him to be robbed or—worse—and he had been glad to get out. God, he'd eat a mile of that fat slob's shit just to see where it came from, to be back with them, safe in their car.

"What you got in the bag, boy?" Hurricane Carter asked.

The surgical screw had worked its way through Captain's scalp. It was into the meat of his brain; it was smoldering. Captain felt the skin all over his body draw tight. Malcolm X smiled with brown teeth, a patch over his shot-out eye.

"Open the bag, boy," Donald Defreeze demanded, smelling of cheap wine. "You're gonna hear from me." Fats Domino sang the blues, and all of the black men from D-block at Attica started to chant, "Open the bag, open the bag." They were all there, the black men who never had a chance in life: the bitter, the anguished, the vengeful. Huey Newton stood up from doing

1,000 push-ups, his black muscles aglow. "Open the bag, open the bag, open the bag, or we'll open your head."

Captain felt perspiration trickle down the crack of his ass. He inched his knees apart, convinced that they would start knocking.

"You gonna be cut, boy." The man was saying it for the last time. He thrust his hand into his loose pants pocket. A cutting instrument would come next.

Captain had to do something. He opened his numb face and bellowed air out over his vocal cords. "Hey," his voice squeaked, "hey." That was better. "Hey, come on you guys, lighten up. I'm going back to school. There's nothing but a bunch of personal shit in there. Nothing that would interest you."

The blacks were not dissuaded. A big buck wearing a full beard knelt on one knee and began to force the latches.

Captain thought about letting them keep it. "You guys can have it. See you around." But where in God's name would he go? They were not about to rob him and let him walk away. Besides, nobody knew he was there. He was a sitting duck.

Audacity, he thought. Don't give it away. Fight for it—for life.

Captain wore heavy, wing-tip imperial cordovan shoes made by Florsheim. They looked right with his outfit and were warm. Captain drop-kicked the bearded black man. He caught him against the left ear with a thunk.

The man dropped to his other knee. Shit, he didn't even fall over. Captain quickly jammed his hand into his outside corduroy jacket pocket and screamed, "All right, you assholes, back off. I've got a gun and—" In mid-sentence a pair of headlights came around the bend, heading south.

The blacks were still deciding how to react to the gun ruse when Captain threw himself through their ranks. He broke into a dead run toward the oncoming lights. He flailed his arms. He screamed.

"Help! Help, I'm being attacked."

The car stopped. Captain ran into the blinding light, past it.

"I'm being attacked. Help, I'm being attacked by a bunch of niggers."

He had never heard himself use that expression before. It came easy. He flung himself against the passenger door. He pushed his face against the window. His burning lungs heaved quick misty breaths onto the dank glass. His left forearm lay on the roof; his right hand clawed at the windshield.

The driver leaned over and rolled the steamed window down past Captain's face. He was a white man. He wore a canary yellow, heavy machinery hat with "GOD" embossed in blue letters above the visor. Captain couldn't compute what he saw.

"What's the matter, kid? You look like you got shit in your pants."

"Thank you, God, thank you," Captain blurted.

The man unlocked the door. Captain stepped away, grabbed the door open and jumped in. "Thank you, God, thank you."

"Slow down, kid. Let's hear it. Come on, spit it out."

"I'm hitching back—to school—in Florida. They jumped me—those—blacks. Stole my suitcase."

Captain pointed to the group of black men who were walking slowly off, dragging their friend and carrying the suitcase.

"That's my suitcase." He slumped into the seat, exhausted, glad to be alive.

"Sssheeeit," the man said slowly. He smirked and hit the steering wheel hard with the palm of his hand. Captain became aware of another set of headlights covering him from behind. He turned to look out over the seat. The car he was in was towing an unlit car; then another set of lights threw onto them. The late-model Chevrolet four-door that he was in towed a Pontiac. Behind this was another car being towed and behind it there was still another car pulling in. Five, then six sets of lights from front cars all towing an extra.

"Shut the door," the southerner said, starting the engine and moving off toward the group of blacks.

The man removed something from the dash, a hand mike, and Captain became aware of a lighted radio in front of his knees.

"This is Tonto talkin'. Young kid hitchin' with me now, jumped by them coons there to the west. They got his suitcase. Goin' up front and hold 'em with my double. Let's go for some baseball." He replaced the microphone and threw another switch. Orange safety lights started to pound on and off from atop both of the lead cars. Suddenly all of the following vehicles were flashing similarly—orange, orange, orange—into the grisly Kentucky morning.

Tonto pulled rapidly up alongside and then swerved in front of the group of young black men, cutting them off. None of them broke to run. It was their town. They continued to move along and drag their friend past the cars into the beam from the headlights. One black man carried the suitcase in one hand his lunch in the other.

Tonto had his door open, was out of the car and then back in, reaching under the front seat. Things were happening fast, in an orange blur. Captain sat stupified, his heart in his throat, watching.

And then Tonto was out and into the white light in front. "Who's gonna die?" he yelled. The gang of men froze and Captain saw why. Tonto held them at bay with a sawed-off, double-barreled shotgun. Then all of the cars were there, and the whipping orange lights splashed among the horizontal white beams to light up that dawn in the craziest way imaginable.

Tonto was surrounded on three sides by men with yellow-visored hats that looked to have "GOD" printed on them. Car doors were slamming; they came from everywhere. They all carried guns—No, not guns, sticks, clubs—bats, baseball bats. The yellow-hatted men were carrying baseball bats. They shared an abrupt laugh, and Tonto nonchalantly squeezed off one barrel where it was aimed. The shot blew what looked like the right shoulder and arm off of his closest black target. The scream was of mutilated disbelief.

The smoke hadn't cleared, but the good old boys went to work with their bats. One black tried to escape. Tonto chased him and brought him back with the short cannon against the man's neck.

"Good God," Captain gasped, starting to moan. He made the noise to fill his ears, to stop the sound from out there.

The boys didn't just break an arm or two. They were smashing for keeps, hitting homers. The killing was being done in the twilight. Picturesque, the bats moved across the murky morning sky. The blows finished down, in darkness. The shadows concealed the spill of corpuscles, but the cries were there and the sound of splintering bone.

Captain moaned louder and cowered.

Some of the boys finished their business with the heels or toes of their boots. There were a few final blows, like driving a heavy tent stake, and it was over.

Tonto's companions gathered around him and his tall lanky prisoner, who was shaking and on the verge of convulsion. The black was lean and tall, a basketball prospect. Tonto ordered, and the black man put his long-fingered hands onto the roof of the car and leaned in. His head hung between his long arms, his face close to Captain's. His teeth were chattering, his eyes bloodshot.

"Legs together."

The basketball player did what was ordered. The orange light played across his shining, wet, ebony face. It was Halloween.

Tonto stepped up next to the man. He pointed the barrel of the squat gun against the outside of the man's right knee. Captain saw it. He moaned, "Noooooooo."

Tonto said, "This'll teach you to run."

Captain screamed over the blast, *"Nooooo."*

Tonto blew the man's legs out from underneath him. It happened fast. Captain couldn't look away. With the explosion, the black man's heavy lips fell apart; he stared back into Captain's eyes while his torso hung suspended in air.

A feeling passed between them. It filled Captain with a haunting sensation. Captain couldn't give to the stare; there was too much energy coming. He took it in. He perceived it as more than the spirit of fear. It was the finish of hope and survival.

Captain watched the demise of an ego, the impotent look of death, the end. Captain's throat closed. His stomach rolled. He gagged on his own bile. When the black face fell away, he choked on the sour liquid. It was tough to do, but he swallowed it.

The Good Old Boys were headed for Tuscaloosa, Alabama. They guaranteed Captain that had he been left to the blacks in Harkinsville, they would not only have robbed him, but that their particular brand of cruelty would have been to "razor off your nuts and leave you to bleed in a ditch." It had happened to stray whites. That was one of the reasons that the G.O.B. ran in numbers and stayed close. "There are towns in the South where a white man ain't safe," they had said. Captain believed them. It was easier that way.

Tonto was their citizen-band code name for the lead car, or scout. Each of the boys had a chance to be Tonto at one point or another during the drive south from Detroit. Tad Willens was the birth name of the Old Boy who had stopped for Captain, the one with the gun. He wasn't really old. The bunch of southern white men that Captain had encountered on the road totaled eight; they were all from the same clique.

Each man had his turn every ninety days or so at providing an old, running, junker station wagon. He would make it decent mechanically and look after the rubber, often lashing extra spares to the roof. All eight would then pile in and share the driving to Detroit, where the old wagon would either be junked or sold. Each man then purchased two vehicles of his own, cheap, at auction. The best eight vehicles would be the lead cars, and the lesser quality vehicles would be towed back into the South. They brought portable safety lights, CB radios for constant communication and plenty of white lightning and Benzedrine.

They drove nonstop. Captain switched from car to car to help keep the men awake. He listened to lots of stories, added some of his own and laughed plenty.

The attitude of the highway patrol and local police was enlightening. They seemed to cater to the eight drivers. The authorities would run their red lights or give a siren a blast or wave, and the boys would tip their yellow hats.

A roadhouse just outside of Birmingham was a regular midday stop on the route home. They were eating hot ragged beef and drinking cold beer when two uniformed state troopers came in behind them. Captain was punchy from Bennies and corn liquor and felt paranoid immediately. He couldn't finish his meal. He wasn't sure about the law, but it seemed that he had to be guilty of complicity. He'd heard about the southern chain gangs.

"Afternoon, boys," the sergeant said, sitting at a table. "Two coffees, Prince," he hollered off to the kitchen. All eight of the boys turned and returned the greeting. They resumed chowing down with hardly a beat.

"You boys come down Route 41?" the trooper asked.

"Yeah," they all answered or shook their heads with full mouths.

"Hear they had a little trouble, side a 41 back on the Kentucky line," the policeman said.

"When?" Tad asked over his shoulder.

"Yesterday mornin'," was the reply. "Make it just about right for you all—if you been going straight through, that is."

"Yeah, guess so. We have," Tad answered.

The patrolmen drank their coffee, and the boys blessed the clear weather. "Don't suppose you boys saw anything up there, did ya?" the talker finally asked.

"What happened?" Dale from car number four wanted to know.

"Somebody jumped on a bunch of niggers, outskirts of Harkinsville," the other cop said. "Did 'em up righteously."

"Ya don't say," was the reply from three stools down.

Good God, where is this going? Captain asked himself. "Hey, Prince," he hollered involuntarily, "you got any bourbon?"

"Comin' up," was the answer from the kitchen.

His thinking was two-fold: not only would the bourbon loosen up his throat and stop him from feeling like a kid, but it would force somebody's hand. They were in a beer and food joint, not a liquor house.

Prince came bouncing out of the kitchen. He was carrying a quart bottle with clear brown liquid in it and no label. "Here ya go, son," he said, pulling the cork out with his teeth. He dropped the cork into his front apron pocket in a move that he'd obviously made before and said, "Ah don't mind if'n ah do," and took a good slug for himself. "Now that's good whiskey," he exclaimed, looking at the bottle with a sigh.

Prince put glasses down for all the boys, and Captain drank

some of the best bourbon he'd ever tasted. It soothed him. The boys joined in, and Captain asked the two state troopers if they'd like a shot.

They declined, saying, "Not while we're on duty."

The nine of them finished the bottle. Captain didn't know if he'd proven a point or not. He'd forgotten what it was and didn't care any more anyway.

Captain paid the bill against much protest, and they all went out to the cars. Captain was riding with Hugh, who was one of the three H's, Hammond and Hardy being the other two.

The sergeant came out and walked over to Tad Willens's Chevy. Captain couldn't hear them. All of the boys waited while Willens and the lawman shot the bull. Finally, Tad looked both ways and whipped out the sawed-off shotgun. Captain groaned. "Oh, no," his mind flashing on the ramifications of what he saw. His heart balked.

But Tad only handed it to the patrolman, who refused it. They both started to laugh like hell. Tad made some gestures using the gun as a bat, and they laughed some more. The gun was stashed, the cop slapped Tad on the back and the cars rolled again. Hugh was Tonto.

"I can't believe—They know, don't they?" Captain asked big-shouldered Hugh as they drove.

Hugh was a brooder, not talkative like the others, but he managed a "Don't you worry your head none about it, boy."

"But it's as though—as though you guys get a—gold star for—" His voice dropped off in disbelief.

Hugh chuckled and put the CB mike to his mouth. "This is Tonto to Tadpole in number six. You copying?"

There was an electrical crackle over the speaker and then, "I'm listening, Hughy, what's up?"

"Cap here wants to know if the state boys gave us a gold star for the baseball game up north?"

There was more crackling and laughs that made it obvious all of the others were listening too.

"Are you listening, Cap?"

"Yeah, he's right here," answered big Hugh.

"We got six gold stars," the audio crackled, and Captain heard whistles and cheers. "And we got five silvers too," Tad added.

The boys exchanged compliments.

Hugh replaced the mike and adjusted his burly upper body for comfort. "That answer your question, kid?"

"Yeah, yeah, it does," Captain replied, and they continued into the South.

Captain unscrewed the top of the plastic orange-juice container and took a long drink of Old Crow and Seven. It made the inside of his nostrils tingle. Jesus, he thought, remembering the Good Old Boys. It had happened years before, but he remembered the time spent with them vividly.

He looked into the rearview again and slid his dark glasses off. He adjusted his yellow hat and rubbed his chin. "No big deal," he said aloud, regarding the shave that he was beginning to need.

He smiled and looked at his teeth. He stared at himself. He searched around his eyes. A bit tired perhaps, but strong, with character, he thought. "You look good," he said. "You are good," he added, laughing.

He put his dark glasses back on and blinked to quicken his pupils open. Losing light, he thought, turning the heavy Dodge onto Western Avenue. "Just a few more minutes," he said, patting the wooden steering wheel. The Good Old Boys—goddamn, they were something.

The Burn

Captain saw it and braked. A new, black, Buick four-door sedan bearing the personalized license plate "INCHES 9." It was parked in the monthly stalls, and Captain was sure that it belonged to Reno Bloom. It had to; who else would have the bad taste. "Inches nine," Captain said and shook his head while he backed the Dodge in three empty stalls away and parked. The beginning of night seeped in through the open areas of the parking structure. Bright yellow illumination reached into the farthest corners of the drab place. Captain sat and listened.

The silence seemed to echo; it hung heavily in the air. He opened the door to step out. The noise bounced off the dense concrete walls, creating in him a sense of desolation. When he shut the car door, the sound jangled his nerves and made him feel conspicuous. He looked quickly around.

Captain had driven slowly through the first two levels of parking before finding the black Buick on the third. Cars were sparse, and he hadn't seen a single person on foot. He scoured the area and couldn't see one now.

He returned to the Dodge and reached in through the open window for his drink. He saw the electrical converter plugged into the dash where the cigarette lighter had been. From the plug hung a bright-orange rubber extension cord. Twenty feet of it lay rolled onto the floor in front of the seat. The iron sat on top.

He took the drink with him while he walked around the black Buick. A decal on the inside of the rear windshield signified membership at the Playboy Club. The owner of the black Buick was a keyholder. He could enter the Bunny Hutch. Captain couldn't help but smile at that one.

"Reno Bloom is a Playboy. How about that," he said. He jumped up to sit on the silver fender of the Dodge and have a drink. "Taking a lot for granted, aren't you?" he asked himself. "Nope. I'm positive it's his. It has to be. It's too perfect."

Captain dangled his boots. He clicked the heels and toes together for a while and listened to the sound. He was becoming accustomed to the site and finally lay back onto the fender.

The wait would be no problem. He understood perserverance. He had learned it hitchhiking. It was the salesman's most important tool. Make enough calls and you'll make a sale. He knew how to wait.

Captain wondered about the network of water spigots on the ceiling. They were so high; would a burning car actually create enough heat to activate them? He bet not. They're probably phony, he thought.

He heard something and sat up on an elbow to watch a mincy Oriental walk by. He lay back down and listened to a car start. A baby blue Triumph roared past him and down the ramp.

Bringing his drink, Captain eased himself off of the car. He listened to the slithery sound that his nylon pant legs made against each other while he walked down the garage to an open space, a half wall. It afforded him a view of the street below. A few of the stores were still open; business was slow. Bloom's was dark except for night lights.

Captain felt a chill of insecurity about his decision. No, he bucked back up; he was convinced. He sat in the opening where the wall began and leaned against the cold concrete. He put his feet up and had a drink.

Then Captain couldn't wait any longer and brought out a pair of rubber surgical gloves from the left pocket of his nylon jump suit. He loved their feel. He rubbed them and touched them. He squeezed them before putting them on. He pulled the thin rubber material over each finger; he was meticulous. Finally he meshed the fingers together, using the left to assist the right and vice versa, exactly as his father had done.

He began to feel calm.

Reno Bloom had apparently closed the store from behind because he was exiting from the alley and about to cross the street. Captain's blood began to race. He strained his eyes to make sure. The man was wearing a houndstooth-checked sportsman's hat, the kind with a little red feather stuck into the side. He wore a smart, three-quarter-length, beige summer outer coat.

"The gnat's ass," Captain mumbled to himself.

He was carrying a briefcase, and it was Reno Bloom, no question about it. Captain's heart was beating so fast it seemed to flutter around his chest cavity while he ran back to the cars. Taking a last slug from the plastic orange juice container and spilling some, he closed it back up and threw it into the Dodge on the way by.

Captain took a final stride and leaped up onto the trunk of the black Buick. The Welby .455 smacked him on the hip bone

109

again. He bounced up and down on the trunk lid; it rippled. He slowed to a nervous but comfortable pace on the springs of the big car and waited. He stood tall and, reaching, he could nearly touch the dirty ceiling.

He thought about Reno Bloom's stupid hat and turned his own hat around on his head. Captain wore his yellow G.O.B. hat backward like a baseball catcher. He made fists to stretch the thin rubber gloves over his knuckles, a feeling he was fond of. Then came Reno, just as he'd expected him. His goony hat first, then his big shoulders and finally the rest of him. Up the pedestrian ramp he came, turning finally around the thick cement revetment and heading directly for his car, the black Buick.

Captain watched the yardage between them narrow and jumped up in the air to land on the trunk lid with the seat of his pants. The black metal buckled. Reno saw it all. His eyes flamed and he dropped his briefcase. He was coming fast.

Captain put his feet on the bumper and adjusted the Welby .455, so that it was at hand. "Hello, Mr. Bloom," Captain spoke like a gentleman.

"Off my car, punk," Reno's voice boomed throughout the hall.

Fifteen feet and closing.

"I want to speak with you about love."

Captain knew that he was smiling now in a nice way. At ten feet Reno stopped and squinted. He was trying to place the face or catch on to what was happening. Then he knew, and his mouth turned down at the sides in a slow growl.

"Now I know who you are. And you want to talk to me about love, do you?"

He started to move again, slowly, one step at a time. "You faggot cunt." He spat out saliva with his words.

Captain watched the big man's hands. They were being formed into chisels, mitsu karate death wedges.

"No, Mister Bloom, not that kind of love. In the name of God, love for people, Mister Bloom, for the downtrodden."

It was no use, Reno Bloom didn't understand. Captain felt a sudden rush of sadness come over him. Reno was close, his strong shoulders were moving. Captain looked carefully into Reno's eyes. He searched for a trace of sensitivity or concern but saw only the creature's black soul.

"Scum," Captain mumbled, depressed.

"Off," Reno's voice cracked as he screamed. His face was purple; frothy spittle surrounded his mouth and he appeared close to convulsion.

Captain couldn't restrain his tears. They ran all over his face and blurred his vision.

"Off," again.

"Make me, make me," Captain teased in baby talk through his tears.

"I'm gonna rip your heart out," Reno shouted hysterically. His powerful right shoulder and arm were in motion. The karate chisel was coming. Reno was driving his wedged hand directly toward Captain's breastbone and heart.

Captain was playing the move in his mind in slow motion, observing the contemptible brute. "Here we go," he muttered to his brain.

Captain pulled the Welby .455 out of his slippery nylon pocket and turned it sideways over his sternum. He could both hear and feel Reno Bloom's fingers snap as they broke against the blue steel cylinder of the British gun. The blow knocked the wind out of Captain.

Reno screamed an inhuman cry and pulled his hand away Captain watched as Reno's eyes filled with cowardice. Captain was smiling again and felt warm and cozy in his nylon jumpsuit.

With a quick sigh of resignation Captain took his turn. He slammed the heavy pistol into Reno's half-open mouth. The power of the blow knocked Reno's hat and toupee clean off; his eyes bulged out hemorrhaging red as if to pop. Captain felt a strong temptation to pull the trigger, but that wasn't what was planned.

Reno's upper lip, most of his lower, his gums and his front teeth had been torn away and jammed into his throat. He started to gag, and Captain knew that he'd be on his knees wretching or pissing in his pants in a matter of seconds.

"Get in my car, cruel motherfucker," Captain screamed, "and swallow it, because if you mess my seats, I'll kill you right here."

II

Iris

Captain continued to put one foot out in front of the other, but he felt weak. Exhilaration from the cool wet sand and salty night air didn't last. Waves of nausea tormented him as he ran. It was a three mile run from the house to the pier and back again. Captain was not yet halfway. The pier loomed up in front of him dark and foreboding. The waves lost their thrust when they slammed into the dark structure. After each blast, the ocean stood still and became an ascending froth around the obstinate creosoted pilings. A clouded full moon assisted Captain in imagining all sorts of creatures hidden in the black wash underneath the thing.

He pushed himself into a sprint, pursued by the same demon who had chased him up dark staircases when he was a kid. Captain strained his hearing and then stole a glance behind him to make certain he wasn't being followed. The beach was empty. The hair on the nape of his neck relaxed, and he slowed his pace. He felt sick and concentrated on loosening his ankles and rolling on the outside of each foot from heel to toe as it landed in the sand.

It was after midnight. A cluster of white flood lights brightened the beach in the distance. Iris was in the kitchen of one of those beach homes ready to drop a steak on the griddle when he returned from his run. She was a good cook, like his mother. Captain needed food. He had been drinking all day and doing emotional things and hadn't eaten a bite.

Iris had met him at the door wearing the bright red nightgown he'd given her on Valentine's Day. Despite the hour, she was pulled together. Her blonde hair was fixed in one thick braid down her back. She stared him in the eye and asked, "Are you safe?"

And Captain had replied, "Of course."

She had come to him just inside the door to put her forehead on his shoulder. Her expression was hidden. "You've been out again, I know it."

Captain had said nothing and headed for a pair of running shorts. He felt lousy, toxic.

Iris's voice had a vulnerable quality that men found attractive. Captain was aware of it then when she said, "The moon is full. Back up in the clouds, it's there and it's full." That meant that Captain's behavior, whatever it was, could be explained by the moon's phases. Iris didn't know anything specific about Captain's deeds while he was away from her. But she had seen him in action on her behalf and probably imagined the worst.

Iris didn't mind what Captain did as long as he was careful, kept in close touch and loved her. Which he tried to do these days.

Captain ran with his head held high, trying to smooth his breathing. His gut was on fire, but he was determined to make it.

"So, you're willing to pay the price are you?" he grunted to himself. Come on, he thought, lighten up. Why make it worse than it is. Captain told himself that if his body took a wracking so that his mind would feel relief, he was for it.

Captain ran into the lighting from the first house. He was close. "Goddamn, I feel sick," he said, "real sick." He thought about medicine. "Chicken shit," he said. "Fuck you," he said back. "I'm sick." He decided where the closest bottle of bourbon was. "How about your promise?" he asked himself. "I'm not breaking my promise, I'm just changing my mind. Come on you big girl, run," he shouted. It made him mad, and he sprinted to the house.

Iris's house was built in three stories. The level on the beach held a gym and sauna, a game room, a bar and two small guest bedrooms. The second floor was all bedroom and bath. This entire second level was richly carpeted in pale blue and had total exposure over the ocean by way of an all-glass front. The third floor faced the sea with a beautiful exterior wooden deck; this was decorated with flourishing green plant life. Then a large fireplaced living room moved into a totally modern kitchen, which opened into a separate two-car garage and Malibu Road. The front door was there also. A richly carpeted staircase ran vertically through the house with landings on each floor.

Captain eased himself through the game room to the bar. He was shaking. He slipped and nearly fell on the wet floor. "Jesus Christ," he said between his clenched teeth. The refrigerator behind the bar held an iced tapper keg of Hamm's beer. He held the refrigerator door open for light. An empty mason jar stood upside-down on a dish rack next to the sink.

After smelling it, Captain filled it with beer. He opened a lower cupboard and found a bottle of Jack Daniels Green Label bourbon. The swallow went down hard. The alcohol scalded his raw throat and stomach. It gagged him, and he threw up again into the small sink. His eyes watered and ran down his cheeks. "Shit," he said, and rinsed the sink.

"Are you all right, honey?" Iris's voice broke over the intercom.

The glass clacked against Captain's teeth as he drank the beer. The noise made him think of Mrs. Pearlstein's golf shoes. He smiled inside and actually felt a little better. "I'm fine, babe," he answered.

"Dinner is coming along. Are you hungry?"

Captain nodded at the wall speaker and then, containing his illness, said, "Yes, yes, I am. I'll shave and steam and be up shortly."

"I love you," she said. There was a click.

Captain drank the canning jar empty, filled it again and poured a water glass half-full of Jack Daniels. Holding a glass in each hand, he opened the door of the sauna using his little finger as a hook. The room was steaming hot.

Captain left the light off and sat on the closest redwood bench. He drank a shot of the bourbon and chased it quickly with beer. It stayed down. A swallow more of bourbon and beer and his stomach cramps disappeared. He got out of his jock and shorts and threw them into a corner.

Captain gulped the last of the Jack Daniels, chased it and lay down on the hot bench. Perspiration poured off of him. He breathed the heat into his lungs and felt his muscles relax. The pain in his calves was the last to go, but it went. "Oh, man," he sighed. "That's better, a whole lot better. In fact, I don't know what the big deal was. I'm fine," he said, laughing at himself, his self-deception.

Standing, he felt faint. He hung his head below his waist until it passed. He snapped on the overhead light and backed up to look at himself in the steamed mirror. After running his hands through his hair, he examined his penis from angles. He tugged at it and watched it grow. He felt good and decided that he looked the same. In fact, great was a better word.

The large wooden drawer in the cabinet next to the mirror held all of the goodies to bring a body back. Shampoos, conditioners, skin cleansers, razor, toothbrushes—they were all there in the type or brand of your choice.

Captain put a new blade in and rummaged the drawer for the shaving cream. A can lay on its side against one slat of the warped rear corner. Next to it sat Mac's old-fashioned shaving mug and lather brush. Captain brought them out. Mac's ivory-handled straight-edged razor was there also. The mug still contained soap. Captain made it wet and lathered his face. The finely bristled brush was soft. Captain remembered how Mac used to enjoy it. He remembered how Mac had enjoyed most things in life and how much he'd loved Iris. Captain shaved and thought about the old goat, the beautiful, old, gentle man.

Captain could see how Iris missed Mac. He felt it too. Many a time the three of them sat together in the steam to enjoy life and to gossip. Mac and Iris loved to gossip. The old man always had a supply of the best coke money could buy. They'd get their noses full, bring an iced champagne bucket and a bottle of the best brut, cut crystal glasses, and they would roost in the sauna and talk.

Captain spent most of the time listening. Mac and Iris seemed to know everybody who was anybody from Palm Beach to Malibu. Their inside knowledge ran from bust jobs to bankruptcy. They could titter together through a steam, swim, dinner and a film when a subject or bit of news was particularly juicy.

Mac wasn't sure but guessed his own personal wealth at between 40 and 60 million dollars. His real given name didn't matter, but Captain remembered it as Hinton or Hillstead; Iris knew. There was no need for any other name. Throughout the world he was known as Mac, the hamburger king. He would put his brawny paw out and say, "Call me Mac," and everyone did.

Mac was a married man and had a family that he was proud of. He said that he just couldn't help himself with Iris. He was crazy about her and called her Chicken. Mac had a massive heart attack and died during the Olympics of 1976 in Montreal. He had taken his real family there for the holiday. He was to have opened the ground at a new restaurant site in Montreal as well but never made it.

Captain made a funny face to stretch his skin and shave. Then he realized something that he hadn't thought of before. He spoke it without moving his mouth. "Sure—Mac knew he was finished. Of course, he did. It makes better sense."

Mac had been to Dallas six or seven months before Montreal for a complete physical checkup. Jack Kennedy would like that, Captain thought. Go to Dallas for your health. "Cock suckers," he said. The memory of Mac's gift to Iris came back to him in a different light.

Mac hadn't been back from Dallas a week when he asked them to his corporate offices in Century City. The big man was unusually chipper. They laughed together, and Iris brought him up to date on all of the gossip while the three of them enjoyed a catered luncheon of milk-fed veal and white wine. Finally, Mac poured them all a glass of his special French cognac, lit a big black Havana, breathed deeply, pulled his six foot four, 265-pound frame out of the chair and bade them to bring the brandy and follow.

Down the fourteen flights they went in his private elevator and into his waiting Mercedes limousine. The driver stopped on Cotner Street in front of Carte and Crate, a prestigious West Los Angeles storage and vault house. A tiny, bespectacled male employee wearing what appeared to be a white surgical coat or butcher's robe, met them at the entrance. The man held a pair of white gloves in his left hand and shook hands with a bony frail right.

Mac had produced a box of amyl nitrate on the way over and although he went very easy on it himself, Captain and Iris had been gluttons and had laughed themselves silly. They were all a bit dingy when the little man sat them down in an off-white showroom. The decor was richly conservative, dark brown leather on thick brown shag carpet. The walls were bare. The ceiling was sprouting with narrow, shaded chromium lamps.

They agreed on mocha java coffee, and Captain settled himself down. Captain liked the elegant smell of the room and felt excited. He remembered how he had let himself go on that occasion because he suspected that the surprise would match the anticipation. Usually he censored those feelings because of his frequent disappointment with results. He would hope and pray and plan and anticipate and imagine a thing, and then it would invariably let him down. Captain was very careful about anticipating especially exciting moments. He was better at letting them slide by so that they could be appraised and savored after the fact.

The little man poked his head around the corner of the oversized polished aluminum doorway and received a nod from Mac. "Come and sit on my lap, Chicken," Mac had said, putting out his cigar. She did and into the room came two other employees—one male, one female—wearing white coats and white gloves. They were pushing a chromium and fur furniture dolly atop which sat a brilliantly colored, five-foot-square, cubist oil painting.

"The papers, Timmy," Mac said to the frail one.

Timmy shooed his two associates out of the room and produced a manila envelope from his coat pocket. He handed it to Mac and closed the polished metal door behind him as he left.

121

No one moved. Captain stared at Picasso's name scrawled in six-inch letters across the bottom of the piece. The colors, the name, the total package did it to him; it overwhelmed him.

Mac snuggled Iris against his barrel chest. "This will take care of you when you get old, Chicken," he said, kissing her softly on the cheek. He began to rock her gently. Mac smiled and looked like a freckle-faced kid. His shock of receding reddish-blond hair was tousled up into the air.

"I don't understand," Iris spoke fearfully.

"What, Chicken, the painting or what's going on?"

"Neither," she finally answered plaintively.

Mac chuckled. "Why not just look at the picture awhile then, and we'll talk later."

Iris nuzzled into Mac, put her hand to her mouth and sighed. Captain heard himself sigh also.

The painting was a brightly colored cubist impression of a naked brunette woman, or women, in what appeared to be a reclined position. Captain decided that it was several views or images of the same woman. The artist's use of color was extraordinary. Some angles and forms met in a complementary texture of similar hues, while others changed abruptly as though to bring an entirely new plane into focus. Double and triple images; side view, front view and back. All contained in the outline of one physique. She was a spectacle and nearly life-sized.

"What's it called, Mac?" Captain finally asked.

Iris's hand hid her mouth, but her outer lips were puckered, making it appear to Captain that she was sucking her thumb.

Mac stroked her blonde hair, and his smile turned sad. It was the same expression that Captain had seen on the big man's face many times. It would happen when he was watching Iris play volleyball or bounce on the fender of his car or walk across the room or just stare him in the eye and ask a question. Mac couldn't

122

look at her for very long and not have his face turn sad. Captain supposed it to be a demonstration of true love.

"It's his portrait of Dora, Captain," Mac answered.

Captain asked, "What's it worth?" and Iris asked, "Who was she?" at the same time.

It wasn't an out-of-line question. Captain and Mac had a forthright relationship, and Captain was sure that Mac would merely tell him, if the question was rude. Besides, Captain thought, when it comes to art, one of the points of identification is price.

"Dora Marr was someone special in Picasso's life, sort of like Iris is to me. He loved her very, very much. The piece is worth a million two. The value is known. That's actually conservative. It's all here." He held up the papers and tucked them under Iris's arm. "It's yours, Chicken. It will provide for you when you get old—not that you ever will." He kissed her cheek. They all became quiet and stared at the painting for a long while. Iris had cried.

Captain gathered the things that had belonged to Mac; the shaving mug, the brush and the straight-edged razor and pushed out through the steam room door into the cool outside room. Wishing Mac well wherever he was, Captain dropped the articles, one by one, into a green plastic garbage can and returned to the steam room.

Mac was a good old cocker, Captain thought. He threw what was left of the warm beer onto the floor near the drain, and the room took on the odor of beer. "That was dumb," he said. The bottle of Jack Daniels caught his eye on the way to the shower. A good swallow went down smooth, backed by some water from the tap. Captain felt healthy.

After a cold invigorating shower, Captain toweled off, perfumed, slipped into a luxurious red terrycloth robe and bounded barefoot up the thickly carpeted stairs to find Iris.

She stood in the middle of the modern red brick kitchen, in front of a stainless steel gas stove adjusting a blue flame. Captain sneaked up behind her. The kitchen smelled delicious with dinner, but Captain was more interested in the sweet, balmy scent of Iris's active body.

He picked up her single long blonde braid and she jumped. "Oh, You startled me."

She didn't turn around but picked a cooking string bean out of the boiling water with her long red fingernails and passed it over her shoulder to him. Captain ignored the string bean and licked the soft blonde hair just under the beginning of the braid on the back of her neck. Iris wrinkled her shoulders and purred. She ate the string bean herself.

Captain moved away and jumped up to sit on the butcher's block next to the stove. "I just threw some leftover junk of Mac's away that was in the steam—razor and stuff—and I got to thinking about the old goat. You still miss him?"

"Yes, yes, I do. He was a special person, a special man. Where do you want to eat?"

"Let's take a tray down to bed with us and try to find an old movie."

"I might have known. Do you want wine?"

"Sure. Remember the time that we all went up to his Malibu restaurant, the night you got up and squatted on the root beer machine, when you pissed in it, and he said how lucky the customers would be the next day?"

They both laughed.

Iris picked a bottle of wine and handed it to Captain with a corkscrew. "Yes, I remember. I remember all of the times at all of his places. I guess we had the most fun up on the highway, though. God, we used to terrorize that place. He loved it—loved fun. God, he loved his places."

"Well, he was the biggest. It showed, his love for the restaurants."

"We're happy, so I'm sure he is," Iris said. "Here, taste this." She brought a string bean and fed it to him.

"Oh, shit," he said. "That is fantastic. I'm starved."

"All right," Iris said, pleased. "The steaks are going on. Take the wine down and put a towel on the bed and see if you can find an oldie. Maybe a creeper, with the full moon and all."

Captain brought two cut-crystal glasses and headed for the stairs. Three steps down, he heard the steaks hit and start to sizzle.

Captain clicked on the large color television but left the sound down. He opened the blackout drapes and looked out with the floodlights into the sea.

After opening the wine, he poured himself half a glass and sat down on the edge of the bed. The wine tasted full and good. He sipped it and watched the sea.

Their life at the beach seemed secure. It was just the two of them now. Mac was gone. Datchel wasn't around to traipse in and out at will and cause problems. Iris's men were quiet. It had not always been that way. Captain yawned, had another sip of wine and remembered.

Captain had not seen or spoken to Iris in nearly ten years when they spotted each other in Alice's Restaurant on the Malibu pier two summers before. Captain had never been close to the women in his family and when they made their home in Paris eighteen months after his father's death, he lost contact completely. He rarely thought of them but for Christmas and Easter. The women were funded by separate investment trusts left by Doctor Blood. Unlike Captain, who but for a subsistence was on his own, the two women had been well provided for. They enjoyed each other's company and loved Europe. The mother's maiden name had been Church; they adopted it, having always disliked Blood.

The sun had been hot, the beach teeming and Alice's busy that Sunday afternoon. Captain had been standing between the Denim twins, the famous nude photo playgirls, who were seated at the bar.

Iris had been wearing a bikini top that day with white shorts and sandals. When Iris ran across a crowded room, people usually stopped and stared; the girl was voluptuous. When she did it in her bikini, they dropped dishes and became disoriented.

She tapped Captain on the shoulder and when he turned, said, "Hello, beautiful."

The Denims began to develop that haughty expression flashy, aggressive women take on when they know that they've been bested. The twins gave Iris the once over, their eyes stopping at her hefty, lotioned, brown bust and turned into the bar. They acted preoccupied, while Captain stared in surprise. Captain remembered how proud he had been of her good looks.

"Hello, beautiful," she said again, smiling and blushing at the same time.

Captain looked into her soft blue eyes and said, "Hello, beautiful." It was all that he could think of to say.

Before Captain had time to think about what he was doing, they were embracing. Not the excited How've-you-been? embrace that one might expect either. They drew very close until their vision blurred. Then they put their cheeks together and hugged for a long time. Captain didn't try to curtail the sexual feelings that came. Iris smelled wonderful.

Back at Iris's table, Captain met Mac and Datchel. He liked Mac immediately and distrusted Datchel.

Datchel was a pure black African whose most recent last residence had been Barbados. She was proud of her tribal ancestry and explained her long, fragile neck as having come from copper

126

wrappings as a child. Her story was never quite the same about how she was rescued from jungle life, but a white missionary played a significant role.

Datchel had been educated in England and was refined. Her skin was blue-black; she was tall, thin and rangy with large hands and feet. She kept a clean, tight natural and wore gold hoop earrings and other clothing that showed off her heritage. Her eyes were slanted and black; there was no denying her beauty. She had been Iris's lover before Mac and continued to hang on. Iris was afraid of Datchel.

Captain's apartment lacked space, and the beach house, with Datchel and her key, plus the ringing phones, was hectic. They drove north in Iris's peach-colored Mercedes convertible through Oxnard and into the San Ysidro Mountains, just the two of them, Iris and Captain; to talk and get to know each other. They took a cottage at the San Ysidro Ranch.

It was raining at the ranch the afternoon of their arrival, and it continued into the next day, a hard, drenching rain. Captain and Iris sat by the fire, drank Pim's Cups and talked themselves out. At one point late into the first evening, Iris stood away from Captain in front of the window and stared out into the storm. Then, keeping her back to him, she stripped herself out of her robe and flannel pajamas. They lay around her bare ankles. Captain thought that her backside appeared smooth and strong.

"Don't you think that we should see each other?" she asked, facing out into the wet weather. "Shall we see how we've grown up?" she asked. "Or is it uncool—and sick?"

Captain couldn't judge and sat there. Iris used her hands to briskly rub her upper arms. "Decide," she said, "I'm getting a chill."

Captain supposed that if they stayed away from each other, if they didn't touch, there could be no harm. "All right," he said.

"Are you sure?" she asked.

"No," he answered and laughed. "But it's not sexual," he said, meaning it. His penis was flaccid.

"That's for sure," she said. "Are you ready?"

Captain dropped his red flannels into a chair and stood there naked except for his fleece-lined chamois slippers. "Yes, I'm ready." As ready as I'll ever be, he thought. In the back of his mind, Captain wished that his penis was hard. He liked the look of it much better when it was hard. But that's the wrong thing to think right now, he thought. Captain felt a chill, shivered and yielded a giggling laugh. He thought that he sounded nervous.

Iris turned, and her large bust swayed around with her. Her stare dropped immediately to his privates. "Uuummm," she mused, blushing and then smiling as though pleased. Iris kept her hands folded over her pubic area, her bust squeezed out between her upper arms. "Now what?" she asked.

"Nothing. Turn around, I suppose," he said, turning all of the way around once for Iris to observe.

"Do you want to see the rest?" she asked, looking down at what her hands were hiding.

"That's okay," he said. "I can see how very beautiful you are, your curves, and your tits." Captain laughed. "Wow, your tits are beautiful—so big. I can see it all fine the way it is."

"I'll bet that you're big, aren't you?" she asked, staring below his waist. Captain could feel her eyes on his penis. Captain knew that he was blushing and didn't speak. "I'll bet that it gets really huge, doesn't it. Come on, you can tell your big sister."

"That's what they say," he said, laughing. Captain put on his flannels, left his slippers and hopped into bed. He slept well and remembered her hugging him briefly during the night.

The sun had broken after breakfast the next morning and made a perfectly clean, clear, hot day. They played tennis, rode horse-

128

back and lay out nude on their private deck to catch the afternoon sun. Iris asked Captain to lotion her up with sun tan oil, and she had moaned while he massaged. Iris loved being massaged. Iris put oil on Captain as well and made no bones about rubbing it over his penis when she had finished his lower stomach. Captain produced a large erection, and Iris had stroked it with both hands. Captain made her stop and went inside to shower. He had masturbated in the shower and felt better.

That night, in the dark, before sleep, Iris had said that she was anxious and wouldn't sleep until she had an orgasm. "A physical thing," she said. "Not love or sex or anything like that—purely physical." Captain listened while she masturbated and quietly tugged at himself too. "Just let me put it in my mouth when I'm going to come," she said, her voice jerking. Captain remembered not knowing what to think; so he hadn't said anything and Iris had ended up swallowing his sperm.

It had not been a difficult thing to rationalize, having only happened that once, and Captain didn't suppose that it mattered if they played around, kissed and things, some touching, now and then. He did think that Iris smelled better than any other woman he'd ever known, and that meant something. But no intercourse.

Captain remembered his resolution. No intercourse with Iris, ever. He remembered his promise to himself. Captain thought about that for awhile. He didn't feel bad about it. Certain promises are made to be broken, he supposed.

It was during this weekend away that Iris let Captain in on her secrets. Mother was well and living with a wealthy German man, a scientist of some kind, in a chateau on Lake Geneva.

Iris has purchased the beach house herself for $285,000. She had put $85,000 down, and she made monthly payments on the balance. Money was not a problem; she was independent.

Until Mac came along there had been four people in Iris's

recent life. The first man who Iris told Captain about was Charles Marantz, the forty-one-year-old aristocrat builder from Scottsdale, Arizona. She had flown to see him, wherever he might be, two weekends a month. Iris said that Charles Marantz lived fast and came the same way. He sent her $5,000 worth of something during the first week of every month. What it was depended on where the man was playing. The goodies ran from gems to casino chips and was often his personal check.

Then there had been Irv Ridder from New Jersey and Nevada who, when in town, enjoyed a fancy lunch that Iris prepared at the beach house. He was fiftyish and portly. He loved to eat and sleep and use the steam and get rubbed down. Datchel did that. Irving bought Iris her little peach-colored Mercedes and made the house payments. Of the admirers, Iris felt most comfortable with Irving.

The third man was Turin Santos, the jockey. Small body, big heart. The man lived to win; that was all that mattered—that, and his beautiful blonde woman. He never got to see her enough and had to constantly be kept in line about how much time she would allow him. Santos owned a showy apartment house near the track, which he'd pumped a fortune into. During the season, after the ninth race, when she felt like it, Iris went there with him, usually an evening or two a week. He didn't give her money, just a sure winner twice a month.

In one way or another, Iris found redeeming qualities in all of her men. She treated them in a way that kept them continually interested, and they had made life comfortable for her. She said that she kept her soul away from them all.

Iris wrung her hands and exhibited a real dread when she told him about the blue-black lady. Datchel had brought the men around. She was internationally social and had made the introductions. Iris had enjoyed the fun for some time. Datchel courted and wooed the men and bought them expensive gifts, signing Iris's name. She didn't take anything from Ridder, because he paid for specifics. She did, however, have her own key to the house and came and went as she pleased. She took half of the $5,000 every month and played a winning horse whenever she liked.

Iris claimed passivity in their love-making but said that there was no denying the African woman's power to provide sexual thrills. Kidding, Captain asked Iris to tell him about it—the details, while he masturbated. Iris had begun the story sexily when she looked into Captain's eyes, then acted insulted and refused.

Iris was at the dog track in Phoenix when she first met Mac at the $100 pay window. They had picked the same winner, found that they used the same system, a tout named Iggy, and laughed together about it. Bored with the dogs and feeling comfortable with Mac, Iris let him buy her a glass of fine champagne. Mac was good spirited and symbolized the American dream. He had worked as a chef for nearly twenty years before earning a real estate license. One thing led to another, and he opened his first hamburger stand in Sylmar, California, June of 1957. The rest was history.

He told Iris that he had a family but was "more and more estranged from them these days. All they want to do is spend my money. Wouldn't mind if they had some depth to them, but no—spend money, that's about all they're good for."

At fifty-two, Mac was a late bloomer and had fallen head over heels in love with Iris. He admitted that he was consumed by her vulnerability.

Iris cared about Mac too. She felt secure with him and loved his brawny Scottish way. "Who cares, Chicken," he would say. "The world is ours." Then he would squeeze the air out of her with his strong arms and chest.

Mac bulldozed his way into Iris's life, and Iris started making excuses to Datchel and the others. Mac took Iris to Paris to buy her a spring wardrobe the second week that they knew each other, and Iris was happy. They returned to find Iris's garage burned down, the Mercedes a total loss.

Datchel had told stories about throwing gasoline on traitors' cars in Spain and thought it a nifty way to get even. Iris never made any accusations but was convinced that Datchel was the culprit. Insurance provided a new car and rebuilt the garage, and Iris became resolved to tighten up her life. She was not a match for Datchel, whose behavior was becoming erratic. Datchel came and went at weird hours and played loud music in the middle of the night, anything to cause a disturbance. Iris asked her to quiet down early one morning, and Datchel had slapped her hard in the face. Iris cried as she told Captain about it.

When their San Ysidro holiday was finished, Iris was in an ecstatic frame of mind. She was excited about having purged herself. She said it had done the same thing for her that confession does for a Catholic. She was wired and happy about her new-found relationship with Captain. "I need someone to talk to, someone I can trust. You're the one, aren't you? Say you're the one, Cappy."

She couldn't sit still and wanted to do the driving back from their vacation; Captain agreed, "Yes, I am the one you can trust, sister. I love you."

"Oh, and I love you," she answered, putting her hand on his leg and squeezing it hard to show how much.

"Then you must trust me to take care of Datchel for you."

Iris watched the road as she drove and didn't speak. Captain continued, "You're caught up in this thing and can't see what is right. She's got your button and will continue to push it until someone—me—until I push hers."

"What will you do?"

"Don't worry about that. Whatever it is will be easy. Assholes go down easy, and Datchel is a real asshole, if you don't mind my saying so."

"It was all so different in the beginning. She was a doll, a beautiful black doll. She did everything for me, wouldn't let me lift a finger. She worshipped me, and I loved it."

"Captain laughed. "Who doesn't? It's nice to be waited on— better if it's love, I guess."

"No, Cappy, not now. Don't hassle her now, please. My house is not in order. It won't be until—I'll check and tell you when—I'll tell you when it's safe."

"Your house—What has that got to do with—? Oh, your house. Your stars are not right, is that it?"

Iris became emphatic. "I'm serious about this, Cap. If you love me and if I'm your friend, you'll wait until—until it's safe."

"Safe for whom? Safe for whom, Iris?"

"Me."

She said it and he wasn't surprised.

"Oh. Well, thanks a lot," he said, acting hurt.

"No, dear. Oh, dear brother, understand—what is right for me is right for us—just like what is right for you as an individual is right for us as a unit. It is—it must be. I have bad, bad vibes about starting anything with Datchel until my house is in order. It's fair, isn't it? Isn't it a fair thing to ask?"

Captain laughed. "Drive the goddamned car, Iris. Of course it's fair. If you want it, it's fair. I will ignore the asshole. But you'll tell me when, all right?"

"Of course." She kissed him and drove on to Malibu.

The rest of that summer had been a party. A harsh word never passed between Captain and Iris. Mac was himself and fit right in. The three of them spent time together playing volleyball, boating or just enjoying the sun. Iris's gentleman callers had given up. Datchel would slide in and out, sometimes overly friendly, sometimes a nuisance. She developed a habit of speaking from behind her shoulder. It gave the illusion of never being able to see the words come from her mouth, just the black cat eyes and long beautiful neck and the shoulder, the raised shoulder.

Captain hated her black ass, but Iris said no.

Through it all, Captain maintained his residence in town. It served to keep his thing with Iris healthy. Observers would have Mac as the man on the scene. Captain found out later that it was during this period that Iris had tried to buy Datchel off. She wired her $15,000 and asked in the telegram to be left alone. Someone threw an African bola through the oceanside plate-glass window a few nights later. Datchel kept the money and continued her reign.

Mac had one of his drive-in restaurants on the Pacific Coast Highway, just a mile up the beach from Iris's house. He kept a set of keys to the place hanging on the key board inside Iris's linen closet. He encouraged her to raid the joint anytime that she needed something and the market was closed.

After a day of fun in the sun, Mac would take pride in hauling a gang of people down to the place, to go into the kitchen and cook for them all himself. More often than not, the hunger pangs would come after a late evening of loud music, drugs and dancing. Mac would turn on the bright neon lights inside and out of the restaurant, fire up the grill and cook for two or twenty. Captain thought that Mac's hamburgers were the best ever.

Captain laughed to himself thinking about the time that he had found Iris and Mac there at 2 A.M. They were half gassed and nude with aprons on and wearing chef's hats, cooking up a storm. Captain had poked his head in to say a fast hello and leave, but Mac had become wide-eyed and excited when he saw him and urged him to stay.

Mac sent Iris to the freezer for more champagne and quickly

134

told Captain how the stray dogs had come running out of the trash area when they had pulled up and how he had run over one of them with his left rear tire. He was sick about it, genuinely upset and had it not been for the loud music in his car, Iris would have heard the yelp and, "Oh shit, help me with this, Cappy," he implored. "I don't even know if the dog is dead. Iris will go on a bummer for life. Here, have a snort of this."

Mac brought out a thick red Parker pen from the pocket of his apron. It was full of cocaine. Mac tapped some onto the flat top of the cap, and Captain filled his nose. Wham, into his brain it went. Captain suddenly felt in charge. He stepped back outside and ran to Mac's car in the rear.

The Lab's head was lit by a slit of light from the kitchen window. It would have been Mac's undoing when they returned. The black dog was pinned under the rear left wheel and was not only dead, but cold. The unfortunate animal's tongue was hung out; his glazed eyes opened wide. "Iris would have fainted," Captain mumbled.

Back inside, Captain threw down a glass of champagne and said to Mac over a loud juke box with at least one blown speaker, "He's dead."

Mac turned his back on Iris and asked, "Where will you put it?"

"I'll put it out in the street, where you put run-over dogs."

Mac's eyes darted around the room. "No. No, meet me out in back by the trash. I don't want—It can't be left near the restaurant."

Captain made an obvious gesture by taking his sweater off and throwing it into a booth, so that Iris wouldn't mess around with "goodbys" or "please stays." She saw him all right, and he yelled, "Right back," and went out to the kitchen and out the back door.

He put the Cad into neutral, released the brake mechanically, above the pedal, got out again, put his shoulder against the door-jamb and pushed. The car rolled slowly back until he could see that the dog was clear. He closed the car back up and went to pick up the animal. He decided on the collar. When he lifted the dog, an identity tag jingled. Captain flashed on a bunch of humanitarian thoughts about notifying the owner but let that go.

Dragging the dead Labrador, Captain entered the trash area just as Mac came bursting out through the back door. Mac was pulling two plastic garbage cans along behind him. "I don't know why they forget to dump the trash," he yelled back over his shoulder, "but that's okay, I don't mind."

Leaving the cans, Mac ran over to Captain. It was dark; they spoke in the shadows. "Have you got it?" he whispered.

"Yes, I do. And it has a name tag on it. It belongs—belonged—to someone."

"Oh," Mac said with disappointment. "Give me the tag."

Captain unsnapped the round leather collar and handed the entire thing to Mac, who threw it next to the door. "Gonna have to send them something," he said. "Goddamn foolish accident, that's all. Move over," he said, nudging Captain aside. Mac pushed a long iron lever that Captain hadn't seen before, and a large, horizontal steel door slid open behind him. "Put it in," Mac said.

Captain didn't question. He picked the dog up by an ear and dropped him in. "Can't leave a dog in the street in front of the place," Mac said. He sighed and dumped the garbage cans into the black mouth of the machine. Pushing Captain further back out of the way, Mac pulled the lever back down.

They stood and listened to a heavy clunk and then the subtle whir of powerful machinery. "What is it?" Captain asked.

"Industrial trash compactor—All of my places have got them."

136

"Jesus," Captain said, impressed.

The heavy machine groaned and lurched against the concrete slab that it was toggled to. Mac put his palms against the iron monster and leaned in on his strong arms. He kicked the machine with his bare foot.

"Goddamn dumb accident. I love animals." He said it to himself.

Captain wanted to get off the subject. "Hey, Mac, what would happen if I got in there?"

Mac's expression changed to a smirk. The question had served its purpose. "It would be goodby Captain."

"But, I mean, where would I go? What happens to what is left over?"

"All the liquids are squeezed out and go into a disposal unit underneath that leads to the sewer, just like with a disposal in a home. What's left is baled up automatically at twenty-five pounds, bagged in plastic and left for the trash man. They're not new, Cap. Almost every restaurant has one. They're handy as hell." In a better mood, Mac put his burly arm around Captain's shoulder and ushered him back toward the door. "The answer to your question, though, is no, you couldn't get in it, because the receiving unit is only three foot square."

"You could put a baby in it," Captain said quickly.

Mac reached down to pick up the collar but let it lay. "Later," he said and then, "Yeah, a baby. Yeah, I guess you could at that. Not a very pleasant thought, though. Come on, let's get some champagne going. We just saved my ass." They walked into the kitchen, and Captain heard two clicks from behind him; the screen door and the automatic trash compactor shutting off.

Datchel

The beach in front of the house glistened silver under the floods as the ocean retreated over it again. Captain blinked himself away from the hypnotic spectacle and yawned. He finished the seasoned wine from the daintily cut glass and felt hungry. At the foot of the stairs he called to Iris. "How are we coming? Need some help?"

"No, I can handle it. Just a few more minutes. Did you put the towel on the bed?"

Captain went into the large, baby blue bathroom and forgot what he was there for. The walls were covered with mirror. He stared and admitted to himself that he looked tired. Finally, he lifted up the toilet seat and his robe and sat down. When he was sure of a clean seat, he always sat to urinate. His father had told him that it put years on your life to relax and let your bladder open instead of standing and pushing.

Captain watched the ornate faucet drip into the tub, the com-

138

fortable, blue porcelain tub. The warm flow of urine started to make its way through his tubes. It relaxed him. He let his eyes close thinking about the insane time he'd had with Datchel in the elegant blue bathtub.

It had happened on Halloween night. Iris and Captain had gone to a bash down the beach. The beach party was a costumed affair with live music and entertainment. It was after two o'clock in the morning when Captain and Iris returned to her house debilitated by too many people and too much dancing, alcohol and drugs. The house was quiet and peaceful, but they were full of cocaine, and sleep was out of the question.

Captain poured them both a white crème de menthe on the rocks, turned on a relaxing radio station, lit candles and stripped back the cool blue sheets of the king-sized bed. Outside the window the tide was low, the sounds from the sea tame, listless. They disrobed and kicked their sweaty costumes into the corner. Iris wanted to go and freshen up. She didn't have to use the toilet, so Captain made her stay. Her smell aroused him.

Nude, they laid out onto the fresh sheets. They took turns sipping white crème de menthe and licking each other's lips; they sucked each other's tongues. Captain was breathing into Iris's ear, drying off the wetness that he'd made when the radio stopped. The music system went dead. Captain figured that a fuse had blown in the amplifier and jumped out of bed to go and replace it.

Iris stared at his standing penis while he moved and smiled her modest, blushing smile. Then she looked away as though unable to take the sight of the stiff thing any longer. She rolled over, turned her backside to him and gazed out into the ocean. Her coy way made Captain hot.

The stereo components were housed in a closet at the far end of the bedroom. Captain found the closet door open but had not yet entered when he heard a loud, explosive crack and Iris's pained cry come from behind him. He whirled around and adjusted his vision to see Datchel step out of the darkness. She was dressed in the costume of a cat, a black jungle panther, and she was wielding a black snake bullwhip.

The flickering candlelight cast funny shadows on the scene. Iris lay back trying to steady herself on her elbows. Her full bust jiggled like jelly against the tendons above her armpits. Her mouth hung open and she didn't blink. She lay there looking helpless, a welting red lash mark ran from her navel, across her stomach and around her side beneath her ribs. Blood began to trickle from it.

"Whore," Datchel screamed, pulling the long whip into readiness again.

Datchel was stunningly beautiful, that before anything else. Her costume was made around a skimpy black velvet bikini. She wore black, knee-length patent leather boots. Pointed black cat ears sprouted from her tight natural. Her makeup was impeccable, and somehow she had glued long, black catlike whiskers to her inside cheeks. They dangled. Her blue-black skin shimmered. Yellow light seemed to flash from her slanted eyes. Captain looked again and Datchel appeared sinister. Her lip curled and Captain heard the snarl.

Iris apparently had had enough, because she rallied and jumped from the bed in a rage. She closed the distance between them fast, her bust bouncing, her fist drawn back and doubled. Datchel turned the whip around in her hand to use the butt as a club, and when Iris was close enough, she swung it hard at Iris's head.

Captain was close now too; he heard and felt the blow. He couldn't get between them in time, and it was a sickening thunk. Iris dropped like lead, and Captain knew in his heart of hearts that she could be a goner.

Datchel stood her ground; her look was cold. She dropped the whip and quickly produced a long steel hat pin from within her natural. She held it ready like she knew how to use it. "Now your little darling is where she belongs, El Capitan. Why don't you get down and stick it in her filthy mouth, brother love. Stick that big dick in her rotten mouth. Teach her to talk to me the way she does."

"I don't know about you two—what's going on between you," he said calmly. "She probably deserved what you gave her, but I'm half ready."

Captain took his penis in his left hand and stretched it toward the floor. He watched Datchel's eyes. He pulled the foreskin over the head and squeezed the veiny thing hard, abusively. He moaned and stroked himself easily. "I'd like to put this in your hot black hole, Datchel. Look at it swell."

A contemptuous smile began to play on her face, and she looked down to watch him work it. Smart as she was, she must have realized her mistake. Datchel tried to recover the seconds, but she was lost. Captain drove his fist toward her face. The only movement that she managed quickly raised her chin away from the blow. No matter, Captain's fist caught Datchel in the front of her long thin neck, on the larnyx, and kept on going. Her spine snapped with a loud crack, and he jerked his fist, still doubled-up tight, out of her throat. Datchel dropped the stiletto and threw her hands to her face. She held her chin and stared. A look of fear came and went; then it was arrogance.

She matched his stare with an arrogant look of the devil. She wasn't about to give it up, not to Captain, not to any man, especially not now. Datchel's hands fell away, and her head dropped forward against her chest. Her knees buckled at the same moment and down she went. She sank into a squatting position with her legs almost crossed and began convulsing.

Captain ran and switched on the lights. He returned to find Datchel curled up, her head hanging lopsided, twitching in a widening puddle of her own urine. Without hesitation, Captain scooped Datchel's jerking body up, ran into the bathroom with it and dumped it into the sunken blue tub. She was not heavy. He opened the drain and turned the water on to run slowly. Bringing a bath towel, he returned to the bedroom and placed it over the urine. He stepped on it briefly and knelt next to Iris.

Captain's heart began to gallop around in his chest when he found a slight pulse on Iris's neck. Perspiring freely, he held his breath and sought out a sign of breathing but could find none. Iris lay in Captain's arms as though she were asleep. He petted her beautiful face and stroked the soft blonde hair over her temples. Smoothing her hair, he found a large swollen lump on the rear of her head. He rubbed it and checked his hand; there was no blood. Captain traced his fingertips over her thinly veined eyelids and smiled at the shock of heavy dark eyelashes that grew from the tips of her lids.

"You've got everything," he said. Feeling peaceful, Captain rocked Iris gently. "My baby," he said, and a drop of clear liquid splashed onto her cheek. He watched the perspiration or teardrop spread out over Iris's pores.

Captain suddenly caught on and moaned out loud, "What in God's name are you doing? She's dying. What would the doctor have done?" He visualized the injury to the rear of her head and could see the broken blood vessels all jumbled together and clotting. The contorted capillaries were neglecting the brain. He knew what would open them up, a vasodilator—amyl nitrate. Stretching back onto the bed, Captain retrieved a pillow. He carefully but speedily arranged Iris's head upon it. Her eyelids seemed to flutter. He watched: nothing. He jumped up and opened the drawer next to his side of the bed, spotted the yellow box and brought it over beside her. There were four ampules remaining. He removed one, broke it and put it under her nose.

"Come on, Dad, we need help." The fumes rolled over his knuckles and up into his face. He avoided breathing. Holding back the urgency, he waited. Captain pushed on Iris's chest. When he let up, she involuntarily inhaled. He pushed again; she inhaled and he waited. Hovering over her as intimately as close vision would allow, he studied her face, paying particular attention to her nostrils. Nothing, not a quiver. Captain stiffened out one arm and leaned heavily, with all of his weight in the heel of his palm, onto Iris's chest. When he was sure that her lungs were empty, he broke another amyl nitrate ampule under her nose and let the other hand come away from her breastbone. The gas rushed into her body.

He waited and closely inspected her visage for a life sign. His temples beat with expectation. A small amount of air slipped from Iris's lips, and then she inhaled slightly. A reflex perhaps, but something. "Goddamn, baby, come on." He held the broken ampule in front of her perfect nose. "Breathe, sister, breathe. Try, try for life, please."

Iris moved her head slightly and released a small breath of air in the form of a purr. Captain froze. She began to breathe, softly at first, but each breath was heartier. Iris worked her heels into the carpet and wriggled her naked body just a bit. Finally, she cracked her eyes and smiled. Captain smiled too; he wanted to cheer but contained himself.

"Oh, baby," she whispered sexily, "you can't imagine what's going on in my head."

"Yes, yes, I can Iris," he answered excitedly.

"Oh, no, you can't," she said, nuzzling her shoulder blades into the soft blue carpet. "Suck on my big titties, honey, come on." She put her hands around her left breast and squeezed it, forcing the areola to distend and the nipple to stand up. "Cappy, suck me." Iris was crawling on her back.

Captain wasn't sure. He said, "Oh, well," and then he said, "Shit," and drew in three mammoth lungs full of amyl nitrate for himself. He felt his vascular system open up, doped blood run for his brain. Captain dropped his head and slobbering mouth onto the end of Iris's soft, upturned breast. The neurons in his brain synapsed; white light exploded from behind his lidded eyes. The room swirled; Captain's mouth slipped off of the wet, tender flesh.

Hunched over, Iris had crawled under him. She chewed on his penis the way that he liked it. She chewed crazily, and it hurt a bit and throbbed. Another ampule popped, Iris inhaled it again and again and passed it. They were into the rush, foreplay vanishing. Iris's silken inner thighs trembled. Her eyes, mouth, nose and vagina drooled. Captain fell on top of her. "Oh, oh. I can feel it pound my stomach. Oh, oh, use it—use it on me. Use me. Plumb me. Plumb my pipes."

The expression excited him, she knew that. It made him feel like a workman: physical, strong, crude. Captain drew back onto his knees, his purplish erection bobbing from his pelvis. He leaned the head of his penis against her bathed vaginal lips.

"Oh, yes." She clawed at his shoulders. He eased it through her puckered lips to test but gave up when she reached behind him and pulled him in by his rear end. "God, oh, God," Iris screamed. Her eyes rolled into her head. She threw her arms around his neck, her legs around the back of his thighs, arched her back and shrieked. Iris impaled herself around him. She jammed the tip of her cervix into the head of his penis. She held on and shook. Captain went for it too. He tried to push her legs up over his shoulders, but even in her euphoria she resisted. "Not too hard, honey. Easy—easy—you'll hurt me."

144

Whether or not that was true didn't matter; she said it, and it made him crazy.

I'm an animal, he thought, pumping. My cock is so huge it will hurt her. He twisted inside of her with all of his strength, listening for a grimace.

"Uh, uh, uh," she grunted.

Iris popped the last amy and passed it up to him. She worked with him, under him, like a rubber doll. The skin around her hips pulled and stretched, her large breasts shook. He felt it start from the tips of his fingers and knew that he was growling. He let himself go. In a blur he saw Iris's eyes fly open wide and her excited smile. She said she loved to watch him come more than anything.

She knew what to say. "Pump me, Cappy, pump me. Plumb my insides out with that big dick. Fuck me, fuck me, fuck me, fuck your big sister. Give me that huge Blood cock. Drive me with it." She urged him on, and he was vaguely aware that she was tightening the walls of her vagina; she muscled him. Suddenly, Captain stopped stroking and cried out in a way that would normally have embarrassed him. He barely heard as he held still inside of her scalding sheath and climaxed. He held fast and peeked to watch Iris move under him, milk him and smile— proud, satisfied, feminine.

Played out, with his knees hurting, Captain fell onto Iris. She feigned discomfort and then relaxed under him. Breathing heavily, Captain licked the perspiration off of Iris's neck and from around the diamond studs in her ear lobes.

"Captain, what happened to Datchel?" Iris asked suddenly. Her body became rigid.

Raising himself up and stiffening his elbows, Captain looked into her questioning blue eyes. Blue on blue, a reflection. He started to laugh and fell back down, forcing the breath from her.

Iris didn't laugh. She kicked her legs up and down against the carpet like a spoiled brat and pushed him off of her. He rolled onto his back and stared at the ceiling.

"Cappy, come on, tell me." She sat upright and shook his upper arm with both hands.

"You don't have to worry about her anymore. Your house is in order."

"What do you mean? What happened?" she asked, flushing.

Captain jumped to his feet and pulled Iris up with him. He turned her and sat her down on the bed.

"Cap, I'm serious. Please tell me."

"I will," he answered. He arranged the pillows against the headboard, pushed and propped her up against them and covered her to the waist with the clean, crisp blue sheet.

Captain picked up the bullwhip, curled it properly and placed it on Iris's lap. She stared at it, trying to remember. A swallow of iced crème de menthe made his taste buds feel fresh. Putting his lips against Iris's, he spit a second mouthful of the peppermint liqueur into her mouth.

"Um—refreshing. Now tell me, please."

Captain handed her the glass and spoke authoritatively. "Stay put. Do not move, do you understand?"

She started to speak, but he put his hand out sternly to admonish her. "Just stay put."

Iris snuggled her back into the pillows, had another sip and said, "All right."

Datchel had not moved; she lay twisted at the bottom of the sunken blue bathtub. Captain stared down at her body. A shiver ran through him. "Goddamn," he sighed.

Captain removed a heavy blue terry cloth towel from the rack and threw it into the sink. He waited with the hot water running until the towel was steaming, shut off the faucet and wrang the towel out. Bringing it, he took another dry towel, a bottle of

146

witch hazel and a tin of talcum powder back into the bedroom.

Iris was sitting up against the headboard with the butt of the bullwhip in one hand and rubbing her head with the other. She had reached her diary. It lay at her side. "I remember now— some of it," she said. "What—what did you—do—to her?"

Captain took the whip away and said, "Move your diary," which she did. "Roll onto your stomach." Iris turned over. Captain put the talc and witch hazel on an end table. He folded the clean, dry towel and wedged it up between her opened legs, against her wet sex. He closed her legs around it. The steaming hot towel was then unrolled and laid out neatly to cover Iris's rump and back. She jumped, then swooned and moved sensually against the sheet.

Captain slapped her hard on the ass and sprang up onto the bed to sit evenly upon her two cheeks. When her back was heated up and soft, he gave her skin a fast wipe and threw the towel aside. Splashing on plenty of Witch Hazel, he began to rub.

"Datchel is dead. I killed her." Iris tensed up, but Captain rubbed her loose again. "There'll be no more threats, no more harassment. The bullshit is over. Just try to forget that the woman ever existed. Can you do that, pretty ass?"

He moved down and sat on the back of her thighs to rub her pink bottom. Captain could feel her thinking. "God only knows how many other people's heads she was twisting," he said, pounding her flesh.

Finally, Iris asked, "Will you tell me about how it happened. I won't ask again if you just satisfy my curiosity this once. Just about when I was unconscious."

It seemed that Iris was taking it well. Captain hoped to continue her feelings in that vein. Accordingly, his explanation of Datchel's death began with, "When she hit you, it was for keeps. I honestly thought that you were a goner."

Iris remained still, took advantage of the massage and listened while Captain explained exactly what had happened. He concluded the story by saying out loud what he was thinking to be the truth, that it was sort of an accident.

"No, Cappy, it was no accident. That is why I wanted to know about it—all of it. Look at this." Iris reached for her diary and opened it to the velvet bookmark. "You were right, and I'll bet that you were just saying it, just kidding around."

"What did I say, about what?"

"About my house being in order." She pointed to her open diary. An astrological calendar lay in front of Captain. He worked on Iris's shoulder muscles.

"I don't understand what I'm looking at, sister. I can't read a chart."

"It's a map, Cappy. It's easy to read once you know how." Iris's voice perked up. "It simply says that today is an absolutely correct day for me, my house is in perfect order. I'm going to begin—I have begun, that is—experiencing a whole new kind of inner peace, a freedom. It's all there, so simple. The stars will guide us if we only allow them to."

Captain worked on her backbone. "It may have seemed like an accident to you," she said, "but I know better. It had to happen; you were just an instrument." Iris paused abruptly and suddenly turned over underneath Captain and stared up into his eyes. "Oh, baby, but I know that you deserve the credit. Oh, my sweet, beautiful thing." She rubbed his forearms in unison. "Did I hurt your feelings, honey? Come, kiss me. I love you so much, the way you look after me, the way you protect me. Why, you probably saved my life." She looked at him sexily. "I know one thing—you sure made me feel good. Come, kiss your big sister."

Captain gave her a wet kiss and exchanged tongues but was not feeling any of the insecurity that Iris imagined. Astrology or no astrology, Iris or not, he was glad about what had happened to Datchel. He was only sorry that it couldn't have been done sooner and at his own pace. Captain would have liked to have taken his time exploring Datchel's sins with her and to have heard her confession before he brought down the curtain. She would have been fun to break. Nonetheless, the African was from the dark side and had to go. "It's done," he said, breaking the kiss.

"What is?" she asked.

"Just it," he said, kneading her breasts and smiling.

Iris became thoughtful and then clapped her hands on the tops of his and held them tightly. "Yes, it is, isn't it. It certainly is."

Captain turned Iris back over onto her stomach and gently patted her down with talcum powder. Placing a cool, fresh pillow onto the length of her back, he lay down on top of it and put his cheek against hers. The corners of their mouths touched. After a few moments she spoke in a hoarse voice from his weight. "Thank you, dear. I feel totally relaxed. Can I ask you what happens next?"

"Yes, I was about to tell you. In a few minutes we'll stand up and put some clothes on you—a jump suit or something like that. Then I want you to go upstairs and make a fire and relax. Take a pillow and the cashmere blanket in the hall closet. If you can sleep, sleep. You probably need it, but do not come back downstairs for any reason. If you're hungry, fix a bite, but stay upstairs—understand?" Captain raised up and twisted the diamond stud earring that ran through her left ear lobe until she lifted her head, flinching with pain.

"Ooouuuch."

"Have you got that? Stay out of here." It was a command.

"Yes, yes. I've got it. I'll stay upstairs—promise—ouch."

Letting go of her ear, he kissed it and jumped up off of the bed. Captain opened her long closet door and grabbed a red, white and blue track suit with U.S.A. plastered all over it. Mac had sent it from the Olympics just before his death.

"Here, babe, put this on and beat it."

She stood up on the bed to slip the nylon suit on. Captain watched her avoid looking toward the bathroom. She stretched to get into the sleeves.

"Your armpits are even pretty."

Iris blushed and hurried what she was doing. She almost turned away, but he could see her second guess that idea. It would only turn her toward the bathroom.

"Don't worry, there's nothing to see in there," he said.

Iris zipped up the jacket and pretended not to hear. Captain spoke again but so that only he could hear. "That's how you survive, isn't it. That's how you stay clean. You see only what you want to see." He thought about it and realized that there had been a lot of that in his family. He decided that it was a most helpful quality in life.

"Did you say something?" she asked, bouncing down to stand beside him.

"No, just mumbling to myself about your assets."

"You're too good to me." Then, excited, "Oh, I love you. My life is going to be so different, so peaceful now. I—we won't have a care in the world. We can go anywhere, do anything; can't we?" She asked the question timidly.

"Sure. Hell, yes."

"Can we get married?" she asked with sparkling eyes.

Iris's open, ingenuous expression warmed him. He took the time to enjoy the good feeling, the love that he had for the girl. The question was not a shocker. Over the past two years Captain had married Iris twice in Las Vegas, once in Vail, Colorado, and once in the Bahamas. It made her happy. "Sure, baby, sure. Hell, yes. Whatever you say."

Captain handed the joyful girl a pair of fluffy beige slippers from the closet and escorted her to the doorway of the bedroom. Pointing her up the stairs, he gave her a good slap on the behind, and she scampered up the heavily carpeted staircase on all fours.

Captain went back to the closet and stood there, wondering what to wear to work in. His eye was drawn to a Bijan's blood-red silk shirt, the most beautiful shirt made, Captain thought. He stared at the glistening crimson material, laughed and decided on bare skin but slipped on a pair of white bikini briefs to keep his genitals out of the way. Up the comfortable stairs he ran, through the kitchen and out into the rear of the newly rebuilt garage. Captain gathered an armful of heavy-duty plastic garbage can liners and shut the hallway and kitchen doors behind him. He waved to Iris, who was in front of the fireplace, and returned down the stairs. Dropping the plastic bags on the floor inside the bedroom door, he went the rest of the way down the stairs to the work out and steam room level. The cupboards and drawers in the rear of this room contained tools and junk.

Captain realized that he was grinding his teeth and stopped. Qualifying his feelings, he was anxious but unafraid. He found a yardstick right away and after rummaging, selected a hacksaw with a rusty but strong blade and an expensive-looking, almost new pair of stainless steel garden shears. Releasing the safety catch, he closed the pruning shears and allowed them to force, to spring open, into the palm of his right hand.

The blades were oiled and moved across each other with a slick metallic cutting sound. The sound was both pleasant and exciting and sent chills through him. He touched the edges; they were very sharp. Captain flexed the shears again and realized that there would be very little they couldn't cut through.

Upstairs in the bedroom, Captain lay the yardstick, the hacksaw and the hand shears on top of the plastic garbage can liners. He dashed back upstairs past the quiet living room and into the kitchen. A toilet flushed in the guest bathroom off of the living room. That was good. Iris was minding.

Captain ran through the cutlery drawer and selected a large steel butcher knife with a blond wooden handle. The cutting edge was like a razor, and he approved it.

He brought a cold beer out of the refrigerator, popped the top and drank two good swallows. His throat was still burning when he glugged down the rest of the can and belched. Thinking about what he'd done, it occurred to him that he'd never chuggalugged an entire container full of beer before. He had always left that to the working-man types. His close friend Hays, the garbage man, was a good chuggalugger. Belching again, Captain felt a tinge of pride sweep over himself.

Captain opened another can of beer and had a pull. He scratched his pubic hair and reached into his French voile bikini to rearrange his constricted penis and testicles. After, they felt better and he had another swallow. Captain looked over his shoulder at his bicep, fixed it hard and held it until it began to cramp.

Bringing the butcher knife and the beer, he went down to the bedroom and shut and locked the door behind himself. The butcher knife went on top of the green plastic bags with the rest of the gear. He sat on the end of the bed to finish the beer. The ocean was low; the calm, tedious.

Porcelain, tile and mirror reflected brightly from all of the light the bathroom bulbs could muster. The circumstances made Captain think of the room as a well-lit surgical theater. A warmness came to him, and he pictured his father. He placed the heavy-duty plastic garbage can liners, the hacksaw, the butcher knife and the clean-cutting pruning shears all together next to the sunken blue bathtub. Standing back from a new angle, Captain took a good look into the bottom of the tub.

Datchel's broken neck was not obvious from where he stood. Her bare black shoulder covered that disarranged part of her anatomy. Her mouth hidden, as in life, Datchel peered past Captain from behind her shoulder. He waved his hand through her glazed stare to try and break it, but she wouldn't give it up. Her body twitched a bit and seemed to swell. She stared. Her arrogance had not forsaken her despite the throes of rigor mortis.

Because of her audacity and ball-busting energy, Captain had always thought of Datchel as a larger person than he now observed. He remembered how she could domineer a social situation by the mere look in her eye and toss of her head. Her feet, which he knew to be large, were hidden from view by the closest side of the blue tub. Neither did her long brown hands appear prominent. Separated from her black soul, Captain saw Datchel for what she really was—a rather petite, young, female Negro. He chuckled to himself about the discovery and was tempted to call Iris and demonstrate that the witch was dead, but decided against it and that he was stalling.

Dropping the yardstick into the tub alongside the body, Captain reassured himself that dismembering Datchel should present no problem. He'd watched his father cut many times and had done some cutting himself. He knew about dissection; he remembered the grisly autopsies. His mind closed in on the first one, the bad one.

They had stood close, Dr. Blood's arm around Captain's shoulder. The pathologist took a deep breath before he began and told Captain, in what seemed a truthful statement, that he hated to do autopsies and made his students do them for him when he could. Captain's father said, "We're waiting, doctor," in a nice way.

The reluctant doctor broke through his hesitation with "Yes, yes, so am I, Kal" and a hearty laugh.

The two men had another shot of bourbon. The pathologist used heavy metal shears to snap open the rib cage; this, to provide access for Doctor Blood to get at and measure the organs. Captain retched and nearly vomited when a sick pancreas broke open in Kalvin's hands. Doctor Blood laughed and said, "Now that is what I call an odor. Don't smell it, Cap; it'll stunt your growth." But Captain smelled it.

The cranial cavity was opened with an electric saw in a brutal fashion, and pulpy brain tissue slopped out onto the aluminum table in front of them. The pathologist nodded toward the unstable stuff as it ran down the table and into the drains. "Booze," he said.

"Booze?" Captain questioned.

"Hell, yes. I've seen 'em turn to liquid, head full of slosh." He looked at Captain, who didn't believe. "No shit. Ask your old man."

Doctor Blood looked up and concurred. "Advanced stages, chronic alcoholism."

"But do people live with their brains turned to liquid?"

The pathologist had a drink from his bottle and was offering it to Captain's father when he said, "Hell, yes." The man shook his head and pretended to listen. "Hell, yes. Can't you hear that?" The doctors laughed and wouldn't talk about it anymore.

"You're stalling," he told himself out loud. Captain picked up the reflective wooden-handled butcher knife and stood closely above the body. He looked at Datchel's fragile, disjointed neck and understood where the first cut would be. Then he wondered what would happen if he called the police and told them the truth. He rolled the knife in his hand and thought about it. The whip was a weapon, and he had used his hands. Actually he had only used reasonable force. Datchel had assaulted Iris, though, and it seemed that Iris should have been doing the defending. Also there were two of them. But then Datchel was the aggressor. He puzzled the facts for a moment and realized that he couldn't, or wouldn't, stand an investigation.

"Who are you kidding? The boys in blue would cut you a new asshole. You're stalling."

It was the truth. He didn't want to get into the tub.

Finally, being very careful not to touch the corpse, he stepped down into the sunken blue tub. Captain thought the hair on his leg brushed against black skin, and he flinched. "You fucking pip-squeak," he mumbled. He stepped around the body and straddled it. His bare feet wouldn't grip the cool, slippery porcelain. They seemed to be sliding inward under his weight. Straining his leg muscles, he fought the sensation. A giddy feeling came over him. He licked his lips, tasted salt and wiped the perspiration from his upper lip and forehead. Surprised at not being able to move, he stood there watching the water trickle out of the faucet onto a bleached blue curve at the bottom of the bathtub.

Gloves—he really needed a pair of gloves. They would make him feel better, insulate him from his own touch. He ran the house over in his mind and couldn't get lucky. The only gloves that he was sure of finding were Iris's bulky rubber kitchen gloves upstairs, and they just weren't right. He thought about it some more, and while most of his brain was occupied with gloves, he reached over and carefully put his pointer finger against Datchel's dead upper arm. Then he pressed the same finger into her flesh. The tissue seemed to be jelling or firming up. The flesh felt thick. He pulled his finger away and watched the white impression stay too long before filling in with dark pigment.

"So what's the big deal?" he said. Convinced for the moment, his nerve returned and he moved. Captain put the butcher knife outside next to the tub, and grabbed Datchel's upper arm and squeezed it several times with both hands. Feeling much better, he touched her back and then ran his hands all over the African's body, squeezing and kneading the flesh as he went. Captain undid the top of the black bikini and let it drop into the tub. He felt her smallish breasts. They seemed waxen. He reached his sharp knife and slit the bikini bottom on the sides. The material fell away and exposed a tan line; faint, but it was there.

Captain was aware of a tingling in his genitals. Datchel's legs were frozen together, her knees touching and bent to accommodate the shape of the tub. Captain turned the body to see Datchel's privates and pulled her black legs apart at the knee. Gripping each knee firmly, he forced, and the legs opened.

"Spread," he said. Perspiration and saliva dropped off of his chin to splash near Datchel's navel. Captain had to look twice, as though his first glimpse had deceived him. But it hadn't. Datchel's pubic area was shaved clean. Captain stood on Datchel's knees and watched her pink crack open. It looked dry and uninteresting, but he licked his middle finger, leaned forward and inserted it quickly into her parting vagina. The uninspired hole was clammy and tight. He withdrew his finger and stared. Datchel's clitoris was tiny, her vulva childlike. A new, not unpleasant, perfumed feminine odor came and went. "Pass," he said, standing off of her knees. Datchel's legs began closing again, slowly. Captain finished the job and turned the body onto its front.

Feeling strong and in charge, Captain straightened Datchel's crooked neck out the best he could. Touching the broken vertebra with his left hand, Captain slid the butcher knife under Datchel's thin neck. He turned the sharp blade up against the fine musculature just beneath the break. He took a deep breath and pulled the knife with all of his might. The body lifted from the tub, the knife did not come through. Datchel's head, her well-kept natural and Halloween cats' ears hung over one side of the blade, the rest of her body hung lopsided over the other. Thickening purplish blood began splashing everywhere. The pale blue tub was suddenly slick with crimson as was Captain's hand, arm and lower body. Blood swirled into the drain.

Captain did his best to ignore the feeling of revulsion that overcame him. Keeping the knife imbedded in neck muscle, he lay the upper torso back onto the bottom of the tub and stepped on Datchel's back and shoulders. He worked the sharp blade back and forth and pulled again, hard, as he cut. The knife came through, and Captain jolted upright from the force.

The loose head rolled over to one side; the tub ran deep in dark red blood. He didn't want to look but couldn't help it; Datchel's head lay on its left ear, half submerged in a frothing red wash. Her eye was open and bulged out toward the side of the tub. Her flat pink tongue hung out between her full lips.

Involuntarily, Captain half jumped and half stepped off the headless body. As he did, a loud slurping moan came from the oozing red stump.

Captain felt his upper body recoil as if to sneeze, but that wasn't what happened. His throat opened, and he vomited in an arc over the bloody work that he had done. His nose burned inside his faint head. Captain felt his empty stomach roll and strain against itself. He gasped and fell back against the side of the tub and dropped the knife onto his bare foot.

He reached out to hold on. Dizziness overcame him. He tasted bile. His knees began to give way. He slipped along the side of the wet tub. Things blurred. He went down.

Somewhere, amidst the darkness in his mind, Captain came to realize that he was lying with Datchel in the wet blue tub; yet, he couldn't move. The acrid smell of his own spew seared his nasal passages. Cold water trickled close by. The furious shivering came again, and over the clatter of his own teeth, he knew that he was conscious. Now, starkly aware of what he'd let happen, he wanted to cry; it was the only thing left. He felt it well up inside of his chest but finally pass. "God," he groaned.

Captain wouldn't open his eyes. She would be there, staring at

157

him. There was no question in his mind that Datchel's head was lying just past her dank-skinned black shoulder, cocked to one side, glaring at him, "Gotcha" in her slanted cat's eyes. A tremor rippled through him from head to toe and back again, and he decided. Without opening his eyes, Captain groped his way out of the slop and up the side of the tub to stand. He was dripping; his mouth tasted of illness, like the flu, when he was a child. He sat on the tub's flat marble edge at floor level, eased his breathing and rinsed his feet under the running spigot.

Carefully, he stood and aimed himself in the direction of the shower. The shivers came again. He walked, one step with each foot, onto the soft blue carpet, opened his eyes into the blinding white light and stepped numbly into the shower. Captain closed his eyes again while he washed and washed. The white bikini was stained pink, but his skin and hair were soon clean. A discomforting bruised lump raised on the top of his foot, and he recalled dropping the heavy knife. He imagined the hack that would have been in his foot had the blade landed differently.

The shower helped restore his peace of mind. He guessed that the worst part was over. Gargling clean water, Captain thought about a drink. His mind ran to bourbon. He spit the water and said to himself, "Later." A drink would come as a reward.

Captain made the water hotter on his shoulders and really began to enjoy. Then he knew that he felt as good as he was going to and any more would be stalling. While toweling off, he set his mind. No, dismembering Datchel was not like cleaning game or helping with autopsies. Yes, it was a big drag that went way beyond proving any point to a recalcitrant sinner, to a beating heart. But it was not the end of the world, and it most certainly had to be done, finished.

Determined, with his teeth clenched, Captain returned to the sunken blue bathtub. Cocking his head, he listened before he looked. The house was quiet; a fan in the bathroom ceiling smoothed the sound of the sea at low tide. Iris was occupied; undoubtedly asleep. Dawn was nearing. The realization spurred his determination.

Captain watched himself in the mirrors while he gathered a green plastic garbage can liner and stepped back down into the tub. With an ease that surprised himself, Captain picked up Datchel's head by a piece of ragged skin hanging from the neck and dropped it into the bag. Setting it aside, he rinsed the tub using all of the power behind the cold water.

He took Datchel's lower legs off just above her black boots, from behind the knee. His breathing wasn't right, and he squinted his eyes to partially blur his vision. Cutting through tendon and muscle was bad enough, but the grisly sound of wrenching cartilage reminded him of twisting undercooked chicken legs free from the bird's unyielding body. His throat was constricted and he breathed through his nose. Perspiring heavily, he gagged all the while. He used the knife, shears, saw, shears and knife in that order until he had cut through Datchel's knees. Removing the lower legs with the feet still intact, Captain bagged them with the devil's head and sealed the bag with the wire that came attached, tying it into a knot.

The tub's edge was where he rested and threw his sweat aside. Captain groaned to try and loosen his throat. It pained when he tried to clear it several times, and he finally hummed loudly. Then he sang, "Mi, mi, mi, mi, mi," like an Irish tenor. He sang, "Old McDonald had a farm, *ee i, ee i, o*— And on his farm he had some chicks, *ee i, ee i, o.*" Captain picked up the butcher knife and went back to work at the thigh. "With a *chirp chirp* here and a *chirp chirp* there—Here a *chirp,* there a *chirp,* everywhere a *chirp chirp*—"

Cutting into the fleshy hip sockets, he became irritated that he

159

hadn't started there instead of at the knee. Without the lower leg, there was little leverage, and he had to use the shears to snap loose the tough internal connecting tissue while he twisted and broke the joints loose. He gagged some more and tried to throw up, but his stomach was empty.

He sang, "Row, row, row your boat, gently down the stream. Merrily, merrily, merrily, merrily, life is but a dream," and laughed as he looked at himself covered with blood in the mirrored walls. "If anyone were to see you," he said to the mirror, "cutting and singing—" He laughed heartily and felt much better in so doing—"cutting and singing—" He held up the bloody shears and posed, "Cutting and singing—they'd surely think that you were mad."

The headless, legless torso lay next to the yardstick in the blue and red bathtub. It measured two feet four inches. All of the other pieces were under a yard in length also, but Captain wondered about Datchel's strong thigh bones and the trash compactor. He questioned whether the machine was brutish enough to consume them; it worried him. The meaty thighs went into a second bag, while the black-skinned torso went into a third bag, with the thin arms folded over the stomach. Datchel's black bikini and what appeared to be horsehair cat's whiskers that had been lying against the tub's drain were added to bag three.

Captain checked the bags carefully to make sure that they were sealed. He then rinsed them clean and pushed them to the rear of the tub. Retrieving a bar of soap and fingernail brush from the sink, he meticulously cleaned the tools. The bathtub itself and surrounding area were scrubbed and sanitized with Pine Sol from the bathroom cupboard. Not a drop of blood remained.

Captain showered again and stepped out of the now-pink bikini. He felt spent, numb, but was worrying about the hour. Had that not been a real problem, he might have laid down.

Captain envisioned the California Highway Patrol or Malibu Sheriff, frequent early morning travelers and snoopers of Pacific Coast Highway environs, well meaning, zealot sleuths, stopping to check his car or Mac's parking lot. Or an early busboy or chef. "Shit, that would be cute. "Good morning, officer." "Oh, hello, Emanuel. Ah, yes. Ah, well, you see, Mac was a friend of mine and said that anytime I wanted to dispose of a body I could use his machine. Yeah, right. Well, have a nice day."

The jump suit Captain selected caused him to smile. He hesitated because Russians were bad guys and because the track suit was bright red with large white U.S.S.R.'s embossed all over it; another treat from Mac at the Olympics and sort of a joke that the old fart thought Captain would like. He did and put it on. Somehow he would be inconspicuous in his conspicuousness. Green Adidas went onto his feet with no socks. Captain stepped in front of a mirror: his hair was still wet; the jump suit fit well. He took a deep breath and thought he might look silly. "Shit, it's still Halloween—almost," he said to his image.

Captain returned all of the tools that he'd used for cutting to the places he'd found them, except for the butcher knife, which he lay on top of a wooden cutting block behind the downstairs bar.

The bags stretched around his fingers and fists when he lifted them from the tub. He wasn't sure whether the knotted plastic necks of the sacks would hold. He carried the bags in his arms against his chest. Hugging the bulky garbage can liners with his arms and feeling their contents made his stomach immediately queasy again. He used the flats of his palms to hold the bags, not his fingers. Downstairs in the barroom, Captain set the bags carefully down next to the door that opened onto the beach.

The cool sea breeze blew around him, salty and wet, while he stood in the opened doorway. He breathed it deeply. The ocean was definitely coming closer again. A faint white rim of light was

161

beginning to edge up upon the horizon and bring a distinction between water and air out there. The air was still dark, but dawn was on its way.

Captain carried two bags first, by the knots, and rushed down the beach to where the break between houses would be. As close as he was to them, the houses were very difficult to make out. They appeared as one long, rough, mountainous shadow against the sky. Not being able to find the exact spot, he estimated and left the bags to return for the third one. Once he had all of the bags situated together in one spot on the beach, Captain walked to and fro until he spotted the break. Gathering all three of the bags in his arms, he ran at the hilly area separating the houses and made it in one try.

It was dark, and if he remembered correctly, the garbage cans would be out in front of the garage. He didn't go out there but placed the bags neatly next to the side of the garage and quickly returned to the beach below, the way he had come.

Captain closed and locked the beach door and ran past the bar, like he figured a good boy should. He passed the bedroom and kept on going up to the living room. Iris lay sleeping, covered by the cashmere blanket, in front of the fireplace. Captain brought a pillow from the sofa and placed it under her head. He felt for the lump. It was there and it was a beauty. He checked her breathing and her pulse; it was only a hard sleep that consumed her.

His keys and wallet were on the kitchen table. He picked them up and stopped at the hall broom closet for the keys to Mac's restaurant. Backing out of the front door of the beach house, Captain pulled the big door shut quietly behind himself. Upon turning, he froze in his tracks. "Now why in hell didn't I think of that?" he said out loud. Datchel's white Bentley four-door was parked in back of the Jensen. "Shit," he said.

Captain stared at the smoked gray privacy windows that

Datchel had ordered specially for her car. Then he snapped his fingers with the idea. He knew what to do. In fact, he liked it better.

He let himself back into the house and stretched Iris's yellow rubber kitchen gloves on over his hands. They were much too tight but suitable for his purpose. Back outside on the front stoop, Captain spoke to the Bentley. "I wouldn't come near you without these." He held up his yellow gloved hands. The keys were in the car where Datchel always left them. Captain sat in the plush seat. He patted the leather dash. "I don't know if you perform like her or like me. Right now it doesn't matter. I could roll you over, but I'm not going to do that. I'm just going to drive you a ways. Don't let me down, and I'll drop you off without a ding—deal?"

He turned the key, listened to the electric fuel pump click and pushed the starter for the answer. The engine engaged fast and ran smoothly. Shutting it off, he smiled, patted the dash again and said, "It's a deal."

A dark sedan passed on the road in back of him. He lifted his foot high above the brake pedal and looked after the disappearing taillights. The clock in the Bentley said 3:58; day was coming. Captain jumped out of Datchel's car and ran to the garage. With his yellow rubber-gloved hands outstretched, he anticipated, turned the corner and reached. The walkway next to the garage was empty. The blood stopped in Captain's veins. His face burned, and he felt a tremendous surge, like embarrassment, rush over him. His imagination flashed. It was as though he were hanging alone, crucified, naked, on a darkened stage somewhere, in front of thousands who had been waiting with bated breath to see. The stage lights exploded with illumination onto his shriveled, tiny penis. He wanted to explain; he felt suddenly helpless. He should act casual, nonchalant. As long as I know the truth in my own mind, he thought, that's all that matters. I know that I have a big one, but the ice man was here and made it small, and I didn't expect to find a thing around this corner—honest—think it—whistle. Captain began to whistle but did the other thing. With a very sudden move, he threw himself spreadeagled up against the side of the garage. He gawked into the hazy dawn on his right, to his left, and above. He tensed and screamed, "The net." A dog barked up the beach. "Drop it—Drop the goddamned net. I won't fight—much."

Captain knew that there was no net that could hold him, no jacket. Unflinchingly, he confronted the barren space between the houses. "Well?" he demanded. The ocean dropped heavily to his right and below, the first big one of the morning. The dog yelped again. He tried to figure it. "Who?—the garbage man, the gardener, the cops—Who the hell—?" His heart sank. Then in the midst of the wracking pain, it came to him.

Captain did not take the time to engage a new emotion before he ran out from between the houses to the street. He turned right, ran past the house next door and ducked into the area just beyond that home. The three bloated, green plastic garbage can liners were there. They sat just as he'd left them, in a neat row—one, two, three—along the outside wall of the neighbor's garage. Captain moved as he cursed. "The goddamned fire." He grabbed the bags and ran for the Bentley. It was simple. The next-door neighbor's garage was almost exactly like Iris's garage had been before Datchel burned it down. Captain had never been alongside Iris's rebuilt garage nor observed it closely from the beach at night. He felt weak-kneed with relief.

The bags fit easily on top of the Bentley's back seat. He shut the rear door, jumped into the car and shut the driver's door next to him. Sitting still with his yellow-gloved hands on the wooden wheel, Captain hung his head and shook it back and forth slowly. "Shit, that was heavy. Scared the shit out of me."

The smoked windows lent an air of intimacy to the Bentley's interior as he drove. He reached Pacific Coast Highway, and the traffic was light. Not that it mattered really; no one could see into the car. This knowledge made Captain feel extremely secure, even cocky. "She should only have known when she ordered the smoked glass, what good use I would put it to." He chuckled and was able to spot Mac's restaurant in the distance. In so doing, he realized that the night was gone forever. The gray commencement of dawn was upon him. The sun, if it was going to present itself, would be next.

Captain crossed the double yellow line in the middle of the highway and pulled into the lot next to Mac's drive-in restaurant. The place was quiet. He swung the big car up and stopped it next to the garbage area in the rear, leaving just enough room to open the doors of the car. Wasting no time, he leaped from the car to begin trying keys to unlock the garbage shed. When he pushed, the door swung open. "Mac wouldn't have liked that," he said into the place.

Captain winked at the trash compactor as he walked by it on his way to the nearest window. He peered in. The restaurant was dark and devoid of people. The back door was locked. Captain aimed the most likely key toward the lock and stopped to think that perhaps the main electrical switch was on, or maybe the compactor worked alone, from its own circuit.

The pause allowed him to see the silver tape that ran along the edges of the glass inside the door. A closer inspection proved that the windows were wired too. "That's new," he said.

He ran to the garbage shed door and inspected it for a burglar alarm: it was clean. He looked again at the silver tape on the door and windows. "I'm sure that's new." He puzzled the situation for a beat. He could get past the alarm—that was kid's stuff—but it would take time and constitute a break-in. There was a round key on the key ring. "Burglar alarm keys are round," he said, but instead of following through, Captain pushed the long iron arm of the trash compactor forward. The black steel hole opened and gaped up at him. A lone piece of bright green withered lettuce shone up from the imperceptible dark at the bottom. Captain patted the compactor's iron belly and ran for the bags. A group of fishermen were entering the pier across the highway. They paid no attention to him.

The green plastic bags went into the receiving compartment of the industrial trash compactor with no problem. Captain felt anxious and was rushing but couldn't slow down. He pulled the heavy lever down and felt Datchel's flesh give beneath his force. The machine was closed. He pulled harder, and there was a click, a clunk and an electrical-sounding hum. Captain was ecstatic, and the machine took over with a lurch against the toggle bolts that held it to the concrete slab at the ground.

Captain listened excitedly and tried to decipher the various sounds that came from within the trash compactor. Then there came a gurgling whir from underneath, where he imagined the liquids being carried away. Suddenly the machine began to strain. Captain put his hand on its side and gave it a pat, while an electrical governor of some kind fed it more juice. He presumed the steel walls to be contending with the bones from Datchel's thigh, the femur. The question continued in his mind whether or not the machine could handle it. Captain laughed in spite of his concern, thinking about the expression on the repairman's face when he came to unjam the thing.

The strain came through the thick metal walls into his hand. The monster seemed to be flexing its muscles. It began to slow down. It creaked and strained and made groaning noises as if it were about to break. Captain was smelling for smoke when there occurred a loud snap. The engine's revolutions sped up again, and Captain cheerfully checked his back to make sure that the coast was clear, which it appeared to be.

It wasn't long before he heard a pushing and sliding sound come from the southerly end of the machine. It was there that an enclosed conveyor system exited the compactor to hang over an open trash receptacle, which sat atop small but sturdy black wheels. He remembered a similar but open conveyor belt that carried baled hay up into a barn when he was a boy. The portable trash receptacle emitted a thunk sound when it received what Captain presumed was the first twenty-five pounds of baled Datchel. The industrial trash compactor then clicked loudly and shut off. He felt a chill of concern while he stood there and waited. Nothing.

Captain pushed the lever to open the machine and looked into the cold black cavity. Although he couldn't see bottom, it appeared clean and empty. Closing it again and standing back, Captain rubbed his chin and thought. He went to the portable refuse container and looked in. Five tidy plastic bags lay strewn on the rusted iron floor. Captain couldn't be sure which neat little bundle was his. He stepped away, understanding that it didn't matter. In fact that was the whole point. It would take a pro to figure out what any one of those bags contained.

"But what happened to the rest of Datchel?" he asked. He stood on his toes and looked back up the conveyor chute. "Will she come out with the next load?" The conveyor chute was empty. He stood there wondering.

When it finally occurred to him, he grinned, patted the powerful machine and said, "I'm impressed." Then with his imagination playing tricks on his vision, Captain watched as the machine's mouth rolled into a contented smile, and he heard it loud and clear when the iron lips parted slightly to emit a haughty belch.

Captain laughed loudly and slapped his thigh but didn't stick around any longer. Checking the coast, which was still clear, he shut the garbage shed's door to leave it as he'd found it, started the Bentley, eased it out to the highway and headed south, down the coast toward the Los Angeles airport.

Not yet 100 yards away from the restaurant, Captain observed in his rearview mirror a dark sedan also traveling south behind him. It appeared to pause in front of Mac's place and pull in. Because of the growing distance between them, Captain had no way of being sure just where the car was headed or who was at the wheel. If it was a cook or dishwasher or waitress—whoever it might have been didn't matter. It gave him the chills, and he didn't want to think about it.

"That was just too fucking close to believe," he said, flashing his eyes onto the road ahead of him and stepping on the gas.

The beach communities were coming to life, putting out garbage and sending people off to school or work. The traffic on the coast highway began to increase as he proceeded toward Santa Monica.

The thing with Datchel done, he felt let down, exhausted. Captain switched things around in his head so that the feeling of accomplishment would help to keep him alert. A longing for sleep came and went with the exertion of his will power. He felt punchy; he needed a drink.

The Set-up

Northbound traffic remained light but for semi-trucks going through to San Francisco and surfers making their way to Rincon and other beaches. Bright rays from the early morning, Pacific Palisades' sun began pushing out over the foothills on his immediate left. The warm yellow light was starting to chase the fog off of the beaches and out to sea. His plan remained unchanged: to take the ramp up into the city of Santa Monica and to use Lincoln Boulevard to reach Los Angeles International Airport.

Now, with time to reflect, Captain thought about what had happened to Datchel; what had been left of her with the liquids removed. It interested him immensely. He had learned long ago that the human body was almost totally comprised of fluids. He couldn't imagine, however, how the point could have been more graphically made. He wondered what was in the twenty-five pound bag; what the remains looked like. He imagined the fluids going down the drain and into the sewer. He questioned if the fluids from the eye could comingle with those of the occipital region of the brain and flash a picture on the side of the sewer pipe as they sloshed along. The right components, bathed in oxygen and blood in the whirling garbage disposal, creating a thought for a microsecond. It was a frightening thing to conjure. It would be "Good God, where am I?" from amidst the impossible screaming razors, the roar of eradication.

Traffic was piling up, and Captain had to wait before entering the ramp up from the coast highway to the bluffs and the city of Santa Monica. People stared at the luxurious Bentley as he drove, stopped and proceeded again. Captain guessed that the smoked windows and nondescript license plate of the car gave people the opportunity to imagine whomever they wanted to behind the wheel.

Knowing that he couldn't be seen, Captain played games with the other drivers, alternately speaking to them about their taste in automobiles, waving to them or giving them the yellow rubber finger. It was fun. He wished he could gather together naked, in one hall, all of the men who drove shiny, nickless Porsches and have a peek. "Goddamn, those boys must have small cocks," he said, watching a black, mirror-finished turbo fight to edge in front of the Bentley and accelerate to be the first one to the bluffs. He chuckled and thought about how much fun those fellows were when he had his Dodge. The old, banged-up, unassuming clunker would set the asphalt afire next to a $30,000 Porsche, spit polished with ego and sperm. Besides the loving memory of Speed that deterred him from letting the Dodge go, it was the expression on those beaten faces that made him keep it. Drained, saddened, alabaster countenances with the look of having just lost 30 K on a crap table.

The traffic lessened on Lincoln Boulevard, and Captain used

the air conditioning. Driving leisurely, he was tempted by a red-headed female, looking as though she were on the way home from a rough night, with her thumb out.

Slowing, he contemplated what might happen. "Come on in, baby. Oh, and here's ten for some head along the way. The gloves? Oh, the gloves. Well, you see, I do hand commercials. All of the men's hands that you see on television are mine. I have the exclusive contract. And I keep them lotioned up and in rubber gloves when I'm not using them. Insured by Lloyds of London for ten mil. Yeah, no shit, now suck."

But Captain knew that stopping would be pushing his luck, and he was glad when he continued by her and the feeling subsided. "Probably a guy, anyway," he laughed, remembering the truly beautiful black girl that he'd picked up hitchhiking in Hollywood. He had been completely fooled. Captain had dropped her in front of Frascatti's on Sunset Boulevard, but not before she had given him one of the all-time best blow jobs he'd ever had. She sat up with a grin and gargled his come before swallowing it. Then she closed her eyes and licked her thick lips with contentment. She was anxious to get out, but Captain held her fast and forced his other hand under her skirt and girdle, just to feel if she had nice lips and was wet. Captain's hand had bumped into the young man's soft but hot penis.

"Please don't hit me," the black boy said, beginning to cry. Captain remembered that the comment seemed ridiculous. He had no intention of hitting the boy.

He gave the surprised transvestite a ten spot for fooling him and for the good head and cut him loose. Afterward, Captain figured that some men would have beaten a person like that. It would have helped them during their impending identity crisis.

The airport was busy, the air loud. Captain felt the pressure but took his time easing the big car through the hubbub. He thought,

171

the more confusion, the merrier for my purposes, so don't let it get to you.

Feigning nonchalance, he watched the cars unload their frenzied passengers. A child screamed bloody murder next to him, and he jump-turned to see a five-year-old with his hand slammed into a rear car door. "Jesus," he said.

With the use of the car's smoked windows, Captain made the tempo change around him It became an old time, black and white movie. Automobiles jerked, and pedestrian traffic bounced along disjointedly. Captain took a deep breath and turned the air conditioning on full blast. His hands had felt damp and constricted by the rubber gloves, but they now began to feel swimmy in them. He was forced to stop in the middle of a pedestrian crosswalk, and what seemed like a gawking crowd of scurrying upright animals flocked past him on all sides. They touched the car and seemed to rock it.

Captain's nerves went raw. He gripped the steering wheel with all of his might, and perspiration dropped out of the yellow rubber gloves onto his lap. "Assholes," he screamed and was finally able to move ahead.

Captain arrived at the approximate place that he had planned, signaled and turned left into the concrete parking structure across the street from and shared by both the Eastern and United Air Line terminals.

He made sure that there were no pedestrians close before he rolled the window down. He then removed his left glove, took the ticket out of the machine, closed the window again using his gloved right finger on the button and proceeded into the garage over the loud clunking sound of metal. His breathing left hand felt so relieved that he decided not to reglove it.

Around the traffic he went and up to the second floor where parking was ample. There were very few pedestrians. Captain continued to the next ramp and up to floor three, which had only

172

two parked vehicles in sight and no persons. The roof parking lot was last and completely empty under the warm morning sun.

With his heart pounding, he wasted no time in swinging the big white Bentley into the furthest stall in the lot, the one closest to the exit sign and emergency stairwell. He looked down the lot to the elevator, which did not appear to be in use. He checked the ramp from whence he had come: nothing. Being careful not to touch anything with his bare hand, Captain gathered his wallet and car keys from the seat next to him. He put the parking ticket into his wallet. Glancing into the mirror, he decided to keep the round, dark glasses. He looked around again, removed the Bentley's keys, locked the doors, jumped out, locked the driver's door and stepped into the stairwell.

He felt excited but under control. Captain dropped Datchel's keys into the empty left glove and put both yellow gloves, folded, under his arm. Forgetting something, he peeked back around the concrete wall to observe the Bentley sitting by itself in the sun. Thinking it all over, Captain consciously looked at his wallet and keys in his bare hands. He squeezed his upper arm against his armpit and felt the gloves. He had everything. It was nearly done.

As luck would have it, no one was using the stairwell while he ran down the three flights to the exit into the alley in the rear. Captain stepped into the alley after looking both ways. A yellow taxi zoomed past.

An unfinished, four-foot cement block wall caught Captain's eye on the other side of the alley. He crossed over to it and situated himself with his face up into the warm sun as he sat down on the rough cement. It seemed a special quiet place amidst the turmoil.

Another taxi came by, stopped, backed up and stopped again. The driver was round faced and needed a shave. He stared at Captain's chest and articulated slowly.

"Are you okay?" he asked.

173

"Yes—yes, I'm fine, thanks."

"You're an American. Shit, I thought—Never mind." He sped off.

Captain looked down at the white U.S.S.R. on his chest. He chuckled and turned the yellow gloves upside down over one of the holes in the closest gray concrete block. He heard Datchel's keys bounce down through the several levels of cement to land on the ground, inside of the wall.

Captain stood and yawned. He stretched widely with both arms and jogged back into the shaded concrete garage and into the first level. The automobiles were bumper to bumper; people were rushing. On his way to the street, he passed a men's room, turned and went back to it. The room was empty of people and smelled of urine. Graffiti was everywhere, even on the ceiling. The yellow rubber gloves went into the wastebasket. He pushed them down out of sight amongst the soiled towels, took a fast leak, tore and flushed the parking ticket and jogged out of the place along the pedestrian walk toward the sunny street.

Upon reaching the open air this time, he knew that he was free. Holding back the excited feeling that was tingling in him, Captain waited for the cars to allow him and some others into the crosswalk over to Eastern Airlines. He wanted to scream, but he spoke to himself. "There is no possible way that this thing could be put back together, no possible way. All Datchel did was travel. Shit, they'll think she went to Angola to help." The thought made him smile, and he ran again, this time past the string of taxicabs and up onto the sidewalk in front of Eastern Airlines.

People pushed and shoved and scurried, but no one paid any attention to him. He liked that. He watched the self-obsessed travelers herd by, their eyes staring off to see themselves, how cool they were going to appear, disembarking.

"Hello," he said into the crowd of faces, but no one heard. "Who's in charge?" Captain asked the nearest redcap porter. The black man stood up from a partially filled luggage rack, brandishing a thick handful of green airline tags and a pen.

Captain stopped cold when he saw that the redcap was Hays, his friend. Captain smiled and put out his hand. "What's the problem?" The porter asked, taking the opportunity to remove his stiff-looking visor hat and wipe the perspiration off his forehead with a shirt sleeve.

"No problem," Captain replied. "I'm just looking for a way to spend a ten spot for a ride up to the bar."

"Guess what?" the porter asked, smiling and dropping what he was doing.

"I know—I've found it." Captain smiled too and felt fine.

"Right this way, doctor," the redcap said with a wink.

Captain sat down and put his feet up on the rear of the electrical cart. The redcap stepped aboard, turned the key and they were off.

"Hold it, hold it," someone called as the automatic doors opened for them. "A lady here for ninety-seven."

The cart stopped, and Captain looked over his shoulder to find an obese woman of indistinguishable age, covered with silver fox pelts and jewelry, with a huge arm outstretched, waddling toward them. Her hair was a mass of red curls piled atop her head. In the other arm she carried a Chihuahua wearing a jeweled collar.

"Wait—wait, I'm coming," she squealed.

"What's your name, pal?" Captain asked, turning back to the driver.

"Sam's my name and makin' money is my game."

Captain opened his wallet a crack and showed Sam the corners of several green bills. "Fuck her, Sam. I'll be late to the hospi-

175

tal." Just like Hays, Sam's eyes opened wide when he saw the money. Captain enjoyed the resemblance.

"Sorry, madam," Sam said. But it was too late. The fat woman had grabbed onto the side of the cart in what could have been a death grip.

"No, no, no," she squealed, obviously used to her own way. "No, no, no. Now you'll just do what I say, do you hear me?" The woman smelled of strong perfume and peroxide.

Sam let Captain see him staring at her hand holding the cart. Then he shrugged his shoulders and held up his hands in bewilderment.

Captain turned and dropped to his knees on the floor of the cart. He threw his mouth over the woman's puffed hand and bit it, hard. She pulled her hand away immediately. Her mouth dropped open. Sam moved ahead. The fat lady didn't scream for a long moment. The Chihuahua was grinning. When she finally yelled, she dropped the dog and clasped her hands to her bosom, as though she were an opera star. Then she let go a bellow, and the entire terminal heard her.

Sam wove the small motorized cart in and out between people, and the shrill, unpleasant noise trailed off behind them.

Sam was laughing so hard that he used the shirt sleeve material that covered his biceps to wipe the tears from his eyes. All that he said was, "Oh, shit—Oh, dear," over and over while he laughed.

Captain had removed Datchel's sunglasses to wipe his tired eyes, lie back and close them. "Man, you look tired, if you don't mind me saying so."

"Probably the light," Captain answered, putting the dark glasses back on again.

"Been up all night I guess, huh?"

"What's it to ya, Sam?"

176

"Oh, nothing, nothing. I didn't mean it no way like that. Just that, I might be able to do you some good."

Captain removed the dark glasses again and looked Sam in the eye. He smiled at the man slyly and slapped the top of his hand that was on the steering apparatus. "Hallelujah, Sam. I hear you loud and clear. Where?"

"In the elevator on the way up to the concourse. You're not the man, are you?"

"I wouldn't tell you if I was, now would I?"

"Naw, shit. No cop would bite a broad the way that you just did. You weren't shittin'. I mean, you really bit her good."

Sam slowed the cart and moved through the people boarding the escalator. He pulled the cart around a corner into an alcove that held the elevator door and pressed the call button. Captain handed him a fifty dollar bill. "Go on, take it. I want you to come back for me too."

"Okay—well—but—I don't have too much. Aah, but it's mighty fine, what I do have." The elevator door opened, and Sam eased the cart in. When the doors closed they were alone, and Sam snapped the emergency switch on. Sam produced a pocket knife and opened it to a blade that had been ground down into a tiny spoon. Then came a small glass vial, mostly full, of what Captain could see was cocaine. Sam shook the snowy crystals and held the bottle up to the light. "Aha, you like?" he asked, observing Captain's stare.

"Yes, I like," Captain replied, keeping his cool.

"It's Merck," Sam said. "You know what that is?"

He handed Captain the bottle and the opened knife. Captain knew that Merck was pharmaceutical cocaine and that it was considered the finest. Pharmacists buy it for $8 an ounce and resell it for $4,000. The Feds watch it like a hawk.

"Yes, Sam, I surely do know what Merck is. Now sit still."

Sam didn't move and grinned while Captain scooped as much of the sugarlike substance into the spoon as he could. "Not too much, not too much," Sam said energetically.

Captain paid him no attention and moved the spoon carefully toward his right nostril.

Suddenly an alarm bell began to ring into the elevator. Captain didn't move but turned his eyes up to Sam, who was smiling anxiously.

"No sweat, man, you got it. Go right on."

Captain pulled it into his nose with a hard snort. *Wham*— behind his eyes and into his brain it went. He heaped the spoon again and repeated the procedure with his left nostril. Sam stood across from him making funny flailing motions with his arms, saying, "Not too much, not too much," and following the tiny bottle without a blink.

Captain moved fast and scooped a third spoonful out and delivered it quickly into his sniffing right nostril. Sam was screaming, "Hey, hey. Hey, come on, man, that's all I've got." Panicking, he reached across the ringing elevator and retrieved his paraphernalia. Perspiration showed on his forehead and under his arms. Captain couldn't smell. "That's all I got," he said again with embarrassment, filling his own left nostril with a small amount. "For now," he added, his smile returning.

Captain felt ten feet tall when he stepped out of the elevator. The bell had stopped ringing, and he was aware of his heart. His eyelids seemed frozen open. The back of his throat felt cold and parched. But he was suddenly well rested, brand new. He felt exhilarated.

"Right here in half an hour, Sam. Don't be late."

"No, no, don't worry. I'll be here. Have a cold one for me and, doctor—"

"Yes?" Captain answered, moving away.

"Watch out for David."

Sam's smile disappeared behind the closing elevator door.
Captain stopped for a moment and wondered who David was but
quickly dismissed the thought to follow a blonde into the open-air
bar across the way. The girl was from Chicago. Captain thought
that she had sexy eyes and looked good. While they drank, she
put her tongue into his ear and rubbed his stiff penis under the
table.

Captain forgot about his appointment with Sam and never saw
him again. But he had wondered ever since about David, who he
was and what there was to watch out for. Thinking about it
always made him feel uneasy.

A Hot One

Cappy, Cappy." It was Iris. She was ruffling his hair and massaging his scalp vigorously. "Wake up. Are you all right, honey?"

Captain opened his eyes into the bright bathroom and sat up. His wrist hurt when he readjusted it from holding his chin. He had fallen asleep on the toilet.

"Are you all right, babe?" she asked again, concern in her expression. "I've got a fabulous dinner for you and a so-so Japanese horror movie on the tube. Honey?"

"Yeah—yes—I'm all right—just tired. I sat down to take a leak and started replaying the thing that happened with Datchel, and I must have fallen asleep. But I'm okay—I'm fine."

Standing up to stretch, he quickly sat back down again to urinate. Iris leaned against the doorjamb, looking wonderful with her hair pulled back and wearing her red silk nightgown.

"You sound like a horse peeing," she said, smiling coyly and turning away to walk into the bedroom.

180

Captain's loins tingled in response. She knew what to say. "Have you ever heard the expression 'Watch out for David'?" he yelled, flushing the toilet.

"You asked me that once before, back after that Halloween with Datchel. No, I haven't," was the reply.

As usual, Iris had laid out a mouth-watering spread. She had carried the food and silver downstairs on a wide, flat, sterling silver tray. She had fluffed the pillows up against the backrests at the head of the bed and put the serving plates out on top of the monogrammed blue towel that she had laid down. Iris pulled her red nighty up over her thighs and being careful not to bounce or spill, sat down gently against a pillowed backrest. Captain brought the wine and sat next to her on the bed.

"Fantastic-looking dinner," he said, filling Iris's wine glass and then his own. Neither of them ate bread or potatoes in any form. So whatever Iris prepared, however extravagant, it would consistently exclude those two items.

The salad dressing was homemade and contained the perfect mixture of oil and vinegar, honey and ginger. Against Iris's protestations, Captain gulped the delicious shrimp and avocado salad. His stomach began to feel appeased. Captain breathed a sigh of relief and attacked the rare porterhouse steak. After a few bites, he slowed down to enjoy the meal. The fresh stringbeans were prepared with shallots and sliced almonds strewn over the top. Iris had made the steak sauce herself. Captain thought that it was a beautiful meal.

On the television a large group of picnicking Japanese were on the run from a fire-breathing iron monster. Trees were blazing and fell across their path as they ran frantically to escape. A small Japanese boy was trying to summon King on his wrist radio.

For the most part Iris was a vegetarian. She would take a bite or two from a good piece of meat on occasion, but Captain always felt that it was done to keep him company. He hated to plow hungrily through a meal while Iris sat at his side carefully picking over a dish of steamed carrots. It made him feel gross. Iris ate a small piece of Captain's steak.

"Look, there's Kong," Iris said, sounding impressed.

"It sure is. He's going to get into it with the iron monster. He's a robot, you know."

"Kong?"

"No, Sphinx Man. He breathes fire. There he goes, see?"

The robot blew flames against Kong, but it served only to anger the enormous gorilla. Kong grabbed Sphinx Man in a bear hug, and they tussled together until they rolled off a cliff into the ocean; there the struggle continued. The sound of the ocean was real.

"Come on, Kong," Iris said, excited.

"Don't worry," Captain interjected.

The monsters finally both regained balance and stood. The sea water only reached their knees. They stood face to face and smashed each other. The blows resounded loudly.

Captain lay back and snuggled into his pillow. Lazily, he put the wine glass to his mouth and finished the wine. He let his eyelids close; contentment engulfed him.

Iris removed the wine glass from his sleepy hand. Captain heard Iris stacking the dirty dishes into the tray. "I'll do that," he offered, without moving.

"Relax. I enjoy waiting on you."

Iris left the bed, and Captain heard her bound up the stairs. He opened his eyes a crack to see what the cheering was about and saw Kong now standing alone with his foot on top of something that he held under the water. Air bubbles came up from the spot, and a large crowd of Nippons cheered from the shore.

"Yeeaa," from Iris who was back with two frosted glasses in her hands. "Surprise for you. Yea, Kong."

Captain sat up and accepted the stinger. It smelled refreshing. "That was fast."

His work finished, Kong was walking off into the sea. The water became deeper and deeper as he went.

"I had them in the freezer. Oh, no, Kong, don't go."

An adult male Oriental wearing thick spectacles and a lab coat consoled the tearful little boy who called after Kong. "No, Kong, no. Please don't leave us. We want to reward you."

"Come on, Kong, stay," Captain said, drinking the blended, iced crème de menthe and brandy.

"Kong, we need you, turn around," Iris said, bouncing on her knees at the end of the bed.

The scientist reassured everyone that Kong would be back when he was needed. That brought a weak smile from the boy, a staring silence from Iris and a brief lump to Captain's throat until the boy dried his eyes.

"Darn," Iris said, "missed it." She took a good swallow and fell back onto the bed holding the drink up high atop a stiff arm.

"Missed what?" Captain asked drowsily.

"Kong. I didn't get to see him."

"What do you mean? He was right there."

She twirled the glass around in her hand and sloshed the ice against the side. "Yes, but not from the front. I didn't get to see him from the front."

Captain was not in the mood, but his penis twitched against his robe. "What's in front that you wanted to see?"

"Wouldn't you like to know," she replied, turning on her side with her back to him and drinking her drink sideways. Her thick blonde braid lay on the blue sheet. The top rear button of her nightie was undone. The silky red material lay open.

"Tell me," he asked casually.

"No," she said quickly, pouting.

He waited, but she gave the impression that she would wait him out. "Why did you—?" His tongue got tied. "What's on the front of the big monkey that you wanted to see, honey?"

Iris said nothing. Captain flexed his sphincter muscle, and his erect penis raised up through his robe. He flexed it again and watched it bob up off of the terry cloth. The end was wet.

"Please tell me?" he asked nicely.

"Why should I?" was the reply.

Iris raised up on one elbow and finished her drink. Her back still to him, she sat up on her side of the bed, placing her feet on the carpet. She pretended to yawn and stretched up into the air. "I'm tired too. I think I'll take a hot bath and—"

Captain reached out and quickly rolled the single braid of Iris's hair around his hand and brought it up tight against the back of her head. "Goddammit, Iris, what's on the front of the big monkey that you want to see?"

She sat there and let him hurt her for a long moment. Finally she spoke with ease. "Let go and I'll tell you."

Captain released her and touched her shoulder gently when he took his hand away. She shook her head and reached back to straighten her braid out.

"He's so big, I thought he'd have something huge hanging between his legs. I would like to have seen it, that's all." She didn't turn around.

"What would you do if you were there with the ape, Iris—and you saw it—and it was really huge like you hoped?" His voice trembled as he spoke, but it didn't matter.

"I'd touch it until his big coconuts got tight, and then I'd lick the end and the big hole, and I'd chew it until—"

"Would you fuck him? Would you let him power fuck you with his huge—?"

"No, no. I wouldn't be interested in that. He's probably too

184

tired for that." She spoke calmly. "No, I would suck him for his milk, his thick coconut milk, and help him to sleep."

Iris turned around and didn't once look into Captain's face. Her stare was on his jerking penis. She pulled his robe open and took hold of it and stood it up. It genuinely embarrassed Captain the way that she looked at it, as though it were an entity, capable of understanding, with a life away from the rest of him.

"I love it when you're this hot," she said to it.

"Don't you want some?" he asked.

"No, no. I want to taste it, to swallow it." She licked the wetness off the end. "I want you to sleep. Tomorrow I want you to come to Montecito with me."

"Jesus," he said softly. "I'll never understand women."

Iris pursed her lips and pushed them over the purple head of his penis and sucked on him. She used her hand to shake the stiff thing in her mouth. The feeling gave him the shivers.

"What's in Montecito?" he asked, wincing.

She took it out of her mouth again. "A house." She looked up at him now, her mouth sloppy. "I'm going to buy us a house up there, and we're going to get married." She smiled and went back to work for real.

Captain started to speak but dropped his head back onto the bed. He pushed the thoughts away and concentrated on the itching sensation along his swollen penis. Then as she gained momentum, he began to count the strokes. At 200, he lost count. His foreskin began to burn, and Iris's specific movements faded away. Captain squeezed his eyes shut, and he began to quiver.

Somehow Iris was able to speak without diminishing the feeling. Her voice was breathy; she was working hard.

"You're ready, big cock. Squirt for me. Come on—fill the pretty girl's mouth."

She began fingering his testicles in a way that pained them.

Then, leaving a profusion of saliva, Iris pulled her mouth away and began stroking his erection furiously with her hand.

Flailing his fists back into the bed at his sides, Captain screamed toward the beamed ceiling as loudly as he could. He felt his system open up for the first spurt and yelled, "Now," for her, or she would have been angry.

Iris dropped her mouth down again and pulled at his foreskin. Captain heard her slurp and slurp while he lost track of things. Then she went really crazy with it still in her mouth. He sat up to see her other hand, under her nightie, moving rapidly between her own legs. That was nice. Iris moved against her hand while she milked him dry and made him sensitive. Captain rubbed the soft blonde hair at the nape of her neck while things calmed down. Finally, feeling mighty fine, he closed his eyes and stopped comprehending anything.

Captain awoke with the urge. Naked, he slid out from the cozy bed and made his way into the bathroom. He seemed to remember being up once before during the night to urinate, but it wasn't a complete recollection. Yawning, he kept his eyes shut and hung his head. When he was finished, he continued to sit until he managed the energy to drag himself back out through the blackout-draped bedroom to flop out face down onto the bed.

Captain lay there until he couldn't stand the anxious feeling any longer and sat up to look at the clock. The spot where it should have been was dark. Kneeling, he crawled to the place and righted the clock from its face.

Iris was gone. She frequently turned the clock over to let him sleep. The time was twelve minutes after ten. "Not bad," he said, scratching his scalp.

Captain rubbed his chin; he needed a shave. He thought about the bright bathroom and couldn't bring himself to face it. "La-

186

ter," he said. His mouth tasted sour, but the thought of toothpaste made him wince.

Finding the drawer where Iris kept accessories, Captain put on the first pair of junk sunglasses that came into his hand. The bedroom door opened into a glare. Daylight filled the staircase. As imagined, the living room drapes were open to the sea. The sun was burning off a hazy morning, and the air was bright. Iris's note was on the living room table, but Captain kept on going into the kitchen. He ground four turns of rough black pepper into an everyday glass and brought a frosted bottle of Zubrowka vodka out of the freezer. The yellowish, buffalo-grass vodka poured thick like syrup. It went down his throat cold and smooth. Captain breathed deeply, the first good one of the day, and mentally traced the icy feeling that rolled through his insides.

Captain brought the vodka, Iris's note and the telephone and slid open the glass door to the terrace. He was met by a strong sea breeze and the crack of a wave from below. Sitting in a white canvas director's chair, he let the vodka and the ocean air vitalize him. He put his feet up on a round, white wooden table. The canvas began to tear under him when he leaned back. He eased up on it.

Observing his naked body, Captain wondered what the weather would be like in Santa Barbara, if it would help his tan. Breathing deeply again, he enthusiastically said, "All right," to the way that he was feeling and read Iris's note:

Sat. morn. 8:15

Good morning my beautiful man:

Off to B. Hills to get a massage and manicure. I have the Jensen. (It was in the way.)

I'll have it gassed and washed.

187

I'm so excited, I'm taking my man to Bernham Wood Country Club for a late lunch. (Very chic—best martini in Montecito.)

I'm a member (Mac).

I want to look at some houses. We'll stay the night (the ranch?).

We'll have a *Ball!*

Make your phone calls and meet me at Chez Jay's at noon. We'll have a drink before we leave. We'll leave one of the cars there—*Fun.*

XXXOOO Iris

P.S. You slept like you were dead.

P.P.S. No breakfast for me—I'm too full of you.

Love you!

Smiling, Captain agreed that Santa Barbara might be a good idea. He planned on it.

He considered not calling his answering service but dialed it anyway, fulfilling his responsibility to the owners of the apartment building. There could be an emergency, he thought.

Nicole answered, a little Latvian who talked dirty with him and was known to sneak away for an occasional quicky. "Hi, Cappy. Where have you been? Jeez, you've got a bunch of messages."

Captain listened and disregarded all but four of them. Three calls were from Mrs. Pearlstein; they caused him concern. The fourth was a message that Nicole said she didn't understand: "Watch out for David." It sent a chill up Captain's spine. She had no idea whether the message had been left by a man or a woman. She hadn't been working. It had come in at midnight. That was all.

"That's a pisser," he said, hanging the phone up briefly, worrying about it and then dialing Mrs. Pearlstein before he forgot her number.

Mrs. Pearlstein was so excited to hear his voice, she began to blubber. "Oh, God, Cappy, did you hear? Have you heard about it? Have you seen the television?"

"No, Ruthie, I don't know what you're talking about. I just got up. Are you all right?"

"Me? Oh, me. Oh, yes—oh, yes, I'm fine, I'm fine. But you didn't hear about him, about Mister Bloom from the department store?"

"No, tell me."

"Oh, my God, Cappy, it's just dreadful. It's something terrible. And to think we just saw him yesterday—It gives me the creeps."

Captain stared out at a large white-topped breaker as it began to swell and roll for the sand. A gust of wind blew the top off of it and slowed its pace long enough for it to be caught and consumed by an even larger wave from behind.

"Cappy—Captain, are you there? Did you hear?"

"I'm listening, Ruthie. You haven't told me anything yet."

"Well—" Captain heard her swallow dryly and then drink something. "Well, they found him—It was on TV—They found him at the cemetery—the Veterans' Cemetery—out—out by UCLA—out by the college. You know where that is, don't you?"

"Yes," he replied.

Captain held the telephone receiver in the crook of his neck while he picked at a hangnail. He pulled it out and chewed at his finger furiously. It bled, and he soaked it in vodka.

"Mister Bloom—Reno Bloom—Well, he screamed—They said that he did a lot of screaming, but the people who live in those houses along the side of the cemetery thought it was college kids—they're always screaming around there—hazing for clubs and things, you know."

189

"Yes, I know," he answered.

"They showed it on TV all this morning—from a distance, mind you—and they showed the lock on the gate—shot right off with a gun—shot off with a gun, can you imagine?"

"Who did it?" Captain interrupted, squeezing his disinfected finger with his thumb.

"They don't know. Some maniac probably. But wait, I didn't tell you—He was stripped naked, can you possibly imagine? Stripped naked and tied over a tombstone. And he was—oh, my—" She let out a sigh. "I just saw the man yesterday. I can't believe it. He was—" She hesitated.

"Yes, he was—?" Captain urged her on.

"He—his skin was burned off. Somebody burned his skin off. The police say that he was mutated—"

"Mutilated," a male voice corrected in the background.

"They say he was mutilated," she said again.

"Who was that, Ruthie, that man's voice?"

"That? Oh, that was Henry. That was Henry—remember?"

Captain laughed out loud and sat up. "Ruthie, you tart you." He drank the vodka.

Mrs. Pearlstein was silent. Finally she said, "That's not very funny."

"Yes, it is, Ruthie. I'm just teasing anyway. Is he a nice man?"

"Henry? Oh, very nice. A real nice person, Captain."

"Let me speak with him."

The phone was shuffled around, and Henry Aldrich finally answered with a boom. "Hello, son."

Captain liked the sound of his voice. It was comforting.

"Is everything all right, Henry, with Ruthie? Don't bullshit me."

"Yes, sure. Everything is fine. You sound like her father."

"Never mind that, old-timer. I just want to know that the woman is safe."

"Hell, yes. We're having one hell of a time—No bull." Mrs. Pearlstein said something in the background. "She says that she didn't mean to worry you about her. It was this fella Bloom she wanted to tell you about. Did you know him?" Henry asked.

"Sort of" was the answer.

"Boy, somebody really put it to him good. It's all over the news this morning. And to show you a coincidence, I knew the exact spot right away, the minute that they showed it. Just past the statue, middle of Vets' Cemetery, corner of Appomattox and Gettysburg, ten or twenty stones from my brother. Can you imagine that? This guy Bloom was tied down to a tombstone and burned to hell. Wow, it's a hard one to figure."

"Was he dead?"

"Was he dead? Was he dead? Holy mackerel, I guess so. He had a slug in him too, in the belly. Yeah, he was dead, all right, but swollen up awful from being burned."

Captain finished the vodka and began to laugh. He held the phone away from his face and cackled. He rocked back and forth in the chair, and the canvas ripped some more. This was aggravating, so Captain stood up and sat down again hard, tearing the canvas out beneath him. He sat on the chair's support struts. Captain felt like he was on an outdoor toilet in the northern woods someplace. For a minute he thought that he was going to go but laughed the idea away.

Captain brought the phone back to his ear with a sigh and listened. It was silent at the other end. "Henry, are you there?"

"Yes, yes, I sure am. I wish I knew what was so funny, though."

"It just struck me funny, that's all—about Reno Bloom. Tell Ruthie this one, see if she gets the humor." Captain began to

191

chuckle again. "I was just thinking—It's nice that Reno Bloom got burned for a change, that's all. Isn't that a hot one, a hot one? Oh, shit."

Captain began to laugh again and rock in the chair. It squeaked loudly and fell apart underneath him. He sat on the rough wooden decking and looked out at the sea. Mrs. Pearlstein was talking, and he raised the phone to listen.

"Yes, I'm here," he said.

"Well—Oh, dear, I think that you're terrible to say that about Mister Bloom. But I see what you mean." She laughed once and changed the subject. "I've got your girlfriend's sunglasses. The restaurant people fixed them, took them right over to an optometrist on Hollywood Boulevard, and they're good as new. They handed them to me when we left. Fast work, don't you think, dear? Very nice of them."

"Yes. Is everything under control around the building?"

"Yes, it seems so. Oh, I need a new—"

"Goodby, Ruthie. I love you guys. Have a beautiful day." Captain hung the phone up.

"That's a hot one," he said to himself and chortled. Captain sat there quietly now. His eyes became transfixed on a murky area beyond the horizon, and his stomach grumbled for food. He decided that when he got the energy to move, he would have a protein drink and a steam, maybe even do some leg raises.

The Gag

Captain heard a noise of indistinguishable origin come from behind him in the house but chose to watch a group of gulls abruptly change direction in flight and start a race for a tiny splash in the water below. A snappy gust of sea breeze came up from the water and seemed to blow through him.

Captain watched a drop of perspiration form on his left eyelash. He blinked it away; the salt stung his eye. Hearing something again, he jumped up to stand stiffly but did not turn around. The gulls were gone and the sky looked dark. His penis felt shrunken. Acting casual, Captain reached a close beach towel and wrapped it around his bottom. Humming a crazy tune that he was making up, he turned to look into the house.

A strong light lit the rear of the kitchen, as though the door to the outside, to the street, was open. He shifted his eyes into the spacious living room. A drape moved and he looked there quickly. Then he understood. The blood froze in his veins, David, he thought. He had damned well better watch out.

The long heavy draperies ballooned out into the large living room again and then settled back in to calmly fold themselves against the window glass. Beginning to tremble, Captain implored himself to make a move. "Why don't you do something?" he whispered without moving his lips.

The booze, he thought, frantically cursing the vague alcoholic notion of what was before him. I'm standing here like a tranquilized dummy, unable to make a decision or move.

Captain tried to get himself into action, but the effort showed only in his being able to nervously switch his weight back and forth from foot to foot. Perspiring, Captain stared. The thick plate glass window reflected back at him, doing bizarre things with sunlight and shadows. Then he saw the movement again and stiffened. A particularly large wave slammed in underneath him causing him to break his trance and look down. He imagined a huge, thick puddle of purple blood, his own, spreading out to soak into the weathered decking beneath his bare feet.

Captain felt the sun begin to come through and warm his shoulders. Suddenly he bolted into the house, through the living room and into the kitchen. An iron skillet was the closest thing at hand. He held it in a defensive posture until he was able to retrieve the largest butcher knife from the cutlery drawer.

Turning back toward the living room, Captain yelled, "Come and get me, David—hobba, lobba, you troll." The beach towel fell off of his waist. Brandishing the iron skillet in one hand and the butcher knife in the other, he charged naked and screaming into the living room. He rushed the billowing drapery. Drawing it back over his head, he threw the iron pan at the shadowed corner of the living room. He threw it as hard as hc could, and it landed loudly against the wall with a thunk.

Captain paused long enough to yell, "Come and get it," like Mac used to when he was playing at being a short order cook at his restaurant, and then he ferociously attacked the draperied corner of the living room, driving the large butcher knife into the folds of material over and over again.

Using his arms as though swimming, Captain swam upstream overhanded against the nubby curtain material, thrashing and tearing. Wading in, he struck low from a side-armed position. The drapery material surrounded him. "Watch out for Captain," Captain yelled, delirious. He slashed one more hard one, and the entire wall of material fell down upon him. The curtain rods and fixtures came too. "No way, you fuckers," Captain growled.

He was on the floor now, stabbing and screaming, "No way. No way." He fought to uncover his head, but pulling at the drapery material encumbered his knife hand, so he let go to struggle in darkness.

Fighting bravely, Captain listened and realized that it was he who was wheezing. His chest heaved as he gasped and breathed again the dusty dead air from the cocoon that held him. I'm smothering, he thought frantically. I'll never make another minute. Goddamn, how many of them are there?

In the distance, somewhere beyond the scene of battle, Captain heard Iris's voice calling his name. With his last breath, he punched and yelled, "My pistol. Iris, get my pistol." The strength from his arms was gone. He let them lie against himself, constricted by the material that bound him. So held, Captain was made to remember the restraining power of a straight jacket.

With his arms paining, he paused to try and breathe a small amount of stale air. He tasted his own blood and listened to Iris call him. She spoke in a concerned tone and seemed to be asking questions.

Captain screamed, "David." He screamed it just once, like a

desperate nightmare scream for help before the terror closes your throat.

Then someone had a foot on his rump, pushing him. Iris was laughing while someone rocked him back and forth against the carpet, using a foot. Iris said that he was being silly. Captain wondered what she meant, what was going on. His naked body itched where it was in contact with the drapes. Synthetic fiberglass, he thought. The drapery material caused a burning sensation, an irritation against his perspiring skin, as fiberglass insulation used to when he was a kid hiding in attics.

"Cappy, it's me, Iris. Don't be afraid."

Suddenly Captain began to sneeze. The dust from the drapes and carpet was into his nose and respiratory system, and he was sneezing long, hard, crying sneezes that made his lungs ache.

"Lay still, Cappy." She pushed at his bottom with her foot as she spoke. "Don't fight, honey. It's me, Iris. David's not here." She laughed and said, "Gosh sakes," and knelt down beside him. Captain contained the sneezing, but his nose and eyes ran profusely. He blew his nose into the darkness that surrounded him. "David is not here, Cappy. There is no David, no one you have to watch out for—honest."

Stopping fast, Captain concentrated and listened intently to what Iris was saying. Wanting to believe her, he began to feel relief immediately.

"Lie still, Cappy. Let me unwrap you. Let go of the knife little brother; you don't need it. It's all been a joke, just a joke— gosh." Iris laughed a comfortable laugh as she pulled at the drapery material. The tone of the laugh convinced Captain that they were alone. He had a hundred questions but wanted most of all to close his eyes and rest. He felt suddenly drowsy, like he could sleep.

An itching sensation rippled up the back of his throat and down into his nasal passages. An overwhelming tickle surged from behind his eyes into his nose. Captain threw his hands there to rub and scratch vigorously. With the sneeze contained, he felt the slimy mucus that surrounded his nose and covered his upper lip. He put his tongue out to touch his upper lip. It was sticky and tacky with gritted phlegm.

Iris made him roll over one more time. She pulled the material from around his head and shoulders. Then there was bright light and fresh salty air. Inhaling, Captain groaned with delight.

"My goodness, Cappy, what have you done?" Iris felt his forehead for a fever and petted his temples.

Closing his eyes from the brightness, Captain filled his lungs with fresh air. He coughed and asked, "What's the joke—the gag—about David? Watch out for David—Who is he?"

"There is no David, Cappy."

If that were only true, he told himself. But lying there a moment longer, Captain assumed Iris to be naive and not to know about these things. His imagination had this fellow David, without a face, and the ghost of Datchel standing behind Iris this very moment. The two ghouls were poised and ready with ice picks in their hands. They hovered on either side of Iris. Captain waited to hear Iris's startled shriek as the monsters started to pick at her kidneys. Captain shuddered aloud as he anticipated the sound of his beautiful sister's voice. He envisioned Iris, her mouth hung open, emitting a grunting sound and defecating into her jeans while the stilettos reamed her gizzard.

"No, no," Captain yelled in a panic. He opened his eyes, sat up and looked quickly around the room.

Iris said, "Cappy, Cappy, easy now, easy," and Captain could see for himself that they were alone. "Cappy, listen to me." Iris got on her knees to face him and said, "Watch out for David is a black man's cocaine riddle, that's all."

Captain tried to figure it out, while Iris was saying that it was she who had called his answering service last night at midnight and left the message "Watch out for David." She had done it to put him on. Iris said that Captain was the most paranoid person she knew sometimes. She laughed about that and said that the drapes were ruined. With a final tug, she completely disrobed him as she set him free.

Sitting there on the thick brown carpet, the sea breeze engulfed his naked body, dried his perspiration and gave his scalp a crawly feeling. Iris stood above him now, complaining to herself about having just broken a new fingernail. She met his stare and smiled. Iris wore all of her makeup, snug faded jeans and a tight UCLA Phys. Ed. T-shirt. Captain felt sticky, a mess.

"Do you want to know the answer to your riddle," she asked coyly, "about your big deal David?"

Captain looked down at the dirt that clung to his skin and went into the muscular folds of his stomach. He glanced at his penis and thought that it looked tiny. Feeling embarrassed, he pulled a corner of the drapery material back over his naked thigh to cover his privates. Iris saw what he had done and said, "Oh, he's shy. My little Cappy is embarrassed, and scared too. Well you don't have to cover it; I've seen it small before." Iris laughed, bit at her broken fingernail and said, "Damn." Captain sat still and stared up at her. "I take it that you want to know?" she said.

"Yes," Captain answered.

"Well." Iris puffed in a proud way. She stuck out her chest. "Well, you'd snorted a whole bunch of the black guy's coke, right?"

Iris began to walk back and forth above him, tapping her right-handed pointed finger into her left palm. "And it was pharmaceutical coke, real strong, the best, right?" She didn't wait for Captain's answer. "And the black guy said, 'Watch out

198

for David.' Don't you get it, Goliath?'' She laughed and looked down at Captain, who still didn't understand. Iris said, "You left the elevator all fired up, thinking that you were invincible, like a giant. You were acting like Goliath, and the porter said, 'Hey, Goliath, watch out for David.' Don't you see? He meant that you're not as big as you think you are. You're loaded on coke and be careful of the things out in the real world that can bring you down. It was the black guy's way of warning you to watch out, be careful, in a friendly way. Look out for the little insignificant guy with the badge in his jacket.''

Iris laughed again and said, "Oh, heck, I might as well tell you how I found out for sure. It struck me the minute I heard it. Beth and Tabby, two black shampoo girls at the beauty shop, came crashing out of the ladies' room last week. I was getting my nails done. They'd obviously done some coke and when they realized that they were acting too outrageous for the room, Tabby said, "Watch out for David," and Beth shut up and walked away quieted down. And Cappy, you've been running around paranoid, wondering who David was and what he wanted you for. Oh, my, I can't believe it. That's a funny one.''

Realizing that what Iris had said was true, Captain felt relieved but foolish. Sitting there blushing, he listened to his sister.

"When you asked me about it again last night, you were so concerned—so worried—and I knew the answer then, but I thought I'd call your service and put you on a little bit. You're always teasing and dishing it out—I wanted to see if you could take it.'' She laughed. "I didn't know that you'd ruin the house over it—gosh.'' Iris went over to the corner of the living room and retrieved the heavy iron frying pan. "What were you going to do,'' she asked, "cook him?'' Enjoying herself, Iris sat down on the pile of drapery that lay next to Captain's waist. Iris removed the drapery material that lay over Captain's private area. Taking his penis between her brightly painted, long, red-nailed thumb and pointer finger, she pulled the foreskin back and forth.

"Did I frighten you?" She directed her question to his penis, which Captain felt shrink up even tighter.

Captain took her hand away and covered himself again. Iris became haughty. "Oh, you're angry at me. Here I figured out the whole thing and you're angry at me." Acting indignant, Iris stood up with the frying pan and headed for the kitchen.

Bringing the butcher knife, Captain jumped up and followed her. He watched Iris hang the iron frying pan back amongst the other cooking utensils that hung above the butcher block. When she turned, she acted surprised to see Captain standing in the doorway. He stood there naked, the butcher knife in his hand.

The smile left Iris's face, and then all expression faded. Captain walked over to lean against the stove. Putting his hand out in a seemingly friendly gesture, Captain beckoned to Iris, and she came to stand beside him. Captain continued to hold his hand out, and Iris, acting tentative, finally placed her hand in his. She watched his eyes and said nothing.

Captain jerked Iris's hand hard and placed her flat palm down over the right front burner of the gas stove. Iris said, "No, no," but Captain put the cutting edge of the large butcher knife firmly against the veiny back of her hand to hold her and took his own hand away. Iris tried to retrieve her hand, but Captain held the blade steady and let it slice into the back of her hand. They both stared at the blood that ran between her fingers and onto the black iron burner of the stove.

Emitting a frightened squeal, Iris let her hand stay and brought her other hand up to cover her mouth. Her stare jerked questioningly back and forth between Captain's eyes.

Captain put his free hand on the stove's front right flame control. Iris's entire body tensed up. She tried again to move her hand, which brought a heavier flow of blood. Huge tears began to swell the lower lids of Iris's pale blue eyes. Her jaw hung in a funny way, and the loose skin over her lower face trembled. Her upper lip showed perspiration.

"No, no, Cappy. Please don't, honey," she pleaded.

"You scared me," Captain said evenly.

"But—but I didn't mean to. It was a joke—a joke, honey—Cappy—a bad joke. It was just a bad joke, that's all." Iris's eyes flashed to Captain's hand on the flame control. Tears flowed down her face.

"Please, Cappy, don't burn me. I have such pretty hands, and I'm so terribly sorry. God, I'm so sorry." Iris began to sob fitfully but through her tears watched Captain's hand on the burner control.

When she finally looked up into his face, Captain said, "I hate being frightened." Captain thought that he sounded childlike.

Iris opened her eyes wide to agree. "So do I. Oh, I hate it. It was mean of me, honey. I'm sorry—truly, truly sorry."

Captain touched the blonde down on Iris's soft cheeks, and he felt his penis stiffen. Holding Iris's sad eyes, he let go of the butcher knife and let it fall onto the stove. Captain brought Iris's trembling hand away from the burner and wrapped her fingers around his penis. Her hand felt sticky.

Iris looked perplexed but squeezed him firmly and tried to smile. Reaching behind her neck, Captain brought Iris to him and let her bury her wet face into his neck. She tugged at his penis and sobbed.

"Are we going to Montecito?" he asked quietly.

There was a long pause, and then Iris answered, "Yeeeeess," in a long, wet wail like a bawling baby.

III

A Favor

Montecito was wonderful.
With Captain's approval, Iris had rented a luxury home for the
week along the third fairway of Birnham Wood Country Club and
Golf Course. The Montecito sky was conspicuously blue. Around
the horizon hung clouds that were billowy and white. The sun
seemed so close and shone so precisely that you could only
glance at it. Behind their rented home a large, turquoise swimming pool reflected a bright, shimmering surface.

Birnham Wood was quiet. Even the distant, occasional passing
golf carts moved in silence. A clean, easy sea breeze rose from
the nearby Santa Barbara Channel. Montecito smelled alive. Captain and Iris breathed the aroma deeply. And there were song
birds. "God, listen to them sing," Captain said to Iris excitedly,
loving the delicate creatures.

Montecito might well have been another world. Captain and
Iris dressed minimally or went nude. Iris didn't go near her

205

makeup, and Captain didn't shave. They began each day with a seven-mile run beneath the tall trees that lined East Valley Road. They ran over the river bridge and past the horses at the San Ysidro Ranch. Returning home dripping with perspiration, they would fall into the pool and spend the rest of the day in a state of happy relaxation.

At night, they lay outside on the patio chaises for long periods of time staring up at the stars. Captain thought that he had never seen the heavens so clearly and was overwhelmed by the sparkling array. One evening while lying there like that, trying to imagine what was up there, Captain peed in his pants, and that seemed all right too. It was all part of it.

The first day of the month fell on the upcoming Monday. Captain wanted to be back in Los Angeles on that day to collect the rents and look after the apartment buildings. The first week of the month around town was always busy. After hemming and hawing with an ostensibly honest real estate man and exhibiting to Captain that she knew her stuff, Iris made a down payment on a particularly lovely ranch house at the foot of the San Ysidro Mountains. The home had a huge black onyx swimming pool and sat on two acres of land that opened onto a street called Park Lane. The entire property was surrounded by an eleven foot high redwood fence and thick bramble hedges. Captain and Iris both liked the name of the street. The home was to cost $285,000 and in everyone's opinion was well worth it. In his private thoughts Captain really liked the place too.

Driving home, they went by way of Ojai, the city in the valley founded by Krishna Murti. Captain and Iris took lunch at the Ojai Valley Country Club, and it was a strain to finally have to face up to leaving the calm green valley where they felt their spirits to be kindled.

Iris was still talking about Montecito and the new Park Lane house when Captain dropped her at the beach house in Malibu and drove into West Los Angeles to do his chores.

He kept the music off and talked to himself the entire way. It was good to be alone. He talked openly about things, his feelings. The weather in town was not bad as he'd imagined, but actually quite bearable. Nothing, he thought, however, compared to Ojai and Montecito. Captain watered and pruned his garden for a long while before going indoors.

As Captain topped the stairs, down the long shadowed hall-way, in front of what appeared to be his own apartment door, he observed a clump of a thing. Stopping to stare, Captain was made to think of a Bowery drunk, his feet laid out in front of him, his back slouched up against a boarded alleyway door.

With his imagination going through a myriad of changes, Captain walked slowly down the hallway to the dark figure. It was an unconscious man propped up against Captain's apartment door. Leaning over to look closely, Captain was startled to see that the person in question was Brad, his ill-sighted bartender friend from the Beachcomber Restaurant in Hollywood. Brad was breathing and appeared to be asleep. Captain was shocked at the man's lack of propriety. This is so totally unlike him, Captain thought, feeling genuine concern for his friend.

Captain pushed at Brad's contorted knee with the bottom of his foot, and Brad awoke with a start. Brad blinked and looked around. He needed a shave. When he looked up to find Captain standing there above him, Brad said, "Good God—finally," and he threw his arms around Captain's legs and hugged them. "God, I'm glad to see you," Brad said, and Captain scratched his scalp, wondering if he had ever really known his friend before.

Captain put his hand on Brad's head as though to pat it but let it lay, and Brad began to sob. "I've been waiting, Cappy. Shit, I've been waiting." Then he let go of Captain's legs and sat back with a slam against the apartment door. "Good Lord, what am I doing?" he asked, wiping his eyes. "I've lost all reason over this thing. I'm sorry."

"Over what thing?" Captain asked. "What the hell's the matter, Brad? What's going on? I've never seen you—"

"It's Penny," Brad cut in. "My baby, my Penny. Look, Cap, look at what we found, what Marilyn found in her stocking drawer. Just look and you'll shit."

While Brad dug around in his wrinkled sport coat jacket, Captain took the opportunity to get his key into the door. The apartment door swung open just as Brad produced something from his pocket and was holding it up to show. Into the apartment they stumbled. Brad ended up lying on his back, flailing his arms.

A yellow and blue Bisodol stomach mint tin lay open, the contents spilled onto the rug in the middle of the living room floor. The spillage, however, was not of Bisodol mints, but of two red rubber balloons, deflated, their necks tied into knots. A glass eye dropper with a shiny hypodermic needle fixed to its end, a small silver spoon and some stick matches lay there also.

Turned up onto his side, Brad stared at the opened tin by looking at it down along the length of his outstretched arm. He closed one eye and sighted in down his arm onto the spilled contents of the Bisodol mint tin. Then he went back to using both eyes to continue the vigil. Brad held a blank expression and flopped his outstretched hand up and down against the carpet in a helpless way that made Captain think of a dying fish out of water. Brad's countenance appeared so distracted that Captain wondered if his friend had lost his good sense.

Brad lay there in that way, staring, and Captain, who was entranced himself, finally broke away from what was before him and quickly moved into the kitchen. Captain roamed the kitchen, making two stiff vodka drinks with Diet Seven-Up and an almost dehydrated lime.

"So what?" he yelled to Brad. There was no reply. Captain found an old but unopened package of Pall Mall cigarettes in the junk drawer.

"What's it mean, Brad?" he yelled. "A couple of bags of dope and a syringe—so what? Is it supposed to be her stuff?" Captain took a good swallow for himself and refilled his drink with straight vodka. He then moved back out into the living room.

Brad remained as Captain had left him, laid out, staring. Captain sat the drink down on the carpet in front of Brad's hand that flopped, and Brad came to life just enough to use the same hand to motion the drink away and say no.

"Fuck you, Brad," Captain said calmly. "You're in my house, lying on your face and I want you to have it. You're not allergic—go on."

Captain left the glass and opened the Pall Malls. Captain removed one cigarette from the pack, went to Brad and put it in his mouth. Captain lit one of the wooden stick matches that had fallen out of the Bisodol tin and held it out to Brad. "Come on, Brad, sit up, close the door in back of you, have a sip of the drink and smoke the goddamned cigarette. Come on."

Captain pulled at his friend, and Brad finally sat up to take the light for his cigarette. He inhaled deeply, coughed, held the cigarette out at arm's length to frown at it questioningly and breathed out a large chestful of smoke. Brad then sat up to reach back and close Captain's apartment door.

Captain didn't speak but stood near him pointing sternly at the drink. Brad finally took it and drank at least half of it down. He winced and had two more good pulls from the Pall Mall, one on top of the other, without exhaling. Brad hung his head and shook it disdainfully. Cigarette smoke came out from under his head, from around his face. It engulfed his upper body.

"That's better now, isn't it? Isn't that better?" Captain asked.

Brad remained forlorn. "Hey, Brad, so you found some paraphernalia—an outfit—in her drawer. So what? Who the hell knows whose it is. I mean, leaving it there sounds stupid. Maybe a friend of hers or—"

"No, no, Cap. She's doing it. She's the one. She's a—a goddamned junkie—my Penny, my baby." Brad appeared as though he would break down again but continued. "She's fourteen years old, Cap—fourteen. Jesus Christ, I saw her yesterday and do you know what she said to me, her own father?—the father who raised her and who she loves—She told me to buzz off, to get off her case. She looks finished, Cap, dead in the eyes, you know what I mean? I could see it in her eyes. She's beat, Cap, beat. Oh, Christ, why me?" Brad began to cry again. He dropped his cigarette into his drink, set the glass at his side and wrapped his arms around his chest to hug himself and to console his shaking.

Letting Brad weep, Captain went into the kitchen and made himself another drink. When he returned, Brad was calm again and sitting with his back against the wall, drinking his drink, cigarette butt and all. This made Captain laugh while he sat in his overstuffed arm chair and put his feet up onto the coffee table.

Captain returned his feet to the coffee table and wiggled his toes. "What's in the balloons?" he asked. "Have you checked?"

Moving slowly, wiping his face on his sleeve along the way, Brad crawled on all fours out to the middle of the living room. Brad picked up the small red rubber balloons and bounced them on his flattened palm. "Now what the fuck do you suppose is in them, Cap? You know all about this kind of stuff." Suddenly dry-eyed and enraged, Brad held the red balloons out to Captain.

Captain saw the pathetic challenge in Brad's anger. He was really saying, Prove me wrong, say it isn't so. Go on, tell me—tell me that they are harmless and blow up and are pretty and red at the ends of sticks; that Penny was saving them for the fair to

210

wave at the elephants when she sits on her daddy's knee. Tell me, Captain, tell me that it's all been a horrific mistake, a nightmare.

Captain thought that there seemed little to do but minimize. He said, "They shoot all kinds of shit today, Brad. The kids, they experiment all over the place. I mean, it could be meth or coke or crunched up Quaaludes or Darvons or, hell, it could be something from Marilyn's medicine chest, maybe some Valium. It sure as hell doesn't have to be—"

"It's heroin," Brad interrupted. "It doesn't have to be, no it doesn't; it could be lots of other crap. That's what I prayed for, but no, it's junk, Cap,—heroin, brown Mexican heroin. Brown Mex, they call it. How do I know? Do you want to know? Ask me how I know that my baby daughter injects herself with brown Mexican heroin. Go on, ask me."

After taking a swallow of his drink, Captain asked, "How do you know that what's in those balloons is brown Mex, Brad? And better yet, how do you know that it's Penny who's shooting it?"

"The police told me, that's who. The goddamned police."

"You've been to the police?" Captain asked.

"Have I—the—the assholes—Yeah, I've been to them, for all the good it did me. We had to drive to hell and back just to find the right jurisdiction, where she bought the stuff, or was given it." Brad thought about that for a brief time and then said, "Aw, no. Shit, nobody gave it to her. Who am I trying to kid? She bought it. She bought it, all right. She just loves the shit. You know what she said to me? Her eyes looked real stupid and dreamy—it scared me at first—and she took me out in back of this place to her trailer—her trailer, *sheeit*—it's where she's staying, I guess—and I got real close to her eyes and saw how doped she looked, and Marilyn was screaming and hollering, and I shook Penny, I shook her hard and I said, 'In the name of God, Penny'—she's always believed in God; she's really such a good girl, with her grades and her chess and all—and I said, 'In the name of God, honey, come home to me and your mother.' I pleaded with her. I said, 'Please, Penny, in the name of God.' And, Cappy, do you know what she said? What she did?''

Captain shook his head no, tried to appear sympathetic, drank his drink and listened.

"She smiled at me, Cappy. She just stood there smiling like a zombie, acting real concerned about me. She took my hand—she wasn't jumpy or anything—she just took my hand, and she said it almost religiously: 'God, Daddy? Did you say in the name of God?' Well, Cap, for a minute there I didn't know what she meant or what to say so I just stood there gawking, and she said, 'Daddy, let me tell you about God. If He made anything that can make you feel better, He kept it for Himself,' and she laughed about it. Do you know what she meant, Cap? Do you? She meant the dope, the heroin. If God made anything better, He kept it for Himself. Good God in Heaven, can you imagine Penny talking about God and heroin in the same breath?'' Brad threw the red balloons down onto the floor in front of himself. "That's what she meant, isn't it, Cap? Anything better than heroin, right? Isn't that what it means?''

"That's what it means, Brad. But what about the cops?''

"Those—those—fools. Inept fools is what they are. To hear it from them, they can't do anything. Oh, they can arrest her. Oh, sure, they can arrest her for possession of heroin and probably for being a runaway, but they'll only turn her over to the officials from Los Angeles County, and they'll bring her home or lock her up—nobody seems to know which—and she swears she'll go right back. She swears she's not coming home. She says we'd have to tie her up to get her home, which I would do right about now.''

"Where the hell is she?'' Captain asked.

A FAVOR

"She's out in Ventura County, out over the line in the boon-
docks, the sticks, where the cops don't care at all. They said that
they've got more to think about than another goofed-up kid,
unless I want her arrested. Oh, they'll do that all right. Can you
see it? Can you imagine how that would look on a resume or a
college thing—an application, if she lives that long? How were
your teenage years? What were your hobbies? Oh, swell, yeah,
swell. Oh, arrested for shooting heroin. Oh, that's swell, a good
hobby. Sure, you're just what we've been looking for, young
lady. Jesus Christ, Cap, to have her arrested for heroin—Hell,
she might even be selling it. I mean, heroin isn't marijuana, is it?
It's a whole lot different than getting busted for grass, isn't it,
Cap?"

"Yes, Brad, it's a lot different. But tell me about the cops.
Why wouldn't they help? What did they say?"

"Well, this place where Penny's staying—I think she's staying
there—it's in the valley, way out in the valley past Woodland
Hills, out of the county. It's in East Ventura County, a little slice
of ground that nobody seems to be responsible for. Well, anyway, it's a roadhouse kind of a place for kids—and grownups
too, I guess. They serve food—food, shit—greasy hamburgers
and fries. It gives them a license to serve booze, and out in back
are some house trailers, and that's where Penny is, in one of those
trailers, or at least the last time I saw her she was. God, imagine a
bunch of house trailers full of junkies and drunks and who knows
what all living together. A bunch of bums is what it amounts
to—trash. God, think about what goes on out there, about sex and
stuff. God, just imagine what they do, with no supervision at all,
just free to do what they want to—to a young girl. Cap,—oh,
God, Cap—imagine what they do, that gang of—of—imagine
what they do to her, my baby, ohh—" Brad cut off, stumbled
into Captain's bathroom and began to throw up violently.

213

Captain recalled Blacky's Bar and Dance Club, located out past Topanga Canyon in the valley. He'd been there; he had, in fact, had fun there, and he knew what went on. If his memory served him correctly, it seemed that there were some small house trailers next to or out in back of the place. It seemed also that working girls, hookers, did business out of the trailers.

To escape his stomach becoming upset by the sounds of Brad gagging in the bathroom, Captain tried not to listen. He twirled the ice round and round in his glass and thought about Blacky's roadhouse. Captain knew that Blacky's was a rough, tough, nightclub where almost anything went. It was a joint that was in the middle of nowhere but, if you knew where you were going, was easily accessible by freeway. A spot where the surfers from Malibu and Rincon and the northern beaches loved to come along with the cowboys and gypsies from Topanga Canyon. They came to drink and dope and brawl and dance among the dope farmers from the San Fernando Valley and the drug pushers and black pimps from Los Angeles. Their women came too. Blacky's music system was big and loud, and he hired hot, nationally known groups. All these elements combined to provide an atmosphere of excitement, adventure and even danger that carload after carload of single females, as well as vans full of college kids, found irresistible. They came as though lured, to dance their brains out, get stoned and in the end, try to find love. Quite often a young lady would lose her virginity at Blacky's, just as a young man might lose his teeth. Some of the stories about the place where gross, but it kept them coming back for more.

I suppose that's the place, he thought. Captain remembered the summer before last when he'd gone out there often to dance and act crazy. "That was during my energetic period," he said quietly, laughing to himself. Then Captain felt gloomy as he realized that if Penny was staying out there at Blacky's, she was

214

probably in real trouble. Captain tried to think about how you got out there. He guessed that it was only a couple of miles from the Ventura Freeway and remembered that it was situated by itself in the middle of a vast no-man's land of desert; the kind of place where the telephone poles and electric lines run up to bring service and then end. The thing that always amused Captain about the big, red, barnlike place was the kind of security that was provided.

Blacky bragged that he handled all of the security himself. Actually this meant using most, if not all, of the local off-duty sheriff's men and their deputies. Captain laughed about the big bruisers with their full beards, coveralls and beat-up Western hats. Captain thought that they appeared comical, remnants from a bygone era. But they were only funny when viewed from a safe distance.

These big men roamed the bar and dance rooms at Blacky's with a beer in one hand and a tent stake or baseball bat in the other. "Bad fucking guys," Captain mused respectfully. Because of these folks, there was little real trouble at Blacky's. Two patrons or more who wanted to fight were escorted out of doors to battle in the parking lot. This happened for all to see, cheer and enjoy under the club's bright exterior floodlights.

Blacky and other big, round-faced, whiskered men who helped him run his roadhouse and, for that matter, East Ventura County were on the take. They sold everything from hot cars and airplanes to homes, ranches, horses, narcotics and women. Because of the circumstances, because they were the law, it was nearly impossible to bring a criminal indictment against them. "Live and let live" is the way that Blacky put it to the press. "Don't fuck with me, man," is what he'd say privately.

Anxious to know if his guess was right, Captain yelled, "Hey, Brad, is Penny out at Blacky's?"

215

The body noises from the bathroom stopped. The toilet flushed, and Captain heard the water run. With his eyes still tearing, Brad emerged from the small hallway, a look of astonishment on his face. He said, "Yeah—Blacky's, that's the place. How the hell did you—?"

"It's famous, Brad. And, Brad, I'd be lying to you if I were to say that it's not trouble. Now tell me just what the police said."

Brad went for the Pall Malls and looked briefly at the stick matches that lay beside the spilled Bisodol tin. Captain thought that he saw Brad's lip curl into an involuntary snarl before he went into the kitchen to light his cigarette with the gas flame from the stove. Brad dragged hard on the stale cigarette and said, "The L.A. County guys out in Woodland Hills and Tarzana were sympathetic as hell. I guess they'd heard the same story over and over again. But they said that their hands are tied. They talked to me real nice but in the end referred me over the county line to the sheriff from East Ventura—a big slob of a guy, a mean-looking, dirty Santa Claus type is what he reminded me of, a big fat slob with rotten teeth—spitting, always spitting brown. He drives a pickup truck with red lights on top of the cab, and a big, mean dog sits in the back snarling his ass off all the time. God, it's like a nightmare."

"Go on. What happened?" Captain asked.

"Well, Marilyn and I went out there the first time—we went twice, but the first time we went, it was afternoon and dusty as hell out there."

"At Blacky's?"

"Yeah, Blacky's place. And Penny was there, playing pinball and drinking a coke. It was hot as hell and dusty, and Penny was wearing a bikini top with those skimpy underpants that dancers wear—yellow though, like the top, and she was barefoot, just lazy as can be. The place wasn't busy, not even open, I don't

216

think. Oh, yes, it was too, but just daytime people were there, not a crowd at all; and Penny walked around with us a little bit and played a song for us that she liked on the juke box. She closed her eyes and kept them closed during the whole record, just swaying and acting dopey, and then she just wouldn't come home with us. I started losing my temper and dragging her, and a great big moose of a guy came and made me let go of her, my own daughter. He pushed me away from her, and he stood in between us and said to move on. He said, 'All right, move on out of here before you get hurt,' and Marilyn started screaming, and the guy grabbed her and said, 'All right, I'll escort you out,' and another guy grabbed me, and they dragged us out and put us into the car and threatened to smash the car—you know, my new Pinto—with bats—until we left—Jesus. So we drove to the sheriff's office, which is another trailer house but bigger, and a brick jail house, a little closer into the freeway but over the railroad tracks the other way. And when I saw him, I played it smart, I thought. I didn't show him the Bisodol tin and the needle, but the other balloon—there was a third one, a green one. And the sheriff said that it was brown Mexican heroin, brown Mex, and that he would go and arrest her for it if we were sure that she had more, or that he would go and get her as a runaway. That sounded like the best idea, but he said that if she had needle marks or was loaded or holding—you know, if she had possession of any heroin—that that would make for a big arrest. He wondered where she'd gotten the dope. He asked us, and Marilyn said that he had to be kidding, that Blacky's place was where it came from, and the sheriff got real insulted and red-faced and stomped around in those broken-down cowboy boots, and he said real loud and mean that Blacky didn't allow any drugs at his place and that he knew that because he worked for Blacky on Friday and Saturday nights, and so did the boys. Then he put the green balloon into his pocket and said, 'The only one going to jail if we go out to Blacky's is your kid, if she is your kid and if there's a goddamn good reason when we get there.' Then he said, 'Now it's up to you. Are we going or not?'

"Well, we just looked at each other, me and Marilyn, and didn't know what to do. So we left to talk it over and decide, and we went back to Tarzana, even to the Highway Patrol, but nothing—no help. So about half-crazy and tired—you know, not thinking right—we drove back out to the bar, to Blacky's. It was dark and the band was there and the kids were all coming, and some really rough looking people too—and Penny. We saw her walking out back to the trailers, just happened to see her. And she was all right, not hostile or anything like I told you before. And I said to her to come along, and she wouldn't. And I sort of came unglued, I guess, because I showed her what we'd found in her drawer at home. She'd been back and forth from the place a lot, I guess, before she finally stayed. I mean, she was acting funny around the house and coming in with excuses and—oh, shit, I don't know. Anyway I threatened her and told her to come home in the name of God and all of that, and she smiled, I told you about that. She just smiled and said the thing about God keeping anything better than heroin for Himself, and when I tried to bring her—I was tugging her—another big guy came, a really big one this time, and he asked Penny what was up, and she said, 'Nothing important. I just want them to buzz off.' 'To buzz off,' Cap, did you hear me? Penny telling her own mother and father to—''

"Yes, Brad, I hear you. So you left?"

"We left, all right. They damn near broke my arm. They pulled Marilyn's hair again too. Jesus Christ, Cap, it was humiliating." Brad demonstrated his hurt by folding his hands together and looking down.

Knowing now for sure why Brad was there, Captain drank his

drink and waited for him to ask the favor. It was Brad's own fault for loving her so damned much, he figured. Captain had thought all along that Brad was stupid to put all his eggs into Penny's basket. But that was Brad's business. The issue that was about to arise here, what was going to occur with the next few words out of Brad's mouth, was a test, a test of Captain's and Brad's friendship. Captain allowed himself to appear serious, even solemn, when in fact in his heart he felt jubilant. Brad had always been there for him, and Captain was completely ready, he was eager, to help his friend in any way that he could.

Brad finally brought his eyes up to meet Captain's. He squeezed his fingers together tightly and made his knuckles white.

"Well, my friend, I'm still listening," Captain said, controlling a smile.

Realizing that his stomach actually felt giddy, Captain forced the feeling of embarrassment aside and said to himself, Well, all right, I enjoy helping people, my friends—so what? It's a good thing, isn't it? Captain nodded his head just a little, allowed a faint smile to come over his face and thought, yes, it's a good thing.

Brad switched his weight back and forth from foot to foot and after an awkward silence said, "Cap, I—I want you to do something for me."

Captain laughed at his friend's discomfort, mostly to try and lessen the man's pain and de-energize the moment, but he thought that Brad looked funny too. "I never would have guessed it, Brad. I thought you came by to use my razor and smoke my Pall Malls." Captain laughed again. Brad's expression remained serious. "Brad, why don't you tell me what you want done and stop acting like a drip. We're friends, aren't we?"

Brad blurted it out. "I want you to go and get her for me, Cap.

219

Force her to come if you have to. I just don't have the—the nerve. I don't have the guts to have to drag her out of there. It's not only those big slobs, either. Shit, I've got my German Luger at home. I could go out there and blast away until—"

"Sure, sure you could, Brad, sure you could. But if you could, why don't you?"

"It's Penny. I'm afraid of her, what she'd say. I haven't been able to close my eyes without thinking about it. You might say I'm being paranoid, but, Jesus, the way she can look at me, even when she was little. I know she'd give me that look. And what if she screamed things at me? She wouldn't mean them, of course, but I hear them bouncing around in my head. I can see her fighting me and staring at me in a way that I could never live down. I know it sounds chicken shit, Cap, but—well—what if she called me a—a—a cock sucker? God! Or if she said, 'Let me go, you dirty mother fucker. I hate you.' Stuff like that. I mean, she's drugged, you know, and apt to do something that—well, that I'll never be able to forget. Going out and forcing her myself could cause a scene that—things might never be the same between us, never again. My girl, my little girl, I don't think of her as being out there, Cap, not grown up enough to—to do anything—wrong. I mean, what if she never spoke to me again. I mean, I don't want to go out there to that trailer and find—her—"

Brad began to sob again. He stood there, tears rolling down his face. "Cappy, I can't go out to the trailer to surprise her at what she's—if she's—I don't have the balls to barge in. I'm afraid, Cap, of what I'll find. She's still a virgin, my baby. Oh, Christ—"

Well, Captain thought. I guess this has gone far enough.

"I'll help you, Brad. How do you want to work it?"

Brad perked up immediately. He wiped his face off on the

sleeve of his rumpled sport coat and began to speak enthusiastically.

"Home is where she belongs, Cap, where we can take care of her, love her back to life. I talked to Tom Duggin. You know Doctor Tom, the silver-haired doctor that comes into the bar—you always call him dapper Tom—you know—"

"Yes, okay, I know who he is. He drinks Manhattans."

"Right, Manhattans, right. Well, Tom's been a customer of mine for years. He's a square shooter. He gave Penny her first baby shots, before Berman the pediatrician took over. Well, Tom's a good friend, and I laid it all out to him, and he said that we should hospitalize her. But that if we could get her home to the apartment, he would come there too and give her something to calm her, to sedate her. He'd give her a prescription. Marilyn wouldn't leave her side for one minute, and we could work in shifts until Penny's system is clean, until she shakes this thing."

Brad watched for Captain's response, while Captain thought about what had been said.

"We'd be home at the apartment waiting, Cappy—me and Marilyn and the doctor—when you brought her home. And another thing, Cap—and probably most important of all—she likes you, likes you one hell of a lot, more than almost anybody we ever had over that I've ever met tending bar. And I've made some good friends, and better than anyone Marilyn has ever brought home, even better than the models she shoots. And some of them are real fun kids, and attractive, popular kids. Sometimes they stay for a bite to eat when they finish or just stay for a drink or something, and they all shoot the shit about modeling and all that. They include Penny and talk openly about their lives, what they like to do and stuff, both the boys and the girls. But Penny still always asks about Captain. She loves your name and laughs about it and kids me when I tell her that you've been in for a drink or lunch. She always asks me, 'Captain, Captain, where is my Captain?' She still counts that day when we took her around the pier and on the merry-go-round and bumper cars—remember when you and Marilyn got so stinko, and Penny and I were almost carrying you guys around, and you were going to jump off the pier to show off? Remember? Penny still counts that as one of her most fun days ever.''

''Okay, Brad, slow down. I hear you. Just let me give it some thought. How is Marilyn? How's her photography? Does she make a buck?''

''Yes, yes, she does pretty good at it. She still works at the apartment in the spare room. Next season she's going to rent a small studio. But she's quite good, Cap. Cap, Cap—come on and tell me—Will you go? Will you go and get her for us? Say you will, please.''

''Just walk right into Blacky's and waltz her right out of there, huh? Is that how you see it Brad? Just a fast shuffle—no problems?''

''No, Cappy, there won't be any trouble with you. People avoid trouble with you, you know that. You're capable of— you're capable—you're the most capable guy that I know. You can handle things like this, tough guys and stuff. Hell, I've seen you. And besides, Penny will listen to you, to her Captain. Please, Cappy, I'll do anything for—''

''Sit down, Brad. I don't like you standing over me shouting. Just let me think about this thing a minute.''

Slump-shouldered, Brad walked back across the room to flop down into an easy chair.

Then Brad spoke evenly, slowly, with a deliberate tone when he said, ''We will give you $3,000, Cap—cash now—if you'll do it for us. Now, tonight—$3,000, Cap.''

Captain stared hard into Brad's eyes until Brad averted his gaze.

"Three thousand dollars, Cap—cash, for your trouble." Brad said it to the wall.

Although Captain was trying to act a bit haughty and insulted about the offer of money, he understood down deep inside that it was understandable, that it was desperation. But as Captain watched his friend's discomfort, he couldn't help think that it almost served him right—for putting all of his faith in Penny, all of his love, for loving her that much. Captain spoke out loud but to himself.

"You've had your neck sticking out a mile. You've just been asking for it." Captain shook his head and spoke to himself. "What a one-dimensional, dumb way to live."

Brad seemed to hear and understand and was back on his feet again, pacing. Then he snapped, "But it's my way, Cap. It's the way that I chose, and I'd do it again. It's made me—I've been very happy—until now."

"Until now, right. But what about now? You're so totally committed to that one relationship that—I mean she's a fucking teenager, Brad; they're all crazy. You can't hold on, she's growing up. Goddamn, man, have you seen the way that you look? I mean, you look suicidal. I mean, Christ Almighty, release her. Release her with love and try to find some balance. She'll wander away from Blacky's, just like she found her way out there, or she won't. She'll just die out there. But maybe there's not one fucking thing that you or me or anyone else can do about it. You're the one with so much faith. Why not back away and let God handle it. Turn it over to Him, pray for some balance in life. You're weighted way too heavy on that kid, Brad."

Brad stopped moving and stood close.

"Good old Cappy, always has to be balanced, doesn't it. I can't believe it. Iris is right about you, you know. You are a typical Libra."

Brad was the one to shake his head now, and then he screamed out, spitting and made Captain jump. "Your way—your way! Don't you understand? Don't you know? There are other ways, Captain. Other ways, other than your way. Your way isn't my way."

Captain thought he saw Brad snarl again in that unattractive, curled-lip way, and he thought that he saw something else also. A different glint in Brad's eye. A glazed look that was more than anger. Captain sensed that Brad didn't like him any more. That he didn't want to continue to be friends. The feeling gave Captain a chill. Brad stood there trembling, with dried white spittle over his mouth, appearing haggard and aged. Captain's stomach felt sick for a moment before he was able to reassure himself that he didn't need Brad. Shit, he thought, he needs me; I don't need him.

While the energy seemed to ebb out of Brad, Captain put what he hoped to be a smug expression on his own face and casually finished his drink. Setting the glass aside, Captain dried his hands on the arms of the chair and went and retrieved one of the small red balloons from beside the spilled Bisodol tin.

Captain wiped his left palm and insured its dryness by blowing on it with a long steady breath. Stretching the neck of the red balloon, Captain tore the knotted end off and poured most of the brown powdered contents into his clean palm. Captain held his hand out toward Brad as he would a cocktail before a toast.

"Well, let's see what God has been keeping for Himself and His friends, Brad. Let's see what He's doing for our little Penny."

Captain brought the brown powder up under his nose and with his palm cupped as though holding liquid and his head bent to drink, he hauled the brown powder into both nostrils with a loud snort.

Brad began a wide-eyed, excited gesticulation that quickly

turned into an audible gasp and an arm-drooping look of bewilderment.

"Fuck you, Brad, and all of your bullshit too. You want me to do something for you. If you're my friend, if you trust our friendship, then you know that I'll do it. I told you in front to just ask me. I was anxious to help. But money? Three grand, you'll give me three grand, will you? Well, fuck you. It shows me what kind of friends we really are—you are. If I asked you to do it for me—the same thing, on our friendship—you'd probably tell me that I was crazy. You'd probably tell me to fuck off. I mean, go out to Blacky's and get down with those fuckers—Shit, you'd tell me to blow it out my ass. But for three grand you'd do it, right? That's what it would cost to get you to move for me, right? Not friendship but money."

Goddamn, he thought, stoned out of his head, I didn't figure it until I said it, but that's the goddamned truth. It would take money to get Brad to move for me, for anything big or difficult or if things were reversed.

Brad didn't move. Captain fell backward into the couch saying, "Holy Toleeeedo, I'm whacked." Jesus, shit, Captain thought. I'm losing consciousness. He talked through it.

"You're looking at me like an old fart, Brad, you old conservative fart you. Come on and take a whack of this shit and see what she means. See what gets your kid off. Oh, my. Oh, my. Lawdy, lawdy, Miss Claudie, Brad."

Captain laughed and dropped his feet onto the coffee table, while inside a fearful feeling welled up through his chest to cause a swelling sensation in his throat. Good God, he wondered, how much dope did I do? Lawdy, lawdy, he thought. Lawdy, lawdy, Miss Claudie. Keep dem eyes open.

Captain felt his head fall to the left, and he would like to have left it there. And then his head was hanging again, and he absolutely could not raise his eyelids. The room was black, and Captain understood that he was sitting there nodding away like a hop head, going deeper and deeper into a coma. Captain wondered what had happened to his friend.

"What happened to Brad?" he mumbled.

In a move that seemed involuntary, Captain drove himself for the door. Being up on his feet helped briefly. The room blurred. The bullies in his brain became dominant and screamed for survival: "This is how you O.D., this is how you O.D." Captain knew that it was true and said something to Brad over his shoulder as he fought to put one foot out in front of the other to move through the door and down the apartment building's darkened hallway. Then he was down and crawling. Feeling nothing, he rolled down and around staircases that fendered and bounced him and made him think of a pinball game. His mind flashed on Blacky's roadhouse, the lights and the sounds of the steel balls bouncing in the game room.

The stairway down to the street felt very hard and cold and rough. Captain heard a crack in his left hand, while he tumbled down the stairs. He turned to see people behind him standing in the doorway. They were a dark blur of a group, and Brad was probably there too.

"I'm a stunt man—just fucking around, doing a roll." He thought he said it but wasn't sure. He laughed. Get up you sucker, he told himself. Get up, get up, get up. Captain kept stumbling and falling when he tried to run down the street. Somehow he turned and managed to trip across the street and run up the sidewalk on that side.

Captain knew the large brownstone apartment building coming up on his left. It was generally well kept and had good green grass, the best on that street. Jumping the short hedge, Captain let

226

himself collapse onto the damp, cool turf. Captain forced his limbs into a spread-eagle position and lay with his cheek against the grass, panting. The yard area was dark, and Captain saw only a swirl of black. A feeling of extreme nausea zipped through him.

While he braced himself for the oncoming seizure of vomiting, the sick feeling was suddenly replaced by a sensation of utter calm and peace. Wonderful moments of tranquility seemed to float by and after a time Captain said, "I don't feel too bad." Feeling safe, almost protected, he lay there thinking, tracing how he'd gotten there.

When he realized that he felt sensational in body and mind, Captain shivered with pleasure and said, "Oh, oh." He said it to himself excitedly. "Oh, oh," and felt himself break into a big grin. Captain stood up, inhaled deeply and said, "Oh, oh." He used the expression as his father had, in joyful exclamation.

Captain sat back down on the grass and said, "Oh, oh, here it comes. Shit, it's here. Wow, what a way to feel."

Chuckling, Captain itched the flat palms of his hands on the stiff strong grass at his sides. Then he had to scratch all over his body and did it voraciously. One of the lower fingers on his left hand seemed swollen but there was no discomfort.

Captain surprised himself when he jumped up to exclaim loudly, "Oh, oh, watch out." Then he said softly, "Good God," about the wonderful way that he felt, and he giggled about it.

Stepping back over the hedge, Captain walked briskly to the corner, crossed the street under the pure light from the street lamp and continued down the sidewalk toward his apartment house. The area was quiet and seemed poorly lit, unsafe. Captain made a mental note to brighten the building's frontal area for the tenants' assured security.

Brad sat on the red brick stairs alone, his back to the stoop, head hung, hands folded, waiting. Brad looked up to say, "Cap, is that you, Cap? Yeah, that's you, that's you." But he didn't move.

Captain figured that with Brad's bad vision he was still guessing. "Yeah, it's me Brad. And guess what?"

"What, Captain?" Brad answered.

"If God made anything better, He kept it for Himself." Captain wheezed when he laughed.

Captain watched through watering eyes while Brad slowly got up, turned and began to walk off down the street. "Hey, Brad, stop. I'll go. I'll go and get her for you."

Brad had turned back around. "You will? You're not B.S.ing me, are you, Cap? You really will?"

Captain stopped his laugh and said it to him seriously, "Yeah, I will, I will, and it won't cost you a dime either. But line up the doctor, Brad. Get the doctor ready, because once she's back home, she's all yours, and it could be a bitch if she's really into it big, because this stuff is dynamite, Brad, dynamite."

Brad was excited. "Okay, okay. Yeah, I suppose you would know that too. But we'll be ready—ready—Thank you, Cappy, God thank you. Marilyn will be so happy. Oh, Cappy, shit—thanks." Brad paused and asked, "And the money—the $3,000—you don't—?"

"No way. I'm doing it for another reason, asshole."

"Shit, you are beautiful. You are the best friend ever—the best."

Brad smiled, and Captain saw the warmth in his friend's eyes. Captain could have sworn that he felt his heart swell in his breast. It must be the dope, he thought. Boy, this is good dope.

Captain backed away toward the building. "The doctor, Brad, have the doctor real close. I'll call you when I've got her, or we're on the way in."

Captain wondered if that was going to be possible. Anything could happen, he thought. "I'll get a call to you, Brad, somehow; so stay off of the phone and be ready. Now get going, friend."

Turning, Captain ran up the front stairs of the apartment building. God, I'm soaked with sweat, he realized. "Be careful, Cap." Brad's voice came from the shadows.

Captain stopped in his tracks and had to smile. Be careful? he questioned. At Blacky's roadhouse? Captain visualized the place, the tough men, what he was up against and turned back to Brad. "Okay, Brad, I'll be careful." You fucking ay, John, I'll be careful, he thought, and he couldn't help but laugh out loud as he entered the building.

The Rescue

Taking advantage of the dreamy way that he felt, Captain lolled in the warm water from his shower. He spent a relaxing time with a bowel movement, the urge brought on, he imagined, by a baby laxative called Mannite, which was often used to cut heroin. Captain dressed in faded jeans, an open-collared sport shirt and a beige corduroy sport coat.

Not hungry but needing nourishment, Captain opened a canned ham, toasted two pieces of frozen bread, made a sandwich and a mug of coffee and bringing the food, used the tedious elevator to reach the garage area. He locked the steel door of his workroom behind him. The overhead light swung back and forth, casting funny shadows, and Captain sat at his workbench to eat half the sandwich and drink the coffee. The sandwich and coffee added to the good feeling that he was experiencing.

Finally, Captain dragged a mesh string bag of Idaho baking

potatoes out from underneath his workbench. Although they were mostly shriveled, he found one that was full and firm, which he liked. Next, he unlocked the steel cabinet at the end of the storage room and brought out the potato gun and metal cylinder.

The potato gun had been Speed's invention. One afternoon while the two of them had been out target shooting at Hutton's rifle ranch in Topanga Canyon, a discussion had begun about muffling the sound of a gun shot. Speed had said that a potato was the best silencer ever thought of and went and got one from Old Man Hutton to demonstrate. Speed started a small hole at the end of the potato with his pocket knife and then forced the potato onto the end of the barrel of a Western Colt model .45. Speed had smiled and said, "Of course it's only good for one shot but—" and he then fired off toward the target. Captain had been surprised that the normally loud boom of the Colt .45 was reduced to a hollow sounding thud. The pieces of potato fell at their feet. Speed had then fired again to demonstrate the difference: a resounding roar.

Speed's knowledge of what a potato would do coupled with his obsession over what he called the .22-caliber murderers brought him and Captain to develop what they called their potato guns. They each had had one. Captain had them both now since Speed's death.

It was Speed's theory that the modern, sophisticated, professional murderers from the mafia, CIA and other agencies, as well as the free-lance assassins who operated throughout the world, were using silenced .22-caliber guns to do their killing these days. Speed said that .22-caliber cartridges were available today that housed solid copper slugs and enough black powder to bring the small projectiles up to magnum force. That they could penetrate steel and you couldn't be heard, even when standing nearby at the time of firing.

For no reason in particular but having fun, Captain and Speed had purchased two new Savage, eight-shot, .22-caliber automatic pistols. These handguns were the choice because of their two-inch barrel extensions. The sights were removed by grinding the tops of the barrels smooth, and threading was then put onto the ends of the barrels using a simple pipe threader.

Captain and Speed had screwed all kinds of experimental potato canisters onto the ends of their guns until they settled on a matched pair of anodized-aluminum salt and pepper shakers. Captain used the saltshaker, Speed the pepper. The holes in the bottom of the shakers were opened up, reworked and threaded to screw onto the pistols' barrels. The fronts of the shakers were sawed off and the edges made sharp so that when the small canister was pushed into the length of a potato, it cut the potato and filled itself up, much like a cookie cutter.

The velocity from the small slugs was so great that the cuts of potato stayed snugly in place in front of the barrels when the pistols were fired. Captain and Speed would take the guns out to the desert or to Hutton's and shoot an entire box of shells each. Every time the sound was the same, comparable to what Captain considered a human belch. Eight shots could be quickly ripped off in what sounded like someone merely clearing his throat. The quiet *sput* sound from the guns was a big hit with both Captain and Speed. "So quiet," they would say, "and yet so deadly."

Captain thought about Blacky's roadhouse and the gang of bad men that ran the place while he gouged a piece of potato into the reworked salt shaker. After finishing the sandwich and coffee, he loaded the eight-shot Savage automatic and stepped into the garage. He locked the storeroom door behind himself and decided to drive the Dodge. The big car roared when it started. Captain said, "I'm feeling mighty fine," and whistling a made-up tune, he headed for Blacky's roadhouse.

232

The freeways were not crowded and that was good, but coming through the Mulholland Pass with its view, Captain could see the murk of air pollution hanging over the night lights of the San Fernando Valley. "Fucking smog," he said.

After a twenty-minute drive on the Ventura Freeway, Captain turned off and drove north into the flat, rural, arid land that characterizes east Ventura County. Captain figured the ocean at about thirty miles to the west and irrigation in the area to be prohibitively expensive. He guessed that that was why almost nothing grew but occasional clumps of weeds and brush. As he drove, oil derricks appeared here and there, doggedly pushing and pulling against the still night skyline.

Captain felt the place before he saw or heard it. A giant string of rickety, unlit billboards lined the road to his right as it dipped for an instant and while down in that blackness, Captain sensed the pounding of electrified musical instruments. An instant later he made the grade, came over the rise and it was all there before him.

People had said that Blacky's roadhouse made them think of fifty yards of the Las Vegas Strip grabbed up and plunked down all by itself in the middle of nowhere. And so it seemed. The neon, God, the fucking neon, he thought, shielding his eyes with his forearm. The big barn was surrounded by cars and vans and trucks all parked haphazardly. People seemed to jump and jive through the parked vehicles on the way to Blacky's front door. The loud music beat the night air in gusts against Captain's chest and made him feel excited.

"A black band," he said, "a good black band." Captain got close and saw that the big boys with the beards were there too. They wore bibbed coveralls and carried clubbing instruments in their hands for crowd control. They sauntered around the area, letting everyone know that they were there. People stepped

233

around them. Then the music became louder, and Captain said, "Goddamn, I'm going to dance my ass off."

Pretending to look for parking, Captain tried to drive around to the rear of the big red barn back by the trailers, but roadblock saw-horses were set up along that access. Captain turned his headlights onto Blacky's back yard and saw the trailers. Before he could really observe anything, however, a cane-carrying, big galoot of a man wearing black aviator glasses and a dark colored Stetson, turned him away. Being careful not to be blocked in, Captain parked across the street on the open flat land with several other vehicles. Young people acting intoxicated and apparently having fun milled around in front of the club. The smell of marijuana filled the night air.

The music had stopped but started again with a solo from an electric guitar as Captain pushed through the long, vented swinging doors. Old-fashioned saloon doors, he thought.

The hall was smaller than Captain had remembered and packed with bouncing or in other ways animated bodies. The rest of the band joined the guitarist, and the floor shook. Captain liked the tickly feeling under his feet. The smoky air smelled of perspiration and stale beer and other things not altogether unpleasant. The boys had wet faces, and the girls looked cute and energetic. They undulated together, all races and types. They wore bright colors.

Dancing by himself, Captain closed his eyes and slipped into the crowd. He moved toward the music. He danced energetically, using his arms to help feel the beat and to push people away. Realizing that he hadn't paid to get in, Captain opened his eyes to squint back at the front door. Two bouncers stood on either side of the entrance, but no money exchanged hands. A free room, he thought. They charge at the others.

Once up to the stage, Captain stood in front of the huge black speaker cabinets and let the music pound over him. Dancing, he let himself float. Captain held his elbow against the potato gun under his jacket. We wouldn't want that to fall out, he laughed.

Opening his eyes, Captain watched some of the crowd disappear through the archways into the other rooms. A long bar ran the length of the room beside him. Red exit signs blazed above two large doors behind and on either side of the stage. The top halves of the doors were swung open into the night air, toward the trailer area behind the club to aid circulation of air. The doors' bottom halves were closed to traffic and guarded by big men who stood drinking beer.

The music stopped suddenly, and Captain pushed his way to the bar. A gin and tonic tasted wrong, so he ordered a can of Coors, which was cold and tasted wonderful. The hell with it, he thought. Maybe Penny will want to dance. "If she feels as good as me she sure as hell will want to," Captain said to a sodden-faced bartender who shrugged his shoulders and turned away.

Two big men sporting beards and handlebar mustaches stopped Captain when he tried to exit out the closest half-opened door into the back yard. Nonetheless, he was able to look out behind the building into the open, dimly lit area where three old-fashioned trailer houses sat. They were metallic with rounded corners and gave Captain the impression of being cozy. The back area was quiet with no pedestrian traffic.

"I'm a friend of Penny's." Captain reached out for the lower door as he spoke. The big man to his right grabbed Captain's outstretched wrist with a large paw and with his other hand against Captain's shoulder, pushed him back into the room.

The man reached out and pulled the top of the door closed enough for Captain to read the sign posted on it:

> If you haven't called or been invited, you'd better have a
> goddamned good reason for coming out here.
> Blacky

"You ain't called or been invited, pal. See you around."

The big man pushed Captain's shoulder hard, turning him back into the room. Captain stumbled but looked back at them. Their heavy beards were parted into big smiles. The sounds from a Stevie Wonder record jumped loudly into the room to fill the void left by the band.

In a bad mood, Captain pushed his way through the crowd and back outside the way he had come. Stevie Wonder didn't sound good. Stevie, he thought, you used to be great, but you're losing it. You're losing it, Stevie.

Captain considered moving his Dodge across the street into the lot next to Blacky's. It would put you close, he thought. "Fuck it," he said, walking around the outside of the red, barnlike building. The big man wearing the black aviator glasses, Western hat and carrying the cane saw him coming and moved through the sawhorse road blocks to greet him.

"Hi, I'm Captain, Penny's friend. I called, they said to come around here, that you'd put me through."

Captain continued to walk past the obese cowboy who, showing remarkable agility, got himself quickly in front of Captain.

"Goddamn, you are huge," Captain said, stopping and acting impressed.

"Turn around, boy, and start to walking."

"Come on, cowboy. I told you that I've got a date." Captain said it impatiently.

"What you got is to be a bullshit artist, boy. Now turn around and start back there to the front of the store."

The man pointed with his cane, and when he brought the cane back down, he let it slide its full length through his hand. With the cane upside down, he leaned on it, putting the palm of his hand and his weight on the rubber tip from the bottom. The curved end pushed into the ground.

With his hands on his hips Captain said, "What kind of shit is this? I want to see my friend, Penny. I can't go in—Can she come out? Or is that against your bullshit rules too?"

"Man, you got a bad 'tude, don't you?"

Captain watched the expression become soft and bland behind the black glasses. The big man continued to lean. Captain didn't move.

"I want to see my friend. Now."

"Not with that 'tude, you don't get to see nobody, punk. Not with that 'tude."

Captain glanced around them. They seemed relatively alone. He unbuttoned his corduroy sport coat. "What 'tude, fatso? What's a 'tude?"

The cowboy moved fast, hooking the curled end of his cane around the outside of Captain's ankle. Captain tried to jump out of the snare, but the man merely followed the move by lifting the cane up to Captain's calf. He pulled the cane hard. Captain was in the air before he knew what had happened, landing hard on his right buttock. The thudding pain from his rear shot through him, but the Savage automatic dug into his groin and ribs, knocking the air out of him and making him wince.

The man stood above him holding the cane next to Captain's neck. He spoke slowly and deliberately. "It's your fucking attitude, man. You've got a shitty attitude. Blacky don't invite no people through here. And, punk, there's a password."

Captain's chest and abdomen were burning, but he rolled away from the cane fast and jumped to his feet. Captain felt the cane tear through the air next to his face. The closeness made his cheek sting.

Stepping back and looking around, Captain produced the potato gun. The big man stopped cold.

"Drop the stick, cow man."

237

The big man let the cane fall from his hand. He stared down at the gun. Stepping up to him, Captain pushed the end of the pistol, the saltshaker potato canister, under the man's fat pectoral fold and held it firmly against the ribs above his heart.

"Back up, fatso."

The man backed away into the shadows next to the building. The music was muffled but made the wall next to them shake.

"What do you weigh, cow man?" Captain asked.

"Three-eighty" was the soft-spoken reply.

"Jesus, you are a big one. Where's Blacky?"

The big man remained silent. His fat lower lip hung wet and full, exposoing his lower set of teeth and gums.

"Don't move, cow man."

Captain reached out and removed the man's Western hat and put it on himself. The large hat hung down against Captain's ears. The sweatband was damp. Captain pulled the man's black glasses off and threw them aside.

"Say *mooo* for me, cow man."

The man's eyes were weak-looking from natural selection, heavily lidded with nondescript, brown-tipped white balls. They roamed around Captain's face searching for an answer.

"Say *mooo* for me—now. I'm not shitting. Do it."

The man's heavy lips quivered. Spittle ran from the corners of his soft mouth into his beard. He gulped and blinked.

"Mooo," the fat man said, licking his lips.

Captain glanced around them and said, "Louder, cow man. You don't think you're still a cowboy, do you?"

Captain laughed, and when the man shook his head his jowls slopped back and forth. "N—No—You're—you're crazy—*Moooo.*"

Captain laughed at the way the big man cocked his head and

bellowed. "That's pretty good. Where is Blacky?" Captain pushed the potato gun into his chest.

"In—in the second trailer."

"Where's Penny?"

"In the first trailer."

"Are they both at home?"

"Yes."

The big man's eyes were darting around nervously.

"There's something you're not telling me." Captain pushed the gun again. "Guards, are there more guards?"

The man shook his head. "No, no, you're safe. I promise you, man, you're safe."

Captain stared at the big man for a long moment, until a set of headlights played over them and continued on. Captain took advantage of the brief period of illumination to look into the compound at the trailers. It took a moment for the idea to register, but he was almost certain something had moved next to the closest trailer. Something on the ground.

Stepping back, Captain retrieved the fat man's cane. He threw it hard in the direction of the trailers, and the Doberman, both Dobermans, jumped to their feet. At least they don't bark, Captain thought.

"So, I'm safe am I, cow man. How do you call them off?"

"Only Blacky can—only Blacky."

Pushing the potato pistol under the fat man's pectoral fold again, Captain said, "Say *mooo* for me again, loud. Say it."

The fat man turned his face upward and bellowed a good loud *mooo* that sounded very much like the real thing. Captain pulled the potato pistol's trigger. Over the loud mooing sound, nothing could be heard. The fat man stared; his wet mouth hung open.

"Guess what, cow man?"

"Wh—what?" he asked.

"You're dead."

Captain watched the muscle tone fall off the man's face. Captain reached out and pushed him, and he fell without a peep into a clump next to the darkened building.

The Dobermans stood stiff-legged, watching, waiting, while Captain struck out boldly toward the closest trailer. The Stetson hat hung down over his eyes. Almost to the dogs, Captain realized that he was in full view of the men inside the nightclub, the guards on the halved exit doors, if they were looking.

He held the Savage potato gun against his right thigh while he walked. He watched the Dobermans come. They were in front of him in a flash. Snarling, they showed their glorious white teeth and yellow eyes. Captain wanted to pet them but got a chill at the thought.

Stopping and holding fast, he removed the cow man's Western hat and held it out for the dogs to smell. They remained rigid and seemed not to be inhaling. Captain fanned the hat toward the dogs using an easy motion of his wrist. The dogs might have glanced at each other, he wasn't sure. The music came again from the club, hard and heavy. It was dulled by the constant droning sound of the air conditioners on the trailers.

Captain stared back into the dogs' eyes, first one, then the other, to finally stop and look hard into the steadfast yellow eyes of the closest animal, the larger of the two.

"Listen, pal, and I'm not shitting, this is a gun that I've got here, and it's quiet. No one knows when I shoot it. I can put a slug into both your heads right now and that will be that. Or you can let me pass. I'm on God's business for a special friend. So live or die, but understand that I don't want to kill you. I think that you're beautiful. Here I come."

Captain held that dog's stare and walked between them. When

they were behind him, Captain could feel the hair bristle on the nape of his neck. His rectum felt ballooned as though swollen with helium, and he wanted to run. He felt the music, or the dogs' breath, boom against his calves.

With the Stetson back in place on his ears and without looking at the club, Captain mounted the trailer's stairs and quickly let himself in. When he closed the door behind him, he saw the Dobermans standing at the foot of the stairs, watching.

The trailer's air conditioning worked well. The interior space was cool. The machine hummed on. Penny was alone, nude, curled up on a small sofa asleep. Captain walked past two unmade single beds as he moved close to Penny to stand above her and observe. A single shaded lamp burned in the room. The light caught Penny in such a way that her face appeared swollen. She lay with her elbows together and her hands to her face as though praying. Her outside bust hung into her chest and showed several severe stretch marks. Captain saw the needle tracks on both of her arms and above the thumb of her right hand. One large black and blue bruise covered most of her right thigh. Penny showed an abundance of hair on her arms and legs except from her knee down where her legs were shaved clean.

How the fuck old is she? he asked himself. Fourteen? Jesus Christ, that's hard to believe. "Sorry, Brad," Captain said softly, "but your little girl ain't a little girl no more."

Captain opened a cigar box that sat on an end table; it contained several red balloons, matches, a spoon and other paraphernalia necessary for a fix. Next to it sat a large box of cotton swabs and a water glass, probably filled with alcohol, which contained a dismantled professional syringe.

Standing back out of the light, Captain went to the small kitchen and found himself a cold beer. The trailer's interior was decorated in a Western motif. Knotty pine walls sported photo-

241

graphs of famous bad men. An Indian blanket covered the floor. A dark Sony television sat atop a powerful-looking Cerwin Vega speaker cabinet in the corner. Captain sat down across from Penny in a comfortable cloth chair covered with a colorful serape.

"Nice," he said to himself, "damn nice. All the comforts of home. Good vibes, security—nice."

Captain felt chilly and figured that Penny must be cold. Then he thought that she was probably too stoned to feel a thing. Sitting there, Captain began to feel comfortable. He put his feet up and nodded his head, understanding that Penny's trip was easy to sympathize with. Shit, he thought. Ride horses, play pinball, listen to music, travel, watch television, get laid and shoot good dope. What the fuck, if God made anything better, He kept it for himself.

Laughing about that, he wondered how she paid her tab. A hooker, he figured. She must be turning tricks or doing something special with Blacky, that might be it. Goddamn, he wondered. If she's happy, how the hell am I going to rescue her? Rescue her against her will? Down deep inside, Captain knew that there was going to be a battle. I hope not, he thought; but then, and he thought about what was out there: the dogs, Blacky, his men. "Shit," he mumbled, "you're fucking crazy." He got up and began quietly rummaging, looking for a truss.

Putting the strength test to a pair of panty hose and impressed with their resilience, he made three pair ready and put them on the floor next to Penny. Bikini panties would do for a gag.

The telephone kept coming into view. Considering it an omen, Captain carefully picked it up, listened and dialed Brad and Marilyn at home. Brad answered anxiously and shaking his head at the absurdity of what he was doing, Captain said, "I'm at Blacky's. I'm going for it right now." He hung up without waiting for a reply.

Sitting back in the easy chair to drink the beer, Captain hid the gun under his jacket. Reaching his leg out, he pushed firmly at Penny's knees to shake her hard. She awoke instantly, bleary-eyed but awake. She sat up and rested on her left elbow. Her bust lay exposed for Captain to observe. The girl had large, dark brown nipples that Captain thought only went with mature women who had borne children. Penny was sexily plump. This added to her bust, which was rounded and surprisingly full.

She lay there with her large, blinking brown eyes directed toward Captain. She had a tentative, innocent look in her eyes that Captain thought was sexy. Penny adjusted her position, and an oblique strip of light a foot wide shifted to lie horizontally down her naked body. It started at her forehead and ended at her knees. One forearm lay into it. Captain saw the brunette hair above Penny's mouth and on her arm and the heavy pubic bush that began to grow surprisingly high just below her navel.

Penny has body hair, he thought, that drives some men crazy. Captain pictured Blacky with his full hair and beard. Hair, he thought: it gets some people off.

"Captain? Is that Captain?" Penny queried, making no effort to cover her nudity.

"It is. Yes, it is, my dear. Want a sip of cold beer?"

Captain handed the beer to her and sitting up straight mostly out of the horizontal light, she drank two full swallows and handed it back. Penny closed her eyes and vigorously massaged her scalp with her fingertips. Then she stood and put on an orange silk robe of Indian design.

Goddamn, Captain observed, she does have a huge bush. He figured that Penny had the most hair between her legs that he'd ever seen.

"Where's Blacky?" she asked, sitting and lighting a cigarette.

"I don't know. I didn't see him."

Penny looked down at her cigarette, and Captain was taken by how much she'd changed. How grown up, how mature she seemed.

"You didn't see Blacky?" she asked.

"No."

Captain watched her attitude change. A changing 'tude, he mused.

"How about Tona? Where's Tona?" Penny gestured toward the sleeping area off in the shadows. Captain shrugged his shoulders.

Penny then stopped and stared at the heroin outfit on the end table. She seemed to blanch and then looked away. She kept looking away in a dreamy way, smoking, and didn't speak. Captain could see that she was loaded but trying to figure what was going on.

"Aren't you glad to see me? Your father tells me that you're my friend, that you like me, or something like that."

"My father—When did you—? Where is he?" she asked suddenly.

"Home with your mother. Where you're going to be."

Captain raised the potato gun out from under his jacket and holding it out prominently for Penny to see, fired twice into the face of the television set, shattering it.

"I don't want any bullshit, Penny. I'm not here to make friends. You're coming with me, or I'll leave you right where you sit, with a hole between your eyes. No one has seen me. I'm safe for the moment. I can kill you right here and now, and your tough friends will catch the blame, if you don't get buried out in the desert. I'm not shittin', Penny. You and I both know that your old man would be better off. Look at your arms. Have you looked at your arms lately? You're a fucking junkie, baby, a fucking junkie. And your old man thinks that he can fix you." Captain

244

laughed. "Shit, I could save you all—your whole family—years of pain, if I killed you right here."

He shot the box of cotton swabs off of the end table, and Penny jumped. He made an obvious move by aiming at the hypodermic syringe in the glass.

Pleading, Penny put her hands out and said, "No, no, I'll go. I'll go. But Captain, I'll come back. I'll come right back, and you won't—nobody will stop me."

"That's up to you, girl—and your people—but you're coming with me now or lay back for good."

Penny said, "Yes, yes, all right," and walked past Captain saying, "All right, my shoes. Just let me get my—"

Penny dove for the door. Anticipating the move and moving fast, Captain dropped the gun, lost the Stetson and leaped to catch her just as she hit the door and it flew open.

When the door opened, it was as though a vacuum had broken to the outside. The sound of music took over from the air conditioner.

Penny screamed, "Blackyyyyyy," and Captain pulled her back from the doorjamb by her hair. She continued to scream loudly. Holding her by the hair, he slapped her hard across the face with his open hand, but she didn't stop. Continuing to hold her hair and making a fist, Captain drove a hard punch into Penny's solar plexus.The yelling changed to a desperate moaning sound, a gasp for air. Penny fell to her knees in front of Captain. He let go of her hair and closed the door. The outside sounds stopped.

Putting her arms around Captain's legs, she hugged his knees. "Please, Captain, please. Don't make me go," she gasped. "They'll cold-turkey me. They'll lock me in my room and cold-turkey me. I'll die. My habit is bad, it's bad, Captain. Blacky says I shoot a hundred bucks a day. It'll kill me. God, Captain, don't you see, I don't want to get straight. I don't want to clean up. I'm fine, I'm fine. Please go and leave me alone."

"Your dad's going to have the doctor, his friend. He'll give you something."

"Bullshit, bullshit, bullshit," she screamed, "Blackyyy," and Captain pulled her hair until she stopped. When Penny calmed, he let go of her so that she could look up at him. Her tears ran with mascara to form black puddles in the corners of her eyes.

She spoke sheepishly. "Please, Captain, please don't make me go back. It's no big deal to you." Sitting up on her knees, Penny began to rub at the crotch of Captain's pants.

Don't do it, he thought. Don't do it, don't do it. But it felt good and he decided, just for a second then, just for a minute.

Penny spoke like a child, a sexy baby doll. "If you let me stay, I'll blow you real good, Captain. I'll let you fuck my young mouth and shoot it down my throat—all of it. I'll swallow it all."

Captain felt his penis stiffen while Penny unzipped his fly. Out away from the center of his brain the good guys screamed, Don't do it, Don't do it, Don't do it, but he decided that it was no big deal and to let her fuck around for a minute, just for a minute.

"Where did you learn to talk like that Penny?" he asked, feeling weak-kneed.

"I know what men like to hear. I know what I have that they want. They want to fuck my young mouth and hairy pussy. No man wants you when you're old."

Captain said, "That's bullshit. Someday you'll get your life in balance and you'll fall in love. You just have to give yourself—"

Penny reached aggressively into Captain's pants, grabbed his penis and pulled it out. He thought about pulling back but didn't move.

"Oh man, is that ever a big thick one. No wonder they call you—they should call you Admiral or General," she said laughing.

In a quick, unexpected move, Penny stopped talking and threw her mouth over the end of Captain's erect penis. She began moving her head up and down. Shit, fuck, he thought, Don't do it, don't do it, but he let her do it. Her wet mouth felt wonderful.

Captain struggled with a picture of Brad pacing the floor at home, waiting. He cursed himself for having no control over his cock. The same old story, he thought. Letting the little head think for the big one. Don't come, he thought. Don't come, don't come, don't come. If you don't come you can rationalize it. She even tried to blow me, but it was no big deal. I mean, I really didn't let her get into it. I didn't come or anything.

Captain watched the young girl slurp up and down over his stiff penis. He was going to make her stop. There was no question about it. He was going to make her stop, but he watched her carefully, storing up the picture that was before him for a later recall and masturbation. Decide now, he thought. Decide, decide, decide.

But Penny made the decision for him. She suddenly bolted from below him and dove for the potato gun on the chair. She made a successful grab and before he could get there, she turned the gun around on him. She got off two shots.

Thinking that he was hit, his stomach sank, but he continued the force of his move. Captain felt Penny's jaw break when his fist crashed into her face. She lay perfectly still where she fell. Goddamn, he thought, you really hit her hard. The doctor will be there, that's good. She'll end up in a hospital. It's a cinch. They'll detox her and fix her face. Maybe it's for the best. Sure it is. Captain felt relieved that there would be no more struggle. I'll probably have to carry her, he realized, but we'll make it. "We got to make it," he said, controlling a frantic feeling.

Then Captain felt the stickiness of blood between his neck and his shirt collar. He froze. "Maybe we aren't going anywhere," he said. A frightening thought came over him that Penny was

247

aiming the gun again, and he quickly moved to her and snatched it from her limp hand. He examined his hands. They were covered with blood, his blood.

"Now wait a minute. Where in the hell?" Stepping over Penny, he went into the small bathroom and turned on the light.

Captain had been shot once. It was both a relief and a laugh. One .22-caliber copper slug had passed through the top of his ear. He put his little finger against it from behind and saw his fingertip. On the sink next to a razor lay a broken piece of styptic pencil an inch long. Captain toweled the blood off of the side of his head and his neck and with a quick movement, wedged the styptic pencil into the hole in his ear. It stayed there, making him look like a cannibal with a bone through his ear. The bleeding stopped immediately. He waited for the sting, but it never came.

Heroin, he thought. I'm feeling no pain. Letting the styptic pencil stay in his ear, Captain put out the bathroom light and returned to Penny. He took a deep breath and said that he was glad to be alive. His penis was still half-hard but he tucked it away. Placing her on the couch, Captain bound Penny's wrists and put the gag close. Her jaw hung funny. Touching his ear, he felt a fool about her putting it over on him.

When he bound her ankles, when he arranged her legs to be tied, Penny's robe hiked up over her buttocks, and Captain saw her vaginal lips protruding from that mass of hair. They shined. They appeared purple colored and reflected the light. Bending over, he smelled them. The aroma made him shiver. He was hard again in his pants and said, "What the fuck, why not."

Captain turned the lamp toward Penny's vaginal area, brought his penis back out, leaned up close to her hairy bottom on one stiffened elbow against the couch and began to masturbate. He wanted to touch her, to separate and tongue her vagina, but he knew that he wouldn't do that. He would love to have stuck his penis into her, and he thought about it while he stared from three inches away and inhaled. He trembled and felt warm. He thought about it but to do it, to put it into her, to touch her, just to touch her while bringing himself off would be an attack. Something in him said, Go ahead on, she's out cold, but he shook his head and said no. Captain was adamant about it. Touching her would make him guilty of the grossest kind of assault.

When he climaxed, he wanted to pump his sperm onto her hairy rear end or her thighs. He thought about it and he had a wonderful orgasm, but he didn't do it. Shooting it onto her, he thought, touching her now would be rape. Thinking about what he could do, what he might have done but being very careful not to touch made the experience exciting. He ejaculated onto the floor.

Gagging her with the bikini underpants, Captain stood Penny up, wrapped her in the Indian serape from the chair and bent down to let her fall over his shoulder. With the oversized Stetson back on his head and the potato pistol held ready under his jacket, Captain left the trailer. Things outside were just as he'd left them. The loud music felt protective, insulative. The Dobermans walked next to him. Penny was not heavy, but with his shoulder in her stomach, she moaned with each step that he took.

Captain could see into the teeming dance floor through the two half-open doors at the rear of the club. No individual came into view, just a feeling of confusion. "Easy, boys," Captain said to the dogs. Captain walked past the darkened clump that lay next to the building obscured by shadows. When he saw his car he wanted to run for it, but he kept pace.

A group of laughing surfer types, boys and girls, passed next to him, and he gripped the pistol butt firmly. "Right on, man," one of them said. "Keep 'em in line," and the group enjoyed the joke. There were other people too, coming and going to and from their vehicles, but no one did more than glance at Captain and his bundle or take a second look.

Putting Penny onto her feet knocked the Stetson to the ground. Captain opened the driver's door of his car and using all his strength, eased her around the steering wheel and pushed her into the passenger side of the seat. She slumped onto the floor. Captain stole a quick glance around the area before getting into the car. He could see a group of people, probably a gang of the big men, coming in his direction fast, through the shadows that lay alongside the club.

Panicking, Captain dove into the car. He dropped the potato pistol onto the seat next to him, brought the keys from the floor, started the Dodge with a roar, cramped the wheel, put his foot on the gas and jerked his head to look for the men. A group of boys and girls, sharing a marijuana cigarette, came laughing and talking out of the darkness at the side of the nightclub. They moved into the light. There was no group of angry men. Captain breathed a sigh, said "Goddamn," and drove into the night.

Brad and Marilyn lived on the top floor of a modern, five-story, security apartment building in the city of Santa Monica, ten blocks away from the ocean. A salty, nighttime sea mist had begun to settle over the area, making things damp when Captain pulled up in front of the apartment house. He parked in the yellow zone and left the trunk of the car open as though on a delivery. With Penny conscious but over his shoulder again, Captain dropped the potato gun into a hedge along the sidewalk to retrieve later. He stood in front of the locked plate glass security door and buzzed Brad and Marilyn.

Suddenly Penny began to kick hard, using both legs together. Captain bit her on the buttocks until she stopped.

Brad responded immediately and buzzed them into the building. Captain passed no one on his way to the elevator, and they rode to the fifth floor alone. When he stepped off the elevator, Brad and Marilyn were there to meet him. Their apartment door stood open down the plushly carpeted, orange-colored hallway.

Dumping Penny into her anxious father's arms, Captain walked ahead of everyone into the apartment and up to the bar. The drapes were open across both ends of the modern apartment, and Captain thought that the view was spectacular. Being as elevated as they were, he thought he could see for miles in both directions.

"Where's the doctor?" Captain asked, making himself a drink of bourbon on the rocks.

"He'll be here. He'll be right along. He's at the hospital, but he promised—" Marilyn did the talking and ran along removing the gag from Penny's mouth while Brad whisked his daughter through the living room toward the rear of the apartment and a bedroom.

Bringing his drink, Captain went out onto the exterior balcony and looked over Santa Monica's residential district that lay lighted out before him. "Nice," he said. "Good air." He was thinking about how expensive it was to live in Santa Monica, when Brad came storming out into the living room, jerking his head around looking for him.

"I'm out here, Brad."

Brad was red-faced and trembling. "What the hell did you do to her?"

"I brought her home, Brad. She's alive. She'll be all right. She needs a doctor. That was your part—"

"He'll be here, he's on his way, but my God, Captain. It looks like her jaw, or skull, is fractured, and she's full of black and blue marks, and she's as good as naked."

"Big fucking deal, Brad. Big fucking deal. She's alive. She'll make it if you get the doctor."

251

"But you beat her up."

Brad moved toward Captain in a glassy-eyed, obsessive way, and Captain turned his ear out for the man to see. Brad got close and then stopped and stared.

"It's a bullet hole, Brad. It could just as well have been between my eyes."

Captain finished his drink and walked inside to the bar. "And where's the three grand?" Captain yelled over his shoulder. He let the feeling of smugness come. He imagined Brad behind him, his eyes flashing, thinking, but, but, but—Captain couldn't help but smile. He poured another drink and didn't move.

Finally, after a long pause, Captain turned around to face Brad, toasted him before he drank, looked him in the eye and said, "Well?"

Brad looked away and chewed the inside of his cheek. Captain finished the bourbon in one burning gulp and stepped quickly up to Brad. He spoke sarcastically. "Thank you for allowing me the privilege of returning your daughter to you, Brad. I loved it, every moment."

Brad looked at Captain, at his ear and then into his eyes. "Yeah, God, you brought her. You brought her home, thank God. I'm sorry, my good friend. Thank you, thank you very much."

Tears began to well up in Brad's weak eyes. Captain watched for a moment and when he could taste his own tears coming, he walked away. A feeling like pride came over him, and he had to catch his breath.

At the front door Captain turned back and said, "Good, I'm glad that you're pleased. Now go ahead, love her and take care of her. I'm exhausted. We'll talk tomorrow."

Captain had his hand on the large brass door knob when the sound of a loud commotion came from the back of the apartment where he knew Marilyn and Penny to be. This was followed immediately by the most anguished animal shrieks that Captain had ever heard from a human being. They were hoarse bleating screams that came over and over. The voice was Marilyn's, the cry seemed of disbelief, and Captain caught the message immediately.

He shook his head to try and clear it for another thought, but he was stuck with his instinct; there was nothing else. A chill ran up and down Captain's spine, and he knew down deep inside that Penny had jumped.

Captain heard himself moan, "Oh, God, no," almost involuntarily, and Brad appeared to actually turn white. Brad stood there immobile, his nose in the air like a springer spaniel, staring for Marilyn.

Marilyn came into the living room with her hand to her throat. Her eyes were bloodshot and roamed the room crazily. "She—she—" Marilyn gasped.

Neither of them seemed to know what to do. What is to do? Captain wondered. What the fuck is to do? He finished opening the front door and stepped away from it back into the room.

Brad and Marilyn ran together past him, out of the living room and down the orange hallway to the elevator. Brad said something, and they ran to the exit stairs at the end of the hallway. Marilyn began to sob. Her voice and the sounds of their footsteps disappeared as they descended the stairs. The exit door finally closed behind them.

In a state of shock, Captain stood perfectly still in the silence. "Goddamn," he said, stunned. Then he felt the chill again and tried to figure if there was any way that he was to blame. After thinking it all over, he guessed not, and the knot in his stomach loosened.

Grabbing the bourbon bottle and a glass along the way, Cap-

CAPTAIN BLOOD

tain opened the first door in the hallway off the living room. He knew it to be Marilyn's workroom, her studio. The room was dark. Snapping the light switch turned on six ceiling spot lights, the only lighting in the room. Illuminated, the room became stark white. Marilyn often hung interesting photographs around the room, but now the walls were bare. The ceiling, the walls and the carpeting were all white. The spots were aimed at a small, white, stagelike platform that stood ankle high in the front of the room. On it sat a white Naugahyde chair. The filing cabinets and dressing screen were painted white also. Captain blinked but still had trouble focusing his eyes. Turning on the light switch had brought an electric sounding hum from three silver umbrella flash lamps that stood around the stage. An expensive-looking camera sat on a tripod near the rear of the room. A small red light shone from its side.

Captain went to the camera and standing behind it, looked straight down into the view finder. The white Naugahyde chair was there to be seen in perfect focus, uniformly framed within four thin black lines. The whiteness of the chair blended perfectly into its surroundings to give Captain the impression that it was floating in air.

He imagined a model posing there in dark clothing, and how the finished photograph would make it appear that the model was sitting in nothingness. "A nice technique," he said.

A rickety card table and two chairs, spray-painted white, sat next to the camera. He sat down, poured a drink, leaned back on a flimsy chair, put his feet up onto the card table, drank the straight bourbon and listened to the screech of sirens from out in the streets, frantically trying to find the place.

Captain sat in that position for a long time, rocking, thinking and drinking. Finally the front door of the apartment slammed, and after a moment someone began to jump up and down, hard, onto the living room floor. Brad began to scream, "No, no, no, no," over and over again in a hysterical way as he jumped.

Captain envisioned the man hunched over, pounding up and down, pulling out his own hair. Making a megaphone out of his cupped hands, Captain yelled, "I'm in here. I'll go if you want or stay if you need me."

Brad stopped jumping and came marching fast into the all-white studio. He held his muscles taut, his arms bent out awkwardly from his sides like an ape. Without acknowledging Captain, Brad paced quickly across the front of the room, up onto the platform, turned and walked back out of the studio the way he had come. After tramping around the apartment, he came back again to repeat what he had done before exactly. Then he went away again to march around and come back a third time. To show respect, Captain put his feet on the floor and sat up straight.

Brad came and quietly sat down next to Captain in the other metal chair. He carefully lay his upper body down onto the card table and began to weep. It made Captain want to cry too, but he held back his tears and rubbed his friend's shoulders. Brad sobbed hysterically and said, "God in Heaven," meekly under his breath.

Captain let him cry and finally asked, "Where is Marilyn?"

Brad choked but he answered, "She went along. She won't—believe—that it's finished—dead."

"Is it Brad? Is it all over?"

"God, yes. She dove right into the concrete. Half her head is—Oh, holy Jesus—"

The Promise

aptain rubbed Brad's shoulders some more, but Brad suddenly sprang up and ran from the room. Before Captain could decide whether or not to follow him, Brad returned. He had a gun, a German Luger, in his hand. Captain felt his stomach sink when he saw it and when he saw Brad's dry-eyed, clenched-jaw expression.

Brad strutted purposefully back and forth across the front of the white room lifting the appropriate foot perfectly each time to make the step up onto the platform and again after turning, to step off. He walked back and forth, holding his skeleton rigid, the Luger beside his leg. Brad began to speak while he walked. Softly at first but soon loud enough to understand.

"We want to get them. We have to get them before they kill all of our kids." Brad stared directly in front of himself while he paced.

We? Captain thought. We've got to get them. Who is we,

256

Brad? he asked himself. Have you got a mouse in your pocket?

"Are you with me, Cap? Penny was your friend too."

"She was—yes, she sure was, Brad, and I feel terrible about it all. But what do you want to do? Who do you—?"

"We've got to get the fiends, the animals who sell the dope to the kids, Cappy."

Brad stopped in the middle of the small stage and sat in the white Naugahyde chair. Using the gun to gesticulate, Brad leaned forward into the light and with a strained fanatical expression in his eyes, implored, "Don't we? We have to get the fiends."

Before he could answer, Captain watched Brad get a new idea. It sat him back in the chair to conjure. He seemed to grow peaceful. Watching Brad's eyes, the quiet insanity that they held, brought to Captain a creeping feeling of fear. Captain watched a weird glint come into Brad's eyes as the man, choosing his words carefully, began to rock slowly on the Naugahyde chair and to speak. "No, no—I'm wrong. That's not the thing to do at all. No, I'm dead wrong."

Brad laughed for an instant in what Captain thought to be a silly, immature way. The small stage creaked under the chair. "No, we won't. But you'll do it, my good friend. You'll get the one—the one head guy who's to blame. You'll get him for me—for Penny, won't you? Just say yes and promise me, please."

Oh, shit, Captain thought. Now what the fuck.

Brad became enthusiastic. "That's it. Do it for me, Cap, for me and for Penny. For all the poor sick Pennys and their ruined lives and families. I mean, it's just, Cappy. There is nothing more just. Get the kingpin dope boss who sells the dope to the kids, the president of the dopers, the top dope, the top one." Brad blurted out a crazy-sounding laugh and continued. "Can you? Will you do it, do this good thing?"

"Listen, Brad, I know how you feel. But the mobs run the dope deals in this country. I don't even know if there is one main guy, a boss. Why don't we—?"

"No, no. It's a business. It's a big business. Sure, killing our kids is big business. But there's a boss, there's a top dog."

Brad then screamed, "And I want the dirty bastard. God wants him. He has to want him." Brad broke into fitful tears again. His shoulders shook. "Please, Cappy, please. Do it for me, please."

The pressure made Captain feel tense. "Aw, shit, Brad. Let's not talk any more. Let's wait for—"

"No, no," Brad said, pointing the Luger at Captain. "No, don't wait. Do it for me, Cap. It's life or death."

Captain wasn't sure just what that meant, but looking into the Luger's long black barrel gave him some ideas. Jesus, he thought, get the fuck out of here.

"Do it for me. Get him, get him. Get the guy who kills the kids."

"Okay, Brad, sure." Captain said, placatingly. "Sure, I'll try to find the top guy. I suppose I can—"

"No, I can see that you don't mean it. I want you to mean it. I want you to promise. I'm going to hold you to it. I will, I will. Now promise me." Brad was excited. "Promise me, say you promise."

What the fuck, Captain thought, go ahead and promise. You can work around it when the man is sane.

"All right, Brad, I promise."

"You do? You do?" Brad said with glee, "On our friendship, promise on our friendship."

Captain didn't want to do that, but he said, "All right."

Brad pointed the gun at him and demanded, "Louder, louder. On our friendship, say it."

"Shit, fuck, all right, Brad. On our friendship, I'll try to find the top guy."

Brad then stopped his agitated movements and stared hard into Captain's eyes. He sat back into the white Naugahyde chair. He spoke in a monotone. "I am holding you to it, Captain—on our friendship."

Brad then turned the Luger in toward his own face, put the long black barrel into his mouth and blew the back of his head off onto the stark white wall behind him.

The Luger fell away. Brad's body, quivering fiercely, slumped into the white Naugahyde chair. With his ears ringing, Captain forced himself to turn away. The smell of burned gunpowder filled the room. Sensing motion on the stage, Captain turned back to watch Brad's body jerk violently forward and nearly come off of the chair. Captain's eye was drawn to the bright red blood that seemed to be splashed everywhere onto that severe white setting. After teetering on the chair's edge, Brad settled back down as before. His arms fell onto the arms of the chair and lay there perfectly. What remained of his head slumped over to his left side.

Overcome with nausea, Captain had to stand. He sprang up, and the chair fell away behind him. His head began to spin with such a strong internal centrifugal force that his body was pulled into the motion. His body twisted into gyrating undulations that moved him around and around and made him feel violently dizzy. I'm doing the hula, he thought, feeling giddy. I'm a hula dancer. When he went down, he took the flimsy white card table and remaining chair with him.

Rolling with the fall and remaining conscious, he continued the motion and raised up to kneel on all fours. He let his tongue hang out and breathed deeply. He stared down into the tightly knit white carpet and experienced the feeling of intense depression that came over him. It made him catch his breath and grit his teeth. Captain emitted a funny sounding squeal and then spoke to himself.

"Captain—Captain, you're okay. You're okay. You're coming down off the junk—and Brad—and Penny—these deaths. But you're okay. Don't be afraid. Stop it, you have nothing to fear. You feel the deaths and the dope. Come on now, get up. It will pass. Get up. Come on, you sucker, get up. Have a drink, a good one—move."

Putting one of the chairs back in place, Captain retrieved the bottle of bourbon and the glass from the carpet. He poured himself most of a glass of the whiskey, sat down and let the bottle slide to the floor. A white telephone on a corner shelf rang for a long time. Captain ignored it and wouldn't look toward Brad. He emptied the glass and concentrated on his burning esophagus.

He stood and after wandering for a minute, found himself standing in front of Brad. Taking a deep breath, Captain looked at him. It was a grisly sight that made him want to turn away, but he continued to stare. The top and back of Brad's head were gone. His face was contorted. Blood ran freely from his ears, nose and mouth. One eyeball had been popped by the concussion and hung by its muscles and cord against the middle of Brad's cheek. The other eye lay closed.

The umbrella klieg lights hummed above him. Captain walked to the rear of the room and looked into the camera's view finder to observe a perfect image of Brad. There was no sane reason, merely the urge, and Captain took the picture. The room exploded with reflective light and for a moment made the bloodied whiteness crisp and clean again. The flash made Brad disappear.

The camera's film feed was automatic. Captain shot the entire roll of film, letting the bright explosive lighting temporarily blind him each time. The red light finally went out. As he turned to move away, on second thought he stopped, removed the exposed roll of film from the camera and put it into his jacket pocket.

Captain stood in front of Brad's body again. He had to look

twice, straining, and was stunned to see movement in the black
pupil of Brad's disgorged eyeball. Reaching out, Captain picked
the eyeball up and stepped in for a closer look. There was movement, but it was himself, his own reflection. The eyeball felt dry.
He let it go and stood erect.

"Goddamn," he said slowly. He said it over and over again,
shaking his head in disbelief.

Running to the master bedroom, Captain pulled the bedding
apart and bringing a large blue sheet back with him, covered Brad
where he sat. He used the telephone on the bar in the living room
and called all of the authorities: fire, police, ambulance, county
sheriff, the paramedics and the California Highway Patrol. He
pulled an overstuffed arm chair against the front door to keep it
open, and with the hair bristling on the nape of his neck, he fled
the place.

When he got back to his apartment, Captain found himself
wandering around looking out the windows at the night, poking
about in the refrigerator, washing his hands in the kitchen and the
bathroom and then in the kitchen again, talking nonsense to himself and not thinking about any of it. Finally he stopped what he
was doing and said, "Shit, man, you are totally exhausted, in
shock. Go to bed. Quit fucking around and get down." He swallowed a Quaalude, took a hot shower, saw that his ear was healing
fine and crawled into his clean bed. Captain customarily thanked
God for the day and said a blessing for Brad's soul.

The promise that he had made his dead friend came into his
mind again. Thinking about it, the magnitude of what he had
promised made him wide awake and angry. "Fuck it," he said
finally. "I won't do it. I just won't do it, that's all. Who the hell
will know? Jesus Christ, Brad, I'd have to be crazy—" Saying it
brought relief and with the Quaalude in effect he fell soundly
asleep.

Captain was awakened once by the sound of windowpanes

rattling. A breeze, he thought, a nice breeze. Opening the windows the rest of the way, he took the opportunity to urinate before going back to bed. He lay awake for just a moment, languishing in the flow of air. "Santa Anna," ne said, "beautiful Santa Anna breeze."

Upon arising, Captain made himself a cup of strong instant coffee. Looking out of the third-story apartment window, he juxtaposed, as he often did, the distant Hollywood foothills and the city's northern morning skyline. This he did to examine the air. The quality of the air often played an important role on his disposition for that day. He had been correct during the night. A breeze had been blowing, and the morning air was clean. Not perfectly clean, but relatively clean compared to most days.

He drank his coffee in resignation, knowing that this country and probably the world, in any kind of unspoiled sense, was gone. "Cock suckers," he said, and then he thought about Montecito's natural beauty and about Iris. He thought about how she loved to suck him, and he masturbated in front of the hallway mirror. Afterward, he slumped into the davenport, prayed for knowledge of God's will and tried to forget about Brad and to give his day some order.

With his coffee in his hand and wearing shorts only, Captain walked the halls of the apartment house from top to bottom, picking up junk and making the place look neat. Out into the morning, he walked around the building, through the garage, checked the elevator, hosed down the front steps and ended up sitting in his garden to read the morning paper and admire the new blossoms on his flowers.

The newspaper carried no news of anything Captain had been involved in on the previous day. He figured that Blacky would merely bury the fatso cow man in the desert and forget it. Chalk it up to a crazy, a bad dope deal, whatever. He figured also that the morning paper was on the streets before Brad's tragedy had been reported.

Back inside his apartment, Captain straightened up the place, returned phone calls, called the carpet man to repair the worn hallway carpet, made up rent receipts and a bank deposit, wrote some checks, spoke with the lawyer who owned the building, said yes to good Ram season football tickets and had a large breakfast.

It was a leisurely yet constructive morning. The kind of morning that usually made him feel a success and competent. But this day he didn't feel either of those things. As the busy work was concluded, as his mind was freed up from what he was putting in front of it, when he allowed himself to think, the tapes began to play in his brain again.

I've been down this road, he told himself. Don't think about it. The man is dead. No one is to know. You are not going to do it, that's final. But the bullies ran the tapes louder than he could his rationalizations. You promised your friend, you no good fucking chicken shit welcher. 'Fraidy cat, 'fraidy cat, 'fraidy cat, pussy, pussy, pipsqueak, 'fraidy cat.

Feeling feverish and with his stomach grinding, Captain called Marilyn. The phone rang, and he thought about all that she had been through. He concentrated on Marilyn's plight to quell the voices in his head. Her relatives answered and said that Marilyn had been sedated and taken to the hospital by the family doctor. He finally showed up, Captain thought.

And he remembered his father, how conscientious a doctor he had been. Doctor Blood never would have allowed such a thoughtless thing to have occurred. He'd have seen the contingencies beforehand and been prepared for them. But he cared about people, Captain remembered. He had understood, in the most fundamental sense, right from wrong.

After hanging up the phone, Captain thought about the doctor being late; that he had to squeeze in one more call before he could go to help Penny. Captain shook his head in frustration and said, "Money talks and bullshit walks, that's all that motivates them. Shit, what a shame."

An ice cold, long-necked, brown-bottled Budweiser eased the constriction in his stomach, but the voices in his mind, his conscience, screamed of the promise louder than ever. Moving quickly, thinking, I'll fix you, Captain reached a bottle of bonded bourbon from a kitchen shelf, poured himself half a glass, put it to his lips and held it there. He didn't drink it and finally put the glass down hard onto the counter top.

"Shit, fuck. Well, who the hell is it, God? Who sells the dope to the kids? Who is the top guy? Come on, Brad, give me some fucking direction."

Captain went to the davenport and lay down. "Make me a channel, God. Come on, Brad, show me." His mind cleared and he thanked them both for that. He closed his eyes and meditated. He concentrated on the white light. He felt at peace. Soon the images came. He let them sort themselves out before him. The show had no ending, but when he'd played the part that existed several times, when he finally got the picture, he sat up and rubbed his eyes knowing exactly what he was going to do, or at least exactly how he was going to begin to do it.

Dressing in jeans, sneakers and a short-sleeved Hawaiian print shirt, Captain went to his basement workroom and tucked a small, .32-caliber, snub-nosed Colt revolver under his shirt into the waistband of his jeans. He wore a good pair of dark glasses, drove the Jensen and headed back out to Blacky's roadhouse. Blacky's was a cassette and a half away. He listened to "The Best of Bread" and sang along, harmonizing.

A few large bearded men were in evidence wandering around

the outside of the red, barnlike club, picking up litter, drinking beer and talking. Captain parked on the opposite side of the building from where he had dragged Penny the night before. There was nothing out on that far side of the club but two outhouses with quarter moons cut over their doors and flat land for as far as he could see.

The sun shone clear and hot. The air was dry. The wind was still, but delicate puffs of dust jumped up off of the ground seemingly of their own volition to swirl around Captain's legs as he walked. The juke box played country music.

The large room was dark and cool. A small group of people were seated at the bar. Another group sat back by the stage with their feet up, watching an old Tom Mix Western movie. A noisy projector clicked the picture onto a portable screen. Captain bought a beer.

The Vendetta

Blacky was not hard to find. He squatted his large head and shoulders into the works of an opened pinball machine. Captain could see no one pay him any special attention as he leaned onto the glass top of the machine. He drummed his fingers against the glass.

"Yeah?" came Blacky's voice from inside.

Captain leaned close to Blacky's shoulder and spoke into the opened machine.

"Blacky, I want you to get this straight the first time, or you'll end your life looking at the innards of a pinball machine."

Captain watched Blacky's beefy body stiffen and then, "I ain't moving. I'm listening," came from inside the machine.

"Blacky, I want you to know that I know bullshit when I hear it; so I expect you to tell me the truth the first time when I ask you this. Otherwise you go the way the flat slob out in the yard went

266

last night. The fact is that I already know the answer to my question, I just need a little confirmation. So don't lie, or you die right here. And, Blacky, I'm not shitting. Now are you going to tell me the truth when I ask you my question?''

"You better believe it," came the reply without hesitation.

Captain could smell Blacky's strong perspiration. When the angle was right it came up to burn the inside of his nostrils. Goddamn, he thought, and women sleep with the pig. But maybe they have no choice. Or maybe they smell bad too. Fuck 'em, he thought, the slobs.

"A lot of dope—smack—comes through here, Blacky. Where does it come from?"

"Mexico," came the answer fast.

"Thank you. Now the big one, Blacky, the one your life is riding on." Captain drummed the glass top of the pinball machine hard. "Who's the man, Blacky? Who is the top smack man?"

"I don't know any guy past my guy, and that's no shit, honest to God—I swear it."

"So who is your guy?"

"Snitches get killed. You're not gonna say where—"

"No, I'm not. Now give or I'll kill you myself, right now."

"Wallman—Wallman—Rick Wallman. You know Rick's Surfboards in Malibu? He's my contact."

"For everything?"

"Yeah. Well, no, not grass. We grow most of that ourselves. The best is right here in the valley, but the hard stuff all comes from Rick. God, man, I don't know who you are, but don't ever tell—"

"Shut up, Blacky." Blacky quieted immediately. "Now, Blacky, I want you to come out of there and walk me out to my car to see me off. Come on out, and act like we're old friends."

Blacky said, "Now?" and when Captain answered yes, the bearded man came out from under the machine.

Blacky laughed and pretended friendship but looked immediately at Captain's empty hands. The big man sweated profusely. His hair was matted against his forehead and his beard was soaked. Captain laughed, said, "Come on," and motioned toward the door with his head. Blacky walked along next to him.

Captain could feel the man's brain working. Blacky turned and looked him over, and Captain could see the nervous temptation in his eyes. When they got to the door Captain slapped him on his bullish back and said, "Go ahead, Blacky—after you."

Blacky held open one swinging saloon door and stopped. He looked back into the room. Captain put the palm of his right hand over the pistol butt in his belt and rubbed it gently. Blacky stared at what Captain was doing and bolted awkwardly the rest of the way out the door. The big slob, Captain thought, watching Blacky's fatty thigh tissue jiggle.

When they arrived around the side of the building, Captain said, "Go to the closest john."

Blacky cast a helpless look around the yard and spoke in a frightened tone. "But why? I—"

"I've got to piss, that's why. Go on."

Captain looked behind them. No one was there to see them enter. He made Blacky sit down over the smelly open hole that was the toilet. Captain brought out the Colt .32, pushed it into Blacky's fat stomach, pointed it downward and gut-shot him twice. The explosions weren't much, and Blacky didn't die. The smell of fresh excrement filled the small enclosure.

Blacky tried to stand and opened his mouth as though to bellow. Captain rammed the snub-nosed pistol up under Blacky's loosely fatted chin, slammed his mouth shut firmly and shot him once through the throat and head. Blacky fell back onto the toilet board with a loud guttural sigh. His eyes glazed.

Captain put the gun away and peered through the toilet's quarter-moon air vent into the yard. The Jensen sat alone in the sun. There was no one. Captain walked slowly to the car, cleared his lungs of the terrible stench and headed for Malibu.

Feeling hungry and having a certain outdoor restaurant along the way in mind, Captain chose Topanga Canyon for the cross-over drive to the ocean. Once at the water he would have to go back up north again to Malibu, but the thought of a good lunch beside Topango Creek made the extra drive seem worth it.

Into the canyon, he prided himself for having made the right decision. The air became balmy and sweet smelling from the wetness and abundant vegetation. The sunny sky was cloudless. "What a gorgeous ass day to be out," he said.

He ate outside on the restaurant's patio and drank a pitcher of beer. A blonde hippy girl, appearing ragged and forlorn, came by and offered to lay him for lunch. Captain said no but gave her a five-dollar bill. The girl wandered away without eating.

Iris's beach house was close to Rick's surfing shop, but Captain decided not to stop. He had a vision of her meditating and being kind to herself. He saw her also with a full face of beauty cream, the scent of which he hated. Let her be, he thought, and take care of biz. Then we'll be anxious to see each other. It will be more fun for Montecito.

Rick Wallman was out in the ocean demonstrating a new surfboard when Captain arrived. Captain crossed the coast highway and walked down onto the sand to watch. The Pacific sea breeze was invigorating. The salt air and hot sun seemed an astringent on his skin.

Captain had been told that Rick would be wearing a red upper body wet suit. He was and was easily distinguishable a hundred

269

yards out to sea waiting for a breaker. Rick's red wet suit stood out among the other bare-topped, black-suited surfers who sat astride their boards around him. Captain thought the tide appeared calm.

Captain walked up onto the Malibu pier above the beach and into Alice's Restaurant. A seat at the bar afforded a perfect view of the man in red patiently waiting for a wave in the ocean below.

Drinking vodka and Perrier water, Captain watched Rick Wallman make the most of two mediocre waves before coming up onto the sand to beach his board. The other surfers followed Rick's example and gathered around the stacked boards to hear him talk. Captain finished his drink and went down to the beach to join the group and listen.

Rick Wallman was slightly built and dark. He was aggressive. Probably loaded on coke, Captain thought. The hard sell, hyperactive type. When Rick finished his pitch, he headed for the stairs up from the beach to the coast highway. Captain stepped in alongside of him to walk with him, step for step, in the soft sand.

Immediately aware of Captain's presence, Rick moved away and looked at him with a wrinkled brow as if to say, Don't walk so close to me, get away, get away from me, shoo. Captain opened his shirt until Rick could see the hatched fiberglass butt of the Colt .32 hidden in the waistband of his jeans.

"What the fuck—?" Rick said, playing the bad guy.

"Leave the board here, Rick, and walk up the beach with me. I've got something for you."

Rick's color seemed to pale. He looked around and his muscles tensed. He appeared ready to bolt.

"I've got a pocket full of money, Rick," Captain said quickly. "I want to give it to you. Blacky sent me."

Relieved, Rick quickly assumed his hot-shot attitude again. "Come on over to the shop," Rick said, heading for the beach stairs.

270

"No way, man," Captain said, trying to sound tough. "There're too many people. I've got twenty grand, man."

"In your pocket?"

"Yeah, in a belt in my pants, in hundreds. Come on, walk up the beach for a minute. It's beautiful for a walk. We'll only be a minute. I don't get to come out this way, come on."

Dropping the board, Rick walked with Captain north on the beach for a short distance. Then he stopped abruptly and said, "Wait a minute, man, wait a minute. What am I doing? I don't know you. I'm not going. I'm going back up to the shop and call Blacky and see what the fuck we've got here. I don't know you. I must be stupid." Rick turned and hurriedly began walking away back down the beach.

"Rick—Rick, wait a minute, man. Wait." Captain called. "I'm not supposed to do any business. I'm not supposed to bring anything back. No trade is supposed to happen. There's no room for a hassle. I'm just giving, that's all, not taking back. I'm dropping twenty K on you, and then we'll go back. I leave, and you call Blacky and make the arrangements. I'm not taking anything back. I'm just a delivery boy."

Rick stopped and thought about it. "You're just giving, not taking?" he asked.

"Right. I'm just supposed to give you the bread and split, that's it. But I don't get to come out here—"

"Okay, sure, okay. Why didn't you say all that in front. Where?"

"Let's walk up to the creek and go up to the tunnel. No one can see us in there, not even with a long lens."

The idea of a telescopic lens caused Rick to look around nervously. Then he nodded and led the way up the beach.

After a two-minute walk north they turned right and crossed up the beach toward the concrete tunnel that allowed Malibu Creek to run under Pacific Coast Highway to the ocean. They walked on

271

the firm wet sand of the shallow creek bed and ended up jumping over to a sandy delta that became a flat islet just inside the gray shadowy underpass. The shallow stream ran past them on both sides.

Green slime hung off of the damp cement walls and covered the rocks. Rusted beer cans were strewn about. The sunny day looked warm and inviting outside at either end, and automobile traffic passed overhead.

Looking both ways in an obvious gesture to demonstrate that they were alone, Rick put his hand out and said, "Okay, so give." His voice echoed in the dark place.

Captain brought the snub-nosed Colt out and put the muzzle against Rick's hairy chest where it showed between the opened zipper of his red wet suit. "I want you to tell me where you buy your narcotics—the hard stuff," Captain said easily.

Acting astounded, Rick stepped back and with a nasty smirk said, "You've got to be fucking kidding."

Captain fired once at Rick's left shoulder. The shot resounded from the heavy walls and made Captain's ears ring. The force of the blast spun Rick around and threw him face first up against the closest concrete wall. His legs lay across the stream.

Moving quickly, Captain jumped over the water and turned the man over to face up from the sand. As he rolled over, Rick Wallman let out a long, sad cry that made Captain, for just an instant, want to feel sorry for him.

Putting the short barrel of the pistol against Rick's forehead, Captain said, "Tell me where your heroin comes from—your source. I won't hear any bullshit, man."

Rick drew his knees up against his stomach and began to sob. He held his shoulder with his right hand. "I'm—I'm bleeding to death. I'm bleeding."

Captain pushed the pistol's barrel hard against Rick's forehead and cocked the hammer loudly. "The name . . . man."

Rick's eyelids fluttered in an uncontrolled way and he answered with a sob, "Hector . . . I get from Hector."

Captain stared into Rick's eyes and let him know that he wanted the rest. "At the station—National Gas Station—12th and Wilshire . . . Santa Monica . . . Hector's National Station . . ."

Captain thought about the location. He knew the station. He asked, "Hector owns the gas station on 12th and Wilshire and deals heroin from there . . .?"

"Yes . . . yes . . . lots . . ." came the now cowering reply.

"Lots of heroin?" Captain asked.

Rick didn't speak but looked up into Captain's face with wide frightened eyes and moved his head to indicate yes.

Captain said, "I believe you," and pulled the pistol's trigger, sending the surfer's brains into the cool Malibu Creek bed below.

On the way back into the city to his apartment, Captain stopped at the National gas station situated at 12th and Wilshire Boulevard in the city of Santa Monica. He had the gas tank filled and got out to stretch his legs. There was nothing unusual that struck him about the place. It was a busy gas station employing several energetic young men, mostly pony-tailed long hairs in grey working clothes. Mechanical repairs were being done in the indoor garage area off to one side where two vehicles sat high above the ground on hydraulic lifts.

The facility sat on the southeast corner of the intersection with a clean looking market and liquor store across the street to the north. A beauty parlor situated kitty corner, started a small shopping area that ran west for the entire block. There were small single-story businesses that ran up and down Wilshire for as far as he could see. A beautifully kept funeral home covered with greenery, sat across 12th Street to the west.

The afternoon sun reflected brightly off of the Pacific Ocean twelve blocks to the west down Wilshire Boulevard where the city of Santa Monica met the sea. Captain walked back to the car. He looked around again and decided that he liked the feeling of the neighborhood. It seemed tidy and the air was good.

He said that he wanted to pay for the gas purchase by personal check, which the attendant refused. Captain then asked to see Hector.

"Hector works nights," was the reply. "Six to twelve o'clock."

"Is he the boss?" Captain asked.

"He sure is," came the respectful answer.

Captain then found the cash, paid the attendant and headed for home.

Rush hour traffic was still an hour away so Captain made his way over to Sunset Boulevard for the drive into town. He drove leisurely, enjoying the sun on his shoulders. While stopped for a red light at the UCLA intersection, a group of students crossed Sunset Boulevard in front of him. Watching them hurry, the intent expression on their faces, feeling their spirit, brought a sudden rush of enthusiasm to Captain and made him smile.

A pretty-featured petite blonde girl, a genuine blonde, dressed in a too short, pleated brown plaid skirt, dark brown summer sweater, white stockings and Oxfords, crossed last, alone. She carried one large bookbag. A closer look showed her to appear a chronic blusher with soft blonde down over her blemished cheeks. An attempt had been made to cover the acne with makeup but the girl's radiant blush came through to give her cheeks a not-unattractive, scrubbed-looking crimson glow.

Captain was sure that she had green eyes, slanted, with long, dark, protective lashes. He wanted the girl to be Charlotte Tully from his high school days, but he knew that was silly. He pretended that she was Charlotte anyway, and it felt tingly and nice in his loins.

Captain laughed as he thought about the unfortunate circumstances that soft, fair, blushing Charlotte used to invariably find herself in. The girl was a delicate, green-eyed, natural blonde with a perfect mouth and sensual figure. But her complexion was a constant problem, and she was forever being asked to participate in front of the class when her skin was at its worst. Charlotte would stammer, turn her green eyes downward and stand trembling in front of the group, her pretty, broken-out face gorged with blood. Captain had fantasized time and again how Charlotte might blush and stammer at the sight of his stiff penis. But he had been much too shy in those days to do anything about it. "Goddamn, what a thought," he said to himself, feeling lightheaded and laughing.

Captain asked the girl in the crosswalk to come along, and while she hesitated there in front of him, blushing profusely, the light changed and the person in the car behind Captain blared long and hard on a loud horn. Startled, the timid blonde creature ran away.

Captain said, "But—" and found himself involuntarily reaching his arms out after her. The horn blew again loudly. Captain slammed the Jensen into park, jumped out and ran quickly back to the driver of the large, four-door black Oldsmobile that was inching up behind the Jensen. The other traffic began to go around them.

"Come on, come on, goddammit," demanded the small, mostly bald man who sat slouched behind the Oldsmobile's steering wheel, a lighted cigar clenched between his teeth.

Reaching into the car, Captain snatched the smoking cigar out of the man's mouth and ground it out against his jowl. The man grasped the steering wheel tightly with both hands and screamed, "Ow, ow, ow," in quick staccato outbursts. The cigar broke apart and scattered.

A greasy looking woman in the passenger seat sat still in her paunch, a dumbfounded, open-mouthed expression on her face. A little dog yapped excitedly and ran back and forth across the Oldsmobile's rear seat.

Captain returned to his car and drove away but turned and came back to the scene to hunt for the girl. He passed the black Oldsmobile on his way back. It moved along too slowly. Captain thought that the Oldsmobile seemed to limp along.

He scoured the closest Marymount and UCLA parking lots. There were other females, but the delicate, insecure-appearing little blonde had vanished.

Captain stopped for an aged New York steak, fresh vegetables, red tomatoes, a chunk of Roquefort cheese and a bottle of good red wine. At home, he messed around in the garden for a while and washed both of the cars, one at a time, at the curb in front of the building.

The six o'clock television news carried the story of Penny's death leap and Brad's suicide. Nothing was mentioned about Blacky or the cow man. There was nothing on Rick Wallman either, which led Captain to believe that Blacky and the surfer heroin dealer had not yet been found.

Sipping a dry Beefeater martini with his feet up, Captain looked at the ceiling of his apartment, let his vision blur and with a decent evening breeze coming in over him, daydreamed about the police. Shit, he thought finally, I'll bet that they won't even try to solve them. I'll bet a hundred people wanted them dead, probably the cops too. "It's a lead pipe cinch," he said, "that we're all better off. It's the right thing."

With the telephone turned off and the curtains drawn, Captain had dinner, drank the good wine and watched a special on public television about a unique species of butterfly. The piece had been filmed in the Congo and told the story of the African Monarch.

Rare footage was shown of the maiden flight of one of these exotic insects with a wing span of nearly three feet. Captain was captivated by the subject and thought that the African Monarch was beautiful beyond imagination.

He said, "Wow," over and over and thought that he would give almost anything to see an African Monarch fly or even better to touch, ever so gently, one of its transparent golden wings. He felt depressed when the film ended but pushed through it to envision again the Monarch's flight, shook his head and said, "Goddamn, what wonderful creatures."

Then he had a sudden chill when he realized that any smart cop might be able to put the right pieces together when these particular dope dealers turned up dead. It came to him in a flash that the police probably knew precisely who dealt the narcotics in Los Angeles and that they might easily be one step ahead of him if they read the progression right.

Shit, he thought, a clever dick will probably know right off where I'll be next. "Fuck," he said loudly. "Now what, Brad?" Captain paced the apartment only once before the answer came and it seemed unequivocal. "Move," came out of his mouth, loud and clear.

Not sure about the number of employees he would find at the station, but remembering the seemingly innocent young fellow who had sold him the gas, Captain brought three pairs of handcuffs, clean of fingerprints, in a cloth shoe bag. Wearing one rubber surgical glove on his left hand, he brought along Speed's copy of the Savage .22-caliber automatic without the potato silencer. He knew that even if caught flat-footed, Speed's gun would show different ballistics than the slugs from his own gun. What's done is probably done, he thought. Nobody will ever have to pay for Blacky or Rick.

He thought about where his dirty Savage potato gun, the dirty

Colt .32 and his other super private things were hidden. His secret place under the basement floor, behind the apartment furnaces, was on his mind and he smiled, convinced that the spot would remain safe forever, or until the building came down and might even sustain that.

He wore his yellow nylon G.O.B. hat, dark glasses, a lightweight jacket and drove the Dodge. The large full moon to the east looked glamorous exsectioned by three wispy thin black cumulous clouds.

The Santa Monica night air was cool. Twelve blocks down Wilshire Boulevard, the ocean shone yellow from the moon. With the exception of the liquor store across the street, the business around Hector's station appeared closed for the night. The red, white and blue National Gasoline station had lots of lights but no customers. Captain could see no one in or around the station. The area was quiet. He drove around the block and finally spotted one lone gas attendant leaning back in an aluminum chair against the front of the station reading *Hustler* magazine.

Parking up the block on Twelfth Street, Captain strolled up to the station from its blind side and looked in. The gas attendant seemed to be alone. Shit, Captain thought, I missed him. In the dark, Captain picked his way over and through the junk behind the station to arrive in back of the windowed garage area. One vehicle, a pickup truck, sat high atop a hoist. The entire area had recently been cleaned. The concrete and blacktop were wet from hosing.

A telephone rang once and was quickly answered by a muffled voice coming from above the interior back wall of the garage, behind a row of tires. Closer inspection showed a greasy wooden stairway that ran parallel with and against the rear wall. Nothing mysterious, he thought. The stairway leads to an upstairs office and probably Hector.

Captain returned to the Dodge and being careful to handle them with his gloved hand only, put two pairs of handcuffs into the pocket of his jacket. Speed's Savage .22 went under his waist band and he headed back up the block to the station.

Watching his own reflection in the windows as he approached the sitting attendant, Captain pulled the visor of his yellow G.O.B. hat down to rest against the top of his dark aviator glasses. He turned and scanned Wilshire Boulevard and the liquor store once more.

Satisfied with the area's inactivity, he put the Savage automatic against his thigh and moved quickly up to the station attendant who let his chair come down on all four legs and asked, "Help you?"

Captain showed him the blue steel pistol and spoke in a gruff whisper, "Look the other way," which the boy did without hesitation.

"Is Hector here?"

"Yes." The boy spoke away.

"Is he alone?"

"Yes."

"Is the men's room open?"

"No."

"Ladies'?"

"Yes . . . Ladies' room is, yes."

"Don't look at me but get up and go there fast . . . right now."

The boy dropped the magazine and moved faster than Captain had expected. They got there immediately.

"Don't shoot me . . . You're not going to shoot me, are you . . .?" The boy cowered and held his arm up to protect his face.

"Look away—not if you keep your mouth shut . . . If you make any noise . . . if you yell, I'll come and put a slug in your mouth."

"Don't worry . . . don't worry . . . Do you want the keys to the cash box?"

"No . . . Just sit down and shut up."

Being careful to use his gloved hand, Captain handcuffed the boy to the plumbing underneath the ladies' room sink. He locked the toilet room door behind him.

Hector was alone and on the telephone. He didn't seem the least bit afraid of Captain's gun; respectful, but not afraid. He was a tall, lanky, straight-haired blond man who wore street clothes with a Western flair. Captain admired the workmanship that went ino Hector's hand-tooled Western boots.

With his eyes not leaving Captain, Hector hung up the phone with an abrupt, "Gotta go." He withdrew his boots from the desk top, turned in his noisy chair toward Captain and sat back with a loud creak.

Acting casual, Hector said, "Okay—Okay . . . you got the gun, you'll have the bucks—No trouble here—" He spoke in a thick Southern drawl. Hector picked up a pack of Camels and put a cigarette directly into his mouth from the pack. He talked from the side of his mouth.

"Listen partner . . . I ain't aiming to hassle you . . . What do you need—how much—make it reasonable and . . . hell . . . I'll give it to ya . . . I don't want no trouble here—You want a smoke . . . ?"

Captain pulled the cigarette out of Hector's mouth, leaving white paper stuck to the man's lower lip.

"Downstairs," Captain said easily.

With a shrug of his bony shoulders Hector got up and proceeded down the wooden stairs to the garage.

"Wait," Captain said and gestured Hector to move under the raised hydraulic hoist which held the pickup truck aloft. "Put your arms around the shaft," Captain said, pointing to the rack's polished steel piston that glistened brown with oil and grease.

"My arms around . . . Oh man . . . it's filthy . . . I'll give you the fucking money, man . . . This shirt cost me seventy bucks."

Hector talked to Captain but his attention was drawn past Captain, out the garage's windowed area down the block to the west. Looking for help, Captain figured, and he turned to quickly see for himself what was out there. There was nothing but the darkened mortuary across the street and the black Santa Monica night.

Captain shoved the muzzle of the automatic into Hector's neck. The gangly Southerner reluctantly stepped under the truck to the piston and tried to be delicate in putting his long arms around the greasy steel thing. Producing the handcuffs, Captain locked the man's arms into place around the cylinder. Captain reached up near the top of the piston, snatched the safety hitch off and stepped back out from under the heavy machinery.

Hector's attitude changed immediately. Captain watched the Southerner's eyes flash around the garage while he tried to think.

"Hey now, hey . . . that ain't even funny . . . I've been in this business for twenty years and I still have nightmares about being stuck underneath one of these things . . . I'll stay here—I mean, I don't mind my clothes getting ruined and all but put the safety back on—Come on, man . . . something could happen when you leave—without the safety catch on."

Captain pulled the handle to lower the hoist. Air hissed and it began to come down. Looking up at the descending machinery, with his eyes abulge, Hector choked on his words. "Hey, hey . . . holy balls—don't fuck around . . . It's not funny, man—I mean it about the dreams . . . Come on, man—"

Hector let out one curt laugh as though he hoped that it was a joke. Then he shrieked, "NOOO." His voice cracked, making him sound effeminate. "Please, man, please . . . please don't do it—stop it . . . stop it in the name of heaven . . . Don't let it come down any more—Stop it . . ."

The truck continued down and Hector was forced to his knees. "I'll give anything . . . please—please—"

Captain stopped the lift approximately four feet from the floor.

Captain began to speak but was cut off abruptly by the ring of a loud bell. A car had pulled in for gas. Hector appeared ready to scream again. Captain said, "Scream and you get the rest—right now . . ."

Hector said nothing but knelt there breathing hard, sweating and looking around for escape like a trapped animal.

"Now . . . I'm going to go take care of the customer . . . When I get back I'm going to ask you the name of your heroin connection—the source . . . the big man . . ."

Hector recovered his composure enough to look surprised and say, "Heroin—me? . . . I'm a gas man, a gas station man—but there's money here . . . the nightmares . . . It's the truth about the nightmares—Please, man . . . lift the . . ."

Captain tucked the gun into his waist band and jogged out to the center gas island just as another car pulled in. "Shit," he said, laughing. He quickly told the occupants of both cars the same story. "Power to the pumps is off . . . there's danger from a gas leak into the electrical supply—Please get out of here . . ." Both vehicles hastened away.

Back inside of the garage, Hector had readjusted his position to sit flat on his buttocks with his long legs stretched out around either side of the piston to match his arms. Hector began anxiously, "Well . . . you see . . . the truth is—"

"Wait Hector, let me tell you something before you go on. I already know the answer that I want. I just want you to confirm it for me, that's all . . . so don't lie, Hector—Don't lie because I'm not going to give you a second chance . . . and you'd better believe that dope dealer . . ."

Hector looked away to think about it and Captain released more compressed air to drop the load down to put pressure on his head which became crooked to one side.

Hector gagged and his contorted body emitted a loud fart while he screamed, "God NO . . . NO." He tried to scrunch down further but had nowhere to go.

Captain stopped the lift. Hector's body began to tremble as though he were experiencing a motor dysfunction, a seizure. His psychic makeup, his chemistry, seemed to change. He gulped air. With his eyes squeezed shut, he broke out into a demented sounding moan and began to sob.

"Meadowbrook—Meadowbrook—Zimms—Meadowbrook . . . Zimms—"

"Meadowbrook—What about Meadowbrook—What is Meadowbrook, Hector?" Captain asked.

But the now mentally disordered, greasy-faced Southerner continued on with the same message, over and over.

Crouching in underneath the rack, Captain slapped the slobbering man hard across the face and eased back out. Hector was quiet, his wet eyes vacant.

"What is Meadowbrook, Hector?" Captain asked sternly.

Hector sighed and said, "Mortuary."

Captain stood still for a beat thinking before spinning around to look west out through the station's windows. Across Twelfth Street sat the funeral home. He saw the darkened sign. It read Meadowbrook Mortuaries.

"Jesus," Captain said, imagining coffins full of heroin. "Jesus Christ." He stood there unable to move and finally said, "Jesus Christ," again.

"Zimm—What does Zimm mean, Hector?"

Hector looked stupefied and unable to answer.

Captain bolted from the garage but stopped at the large opened doors and walked back to the lift control. "Hey Hector . . . Hector . . . can you hear me—?"

There was no reply. Hector's head appeared forced down

against his shoulder. His back was arched under the strain. His eyes were closed. Spittle ran freely from his mouth.

"Hey Hector—just for the record—so you understand . . . I know a nice lady named Marilyn, who never hurt a soul . . . who once had a Brad and a Penny . . . and thanks to you, she knows more about nightmares than you'll ever know—knew—" Captain pulled the hoist's release handle up and left it that way.

Hector began his anguished moan again and it grew louder and more insistent while Captain walked away. Then there occurred a loud snap. The sound made Captain's stomach turn, and the moaning stopped.

Meadowbrook

Breathing deeply of the clean damp Santa Monica night air, Captain crossed Wilshire Boulevard to sit on a bus bench. He looked across the street at Hector's brightly lit National station on one corner and the darkened Meadowbrook Mortuary on the other. "What do you think, Brad—Those lights have got to go, don't they . . .?"

He ran across to the gas station, found the main electrical power switch and put the entire corner into darkness. Back at the bus bench, the station appeared closed for the night.

Feeling tentative, Captain sat and stared at the dark mortuary. "Are you afraid of the boogie man?" he asked himself, laughing nervously and feeling giddy. "Yes—yes . . . you fucking ay I am—"

He tried to figure what was in the dark old house of the dead. He envisioned ghoulish things like rooms filled with bodies. He saw them neatly laid out next to each other, row upon row. Some were nude and waxen, some were wrapped like mummies. Zombies stalked around the place with their arms outstretched, waiting for a fix, and Hector was there, in the basement, squashed flat like a pancake onto the concrete.

Hector saw Captain and became a television hot cake commercial. He beckoned to Captain to come in and try some, he danced with the rest of the stack. His eyes were melted butter and ran down his cheeks. Then Hector was an uncooked hamburger patty. He was raw, ground, gristled meat. Thick red sauce oozed from his sides. He danced and sang, "Come on in—come on in."

Captain saw himself standing there on the basement stairs watching Hector dance, sing and bleed, when he saw the dreaded monster named Zimms, the hooded Zimms monster with whips in both hands, appear and tap him on the shoulder.

"Shit . . . fuck . . ." Captain said, jumping up from the bus bench. "The place is probably full of stiffs . . . Shit, what a thought . . ." He sat back down on the bench and let a few cars go by. Finally he said, "Go on you fucking sissy . . . go have a look . . . You've got a gun . . . a look won't hurt you . . ."

Holding his breath so as not to smell the formaldehyde and trying not to think, Captain ran across the street and up the old mansion's three cement front stairs to stand at the heavy, carved wooden front door. An ornate golden mail box slot was in the middle of the door. There was an inscription on it. Captain leaned into the shadows and squinted to read, "Lloyd and Trudi Zimm," etched into the face of the mail slot.

The Zimms, Captain thought. Son of a bitch, is it possible? God damn, what a set up. Is it possible, he wondered, that it ends here? "Naw," he whispered, "I'll bet not . . . but wow . . . what a brainy way to go . . ."

Captain stared at the door bell button and spontaneously

pushed it. After a moment, a small bright light popped on to illuminate an intercom box to his right.

"May we help you?" inquired a pleasant sounding female voice.

"Yes—yes . . . Rick Wallman here . . . Rick's Surfboards, Malibu . . . I've got an urgent message from Hector."

There was a click and then nothing.

Captain was sure that he heard a telephone ringing somewhere out in the night. It was a difficult thing to pinpoint but he was quite sure that it was Hector's telephone at the gas station. After ringing a long time, it stopped.

A white light above the mortuary's entrance came on. It was an intense light that made Captain appreciate the visor of his G.O.B. hat and his dark glasses. The intercom clicked.

"What is the message, please?"

Captain felt a presence on the other side of the oaken door. A panel of the dark wood in front of his face showed itself to be made of smoked glass where the bright light hit it. Captain was sure that someone stood just past the door observing him.

"I won't give the message to just anyone. I was told to give it to the Zimms only."

"I am Mrs. Zimm," the pleasant female voice continued, "and would you please remove your glasses and hat so that I might see with whom I am speaking?"

"If you will open the door so that the courtesy will be mutual," Captain said, smiling and hoping.

The panel of glass in the door slid open to reveal a face. Captain stepped close and at the same time brought the Savage automatic out to hold at his side.

"Well, I am Mrs. Zimm and I am listening." The woman's face was back lit and could not be distinguished.

"I would like to come in and talk. Is that a big deal?"

287

"Yes, it is a big deal. It is late, and I don't know you. This is as far as you go. Tell me what you want—now, please."

Acting insulted and huffy, Captain said, "But wait a minute," and turned to look out into the night behind him. Things were at a standstill. There were no people. Turning back, he put the barrel of the automatic into the opened hatch, pointing it directly into Mrs. Zimm's face.

"Don't jerk or jump away, Mrs. Zimm, or you'll be your own best customer." Captain got very close and peered in at the woman who did not move. "Don't think. Just open or die now," Captain said emphatically.

"I have to move for the lock. I can't reach it."

"Go ahead, unlock it."

Captain put the pistol through the square peephole in the door to follow her. He could see her now: middle-aged, gray hair, well kempt, European-looking. Craning his neck, he could see the polished stone floor. Mrs. Zimm wore black leather wedgies.

When the door was unlocked, as it began to open, Mrs. Zimm gave it an extremely hard, jerking pull. The Savage flew out of Captain's hand into the mortuary's front room. Captain was able to observe it momentarily sliding across the marbled floor before it disappeared from view.

He was in the place in a flash, racing Mrs. Zimm for the gun. On the way Mrs. Zimm stopped, turned around quickly and put a stiff leg between his. Captain understood the judo move, and as he rolled onto the floor to arrive at the gun first, he thought it had been a stupid choice. As he sat up, the pistol in hand, a man dressed in a neat dark business suit and silk rep tie, showed himself at the head of the long, polished flight of stairs that graced the rear of the room. The man was illuminated by a large crystal chandelier that hung high above the middle of the staircase.

The impressively dressed man saw what was happening below

him and turned immediately to leave. Captain fired five shots at him in rapid succession. There was one pinging sound and a ricochet. The man turned back around. Captain could see that he was dead and held fire. The man fell headlong onto the stone stairway and came tumbling down the entire flight of stairs to flop out onto the floor in front of Captain and Mrs. Zimm.

Mrs. Zimm seemed to lose her self control. Captain thought she went a bit crazy. With no concern for her own safety, she attacked Captain from the front. She screamed and raged in German while she tried several unsuccessful karate moves against him. She settled for pummeling blow after blow on Captain's head, arms and shoulders. After a time Captain shot her twice, once in each thigh, and the shocked woman went down.

After shutting the front door, Captain dragged Mrs. Zimm by the hair, past the dead man who lay on his back with his eyes and mouth open, to sit and prop her up against the marble stairs and the hand railing. She started to fall, but he made her hold onto the railing.

Captain separated her chattering teeth with the barrel of the pistol and put the barrel's tip against the back of the woman's throat. She gagged slightly. Her upper teeth clicked against the blue steel barrel. Her teeth were real and looked strong.

"I have one shot left, Mrs. Zimm. Where does the heroin come from? Don't try to fool me. I am not afraid to kill people like you. Now tell me, where does it come from? Who is the boss, the top dope dealer? Tell me."

Mrs. Zimm appeared to calm as her eyes exhibited an understanding of the reason for Captain being there. Not just a maniac off of the street blowing the place up, but someone, something, that she had to know deep down inside might one day happen.

"Heroin, Mrs. Zimm—I'm here because of heroin. Now tell me—"

Mrs. Zimm's eyes took on an expression of resignation. She

shook her head up and down in spite of the pistol in her mouth
and closed her eyes. She squeezed at her thighs where she'd been
shot. Then she opened her eyes and put a bloody hand up in front
of her, palm flat like a stop signal. Captain withdrew the gun
from her mouth.

Swallowing hard, Mrs. Zimm spoke with a German accent.
"We were getting out next month. Do you believe it?" She
looked at the dead man. "We were getting out. We'd made it, a
fortune. Lloyd wanted to live in Paris, to live out our lives in
peace. We were getting out of it. Oh, Lord, the irony of it all.
Oh, Lloyd, no." She looked again to the dead man, Lloyd, her
husband, but controlled her tears.

With her eyes still fixed on the dead man, she slowly shook her
head and spoke. "I don't know who you are, but I'll tell you what
you want to know, which is nothing really."

"Who is the top dog?"

"I don't know, so help me. You're going to kill me anyway,
aren't you."

"Probably, just like you've killed—"

"I know, I know, don't explain. We've got it coming, I
know."

"Who is your boss?"

"We have none. We're autonomous."

"You mean—"

"I mean that we are supplied with everything we need from
Meadowbrook in Pasadena and are audited four times a year by
an accountant, a different accountant each time."

"How many Meadowbrook Mortuaries are there? Who's the
owner?"

"I don't know. The big one—the home base—is in Arizona, I
think. I'm not sure that it's a secret. We just didn't want to
know."

Mrs. Zimm lunged at Captain, grabbing the pistol by its barrel.

Her strength surprised him, and she nearly got the best of the struggle before he was able to direct the gun toward her face. He shot her.

The last .22 caliber brass slug went up through the bottom of her hand and into her brain by way of her right eye. Bright red blood gushed to pour off of the tip of Mrs. Zimm's nose, and she fell back dead. She began to slide, and Captain allowed her body to roll across the last few bottom steps and topple over on top of her dead husband. She lay there face down, spread-eagled over him, her cheek against his. It was an eerie sight that Captain could not take his eyes away from until he shut the mortuary's heavy oaken door behind him.

"Son of a bitch," he said and jogged to the car.

Captain's absolute all-time favorite painting, Gainsborough's masterpiece entitled "The Blue Boy," hung in the Huntington Museum in Pasadena. That much of the drive to Pasadena will be fun, he thought. And if the smog is not bad it could turn out to be a good day. Before falling asleep, after his prayers, Captain tried to recall the look in the Blue Boy's eyes, the look that sent chills through his body and made him shake his head in amazement every time that he saw it. Anticipating the pleasant sensations that he knew the painting would bring to him the next day, Captain snuggled in and slept with a smile on his face.

News of the discovery of Rick Wallman's body in Malibu was in the morning papers. There was nothing about Hector or the Zimms but it was a cinch, Captain thought, that those discoveries are being made right now.

He wanted to quit. To stop following the trail and spend the day in a quiet, safe way; perhaps with Iris. But when he looked down over his garden, Brad's sad image came. It made Captain shake his head in a solemn way, say, "shit" and head for the freeway.

He read another set of uneventful newspapers over drinks at the

Old Log Inn in Pasadena. He mused about the fun he and Gracie had had in the same comfortable bar four or so years before. Gracie had been an aspiring actress who studied her craft at the Pasadena Playhouse which was situated just down the block from the bar, to the south. He had met her at a Will Rogers polo game during that summer past and visited her at her small Pasadena apartment frequently after that. They had done all of their drinking at the Old Log Inn. Captain remembered that he could never hold it with her. God, he thought, remembering, that was terrible of me. There was something about her that even now eluded him, something about her skin or her temperature, something that would not allow him to prolong his orgasm, ever. Weird, he thought, that I was like that with her. I still don't know if it was good or bad. "Good for me, I guess," he said, shrugging his shoulders but not really believing it.

Although Gracie had been beautiful, she never made it. She ended up back in Toledo, or so he remembered. Too bad, he thought, that she took everything so seriously. "Acting is serious business," she would say. Dedication was her favorite word. It's too bad, he told himself, that Gracie never had a chance at the new Dolly Parton philosophy. Captain had heard Dolly say it herself on television. "Show business is a big money-making joke, and I've always liked telling jokes."

Captain ordered another drink and thought that he would like to suck on Dolly Parton's big tits. But then he remembered that she was married. It would still be difficult to say no, he thought, if they were out there bare, with hard swollen ends.

He wasn't positive, but it seemed that the Meadowbrook people in Pasadena had begun to feel the progression of the killings. The old brownstone mansion appeared to have extra help. Big, tough-looking people who are dressed inappropriately for doing funeral business roamed in and out of the establishment's doors and around the grounds.

292

Nevertheless, Captain got a gun on John Chrome, the mortuary's proprietor, and they went for a ride in a hearse. They went to look at a crypt, and John Chrome told a convincing story before he died.

Captain found out that the Meadowbrook Mortuary chain was definitely the key to the movement and sale of Mexican heroin in the United States. Chrome thought that there were forty or more Meadowbrook Funeral Homes situated throughout the fifty states and Mexico. Meadowbrook's home base was in Tucson, Arizona. Chrome's heroin for the Pasadena outlet came from Meadowbrook in San Diego. The narcotic was transported inside cadavers.

The Pasadena operation was autonomous in terms of local sale and distribution of heroin and had police and legislative protection. Chrome imagined that all of the Meadowbrook locations were protected. The funeral business was lucrative and showed a profit every year. The funds from the two businesses were not co-mingled. The heroin trade was conducted on a cash basis only. John Chrome deposited the cash, minus his share, on the tenth of every month in a large safety deposit box in the bank where the funeral home business was done, where he was known and respected. The safety deposit box was frequently moved within the bank, and he was given new keys and instructions. The cash was always gone from the box by the tenth of the next month when he returned with more.

Both businesses were audited four times a year by different accountants from Meadowbrook's home base. The accountants asked lots of questions of Mr. and Mrs. John Chrome. The Chromes asked none of them. The accountants altered prices, made policy and changed passwords for the telephone calls that might or might not come.

John Chrome and his wife had been in the funeral home business for thirty-three years. They had been dealing heroin and running Meadowbrook Pasadena for eleven years, ever since Mrs. Chrome's enormous gambling debts became a life and death problem, which put them in touch with the first Meadowbrook accountant they had ever met. He had made them an offer. Mr. and Mrs. Chrome had accepted and become millionaires. John Chrome would never spend his.

The Pasadena afternoon was warm and smoggy. A bright, polluted haze stifled Captain's breathing, made his eyes sting and caused his skin to feel dirty. I'm never, he thought, coming to Pasadena again ever. He felt irritable.

Parking was a problem, and the Huntington Museum itself was much more crowded than he had anticipated. Captain sympathized with the elderly museum guards clad in worn brown uniforms, who strained at keeping ill-mannered, candy and ice cream-toting urchins away from the priceless pieces of art. One little black boy, balancing a sloppy red sno-cone, continued to duck under the security ropes and get dangerously close to a large Rembrandt.

The two heavy-set black women who accompanied the group of youngsters ate greasy-looking fried chicken while they walked along. They licked their fingers, laughed together and ignored their misbehaving young. Observing this scene, Captain suppressed a real, frantic desire to run and punch the inconsiderate women.

A nervous, white-haired guard went to them and with his palms turned up in a helpless gesture, implored them to help. The large black women looked at him as though he were an insect, ate their chicken and continued on. Captain knew what they were thinking. He could see it on their arrogant faces: So what if Leroy does throw a sno-cone onto the picture? Who painted it, anyway? Some honky who probably had a slave.

Captain urged himself out of the room and through several others until he came to the main gallery. He went and stood before "The Blue Boy." Dirty sunlight flooded in through a skylight. Captain moved closer and had to squint to see what he wanted to see, Blue Boy's expression, the look in his eyes. Captain saw it, and it was not the happy look that he had remembered. Blue Boy stared past Captain, across the hazy room of disquieting people. Following the look, Captain found Gainsborough's "Pinky," the painting of a beautiful shy young girl. She looked across to her Blue Boy.

Captain looked book at Blue Boy too. He heard him say it to her. He watched Blue Boy talk to his Pinky love. "Let's get the fuck out of here," he said. Captain smiled but felt sad. They have the evenings, he thought. They have the nights alone together, and that must be nice.

He wanted to ask Blue Boy about the quiet nights with his sweetheart, but the loud gang of children entered the room. They all seemed to scream at once and fly around the gallery. Captain watched Blue Boy. His eyes appeared forlorn. Blue Boy saw them coming and said, "Goddamn." Captain said, "Yes, goddamn."

He moved past the two black women as he hurried from the place and when close yelled, "Pigs," at them. Not startled, they ate their chicken and talked. Captain's eyes teared as he ran. From the smog, he thought, from the smog.

Captain was in a quandary. Coming in from Pasadena, he had stopped at Frattelo's and brought home a plate of what he considered to be the best spaghetti and meatballs in Los Angeles. But after three bites of the delicious food, he was unable to go on. He drank the entire bottle of red wine but couldn't quell the growing notion that someone, somewhere, was getting wise to him. Perhaps Mr. Big himself, he thought. "The rest of this thing could be fucking dangerous," he told himself. "And I'm not kidding."

He sat there brooding. "It's time, goddammit. I can sense it.

295

Something is out there, call it a hunch." Feeling frustrated and angry, he said, "Jesus Christ, Brad, you don't want me to get caught, do you? Or killed? I can't help anybody if I'm dead." Looking toward heaven he said, "Well—?"

Captain decided then and there not to go to San Diego the next day as he'd planned. He felt what he considered the very real possibility of imminent danger waiting in San Diego. "Call it a hunch," he said, "or whatever, but that's one trip I'm not going to make. There's another way to find him—a short cut, and I'll find it." Relieved, he breathed deeply, finished the spaghetti and with the lights still on, fell fast asleep.

Using some tradesmen payables and two straggler rent checks as an excuse, Captain went the next morning to the Beverly Hills office of John Frost, the attorney.

One of the best real estate men around, Frost was the principal owner of the apartment building where Captain provided management and lived. When business was concluded, after a discussion with John about the philosophy behind rent control, Captain took leave to use one of the telephone lines in the lawyer's unoccupied conference room.

The story that Captain related to the Meadowbrook Mortuary people in San Diego concerned a made-up friend who had just died in Mexico City. He said that he wasn't sure where to bury him, in Mexico or the United States. The mortuary people said that bringing the remains back to the states was no problem whatsoever, that they were licensed to do it without red tape, that the hearses or airplanes had special international permits to bring the body back across the border without problems. The mortuary needed only a letter with the details and a check or money order. Shit, Captain laughed to himself, they should be paying me.

"I believe my friend's mother lives in Arizona. Could I bury him there?" he asked.

296

San Diego replied with an emphatic, "Yes, of course. That can easily be provided for, in either Phoenix or Tucson, Arizona. Would that suit you, sir?"

"Yes, probably. Which is the best facility? Isn't one of them your home base?"

"Yes, sir. That would be Tucson, sir."

"Who is the president of your company? Who heads up Meadowbrook Mortuaries in Tucson?" He asked it as casually as he knew how.

There was a pause from Meadowbrook in San Diego. Then, "Why, we are incorporated, sir. We are a corporation."

"Who heads the corporation?" Captain asked.

"Are you unhappy with my handling of this affair, with my service?"

"No. no. You do a fine job. But who's the boss, or is it a secret?"

"No, of course not, but we do not give out that information over the phone. I'm sure you understand, and thank you for calling, sir. Call again if we can be of service to you or your deceased." The line went dead.

Captain called Meadowbrook Mortuaries in Miami, New Orleans, Dallas and Houston and got about the same story as he had in San Diego. Finally, with a woman at Meadowbrook in St. Louis, Captain was able to tell a tale of gratitude. He spoke of the fabulous service that Meadowbrook had provided for his family in Tucson and asked who the wonderful chairman of the board was, that a thank you might be sent to him personally.

She said, "I understand. The person you want is Mr. Ritter."

"Is he the boss?"

"Yes, he runs the home office."

"But is he the overall boss?"

"Yes," she replied. "I think so."

Captain thanked her, hung up and sat back in the leather chair. "Mr. Ritter, huh? Put on your high-heeled sneakers, pal, 'cause we're going out tonight—right, Brad? Right, you goddamn well, better believe it."

Back at home when Captain called Iris to tell her he was leaving the city for a day or so, she acted silly on the other end of the telephone while she described what she was viewing through her binoculars. Two successful young fashion models from New York—he a blond, she a brunette—had leased a beach house two homes down from Iris's. Their sandy front yard was fenced and but for Iris and her field glasses, private from onlookers.

The couple lay nude together in their beach front yard making love. Iris's voice became thick while she described in detail what she saw and what she thought they were feeling. Captain suggested that she masturbate. She answered tentatively, "I am."

Captain said, "Tell me all about it. What you see," and he joined in. He started and stopped and prolonged his orgasm until Iris was ready, and then they climaxed together.

Afterward, they both laughed with embarrassment, trying to imagine what a person would think who had been listening in on the phone line to the oohs and aaahs, the grunts and groans of their orgasms.

"Where are you going?" she asked, short of breath.

"Tucson," he replied.

"What for? Can I come?"

"To see a guy. No, you can't. What are they doing now?"

"Just a second, let me adjust. She just put a towel between her legs. She's watching him take a shower. Uumm, he's built real nice standing up. He hangs down through the soap suds. He's stretching his thing, trying to show it off—uumm—"

Captain felt his metabolism change, a sensation he hated. Jealousy and anger flowed into him. He said, "goodby."

"Not as nice as you though, Cappy. He's nothing like you," Iris inserted quickly.

That was better, and Captain said, "I'll call you. I'm anxious for Montecito."

"Oh, yes. Me too. And, Cappy, I've got the wildest secret to share when I see you. I'm dying to see the expression on your face. And I bought that black desk for the den."

"Iris, tell me the secret now. You know that I hate secrets. It will preoccupy my thinking."

"No, I won't."

Captain screamed, "Goddammit, Iris, tell me, or I'll come out there and kick your ass." Then he spoke quietly, childlike. "Please, I need to know. Come on, it's important to me that I know."

Iris said, "Well, all right," and she told him her secret. He listened and when she was finished he sat there bewildered.

"Well—I—" he stammered.

"Don't worry about it," she said. "It's no big deal really. Actually, I think it's fun."

"Yes, well, I'm going to go now."

"All right, but, Cappy, be careful. Please be careful, whatever you do, please."

"Yes, Iris, I will, I promise. I love you." Captain hung up and sat thinking about what she had told him, about her secret.

Tucson

Captain loved to fly. He regarded air travel as a real luxury and looked forward to the experience every time it presented itself. The word that Captain used to describe the air flight to Tucson was *fabulous*. The ride was fabulous, the visibility fabulous, the service, the drinks and the stewardess were all fabulous.

The Tucson air seemed clean, dry and salutary, making Captain think of a smogless late afternoon in Palm Springs, California. The sun was orange.

Hertz Rent-A-Car provided Captain with a new, four-door, air-conditioned Chevrolet. An old-timer who advertised in the personal column of the Tucson Sun newspaper, sold him a snub-nosed, .38-caliber police special revolver and a box of shells for $150, no questions asked. Captain checked into the Kings Arms Motel, a snazzy-looking place less than one mile from Tucson's Meadowbrook Mortuary.

The water in the swimming pool contained too much chlorine, but he swam thirty laps with his eyes mostly closed anyway. When the pain came during the last ten laps, he asked himself why he was doing it and why not stop, but he knew: he could feel the suntanned, long-legged brunette watching him. She sat alone at an umbrellaed table behind the diving board area, drinking a martini. Captain thought that her eyes were slanted in an unusual way, and he imagined a sly sexual glint from them as she slid into his motel bed.

He completed a perfect flip turn and raced the final lap for his planned finish beneath the diving boards. His musculature seemed on fire. Touching home, he broke water smiling, pulled himself out of the pool with one last effort and stood there, his muscles flexed.

"Wow," he said, grinning. He looked to the sexy lady. She was gone. Captain could feel the expression fall off of his face, and he quickly turned away experiencing more disappointment than he knew he should. He felt sick. A normal, everyday person, he thought, wouldn't take it like this.

Just to show whoever might be watching that it didn't matter, Captain climbed the thirty-foot ladder to the high diving board. The dive never developed properly, so confused was his thinking, and the back of his legs slapped the water hard when he hit. With his calves paining from the impact, he swam underwater to the shallow end of the pool.

Alone under water and out of breath, he felt an urge to cry, but he jumped from the pool smiling and went to the showers. He had a bottle of bourbon sent down while he steamed and after two nips felt better. He laughed about what had happened. He felt good.

There was no problem finding a late-model, four-door Chevrolet in the Kings Arms subterranean parking lot, a vehicle nearly identical to the one Captain had rented, which also had current Arizona license plates. He removed the front license plate from the stranger's car and after stashing both plates from his rented car behind a steel girder, fixed the stranger's front plate to the rear of his rented Chevrolet.

After soup, a sandwich and a split of iced champagne served in his room, Captain went to the bar. The slant-eyed, suntanned brunette was there and was all business.

Disillusioned again, he thought, with a lump in his throat, but he paid her price. Upstairs he couldn't help himself and tried to love her, to talk gently and caress her pretty ears, but she looked at him funny, as though he were peculiar. Like something is wrong with me, he thought. Is something wrong with me? After becoming a sexual technician, she dressed hurriedly and left. Captain fell into a deep, agonizing depression and finally slept.

In the middle of the night he awoke with a longing for Iris that he had never experienced before. He thought about what a good girl she was basically, and he thought about what she'd told him, about her secret. He said, "Come on, Brad, let's get on with it," and fell back asleep dreaming about Montecito.

The next morning brought a still, hot day. The Arizona sky was cloudless and powder blue. The motel employees appeared lethargic working in the sun. Captain saw the long-legged brunette prostitute in the motel lobby and waved before he could stop himself. She ignored him. He said, "Shit," under his breath and with a thermos of coffee headed for Meadowbrook Mortuary.

Captain was surprised to find a thriving National gas station on the corner opposite Tucson's Meadowbrook Mortuary. A black Cadillac hearse and two Cadillac limousines sat next to the station, being washed by a gang of Mexicans. He pulled in for service, got out and spoke to the attendant while the car was being checked.

"Fucking car. Vapor-locked or some damn thing on the way getting here. Almost didn't make it, and I hate funerals."

"You going to one?"

"Yeah, my buddy. I think that it's today." Captain laughed and asked, "You know a guy over there named Ritter?"

"Sure, he's the boss."

"I wonder if he's in yet?"

"Yeah, he is. That's his car over there."

"Which one?"

"The black Chrysler, over there."

A shiny, new, black Chrysler four-door sedan sat under a green fiberglass canopy that covered it and three other expensive vehicles.

"We wash 'em every morning, and take care of 'em, keep 'em right. Ritter is a fussy guy."

"Yeah." Captain stared at the black Chrysler and decided what to do. "Thank you, Brad," he said quietly.

"You're welcome" came from the attendant.

Surprised, Captain paid cash for the purchase and walked into the office with the attendant. "Is your name Brad?" Captain asked.

"Yep, has been for thirty-one years," the man said.

Captain went back to the car shaking his head and laughing. "You're too much, God. You're too fucking much."

A phone call made from the corner told him that the mortuary closed at ten in the evening. He asked if Mr. Ritter would be available until ten, and the female voice said, "Yes, he closes up."

Captain played in the sun all day, ate when he was hungry and was back at the mortuary, staked out up by the street, by nine-thirty in the evening. Ten o'clock came and went, and the National station closed. All of the other vehicles were gone from

303

under the green canopy but Mr. Ritter's black Chrysler. At eleven o'clock Captain realized that Mr. Ritter must live in. Of course he does, he thought. The feeling of disappointment was just setting in when the mortuary's side door opened and a man came out. The man wore beige chamois bedroom slippers, slacks and a sweater. The collar that came out from the neck of the sweater looked to be from a pajama top. The man drove away in the Chrysler.

Feeling excited, Captain followed the black car while it went less than a mile to slow in front of an all-night delicatessen. Mr. Ritter leaned across the seat to look into the good-smelling place. He parked around the corner on a darkened side street and walked back to the deli.

Captain pulled in behind the Chrysler and backed up to leave not quite a car space between the vehicles. He let the engine idle and turned off the Chevrolet's lights. The street was quiet.

Mr. Ritter returned with a brown paper bag in his hand and when he stepped from the curb behind his big Chrysler, Captain put the rented Chevrolet into gear and accelerated. Ritter turned, and Captain saw his astonished expression as the Chevy slammed into the Chrysler. Captain thought that he could feel Ritter's legs absorb the impact of the collision. He backed quickly away, and the funeral man fell down between the cars.

Mr. Ritter's broken legs stuck angularly up in the air, half crooked toward his body. He writhed back and forth on his back from shoulder blade to shoulder blade and the sound *Neeee* came in an anguished squealing tone from between his clenched teeth. Captain knelt beside him.

A set of headlights suddenly bathed the scene in bright light. The vehicle was soon there too, but Captain waved it past, and after a brief pause it continued on down the dark street. Captain clamped a hand over Mr. Ritter's mouth and jammed the snub-nosed .38 into his ear. He cocked the pistol's hammer.

"When I take my hand away, you'll give me the answers that I want, or I'll blow your head off. Are you Ritter?"

He removed his hand.

"Yes, *neee.*" Captain covered his mouth.

"Are you the kingpin, the head of this heroin thing?"

Mr. Ritter shook his head vehemently from side to side and when Captain removed his hand, said, "No, no, no—*neee.*"

Shit, Captain thought.

"Give me a name, Ritter."

Captain took his hand away, and Ritter gasped, "Trench—Trench, you fool. It's Trench. God, my legs—my legs—"

Captain held his mouth, and Ritter frantically splashed the flats of his hands into the deepening puddle of blood that surrounded them.

"Who is Trench?"

"God, please, the pain—"

"Who is he?"

"The top—he's at the top. My legs, God—"

"Where is he?"

"At the farm, the farm."

"What farm?"

"Meadowbrook Farm."

"Is it in Tucson?"

Mr. Ritter had begun to cry, but he managed, "Yes, yes. Call an ambulance, please. Yes, the farm, out on Algonquin. Please help me."

"Now hear this, Ritter. I want to know—"

The funeral director let out a long hoarse sigh and fainted. Captain began to shake him but after a moment checked his pulse. There was none. Mr. Ritter was dead.

Algonquin Road ran for miles, as did the white wooden fences of Meadowbrook Farms. Nocturnal domestic animals grazed on either side of the blacktopped roadway. Oil derricks moved against the night sky.

"Meadowbrook Farms—World Champion Thoroughbred Horses" was branded into a large wooden sign that hung over the farm's entrance. Lights were on in the buildings at the end of a long driveway. There appeared to be several structures. Driving slowly past the farm's floodlit entrance, Captain saw no gate and no obvious security. A roadside sign came into view, depicting a four-leaf clover. Its lettering read, "Meadowbrook 4-H Club." Jesus, Captain thought, the man's got all the bases covered. Captain laughed when he thought about it.

Driving off down Algonquin Road, he tried to decide what the 4-H's stood for and settled on Honesty, Home, Happiness and Health. "You've forgotten the fifth H, Trench—Heroin, the big one that'll make you forget all the other four." He stopped laughing when he realized that what he'd said was the depressing truth.

Further on down the road, Captain came upon a small country gas station that appeared open and an adjoining tavern named Pete's Roady that looked closed. The station had the feeling of an independent operation but pumped National gas. Next to the station in the shadows was parked a sixteen-wheel diesel tanker truck with "Meadowbrook Refineries" printed in bold letters along its side. The truck was licensed out of Texas.

"Son of a bitch," Captain said, pulling into the station.

He wondered what it all meant. The bottom line, he thought, is that this guy Trench is super big. "Oil, fucking oil too." This is the kind of guy, Captain thought, who has it his way or kills a Kennedy. "Money talks and bullshit walks," he said.

The gas station attendant seemed half-asleep until Captain asked, "Does Trench own all of this?"

The attendant perked up and sneaked a good look at Captain. "This is all Meadowbrook," he answered in a drawl.

"So it's all Trench's, right?"

"If you say so. You gonna ask questions or buy gas?"

"Ask questions."

"Well, some people don't like to be discussed. I don't suppose it's none of your damn business anyway, is it."

Demonstrating to Captain what he thought of him, the attendant stared into his eyes, spit brown onto the ground next to the car and went back inside.

Captain drove around in the desert breathing the dry, black Arizona night air before going into Tucson proper to sightsee and stop at three different bars to drink and think.

Feeling good back at his motel room, he tried to call Iris. She was not at home, and her answering service knew nothing of her whereabouts. He went to the motel bar. After five intermittent phone calls to her from the bar and no response, he suddenly became obsessed with the image of another man making love to her. Iris laughed and held her legs back for the dark hairy brute to pound her. The man growled and slobbered over her neck and bust like an animal. Iris's nipples stood erect; she loved it.

Captain could not stand the thought. He pulled at his hair. He got drunk.

Iris called early the next morning and assuaged what he could remember of his emotional pain. The physical pain, the exploding head, was handled by two Excedrins and two double screwdrivers, rushed from the motel bar with the promise of a five-dollar tip. Finishing the second drink in a hot tub, Captain seemed to remember someone trying to come into his room in the middle of the night.

He thought that he remembered yelling, "I've got a gun," and the problem going away. "What the hell does that mean?" he asked himself. "Whether it happened or not, it probably means be careful, that's what it probably means," he answered.

Cry

After a good breakfast, a bottle of beer and four coffees, Captain drove out to Algonquin Road and down to the Meadowbrook Farm entrance. He hesitated there under the large branded sign, but the place seemed so peaceful that he said, "The hell with it," and drove in.

"I'm looking to buy a horse," he said, listening to the way it sounded in the car. "Let me see a good thoroughbred." Captain was prepared to spout some fast reasons for his being there, but no one looked twice as he drove onto the spread.

Not the least bit of suspicion could he see in any person while they ambled around the place from barn to barn; mostly young, rural, vital-looking people dressed in casual wear—boots, jeans, farm clothes. Captain estimated that with the tractors and jeeps, the parking lot held forty vehicles. A group of Mexicans trimmed the hedge and worked around the large, two-story main house.

All of the buildings were painted white and had a sanitary look.

The trim was painted a glossy dark green. The lawns appeared healthy and damp.

Walking from the parking lot, Captain actually got a smile and nod from the friendly looking people he passed, which he acknowledged. Stopping in front of one open barn, he peered into the dark to observe the glittering, unmistakable grill of a Rolls Royce. There was a poultry barn and one long, flat building called Experimental Rodent Station, from which the muted sounds of chittering small animals came.

Deeper into the large open compound, Captain began walking past barns that held horses. Trainers walked the shiny beasts to and fro, and an active workout ring was visible at the end of the street. A rolling green pasture lay beyond, where three glamorous dark brown show horses played together, their coats reflecting the sun. To the south, beyond a rise that hid a hangar, if there was one, a concrete runway headed for the horizon to end in a glaring mirage of steaming wet cement.

Walking, Captain liked the feeling of the place. To his left there appeared a small, conspicuously white, antiseptic-looking, one-story building. The windows were closed and covered, and the large, heavy front door appeared shut airtight. "Insemination" was printed in neat block letters next to the door. A yellow Corvette convertible with the top down sat in the shade beside the building, a red and white M.D. decal on its bumper.

A metallic unlatching sound came from the insemination building's front door, which then opened with a loud whoosh, making Captain think of opening a meat locker door or the door of a Hollywood sound stage. Out past the thick door, giggling with embarrassment and blushing, stumbled a teenage boy and girl dressed alike in bibbed denim coveralls. Acting silly, they messed around with each other; they teased each other by pushing, pinching and pulling at coverall straps. Seeing Captain, they paused and held the door for him to enter, which after a moment of indecision he did.

The couple's nervous laughter was cut short when the door clanked shut behind him. Captain stood in a white concrete hallway that seemed to run the length of the climate-controlled, chilly building. Feeling suddenly alone and frightened, he shivered and touched the butt of his pistol. The smell of animal dung and strong medicine came into his nostrils, and he sneezed. The heavy walls and the apparent vacuum in the chamber changed the sound to a thump and quickly absorbed it.

He swallowed twice, forcefully, to clear his ears. Above him white, hooded, evenly spaced, porcelain ceiling lamps cast intermittent halos of light down the length of the hallway. Standing still but rubbing his arms for circulation, Captain thought that it was an eerie place, like a death house hallway, the final walk to a shower of Cyclone X.

He looked at the push latch on the heavy door behind him and thought to lean on it, to get into the sun, but he sighed and let his curiosity draw him down the cheerless refrigerated corridor.

The hallway turned to his right at the rear of the building, bringing Captain face to face with a wall of blue ribbons, plaques and framed photographs. A humming fluorescent tube light illuminated the display. Looking at the photographs made him laugh and feel better immediately.

"Jeeeesus," he said, "what they get away with down on the farm."

There were six color, eight-by-ten photographs. The series pictured a black stallion, led by an attractive blonde woman, performing sexual intercourse with what appeared to be six different mares. The blonde woman smiled while she reached to

311

hold the mares' braided tails to one side or up and pulled back over their rumps for the stallion's unencumbered penetration. The glistening black stallion was identified as Algonquin, the Arabian King.

The corridor turned again, and Captain followed it into a well-lit room that contained three animal stalls built against the room's far side. They stood empty. The room was painted totally in beige enamel. One more step into the room past the protruding concrete entranceway, and Captain matched eyes with a shining black-coated horse who stood no more than eight feet away. The horse's ears were back, and he appeared embarrassed. The animal's head was cinched up tight by his halter to a crossbar and because of a beige wooden panel that stood between Captain and the horse, a chest-high division that partially separated the room, Captain was unable to observe the horse's form below his glistening shoulder.

"Easy, big boy, take your time. Mama doesn't mind." came from a throaty but gentle female voice on the other side of the room division.

Captain smiled when his mind went to Lauren Bacall and the way that she used to say it to Bogie: "Easy, big boy, just take it easy. Mama's right here." The voice had an athletic, breathy quality.

Captain looked at the horse's face again and could have sworn that the black face blushed. It showed in the wild-looking, red-veined whites of his eyes as he tried to force his stare away. The skin over his jowls seemed to sag and tremble.

The room was in neat order and full of veterinary supplies, and Captain understood that he was in some sort of special animal hospital or infirmary. Aware of the chilly climate again, he shivered inside and felt out of place. He wished to evaporate, to be out in the sun. He thought about Montecito and the new dazzling black swimming pool. He quickly searched his consciousness for answers and came to think about the photographs of Brad, sitting in the white Naugahyde chair, his head blown away.

"Come on, boy, come on. Squirt for Mama," she said.

Crouching over and tiptoeing along next to the room division, Captain could hear a rhythmic sound from the other side that made him think of skin being manipulated by skin. The soft female voice found the tempo too, and Captain, feeling like a peeping Tom, peeked around the edge of the beige enamel wooden division to observe what the blonde woman wanted when she rhymed, "Do it, do it, do it, do it," her voice becoming frenzied.

He saw, he gawked and thought that he might laugh. Clapping his hand over his mouth, he pulled back for cover. He had seen it and so had to believe it.

He knelt on the cold cement floor and understood why the young coveralled couple had been so embarrassed, why the black stallion was embarrassed and why he now felt his face flushed with embarrassment also. It was the attractive blonde woman from the hallway photographs. She was on the other side of the room division, kneeling beneath the belly of the black stallion, masturbating him.

Hearing the movement of flesh next to him, Captain pictured what he knew it to be, what he'd seen. "Goddamn," he whispered, breaking into a sweat. He felt his penis jerk.

With his head around the room division again, he watched the woman work. She perspired. She knelt on a folded saddle blanket in front of the black beast's haunches and because of the posture in which she held herself, could not see Captain.

"Come on now, boy, do it, do it, do it, do it for me."

While he stared, he was struck with what he thought was a peculiar notion; that there was something maternal about what she was doing. She projected a quality that made Captain feel what she did was the kind of thing that any good mother would do for her son. And then he saw another look come over her face and knew that that was bullshit.

A tube of lubricant lay at her knee. The stallion's four hooves were locked into place by some kind of stationary iron shodding apparently forged for just that purpose. The animal stood stiff-legged. The muscles in his hind quarters were taut and quivering.

The blonde woman looked about forty. She wore no makeup and worked with her yellow hair pulled back into a pony tail. She wore a short-sleeved, red gingham blouse and no jewelry. Perspiration from her upper lip rolled down into the corners of her mouth. She shook her head or blew the sweat away. The horse's penis was colored pink and black in a spotted configuration that made Captain think of camouflage. The woman used both hands to pump the tremendous organ. Two feet, he thought; the damned thing is two feet long.

His face burned and an urgent feeling of anger flooded him. Jealous, you're jealous, he thought. He stared at the stallion's glistening stiff penis, and it made him mad. You're just jealous, he thought, and then, no, that's silly. That's just silly, forget it. But he couldn't. You asshole, he said to himself. It's a fucking horse, a 2,000-pound horse.

But he watched the blonde woman stare at the end of the spotted thing. She pulled it and pushed it and held it close to her face and seemed to stare into the hole in the end. She stared intently with a wrinkled brow, as one would look into a spyglass. She licked the sweat off her lips.

It's got to be her job, he thought. It's her job to do this thing. But assuming that didn't help his upset stomach. Captain

314

watched the blonde woman stare at the black stallion's huge slippery penis in a heated way that he was sure meant much more than business or a job. Afraid to think it in the open, Captain kept the thought recessed into a secret corner of his mind, but he flitted by it. Ruined, the broad is probably ruined. I'll bet she never looks at a man's cock like that, the cunt.

The stallion began to shake. His blue-black coat seemed to separate from the flesh beneath it and float on a rippling wave of fluid or air. The animal held his braided tail tight up against his rear end, and Captain watched his blood vessels distend along his trembling body all the way into his bright pink ears. His bulging brown eyes looked backward at Captain.

The blonde woman said, "Aha, aha, here we go."

Continuing to pump with one hand, she reached away to grab something made of clear plastic with the other. The horse looked to put all of his muscle into the shocks that held his hooves. The tendons in his neck strained in a quick series of jerks, and air bubbles appeared to go racing all over his body underneath his shining coat.

In licking the perspiration from her lips, the blonde woman made her mouth sloppy wet, and Captain thought that it looked sexy hung open. He watched her juicy mouth. He had a complete erection. He felt heady, faint.

"That's right, big fella." She gulped as she said it.

The black stallion shuddered, cleared his nostrils with a loud blow and emitted his sperm with an audible gush into the plastic container, which the excited woman fitted over the head of his surging penis.

"Oh, yes," she encouraged, "come on."

"Holy Christmas," Captain mumbled. His legs wobbled, and he had to grab onto the room divider to stay on his feet.

The blonde woman then quickly turned her stroking technique

into a milking pulling motion. She started with her grip back, the length of her straightened arm, at the animal's testicles. Squeezing, she milked the bouncing spotted penis forward.

Continuing to labor, the woman let out a sigh and focused her attention on the proper use of the now-heavy plastic semen gathering device. Then without looking up, she said, "Who's there?" She spoke casually, without embarrassment.

Stunned, Captain looked around to see who she was speaking to, but she stopped what she was doing for a moment and craned her neck to look up at him and into his eyes. She smiled and said, "I could hear you breathing. Hello."

The stallion shook violently at his restraints and whinnied. "Oh, yes, hello. Sorry," Captain managed from a dry throat. He thought that he sounded immature and couldn't look back at her.

"Sorry about what? You didn't bother anything. I've got it all. Here, wipe him off. Hurry up."

The blonde woman removed the head of the horse's penis from the plastic receptacle and directed the entire wet spotted thing toward Captain.

Stepping back away from the room division, out behind the horse, Captain said, "But, I—I—" His heart seemed to beat in his throat, and he wanted to bolt from the place.

With both of her hands full the woman spoke seriously, and gesturing with her head, she said, "Come on, come on. I've got two minutes. Just wipe him clean."

Captain watched her search his face. He couldn't move. Shrugging her shoulders disappointedly she said, "All right, just hold this so it doesn't—Oh, never mind. I'll do it myself." Paying particular attention to the bag of semen that she held aloft in her left hand, the woman stood and with a sneakered right foot pulled a plastic tarp underneath the horse to lay his sagging penis on.

She glanced at Captain from under her lids in a way that made him feel unassured and uncomfortable. Reaching his right hand out to her, he said, "But—"

She said, "Yes?"

"Wait, I'll do it. Here let me."

Captain went to her and knelt down in one quick, resolute motion. She took time to smile at him. Approval showed in her deep blue eyes. The look was soothing. He felt better and tried to smile.

The horse's penis was hot and wet. Goddamn, he thought, is it ever heavy.

Standing above him, she said, "Thank you. There's a towel, and that bottle there is alcohol."

She looked intently into his eyes. As though she likes me, he thought. And she hurried away to the rear of the room.

Watching after her clean athletic figure, Captain decided that she had an air of self-determination, of strength, about her that looked dependable and that he liked. He guessed that he might even like her, even though, of course, she was probably ruined for a man's cock.

When she stepped from view, he heard a refrigerator door close and then the whirring sound of a machine. Captain stared at the thick piece of horse flesh that he held in his hands. He was afraid of thinking it, so he said it once emphatically and then forced it from his mind.

"Never, and I mean never, should Iris be allowed to see a prick this big."

Holding it out to look at it up and down again, it flexed in his hands and he said, "Jesus Christ." He used the towel and alcohol to bathe the stallion's spotted penis, and he couldn't help but laugh.

"Christ, what would my friends say if they could see me

now." He imagined them standing around him, good-naturedly enjoying the joke. He tried but could not conjure a picture of their smiling faces. Weird, he thought, but I don't know my friends. "Who are my friends?" he wondered out loud.

"What was that?" came from the blonde woman who stood shaking a bottle at the room's end.

"Nothing. What do I do now?"

"Is he clean?"

"Yes."

"Then just sit tight. He'll retract any minute now. When that happens, let go."

As she spoke the horse's penis began to shrink. Its volume reduced to make it jerk and then pull rapidly away from Captain's hands.

"That's fine. Let go now. Thank you," she said.

The stallion wouldn't match stares when Captain walked past him to use the wash basin. Drying his hands, Captain caught the horse's eye, shrugged his shoulders and said, "Hey, what do I know?" but he could see that the horse didn't like him. Captain whispered, "Fuck you" into one proud pink ear as he walked back by.

"I'm Doctor Leighton. Do I know you?" the blonde woman inquired.

"No. No, I'm looking at horses. My name is Blood, Captain Blood, and I want to buy—some horse."

He watched her reaction carefully and could sense no change.

"Some horse?" she asked, smiling.

"Yes, some kind of good horse. I want some good horse."

"All right, if you say so." She said it as though what he was saying was juvenile, stupid. She turned her back, and he guessed that she was right. He blushed.

"What kind of doctor are you?" he asked.

"What kind do you want me to be? I'm all kinds. Take your pick."

"Are you a veterinarian?"

"Among others, yes."

"My father was a doctor—a good one—famous. I like doctors."

"I don't," she said. "I don't trust them, the life and death boys, and money—the life and death for money boys," she laughed. "No ethics any more, just gold." She walked to the black stallion, patted him good, scratched his ears and said, "Isn't that right, big boy?"

She laughed and walked back to the rear of the room where she finished what she had been doing there and came back to wash her hands and rinse her face and neck with cool water. She used a clean towel and said, "There, that just about takes care of that."

Sitting on the edge of a stainless steel table, the blonde Doctor Leighton lit a cigarette, rested her feet on a wooden stool and smiled. Captain could see that she was at least forty, but he thought that she looked good. Her skin was tanned and smooth and but for a sign of crow's feet next to her eyes, wrinkle-free. Her eyebrows were well shaped and appeared close to natural brown in color. Her dark eyelashes were of medium length and curled up out of her eyes.

She allowed him to look deep into her eyes, and he wasn't sure if it was a spacy, cosmic or possibly eccentric inclination that he found within or a vacancy sign. She blinked him away.

"Where is Trench?" Captain heard himself ask suddenly.

She didn't blanch, merely looked at her cigarette, blew out some smoke and said, "Around."

"Close?" he asked, feeling a surge of panic.

319

"No, not close."

Letting her glance fall down onto Captain's crotch, she stared there and smoked. Then she looked back into his eyes, pulled the ribbon out of her hair and shook it to let it fall down over her shoulders. Bleached hair, Captain observed. But as she shook her head, her hair fell into a neat, sun-streaked, layered cut that Captain thought was pretty. Good hair, he said to himself.

Smiling, she asked, "What did you think about what I did to the animal?"

"Ah, well, you mean to Algonquin?"

"That's not Algonquin. Algonquin has been dead fifteen years. This beauty's name is Jinx. He's Algonquin's grandson. But what did you think, frankly?"

Captain thought that he saw a flicker of maternalism from her again. He felt at ease. "Frankly, it turned me on."

"Do you want me to do it to you? I wouldn't mind."

She put her cigarette out and clasped her hands together over one knee. She smiled at him in her easy way.

Captain didn't know what to say. He felt his blood get hot and run around in his loins. "Let's face it, it's a very sexy thing to watch if you've never seen it before."

"If it made you feel that way, I'll relieve you, if you like. Nothing personal, mind you."

Feeling embarrassed and looking for something to say, he asked, "Don't you use machines to get the sperm these days?"

"No. Oh, there are machines, but they're too brutal. No, by hand is still the only right way."

She stood up away from the table. "Well?" she said and rubbed her hands together.

While she stood there smiling, Captain observed that she had no bust to speak of and that her teeth showed tobacco stains. But still, he thought, there's something about her, her matter-of-factness maybe, that I like.

"Are you sure that you don't mind?"

"Not at all, as long as you don't take forever. My arm is weak from Jinx. I hope you understand that I offer because I know you; that is, I know more about the male animal than maybe any other person anywhere in the world, honestly. So I am sensitive to males. If I let Jinx here get an erection and worked on him but didn't finish him off, it could kill him. I'll bet you didn't know that, did you?"

"No, I didn't. Kill him dead?"

"Yep, it could. It would for sure make him impossible to deal with or control until he was relieved. And even then he'd stay ornery as the dickens for a long time. So I understand your needs, and if you want me to help you, I will, that's all. Because I don't want you to be sick on account of me and Jinx and what you saw here."

Madam, Captain thought, you are definitely not playing with a full deck, but I like you and would love to have you pull my cock.

"Where?" he asked.

"Wherever you want. I have no secrets, but if you want privacy, in the bathroom.

Jesus, he thought, she'd do it right here. Goddamn.

She was into the tiny, immaculately clean beige room that housed a lavatory and sink. "Come on in. Take your pants down, come on." Looking into his eyes, she laughed gently and said, "Come on."

Captain pushed the .38 revolver along his waistband as he stepped into the room. He unzipped his fly.

"Drop them," she said. "Put the gun on the toilet or hold onto it if you want."

321

"The gun?" he asked.

"Yes, the gun in your belt. Do something with it and drop your drawers."

Christ Almighty, he said to himself, be careful. He held the .38 in his right hand while he dropped his jeans down to his knees. The room smelled of disinfectant. Captain pushed the door shut behind him, and the sound of a drawing fan began.

Doctor Margarette Leighton knelt down and pulled his trousers to his ankles. She stayed bent at the waist to examine Captain's penis. Her touching it sent a chilling sensation over his body. He felt his penis fill with blood.

"Aren't you going to use some lubrication?" he asked.

"No, no," she said in a perfunctory tone. "I'll do it dry. I'll use your foreskin."

The doctor's blonde hair fell over her face and neck, and Captain saw that her hair was dyed well into her healthy-looking scalp. That's nice, he thought; she looks after herself.

"You look fine," she said.

Doctor Leighton stood up, shook her hair out of her face, put her left hand flatly against Captain's right front shoulder as a brace and began to slowly move the skin back and forth over his penis.

"All the way, come on, completely hard," she said, and then, "Oh, that's good. Oh, that's choice."

She squeezed his perfectly erect penis, and he flexed it against her tightened fingers. Laughing, she began to masturbate him furiously. After a moment she took her eyes away from his to stare at the action and say, "Come on, boy, do it. Come on and do it, do it, do it."

Captain said, "Oh, good God, I have never—"

The room began to smell of the two of them. "Come on and squirt. Come on, do it, do it."

"Put it in your mouth, doctor. Will you put it in your mouth, please?" he heard himself begging.

"You've got to be kidding," she said matter-of-factly without looking up.

"But isn't it sexy to you? Don't you like my cock?"

Nearing an orgasm, Captain began to shake. He heard the doctor laugh in a friendly way and say, "Yes, yes, I like your cock. It's a beauty, and it's, oh, so sexy. Now go for it. My arm won't last much longer, not after Jinx. Come on, squirt it."

Captain was going to climax. He put the tip of the .38 against the soft tissue behind the doctor's ear and pulled the hammer back loudly.

"Suck it. Suck me off, you bitch. Take it in your mouth and swallow my load. Come on, please, or I'll kill you."

Laughing, the blonde female doctor said, "No, I won't and, no, you won't kill me either, or I'll stop. And besides, I won't tell you where Trench is."

Losing control, Captain screamed out into the tiny room. He yelled like a pained animal. "Beat it, beat it—harder, Doctor. Beat my meat. Beat it. Yes, yes. Now watch it, watch the hole in the end. Yes—"

Doctor Leighton did as he asked, and they both watched as thick globs of spermatozoa poured from the stretched, shining end of his penis. "That's what we want," she said. "Come on and spurt. That'll make us feel better." She went to her pulling, milking motion, and Captain dizzily watched her gather his semen into the opened palm of her left hand.

"Be careful with that gun," she said, and she poured the contents of her left hand into the small sink. As the sperm ran to the drain, she put her finger into it. "Good consistency, good thick sperm. See how thick it is? Is it always this thick? Do you remember?"

323

"Yes—No—I don't know. I don't remember. Yes, I think so, goddamn." His knees felt weak. Where am I? he asked himself. What the fuck am I doing?

Using toilet paper and the wash basin, Doctor Leighton gave Captain a cursory but sufficient cleansing. She then bent down and pulled his pants up for him. Smiling, she slapped him hard on the buttocks and said, "Come on, help me with Jinx, please."

He assisted the woman in returning the black stallion to his stall. The big horse seemed relaxed, which helped Captain to feel the same way. When Captain was alone near Jinx's head, he got his eye, winked and whispered, "I guess we know a good hand job when we get one, don't we, boy."

Jinx stepped on Captain's foot. "Ouch, Jesus Christ," Captain yelled, "you damn near broke it."

"Well, use your head and get out of the way when you're around animals. Think, Captain, think," came from the maternal-sounding blonde doctor.

After Jinx's stall was secured with a huge combination paddle lock, she asked, "Are you hungry?"

Captain thought that he was and said so, but as they walked together from the place, down the long, cold, tunnellike corridor beneath the intermittent wreaths of white light, Captain said, "I want Trench. Where is he?"

She leaned on the heavy door latch, but before it opened she stopped and stared up into Captain's eyes. It was a deep, soul-searching, serious, blue-eyed look. Then the stained-tooth smile came and she said, "You are insane, aren't you? Completely crazy."

"What do you mean?" he asked.

Doctor Leighton broke the heavy door open with a whooshing sound and taking Captain's hand, led him outside into the dry, sunny afternoon.

324

"Woweee, what a wonderful change," he said, stretching his arms up into the hot, bright Arizona elements.

Acting in a good mood, Doctor Leighton pulled Captain along to the yellow Corvette convertible parked next to the building in the shade. "I didn't mean to insult you, Captain. I didn't mean it that way. But you have to admit, what you're doing is a bit strange."

"What am I doing? Nothing I'm doing is strange."

"Do you know Jack Trench, honestly?" She watched him for his response.

He answered with a shrug as though it were no big deal. "No, I don't. So what?"

The Freak

The Corvette's black leather seats were warm and tacky but comforting as she drove out the farm's long driveway. Glancing over his shoulder as they passed the parking lot, Captain could not see his rented car. He turned to take a good look, but a grassy knoll got in the way of his vision. It's got to be there, he thought. I just missed it. I'm sure that it's there.

Just before the main gate, Doctor Leighton pulled off the road to the right to allow a lone man on horseback to pass by the car. The horseback rider was a dark, coarse-looking individual with a jutting Neanderthal-like forehead. His eyes were hidden beneath thick black eyebrows.

"Hello, Cry," the man snarled, tipping his black Western hat. The man spurred his horse, which galloped past them down the driveway toward the farm.

"Who was that?" Captain asked.

"Just a wrangler," she replied, pulling the Corvette onto Algonquin Road to drive north into Meadowbrook country.

Captain put his hands up and let the hot desert air blow through his fingers. "Wow, that feels nice. Did that wrangler back there call you Cry?"

"Yes."

That's not your name, is it?"

"No, but some of the men call me that."

"Cry?"

"Yes."

"I don't know," Captain said, "what kind of a name that is, but I think that I like it—Cry. Hello, Cry. Nice to meet you, Cry. Hey, where are you taking me, Cry?"

"Up the road for a beer. Don't worry. It's more a name to make fun, Captain. It's a name that they tease me with, more or less. Only the men that I've been intimate with use it."

"That guy back there on the horse, he was a bad looking guy. Is he one of your boyfriends?"

Doctor Leighton looked over at him and smiled. "I use him, and some others."

"Goddamn, Doc, I enjoy your—I love your openness around me. It makes me feel comfortable, like you trust me."

"Why not? You're not going anyplace. You won't tell." She apparently read the fearful expression that came over his face, because she immediately added, "Will you? You won't go telling my secrets, that's all I meant." She rubbed his crotch in a friendly way and pulled into Pete's Roady, the cafe next to the small Meadowbrook gas station where Captain had stopped the night before.

Looking out through a dusty, mended screen, they sat in a booth at the front of the cafe watching the heat rise from the blacktop over Algonquin Road. The yellow Corvette sat out there on the hard, dry ground in front of them, soaking up the sun.

A dirty, coffee-drinking, mechanic-type man sat in the shadows at the rear of the place reading a paper. He was the only other patron. He raised his coffee cup, smiled a toothless grin and yelled, "Hi, Cry."

She waved back, and Captain said, "Him too?"

Doctor Margarette Leighton didn't speak a word on the subject; she only smiled.

Pete was a stout, bulbous-nosed Mexican woman dressed in a Christmas-patterned muu-muu. She and the doctor were obvious comrades and chatted briefly in Spanish before sharing a joke. Pete then tried to sell the day's chili in English, which sounded fine to Captain.

"Let's drink a little first," Doctor Leighton said.

Pete put her hands on her broad hips and leaned away to stare at her friend through a squint as if to say, "Drink, are you sure about that? Oh, come on now, you don't want to drink."

But Doctor Leighton said, "Come on, Pete," and the large Mexican woman waddled away without taking their order. "Pete was my nanny from the time that I was ten. Can you believe it? She used to live at the big house with us."

"What big house?"

"The beautiful big house, the main house back at the farm. I was raised there from the time that I was ten. It was our home—my mother's and father's—before it was Meadowbrook. Pete worked for us then."

Pete returned with two cold, opened bottles of Suprema Mexican beer in one hand and a bottle of tequila and two glasses in the other. Margarette Leighton went for the tequila in what appeared an immoderate way. The liquor held all of her interest while she hurriedly poured herself a good-sized splash, licked her lips and swallowed it down. He could see that she loved it too much, and when she chased the drink with cold beer and sighed with a glance toward the rafters as though life were suddenly perfect, Captain speculated that she was alcoholic. But far be it from me, he laughed to himself, to ridicule a drinker, and he had a decent swallow of warm tequila for himself.

The cold Suprema beer tasted wonderful behind the straight shot, and Captain felt warm and heady almost immediately. He watched as the blonde woman's eyes and cheeks reddened from her allergic reaction to the alcohol. He touched his own forehead and it seemed clammy and hot. They poured more tequila.

"So you were born back at the farm?"

"No, not born. I was born in Buena Park, California, a block from Disneyland. My father was a veterinarian, took care of Walt's animals until I was ten. We moved to the farm when I was ten."

"And you lived here ever since?"

"No, no. Heavens, no. I've been educated all over the world. I've got seven degrees." She drank to that and said, "Honest."

"I've never been to Europe," Captain said, "but my mother lives there and likes it, I think. Could you live in Europe?"

"No, I like it here. But I have lived there." She yelled at Pete for cold beers.

"What are European women like?" Captain asked.

"They're as different as American women."

"What does that mean?"

"That they are all different types. What type of woman do you like, Captain?"

"I don't know. I'm not sure." He wondered how to explain what he liked without being vulgar. How, he asked himself, do I tell her that I like women with large, protruding vaginal lips and substantial clitorises, usually brunettes. Then he thought of Iris's nice vaginal lips and clitoris and that she was a blonde, and

Marie, another blonde who he remembered loving a lot who he'd thought had a small, neat pussy. Women raced through his mind: their dispositions, their breasts, their feet, their smells; but he couldn't stop the contest long enough to settle on one type or even one face.

While straining to think, he blurted, "I—I like the type that likes me." He felt himself blush and had a large swallow of tequila.

"I'd never have guessed," laughed the doctor, touching his hand understandingly. "Oh, Paris," she said. "They'd love you in Paris, if you have money. They love American men with money. I hated Paris. Lived there but hated it." She reflected for a moment and laughed. "I just thought, no wonder I was confused and flipped out in Paris—When you're born and raised at Disneyland, what can you expect to understand about Paris?" She laughed, and Captain liked that one too.

"But I'm Irish," she said. "Old Mumums and Dadums always wanted to live over there. When I went away to college, Jack moved them over, retired them, to Ireland. He bought them out first, I guess." She laughed. "Not that it would have mattered. I can hear benevolent Jack." She gestured with her glass. "My dear Mr. and Mrs. Leighton, you will go to Ireland, as you've always wanted, enjoy your remaining years over there and die in peace—or die here, now."

She drank a good swallow of tequila. "But they loved it. I went over to visit and couldn't stand it. When Dad finally died, I went back over again for the burial and the wake. God, when I saw all of those drunken Irishmen pull my father's body out of the box to dance with him, I fainted dead away. Only time in my life I've ever fainted. But they scooped him right out of the coffin and passed him around to dance—His friends, can you imagine?"

She shook her blonde head. "Golly, the memory of that—

Actually, I've got nothing against Ireland, I don't think, but the wakes, the drunken Irish wakes. You can have—"

"Did Trench really threaten your parents?"

"Naw, I was just kidding, I think."

She grabbed his arm and urged him to see the humor, and they laughed together, clicked glasses and drank.

"Why did you say that I was crazy back at the barn?" Captain asked into a flushing face.

"Because you are. Anybody who comes looking for him is either crazy or stupid; yet you walk right in hunting him. God Almighty, Captain, when I think of it—Is that your real name— Captain Blood?"

Captain told the story about his father being an Errol Flynn fan, how his father had insisted on the name and how his mother had thought that it would have been a more suitable tag for the family dog.

Doctor Leighton thought that it was a great story and drank to it. They sat quietly for awhile in the warm room, letting their systems settle.

"I've got that good old feeling, Captain," she said, and Captain said that he did too.

"Why is everyone so protective about Trench, so secretive?"

"Oh, good God, Captain Blood, you can knock it off. You come looking and you don't know? Well, they know about you, you can bet your last peso on that." She laughed. "They sure as the dickens know about you, Captain Blood. And here you sit—I don't know, I've got to hand it to you, I guess. Maybe you're just one of many. Are you a landing party, Captain Blood? Are the Marines behind you?" That one really made her roar.

Captain touched his gun. "Where is he, Doctor?" He reached across the table and grabbed the blonde woman's arm. "Where? Goddammit, where is he?"

331

"Ouch—Ouch, you're hurting me—don't—He is around, I told you. He is around. He'll be around tonight for sure. You'll meet him. You've got no other choice now."

"Now what the fuck is that supposed to mean?"

"Just what I said, but you're safe." She became serious. "That's the truth, honest. You're safe for now. He usually doesn't hit from behind, that's one thing about him. He doesn't need to. Don't forget, this is all his." She gestured to the surrounding countryside. "Besides, I'm sure that he's dying to meet you." She laughed and drank beer until her eyes watered.

Captain leaned up to the dirty screen and stared up and down the deserted road in front. "Nothing," he said, shrugging. "Nobody."

She patted the back of his hand. "Oh, good God, don't look so worried. Here, take the keys to my car and make a run for it. Go on, you can make it, I guarantee, honest Injun. Head south, back past the farm. Go on."

Captain felt a sudden urge to move. His muscles tensed, but he stayed still. "What's going to happen?" he asked, trying to remain calm.

"You two are going to meet at high noon tomorrow in the middle of the barnyard. And when the shadow of the cockswain falls evenly between you, you'll both draw and—bang—the town will be free. Or we'll all have to suffer worse than ever for befriending you, for jacking you off." Laughing, she slapped the table top and lit a cigarette.

What the fuck, Captain wondered, have I gotten myself into? He looked out at the yellow Corvette and while so doing, she pushed her car keys across the table to him. "Go ahead, go." She pointed toward the open road, smoked and sipped tequila.

"What's going on? What have you heard about me?" he asked.

"Nothing. I've heard absolutely nothing. But I've been around a long time, Captain, and I'm a good guesser."

"But how do you know that he knows I'm here, or expects me, and that I should be careful and all of that bullshit?"

"I know Jack Trench and I know his business, and I've seen them come and I've seen them go, with guns in their pants. Jack's business is exciting, and he's still here. They come and go, but he's still here. I haven't seen anybody with a gun as cute as you, though." She laughed.

"Does he know that I'm here?"

"I would guess so, probably. If you're here looking for him, sure. If you're here to use that gun, you must have a good reason, and he must know it. He makes it his business to know things. That's all, that's all I'm going by. I'm guessing."

"How do you figure into all of this? How do you know about things?"

"Because I'm the one that makes it all happen, all of it." She laughed boastfully. "All of the honest stuff, that is, and the man trusts me."

"What do you make happen?" he asked.

"Meadowbrook Farms—the finest thoroughbreds in the country and most of the world. Do you know what that bag of semen that I took today is worth?"

"No," he answered.

"Jinx will artificially inseminate one lucky mare somewhere else in the world with what was in that bag today, and it will cost the other side $100,000, assuming that it takes. One masturbation of one black stallion on one given occasion—a hundred thou. Not bad, huh?"

"No, not bad."

Doctor Leighton, who had slowed her drinking a bit, poured each of them a new half-glass of tequila and reached over to take Captain's hand. Calmly she looked into his eyes.

"Don't be afraid. You won't get hurt if you're with me. You've got your gun. There's nothing to be afraid of."

"Who says that I'm afraid?"

"I do. I can see that you are. But don't worry; you're with me and I am catered to, protected, loved, adored, well fucked and handled with T.L.C. I am kept happy because I am the best thoroughbred vet in the world—in the world, Captain, honest. Jack is gone until late, anyway. If you want to drink with me and play around, you'll be okay. And when he gets back, I'll introduce you to him, if that's what you want. And then you're on your own. You can go and hide in the barn if you like." She laughed.

Jack is gone, Captain thought, until late. Hearing the words made him feel much better.

"How late is late?" Captain asked.

"Late, probably after midnight. You'll hear him arrive, Captain. He'll come in his plane."

Goddamn, Captain thought, feeling suddenly anxiety-free. The keys to the car are here, I'm armed, we're alone, the big man is gone until late and when he comes home, he'll announce his own arrival by the sound of his plane. What else is there? he asked himself. Shit, he thought, feeling cocky, maybe I'll go down to the airstrip and ambush him when he lands.

He looked across the table at the doctor. And what, he asked himself, does she know? I guess this and I guess that. Bullshit, she doesn't know a fucking thing and neither does he, or somebody would make a move. All that guessing crap is in her quirky mind.

"Doctor Leighton, you have a good imagination."

"What do you mean?" she asked.

"I mean that you think fun things, but the way you drink that booze, aren't you afraid you'll screw up your brain? Do you ever black out?"

"Naw, never. I black out my blackouts."

They both laughed and clicked glasses.

334

"No, I really don't ever black out. Drinking enables me to mitigate my feelings, that's all. I am lonely, Captain."

He thought that she looked pathetically sad and drawn as she said it, for just that instant while she thought about it, before she smiled again and asked, "How about you, do you black out?"

Feeling insulted, he answered, "Hell, no. I remember everything, absolutely everything, always."

"So," she said, with her knowing smile, "which is worse?"

He had to think about that and catching her point, he finally agreed with a smile of his own and said, "I don't know."

A deep, understanding look passed between them until Captain asked, "What does he look like—Jack Trench?"

"You're kidding. You don't know? You mean, you've never seen him?"

"That's right."

She seemed puzzled. "Well, if you two don't even know each other, then maybe you are safe, I don't know. What do you want here?"

"Never mind. What does he look like? Tell me."

Smiling coyly, she picked at a beer label and made him wait for the answer. "You're not teasing—You don't know him?"

"That's right."

She watched his expression as she spoke. "Jack Trench is a dwarf."

"A what—? You're kidding."

"No, it's true. He is a Castillian dwarf. Do you know what that is?"

"I'm not sure."

"Jack Trench is high Spanish, a pure-bred Spaniard—purer, better than all of Mexico, so he says. And the funny part is that it might well be true. But he is a dwarf. He stands only a head taller than this table."

Staring at the table top, Captain tried to picture the little man and got a vision of a circus clown, a midget in white face and full makeup, with a sad red mouth, awkwardly waddling along a boardwalk.

"You'll probably see for yourself," she said evenly.

"Yes, I will," he said. "Is he deformed?"

"Yes, but I'm going to let you find out about that for yourself."

"Why? Tell me. I want to know what he is."

She said, "No," and shook her head.

"Why not tell me?"

"Because I don't like to talk about it, that's all, nothing more. I'll tell you one thing, though, that you should know. During his life, Jack has gone through more pain and survived than any other human being I've ever personally known. And you know what the endurance of pain brings, don't you? Or do you?"

"Physical or emotional?" he asked.

"Both."

"Yes, it brings growth and maturity."

She laughed. "Growth and maturity my fanny. Maybe that's what the pain you know brings. The kind I'm talking about—the kind of pain that makes the big boys and girls weep like broken children—brings only one thing, if you survive it . . . strength. Jack Trench is one of the strong ones, Captain." She thought for a moment, they drank together and she said, "Listen to this one incident that comes to mind. There are so many but—A few years ago he was out alone driving the fence line along the deep south pasture, way back into the old Mexican county where the land is rough—raw, unbroken ground. Jack suffers from epilepsy, and on this day out on the line, when he got out of the Rover to straighten a stake, he had a seizure. A grand mal epileptic seizure, Captain, so severe that it broke his back in two places.

When he came to, he was mostly paralyzed and couldn't get back into the jeep. So he crawled, Captain, he crawled on all fours and his belly and his chest. He crawled back in. It took him three days and two nights and a go with a pack of wild animals."

Doctor Leighton took on a faraway but apprehensive look while she stared out the window and remembered. "It was an impossible chore, Captain, impossible, but he made it. His clothes were gone, the skin was torn off the front of his pathetic little body. I treated him, and I saw the pain festering in those black eyes of his, but never a word, not a complaint. He was up and around in a brace in three days. He's strong, Captain. Whatever your business is with him, you'd better know that."

A depressing pall seemed to hang over their table. Captain tried to break it by drinking and joking. "But he was smiling, wasn't he? I mean, he saw the humor in the long crawl, didn't he? Wasn't he happy to be alive?"

Doctor Leighton's expression remained serious. "No. No, he didn't smile at being alive, Captain, because Jack Trench has no sense of humor about life, about anything. He's just strength, Captain. Dealing with life has made him unbearably strong, and brutal."

Jinx

See you, Cry Baby.'' The mechanic threw his newspaper into a corner receptacle, patted Doctor Leighton's shoulder, winked at Captain knowingly and smiled as he passed them. The cowbell on the screen door clanged when he strode from the place. Pete yelled after the man from the kitchen, "See ya, Barney."

"All right, tell me why they call you that? Come on—"

Doctor Margarette Leighton yelled over her shoulder at Pete for cold beer.

"How do you feel?" she asked.

"Half stoned but good, warm and good."

"Me too."

"Come on, Doc. Why do they call you Cry and Cry Baby?"

"You mean the rough-looking men, don't you, the ones I've been intimate with?" She was teasing and he liked it.

338

"Yes, the crude-looking men. Why do they call you that?"

"It's their joke. You know how men are when they get together and talk about the women they've had, they laugh and make fun." She laughed, drank and lit a cigarette. "I'm glad you don't smoke," she said.

"So am I. I know that one will kill you. But go on, about your nickname—"

"Well, they don't understand that their coarseness doesn't bother me. In fact, I like it. So let them talk, let them brood around like big, stupid bucks calling me Cry. It's of no matter to me."

"But why that name, may I ask?"

"Sure, but it might make you hot again, if I know you at all." She laughed and looked deep into his eyes until he felt his penis jerk.

The fucker, Captain thought, she is a turn on. "Yes, go on. Go on, tell me, please."

Sighing, she yawned, sneaked a glance at Captain from the corner of her eye and spoke matter of factly. "I am a virgin, Captain. That is, no man has ever been in my vagina, and no one ever will, and that's that."

"But?"

"But I let them get around in back of me, if you know what I mean. I don't look at them once they get behind me, I just bend over and let them have a field day, and I dream."

Captain's penis was completely stiff. Reaching under the table, he took the woman's hand and brought it back to feel his hard penis.

She smiled, and her face seemed to take on even more color. She kept her hand where he had put it and squeezed his penis firmly in what he thought was a professional manner.

Swallowing loudly, Captain said, "The story is beautiful. It's very sexy too."

"I told you that you would think so," she said. "I'm sensitive to men. I know what you like."

"Why are you so open about it? Why are you willing to be so open and free?"

"Why not? It's merely the way things are. It's not dirty."

"Why didn't you suck me, back at the barn?"

She squeezed him hard and took her hand away. "Because you're not my type—honest—at least up until now you weren't. And I don't do that anyway, what you said."

"Oh" slipped out of Captain disappointedly before he could censor it.

"Oh, no, now don't feel bad. You're just not rough enough, that's all. You appear to be sensitive and rather exclusive, in your way. I like them rough and tough and hard. I like them to rip away and—"

"And it makes you cry, right?"

She smiled and looked straight into his eyes without blinking. Almost, he thought, as though it were some kind of a challenge to see if she could say it.

"It doesn't take very much to do that, but yes. It is involuntary, like a reflex. They put it in, and I cry."

"Holy Toledo," Captain said softly. "They put it in your—your—"

"In my rectum, yes."

"Did you say that you dream?"

"Yes."

"What about?"

"It depends on my mood."

"Well, tell me one mood."

"I have only three: Algonquin, Trinity and now Jinx—the three stallions, the three black devils."

"Do you like black men?"

340

"No, that doesn't interest me in the least."

"But the horses?" he asked.

"The stallions, yes, they do. They hold all of my interest."

With her elbows on the table, she folded her hands, put her chin on them and stared at him affectionately. "I love them, Captain. They are my life. They are everything to me. I told you about being lonely. I am without people really, but I am not alone. You saw Jinx. Tell me a man that can come up to him. Think of one. Clark Gable? Tyrone Power?" She laughed. "What a joke. Jinx wouldn't even let one of those people get on him, not for a second."

Trying to act calm, Captain asked, "Where do you live?"

"I live in a lovely bungalow back on the farm grounds."

"Alone?"

"Yes."

She smiled in an encouraging way, and he said to himself, What the hell, why not?

"Can we go, please, to your bungalow for awhile and can I hear you cry? The thought of it is making me a little nuts."

Captain squeezed his own penis in an obvious gesture, breathed deeply for her benefit and stared. "Please?" he said.

Reaching and placing her hand on top of his, she said, "Will you tell me a story too? Then I would let you, if you can tell me a good story while you're—at work."

"A story?" he asked, but before Doctor Leighton could answer, he caught on and excitedly said, "Yes, yes, yes, of course I will. But I will want a silk scarf to tie around your eyes for blinders, so that you don't see Jinx behind you. Yes, Cry, I know what you want to hear, and Jinx will make it real good for you, I'm positive."

Standing, uneasily at first, Doctor Leighton yawned again, stretched and said, "Then what keeps us here?"

341

"The tequila," Captain said, joking.

"Not really," she said, bringing the bottle of tequila and a cold beer.

"Be careful, Margarette, don't drive. Let him drive," came Pete's loud voice from behind them.

"You drive, Captain," she said. And he did.

Hurrying to get there before she changed her mind, driving too fast, Captain felt Doctor Leighton's hand on his leg and then a hearty pat on his thigh.

"Slow down," she said. "Don't worry, you'll get what you—Don't worry, Captain, I'll cry for you."

Captain slowed the car but thought that he would squeeze the fiberglass steering wheel out from between his fingers. "I've never known a woman like you before."

She sat with her eyes closed, her face up into the sun, the bottles in her hands. "Be careful," she said, "the turn is up ahead. Don't be impatient."

At the same moment that he saw the black clump of a dead animal in the road up ahead of them, the smell was upon them. Doctor Leighton broke her sunning trance and sniffing, looked around. Shielding her eyes she said, "Skunk," and Captain agreed. When she saw it in the road, she became very excited and yelled, "Stop, stop."

Shit, fuck, Captain thought.

The yellow Corvette was still moving when Doctor Leighton alighted and without checking for traffic, ran out into the roadway to administer to the animal. The stench of skunk was overwhelming, and Captain held his nose. Captain looked down at the spot on his pants and said, "Shit."

He had a drink and yelled, "Can I help?"

The doctor called back, "No, he's dead."

After a short time, she dragged the black and white animal off the road, left it in back of the car and got in. "Too bad," she said, appearing preoccupied. She drank tequila out of the bottle, chased it with beer and said, "Let's go." Then she looked at him and smiled in that sly, deranged way, and Captain's juices began to flow anew.

Passing the farm's parking lot, Captain glanced over to find a large, green baling machine parked between him and where he had parked his rented Chevrolet. It's got to be there, he told himself. Of course it is; it's behind the big tractor, that's all.

The bungalow in which Doctor Margarette Leighton lived was set off from the rest of the Meadowbrook compound and nestled at the edge of a golden-colored field of swaying, unharvested wheat. A neatly painted 4-H Club sign was posted next to the field. Kids planted this, he thought. It probably used to be desert and sagebrush.

Captain thought that the wheat field was magnificent, and when a gentle breeze bent the shocks of wheat in his direction, he tried to smell them, but the faint odor of skunk lingered in his nostrils.

"Beautiful," he said, nodding toward the field.

Appearing pleased, she smiled and said, "Yes, isn't it."

The white wooden exterior of the small one-story house matched the other buildings in the compound with dark green trim and a green shake roof. The surrounding hedge and colorful garden were well kept, the lawn thick and strong looking.

Inside the breezy, knotty pine living room, Doctor Leighton told him to brush his teeth and announced that they were switching to martinis. He followed directions and coming back from the bathroom she handed him his iced glass as she passed him, carrying hers. The dark brown carpet looked thick and cozy against her bare feet. He threw his shoes next to hers. The floor felt luxurious as he walked. He yawned.

She yelled, "I'll shower. Undress and meet me at the pass."

He heard her shriek when the water went on.

The martini bit his throat, but he drank most of it while he examined the photographs, plaques, ribbons, the silver and gold plates that adorned the polished pine walls, distinguishing the doctor's work with animals.

The quiet, sunny afternoon and natural, rich surroundings continued to draw his attention out through the wood-framed screened windows, out into the open day. The unpleasant odor had disappeared. The air smelled clean and sweet.

"Nice," he said, making a new shaker of martinis, "damn nice."

Bringing the full shaker, he searched for and found the lady's bedroom. The carpet was thick and dark green. The walls and ceiling of the room were covered with what seemed to Captain an overpowering wallpaper pattern. The background was dark green and wet looking, the foreground was comprised of a jungle design of thick and thin, seemingly three-dimensional, white vine-like foliage.

The walls seemed to move together in some hallucinogenic way, and he found himself backing out of the place. Telling himself that he was acting silly, he stepped back into the room. He felt the ceiling and walls reach out to him. He stood still and let them encircle him.

"Goddamn," he said, "it's alive."

Forcing his eyes off of the room's interior, he looked out through the opened window into the golden harvest of wheat that went on for as far as he could see. It moved in the breeze, giving him an easy, relaxed feeling. He concentrated on the out-of-doors and sipped the martini until he was completely comfortable. Then he went over and touched the nearest wall. It was slippery yet textured.

"Goddamn—weird," he said, still unable to adjust his eyes to the pattern.

Stepping back, he felt his eyes swim over the jungle design. He shook his head, touched the wall again and spoke to it. "Boy, are you weird."

Captain stripped the bed clothes back from the big green bed to reveal a neatly fitted lime green bottom sheet. The bed appeared cool and sent a shiver through him that made him want to lie upon it. He put his pistol close at hand under the side of the bed and lay all of his clothes in a neat pile next to it.

Shivering again, he sat on the end of the bed to finish his drink. Breathing deeply of the healthful air, he sat still and stared out of the window, letting himself become mesmerized. "The amber waves of grain," he sighed, feeling good about America.

Another swallow finished the martini, and he dove onto the lime green mattress. The bed was firm and cool but more than that, he could see himself. His reflection was there on the wall closest to the door he had entered. The heavy verdant feeling was there and the entanglement of stark white vine, but he was there too, bouncing on the lime green bed and grinning. The thought that came wasn't appealing, but he laughed and accepted it. Like a baby, he thought. Like a big, naked baby.

Doctor Leighton then appeared, small-busted and large-boned. Her pubic hair looked bleached. With a faraway look in her eyes, she smiled and touched her temples and then her hair, which was pulled back and held that way by a long, hanging, black silken scarf.

"Are you going to bone me, big boy?" she asked sexily, moving her broad hips from side to side.

"Not unless you're a fish," Captain said, laughing and not being able to help it. He fell back onto the bed.

Jesus, he thought, letting his eyes go with the white-veined ceiling. Why does she try to act sexy now? She's not sexy; she's eccentric.

He felt her sit beside him. She shook her head just right until the soft black scarf hung down onto his stomach. It felt good, but his mind flashed ahead, and he hoped that she wouldn't want to get into a kissing thing.

Moving her head and shoulders, she dragged the scarf up and down his torso. He closed his eyes and tried to shut his brain off. He worried that the stories at the roadhouse had been a lark, and he worried that his penis might never get hard for conventional sex with this woman. Stop, stop, stop, he screamed to himself. Feel the soft scarf, feel the nice scarf.

Doctor Leighton finished her drink and after a moment said, "When will Jinx be here?"

Sitting up on one elbow, Captain observed that the woman's eyes were closed. She leaned back onto two stiffened elbows, her smallish breasts thrust upward. A slight smile played over her lips. She rocked back and forth against her arms.

The immature inflection in his voice made him feel self-conscious when he began to speak excitedly. Slowing his speech and deepening his voice, Captain strained to use the best of his imagination.

"Yes, Jinx is on his way. I hear him coming. Clop, clop. Goddamn—" He jumped from the bed and tromped heavily on the floor—"Goddamn, the whole house is shaking from his power. Feel it?"

Doctor Leighton didn't speak but smiled with her face tilted upward, her eyes closed toward the ceiling, listening. Captain was able to get the small place to resound from his stomping.

"Jeeeesus Chreeeeist, lady, this horse is beautiful. God, his coat shines like velvet. He must have a good, a great doctor, the best. But don't look. We wouldn't want him to see you looking at him, staring at his huge dangling prick. Wow, what a powerful spotted shaft. Keep your eyes closed. Don't dare look. God, no. He would see the need, the desire in your eyes. We won't embarrass him with that."

Captain pulled the black silk scarf out of Doctor Leighton's hair and wrapped it around her head over her eyes several times and tied it. "You need blinders, girl, or you'll stare, I know you will."

"Yes, I will, I would have," she said, bouncing on the bed excitedly.

"No, Jinx, don't. You'll hurt her." Captain said as he made a loud whinnying sound. He began to nip the masked woman on her shoulders. He snorted and whinnied and bit her on the neck.

Doctor Leighton kept her arms stiffened and began saying, "Oh, baby—Oh, baby." She wriggled and pushed her bottom into the firm bed.

When Captain whinnied again, he looked in the mirror to see himself crack a big grin. He was glad that the doctor couldn't observe. It was because he sounded just like a goat. I'm not whinnying, he thought with embarrassment, I'm neighing. Why, he asked himself, don't you just go *baaaaa* like a sheep? But the blindfolded blonde doctor appeared to love the sounds.

She asked, "What is he doing? Does he see me?"

Captain whinnied. "Does he see you, honey? He is pawing the ground right next to me and nudging me with those big flaring nostrils. He wants me to move aside so that he can have you. Back, Jinx, back, boy. It's too big. You'll hurt her. You'll make her cry."

"No, no he won't. Let him. Let him have it," she said, working her mouth in a peculiar way as though chewing a stiff piece of gum. Frothy saliva showed at the corners of her mouth. "Let him. Let him have some," she said, bouncing on the bed.

347

"All right, Jinx, but be careful. Don't tear her. I'm going to let him put the big spotted thing into you, Margarette. Don't try to stop us. Turn over."

She quickly turned over on the bed to kneel and point her bottom side out at Captain.

"No, at the end of the bed, so that Jinx can watch."

"Yes, yes, yes," she said excitedly, finding her way to the bed's end.

He didn't touch her with his hands or the rest of his body, but swung his hips past her to slap his stiff penis against her. Doctor Leighton tried to follow his movements with her bottom. He stepped away and nipped her rear end hard and her back and he whinnied loudly, the best that he could. He finally laid his full penis against the crack of her ass.

"Oh, hot, hot cock," she murmured.

Leaning over her back, he began to braid her shortish blonde hair. "Your mane will get in his way," Captain said, watching the mirror and flexing the length of his penis against her crack. While he teased with her hair and attempted to make horse sounds, he realized that she had her hand under her belly and was directing his penis into her rectum.

Standing but leaving his penis in her tugging hand, Captain said, "Go ahead, boy, do it, do it, do it." He heard his voice tremble and felt the goose bumps come.

Doctor Leighton repeated, "Do it, do it. Come on boy, do it." She put saliva onto Captain's penis. She began to speak frantically and wiggle her bottom. "Put your hands on my hips. Help him, Captain Blood, help him. Put your hands—Yes, yes, that's right. Now shove it—hard, hard. Shove it. Oh, my God, there. Come on, push. Oh, yes, go, fuck me in the ass—hard. Come on, boy."

Captain felt the head and then some more of his penis pass her rectal ring, and as this happened Doctor Leighton broke into a long, loud series of boo hoos. She cried hard, in anguish, and through it yelled, "Do it, do it, do it. Fuck me real hard, you cold black devil."

Captain pushed once more, and when he realized that he was in her, at that instant she sat back onto him to impale herself. She let out a startling death cry of a scream and bawled.

"Holy Toledo," he said, feeling the tightness around his penis. I've never, he realized, done it like this before. I've never been in an asshole. They said that my cock was too big. Goddamn, it's wonderful, he thought. Pushing his groin and pubic hair against her bottom, Captain yelled, "Go, Jinx, you fucker, go. Take it to her."

Doctor Leighton tried to catch her breath with a loud hoarse inhalation of air. She began to weep fitfully and sob, "Oh, no. Oh, no. Oh, no," again and again.

Watching himself do the deed in the mirror, Captain went with the good feeling. Holding her rump with both hands, he began to pump into her muscular rectum with rhythmic driving thrusts. He saw the tears covering her face, and he watched her varying tormented expressions in the mirror. He admitted to himself that watching the perspiring naked woman beat her fists into the bed and wrench at the end of his penis excited him. Captain wondered if Iris would let him do it to her in the ass. What prudes we really are at heart, he thought. We've never even contemplated doing it like this, never discussed it. Shit, fucking squares under it all.

The entire area of the crack at Doctor Leighton's bottom was wet, making intercourse easy. A not unpleasant scent filled Captain's nose, which made him drive even harder. He slammed into her. Without giving it much thought, when he pulled his penis most of the way out, he reached under to touch the doctor's juicy vagina.

Continuing to cry, she quickly pushed his hand away, but not before he had felt what was there. It stunned him. His movements slowed and became mechanical. Stop it, stop, stop, don't think about it, he screamed at himself, but he thought about it. Doctor Leighton's vagina was huge and hung gaping. He knew a Jewish word that was conceived to describe such a hole: *luch*. Cry has a huge *luch*, he thought, and he used the guttural sounding word in a softly spoken sentence and made himself laugh. "Lots of *luch*," he said, laughing quietly.

Captain listened to her sob and again resumed the pleasure of working hard at rectal coitus with the woman, but his mind was somewhere else. He felt her big hole again, and she pushed his hand away. She fucks horses, he thought, sure as shit that's it. She's a virgin, all right. What did she say? he remembered, No man has ever been in my vagina, right? Right. No man, that's for sure, but those big, spotted horse cocks have been in there. Shit, yes, he thought, it's a lead pipe cinch.

"Can you come this way?" Captain asked, perspiration dropping off of his face onto her back.

Sobbing hysterically, the answer came in a loud rhythmic moan, "No, do it, do it, do it."

"But can you have an orgasm?" he asked, his face close to her ear.

She wouldn't answer, so Captain began to pound into her as hard as he could. Reaching, he held her shoulders and reminded himself of a piston steam engine at work when he watched himself in the mirrored wall.

Doctor Leighton turned her mouth into the bed, which muffled her cries and left the warm, sex-scented Arizona air calm but for the slap, slap, slap sounds of flesh that echoed in the green and white hallucinogenic jungle room.

"Come for me. Can you come for me?" Captain blurted,

350

spitting onto her back. He heard himself screaming now too. With each thrust the pain in his legs and abdomen became greater, but he bore down as though in an athletic contest. Holding his breath like in weight training, he slammed her as absolutely hard as he could. His testicles ached. Suddenly blood appeared. It splashed between them and up onto her back, but he didn't stop.

"Come," he gasped.

Doctor Leighton then stopped crying long enough to wail out, "No, animals don't. Now get it, get it. Do it for Mama."

The desire to stop began to overwhelm him. The last six miles of a marathon run. His muscles tingled from oxygenation and his head swam. His knees gave out, and he fell with a wet slopping sound onto her back. His penis stayed intact in her bleeding rectum. Doctor Leighton continued to cry like a tormented child, and Captain added the sound of his own gasping breath to the room's resonance.

Doctor Leighton began to utter a purring sound while Captain allowed himself to lie heavily upon her, unmoving. She gasped out, "Did you do it?"

"No," Captain replied.

She crawled away from him and at the same time removed the silken blinders from her eyes.

Captain lay still, watching himself breathe through an open mouth in the greenish mirror.

"My goodness, after all that. You are the one, aren't you. Have you got blue balls?" She asked the question directly, without a trace of a tear. She rubbed her eyes. "Let me see," she said, and rolled Captain over to lie upon his back. Kneeling down, blocking Captain's reflected vision, Doctor Leighton explored his testicles with her fingers and touched his half hard penis gently. He felt his penis grow full again.

"I thought so," she said in a most salutary tone. "We can't

have you going around like that." She left him lying on his back and returned quickly with a handful of some thick lubricant. Vaseline, he thought. While she rubbed it over his stiff penis with one hand, she pulled him to his feet with the other and brought him to stand close to the mirror.

"Watch me do it to you. It will be very sexy. You'll do it right away, I know you will."

She rubbed his hard penis vigorously but with smooth, even strokes. Utilizing the mirror, they looked away from the action, into each others' eyes. She smiled coyly, winked and looked back at what she was doing. Captain looked back too and noticed a thin trickle of blood making its way down the inside of the woman's right leg.

"Why don't you let me fuck you?" he asked, feeling close to orgasm.

"Because I told you, I don't do it with any man. I told you that. Now come on and concentrate. Do it for me, you're nearly there. I want to see you do it. Come on."

"But don't you want an orgasm for yourself? I know a Hollywood girl who runs around at open sex parties—orgies, I guess—and she runs around insisting to couples, 'Everybody gets to come. Don't be selfish, everybody gets to come.' I believe that, sort of. Don't you?"

The doctor stopped what she was doing and turned to him. She spoke in a scolding tone, and he thought that she might put her hands on her hips. "The female animal does not experience orgasm, Captain." He started to speak, but she cut him off. "I know, I know what you've heard, but it simply is not true. Oh, it can feel fabulous and tingly and wild, but no female animal actually reaches a climax. I know—I'm the doctor."

"Bullshit," Captain said.

"No, believe me, Captain. It's all in their head. They think

352

that they reach some kind of peak, but that's all that it is—a thought. I know, I've done the tests. Believe me, I've tested nearly every female animal that lives, and they have no orgasm. Why should a human female be different? I'm a woman and I don't, and God knows that I've tried."

For a moment Captain thought that he could save her. That he could lick her clitoris for hours or make super good love to her and show her how to come. But he glanced at her in the mirror and while appearing to be lost in thought, looked her body over from her bleached blonde head to her large flat feet, and he knew that there was no offer that he could make.

"Maybe you're right," he said. "I mean you're the doctor, and you would know. Go ahead and finish me. I'm ready to do it for you—for us."

She laughed and began to fondle him. "All right, come on and shoot that big thing off."

Oh, goddamn, Captain thought. She thinks I've got a big one, even after the horses. Oh, goddamn. He began to swoon but steadied himself with a hand against the mirror. His penis burned, and he watched her stroke him. Then he watched her collect his spurting semen in her cupped left hand. Pumping him smoothly, evenly, she bent over and closely watched his emission. Her interest appeared very sexy in the mirror and added to the excitement.

"You got me," he moaned, his entire body jerking. Captain looked up into his own face to find it trembling, distorted and swollen red. He closed his eyes.

Finishing things in a professional way, Doctor Leighton smiled, looked Captain in the eye and said, "Boy, are you easy. You just like to hear that you have a big one and that does it for you." She stood on her toes, kissed him on the cheek and went away saying, "Men, golly, men." After a moment she ducked back into the room to throw Captain a cold can of beer and a towel. Then she disappeared again, shaking her head.

Captain wiped himself clean, had a swallow of iced beer, which tasted delicious, and sat with a sigh on the corner of the lime green bed. The day was getting late. Long rolling shadows played across the wheat field outside. The sight caught his vision and held it. "Beautiful," he said, "truly beautiful."

The onset of a balmy evening breeze wafted through the room. He shivered, sneezed, said, "Beautiful," and yawned. "What do you think a clitoris is for?" Captain yelled, lying back onto the bed. There was no reply. He listened for running water but heard none.

I've got her, he thought. No other female animal has a clitoris, I don't think; just the human. "I'll bet that I've got you with that one," he yelled. When there was no response, Captain yelled, "Cry, can you hear me?" She's thinking up a good answer, he thought, smiling to himself.

He thought about what the blonde doctor had said and was genuinely curious about her understanding of the female orgasm. He thought about some of the women he had known and their climaxes. He remembered Sylvia and how she had urged him to beat her very first one out of her. He had lain on his back and she upside down on top of him. He had sucked her clitoris and whipped her ass real good with a long-handled wooden spoon, both at the same time, until finally she reached her first orgasm. And then she wouldn't stop, he laughed. "Still hasn't," he murmured, thinking about the last time he had spoken to the girl and her preoccupation with sex. But that was surely a real orgasm, he thought.

He was certain that Iris experienced an orgasm. I am, he decided, absolutely positive that she does. He laughed and thought that it would be fun to call her in Malibu and ask her. Then

354

Captain felt an overwhelming wave of lonesomeness for his beautiful blonde sister. Picturing her, her face and figure, he realized how truly gorgeous she really was. I am spoiled, he said to himself and knew that it was the truth.

He thought about Iris's secret. He envisioned her flat stomach and laughed. He wondered about her health and decided that she was fine, just fine. I love her, he thought. I hope that she's having a good day, alone.

He laughed and yelled, "Hey, Doc, I know a lady intimately who absolutely does experience an orgasm when I lick between her legs." Sitting up, he yelled toward the cool-looking, darkened hallway. "I can feel her orgasm, the impulses on my tongue." Captain moved from the bed into the shadowed hallway to make his point. "Hey, Doc?" There was no reply, and suddenly Captain knew that he was in trouble.

Turning, he bolted back for the bedroom and his gun. He sensed movement in the shadows behind him before something very hard slammed into the back of his head. Falling against the wall, he fought the pain and he fought going down, but consciousness ceased.

The Mask

The loud chittering sound of small animals was there. Their stench was there too. Realizing that he was bound naked in an upright position, Captain quickly opened his eyes. Intense laboratory lighting shot a sharp, bright pain into the back of his head where he had been struck.

Wincing, he said, "Goddamn."

He squinted and saw small metal cages stacked from floor to ceiling. They were aisled for access and ran the length of the beige tiled building. Captain shook his head to clear the ringing. The high-pitched animal sounds made him think of birds. Are they bird cages? he wondered, but then he caught a glimpse of the scurrying creatures and knew that he had been right at first. "Rodents," he mumbled, "guinea pigs. What the fuck—?"

He became aware of the presence of two men. One shuffled and moved nervously where he stood off to a side of the room. The way that he held his hands, the way that he rolled them together up close to his face made Captain think of a kangaroo. The other man sat very still at a porcelain table and chair set arranged just below and in front of the spot where Captain was hung.

This quiet man appeared to sit hunched while one forearm was awkwardly bent upward onto the table top. He had curly black hair and eyebrows, black sunken eyes and appeared impatient and angry. When the man at the table saw that Captain was fully awake, he began drumming his fingers on the shiny table top. The man adjusted himself for comfort, and Captain thought that his right shoulder was misformed, humped.

Testing his restraints, Captain found that he was tied securely to a thick wooden beam and crossbar. He imagined the device to be like a large, strong painter's easel. His feet were tied together at the ankles and held a foot or so off of the floor. His arms were held straight out from his body by tightly wrapped lengths of farm twine tied at each of his wrists.

He looked down at his shrunken penis and felt himself blush. He put all of his strength into his arms to test his predicament and found that his legs and left arm were held absolutely tight and would stay that way until freed. His right wrist, however, came away from the heavy wooden beam enough to create hope of escape. I'm stronger, he thought, than either one of these ass-holes will ever know, and he strained the muscles of his chest and right arm some more. There is definitely hope in that arm, he thought, continuing to try and stretch and loosen the twine through sheer brute force.

"Are you Jack Trench?" Captain asked finally.

The man continued to drum his fingers and without the slighest change of expression, said, "Yes," in a high, strained-sounding voice.

Then Trench turned to the tall, thin, hyperactive-looking man who stood nervously off to one side of the room. The skinny man continued to do funny things with his hands near his face. Like a mouse, Captain thought; not a kangaroo, a mouse.

Trench said, "Squeak, bring the mask."

The thin, anxious man grew extremely excited and made a squealing sound. He rubbed his hands together under his chin and with his eyes flashing, exited the room dancing sideways. Like a crab, Captain thought. He moves like a crab.

"Do you know the trouble that you've caused me, you piece of shit?" Trench spoke to Captain in a manner that gave him the chills.

Captain could see that Trench hated him in a deep, unforgiving way that no amount of talk would ever change. Captain had always been frightened by that kind of hatred. It left his stomach cold and gnawing. A resentful poor boy from downtown who Captain had often fought while still a schoolboy had hated him in that same way, with the same loathing glare in his eye. They fought, and Captain would knock him down and always win, but the kid would look up bleeding, with that terrible kind of unforgiving hatred in his eyes and say, "I'm going to get you. Someday I'll get you."

He remembered becoming morbidly depressed after those bouts. So much so that his father had cornered him and made him talk about it. Doctor Blood had listened and said, "This thing is really affecting you, isn't it. You're frightened and trembling. What are you so frightened of?"

"Of the way that he looks at me," Captain had answered, and Doctor Blood had hugged him and said, "I can't help you with this. I want to but I can't. And besides, these things have a way of working themselves out."

And they did. The next semester found Captain's nemesis stricken with a severe case of poliomyelitis from which he never

THE MASK

recovered. Captain felt truly sorry for the boy, but it was a relief not to have to see those eyes.

Jack Trench looked at Captain in that same dreaded way now. Frightened as he was, Captain couldn't help but think about it and figured that not only had he thrown a monkey wrench into the man's heroin trafficking, but that on a more basic level, the crippled man who sat glaring before him was, like the poor boy in school, jealous of his good looks and hateful of the confident attitude that accompanied them.

"There are photographs in the trunk of my rented car of a guy who blew his head away because of your heroin, Trench."

Trench looked away and contemplated what he'd heard. Then he slowly shook his head, making Captain realize that he had already seen the photographs but until now hadn't understood them.

"Big fucking deal, one guy. You've cost me—Do you know what you've cost me in top people, you fucking punk?"

He screamed, "Jesus Christ," and slammed his fist against the table top. In a rage he stood up. The chair fell over, and Captain observed for himself that Jack Trench was a dwarf. The awkward little man tottered there on two short crooked legs that seemed barely capable of doing their job. His back was misshapen as well, and his head appeared too large for his body.

Jack Trench was red-faced with anger. His full head of curly black hair showed purple under the fluorescent lights. He took a handkerchief from his pocket and wiped his brow and eyes dry of perspiration.

"Cocksucker," he said up at Captain.

The tall, mouselike man named Squeak came scurrying sideways back through swinging doors carrying a small cage. He placed it carefully on the porcelain table in front of Trench, who transferred his weight from leg to leg as he stood seething

359

and attempting to adjust his tiny black suit coat over his deformed shoulders for comfort. The cage appeared to have belts or straps hanging off of one end, and in it there was no mistaking the sight of a very agitated gray sewer rat.

Appearing more and more as though he were operating off of a tightly wound internal spring, Squeak laughed a squealing laugh and said, "Brains, brains," to the rat. He rubbed his long-nailed fingers together under his chin, and Captain saw that the man had huge ears, large flaps of sheer pink skin that lay against his baldish head with enormous holes for hearing. "Brains, brains," he said excitedly again, making the same motions with his hands.

The animal became frenzied and ran all over the inside of the small, peculiar-looking wire cage. "Oh boy, brains," Squeak said, and giggling, he looked up at Captain to smile one of the most insane smiles Captain had ever seen.

Then what was going on came to him. Captain got the grisly picture all at once. He felt his stomach roll and had to restrain himself from vomiting. He realized that the brains Squeak was talking about were his own and that the cage that sat on the table before him, built with a skull-conforming rubber fitting at one end and straps and buckles, was going to go into place over his face.

Unable to look away and so staring at the cage on the porcelain table, Captain could see it had been constructed for just that one purpose. There was a piece of sliding wood that kept the rat at bay until the mask was secured. He saw the thing but couldn't believe it.

In a state of sheer, iced terror, Captain thought that the mask was terrible beyond his wildest imagination. "Oh, no, God, no," he said, drooling down his chin.

The rat stopped his anxious behavior long enough to put his

whiskered nose up into the air and sniff. The rodent's eyes were the color of milk and added to his horrific appearance.

"Blind, he's blind," Captain whined. Some sort of test animal, he thought. The rat sniffed the air in Captain's direction. "Good God in heaven, *no*," he cried, seeing the animal actually lick his chops.

Feeling suddenly weak, with the cold surgical screw burrowing into his scalp, the urge to beg came over Captain, but when he opened his mouth to speak, Trench cut him off with an order to Squeak. "Give this hero motherfucker the mask."

Captain pulled at his right wrist until he thought that he might actually pull his hand off. It was coming too, but he understood with the coldest of chills that it wouldn't be in time. He heard himself moaning. He bucked against the restraints as though charged with electricity, but the ghoulish person named Squeak was on a stepladder next to him, following his flailing head back and forth with the rubber-cushioned end of the mask. Although the white-eyed rat could not be seen, Captain heard him squealing and jumping around, scratching at the board that separated him from Captain's face.

Captain was aware of two people screaming in the hollow-sounding room. He screamed, *"NO, no, no,"* as he threw his head back and forth, and Squeak yelled, "Brains, brains," to the crazed rat.

And then with a perfectly timed lunge, the mask was over Captain's face, the buckles pulled tight and fastened behind his head.

Captain felt about to expire or lose his mind. He felt the weight of the device pull on his neck as Squeak let go of it. The mask was in place and Captain knew it. "Holy Father in Heaven, help me. Brad, don't let them."

Captain knew that he was crying when the room grew still. His sobs were the only thing to hear. Through his tears he stared at the grained wooden board that separated him from the rat. He held his breath and listented. The room was completely quiet, even the animal was unmoving.

Trench yelled, "Bon voyage, Captain Blood, handsome hero motherfucker."

Captain sensed Squeak fiddling with the board in front of his face, and he heard a door slam.

During the next instant, fluorescent light flashed into Captain's eyes, his entire body tensed and the sharp claws and teeth of the ravaging rat fell heavily onto his face. The rodent's terrible reeking gray fur was on him and the weight of his thick slippery tail. Captain gagged.

Squeak shrieked with delight and screamed, "Brains, Mickey, brains," and the horrific beast tore into Captain's nose.

Captain immediately tasted the blood that gushed back through his nasal passages into his throat. Screaming out in hysteria, he feverishly pulled at his right wrist.

Squeak was yelling too and clapping his hands. "Go get the brains, Mickey. Go for the brains."

Captain flashed Doctor Leighton and Walt Disney into his prayers and begged them to call the rodent off, but Walt Disney laughed and turned away saying, "Mickey Mouse he ain't."

The rat bore down voraciously, and Captain heard cartilage snap in the front of his face. Captain peed over his legs and out into the room. He fought fainting.

Throwing his head to the left, Captain was able to dislodge the animal momentarily, but the beast flew back to tear into his right cheek. He heard the rat's gnashing teeth. Blood flew into Captain's eyes. His vision blurred. He screamed. Squeak whistled and cheered.

Throwing his head didn't work, but he threw it hard again anyway. He tried to snap his neck by jerking the cage to the right and to the left. Gnawing, the rat hung on. Then the animal fell away again, and Captain made the decision. He opened his own mouth as wide as he could and did not have but an instant to wait. The ferocious rodent screamed back to tear into Captain's tongue. The pain was more severe than the previous attacks had been, but quickly clamping his own mouth shut hard, Captain caught himself the ravaging animal's small, energetic head. He crushed the rat's skull between his teeth.

Captain threw his head to the right, and the dead animal fell to the bottom of the cage.

"Mickey, Mickey. What have you—my Mickey, *no*—" The insane man named Squeak was screaming and up the ladder in an instant.

Captain's right hand came free. Make it good, consumed his intellect, and reaching at first to aim, Captain drove his thumb into the outside corner of Squeak's left eye socket. He didn't have to stretch an octave and dug his middle finger into Squeak's large left auditory canal. Continuing the motion, Captain used all of the strength that he could muster to make his thumb and middle finger meet, somewhere under Squeak's temple.

Squeak's voice lost its shrillness. He screamed, *"Zaaaaa,"* hoarsely into the room. The caged animals went silent. There wasn't a chitter. Squeak fell off of the ladder and hung there with his skull in Captain's grasp like a bowling ball.

Captain shook the dead man until he was sure and then let him fall.

The masklike cage came off easily, and Captain was free and on the ground in a matter of seconds. He fell to his knees and vomited. A hose lay rolled in one corner, which Captain used to rinse himself off. He looked for a mirror or alcohol for his face or a towel to hide his nudity but found none. The room was still.

He said, "Lord Almighty, I'm free. I'm free at last."

Running around hysterically, Captain tried to slow himself down, but paying that thought no attention, he ran to the cages and opened what seemed like 100 of them. He leaned on the stacked cages, and toppled them onto the floor.

The experimental rodents, many of them white-eyed, came alive and screamed all at once toward Squeak's body. They moved like a wave to cover Squeak and burrow into him. His corpse appeared to jerk from their force. Paying Captain no heed, the rampaging animals seemed to fly past him. They devoured Squeak in a sickeningly noisy, wet-sounding way and Captain thought that he could see Squeak's toes curl inside his shoes.

It was night, and the exterior compound was brightly lit. Captain stepped into the nearest shadow and fled the place in what he knew to be the direction of Doctor Leighton's bungalow. There were people about. Sneaking, using the darkened grassy or blacktopped areas behind buildings as a route, Captain escaped detection and finally, with the help of a quarter moon, arrived to hunch down next to the hedge at the side of Margarette Leighton's bungalow. The yellow Corvette was where he had left it. But for a small light coming from the living room, the place was completely dark.

The wheat field was in shadow, but he knew that it was out there, and he tried unsuccessfully for the scent through the taste of blood and bile. He suppressed a desire to run out there and hide, to let it cover him like a blanket. Falling back onto his haunches, he crossed his legs Indian fashion and looked up into the black, star-filled Arizona sky. The quarter moon shone clean and clear.

Folding his hands he said, "Father, this is your son, Captain, speaking. Thank you for my life." He paused for a while longer and felt his heart stop pounding. He found the nerve to touch his face, and blood seemed to be crusted everywhere. He said, "Oh, no," and moved quickly to stand next to the screened window of Doctor Leighton's bedroom.

From what he could make out, she was in there sleeping. Nothing about what he saw made Captain feel defensive. Sneaking around to the front of the small house, he found the screen door locked but the front door open. With one swift move he punched his fist through the screen, unlocked it and was into the living room. He moved unhesitatingly to the darkened bedroom and was able to distinguish one form in the bed. On all fours he crawled around to the side of the bed where he had hidden his pistol. It was the blonde female doctor, snoring lightly, smelling of alcohol and tobacco, who was asleep in the bed, alone. He reached and reached again.

"Shit, fuck," he said angrily. The gun was gone.

With his left hand firmly over Doctor Leighton's mouth, he put his other hand behind her head to hold her. He shook her head and spoke softly. "Wake up, you fucking cunt. Wake up so that I can put you back to sleep again for good."

After bolting awake, she got the message and lay back.

"I'm going to take my hand away. I need some answers and your car keys. If you yell, I'll rip your throat out, and that's no shit."

She shook her head up and down in understanding, and he let go of her.

Doctor Leighton reached immediately for Captain's face and touched it gently all over. She whispered, "How in the world? Where is Jack? What time is it?"

"I don't know where Trench is, but the rats are eating Squeak, and I have no idea what time it is."

"You mean you—?"

365

"I escaped, yes. I'm on the run out of this fucking place."

"And Jack?" she asked anxiously.

"He left me to Squeak and his face cage."

"But how did you—?"

"That's not important—I'm here. Where is my gun?"

"I don't know. They took it. Wow—" She sighed, and he let her fall back onto the bed. "I can't believe it," she said, touching his face again. She jumped out of bed to pull him down the hall and into the bathroom. She closed the door behind them.

When the bathroom light went on, Captain saw the woman's swollen purple right eye before he noticed anything else. She was naked also. She used soap and water, alcohol and a clear, stinging antiseptic solution on his face while they whispered. Captain stood with his back to the mirror, afraid to look.

"This isn't too bad," she said. "You'll be fine. A couple of stitches if you want it to be perfect and a tetanus shot. Be sure to get a tetanus shot."

"Did you sell me out?" he asked.

"No, silly, no. I didn't know he'd come back, word of honor. I'm still not sure how he got here, or when. Probably a car or a chopper down in the valley, or maybe he was here all along, I don't know. But, good golly, Captain, do you think that you're the first one to come looking to get Jack Trench? I mean, he is the head of the Mexican Union, and, good gosh, he's got an intelligence network that literally goes all over the world."

"Union?" Captain asked.

"Mafia—the Mexican mafia, they call it. You know, don't you?"

"Mexican mafia—Trench is the Mexican mafia, you are shitting?"

"You didn't know? Oh, you are too much, Captain Blood. Who do you think that he is?"

"I don't know," he shrugged. "The big dope dealer?"

She laughed and said, "Well, you're right about that. That's who he is, among lots of other things, and he knows about everything that goes on. There is a policeman in Los Angeles who knows you too—comes down here to visit over Christmas every year, always chases the guys, the young guys. He likes boys—Pepper—Do you know an L.A. cop named Pepper, a homosexual?"

On second thought, Captain was not surprised and shook his head. "Yes, I know Pepper."

"He called Jack about you. I heard Jack tell Squeak before they took you. They thought that I was still unconscious." She pointed to her black eye and swollen face. "He works for Jack, you know, Pepper does."

Captain shook his head. "Yeah, it figures. Ouch—careful."

"Hold still, I'm almost finished."

"I wonder what they know, the L.A. cops."

"I don't know what you've done, but it sounded like company business to me. You know, a family feud, internal. Jack said that Pepper's hunch was right, that's all. He works for Jack first and Los Angeles second."

"So they probably have no idea about Pepper's hunch."

"I wouldn't worry about Pepper," she said, using a Q-tip on his nose.

"I agree," Captain said.

"But I didn't do it, Captain—sell you out, honest. Nothing that I do matters one way or the other anyway, except where the horses are concerned. I am the best thoroughbred vet there is, I told you that and it's true. I saved Trinity's life, Jinx's sire. I saved him from sleeping sickness after they'd all given up on him, not to mention the sperm count that I get from the stallions. I'm protected here."

"But can you ever leave?" he asked.

"Sure, I have. But they find me and bring me back. I get drunk and end up in Arabia or someplace where there are thoroughbreds, but I come back. I love my horses. You probably don't understand that, but I love them. They are my family, my life."

"Ouch—and Trench, is he into horses too or is it cover?"

"No, he's into them too." She laughed and said, "Hold on." She turned off the light and with Captain holding her hand, she moved quickly through the dark house to retrieve a bottle of liquor and a can of soda pop from the kitchen. Back into the bathroom, they both had a stiff swallow of vodka and chased it with Diet Seven-Up.

"You know about the rat mask?" Captain watched her eyes.

"Of course. He's got all sorts of things that he's thought of like that, really bizarre things, brutal things."

"Why is he so cruel?" Captain asked.

Smiling, she said, "As bad as he needs me, he'd kill me if I told you, so don't tell him, okay? Just die if you're going to without telling that I told you, okay?"

"Oh, sure, lady. I'll go nice and easy. Jeez—" Captain wanted to run, but he shook her and said, "Go on, tell me. And then think about a gun. I need a gun and your car keys. Is my car gone?"

"Yes, sure, long gone I'd bet. All I have is a carbine, a Winchester carbine. It's in a saddle scabbard in the front closet. Do you want it? Would it make you feel better?"

"You're fucking ay it would. Is it loaded?"

"No, but there's a box of shells there too."

Hand in hand they went back through the darkened house to retrieve the Winchester saddle gun and the box of shells. Captain stood right there next to the closet in the darkened living room and loaded the compact, lever-action rifle. With a shell in the chamber and five more in the magazine, Captain left the rest of the cartridges and returned to the bathroom with Doctor Leighton.

Another swallow of vodka and things seemed more relaxed. "You won't make it in the car. The gate is closed, and there are men around."

"I want Trench first, and then I'll worry about leaving."

"Bravo," she said and drank to him.

"What other way out is there—horseback?" Captain asked.

"No, by air. Take a plane."

"I don't know shit about planes."

"That's all right; there're always three or four men—pilots—twenty-four hour shifts—in the office at the hangar. Jack wants them on call all of the time."

"Why tell me this?"

Because all of a sudden I feel that it's probably you or him, and I've got a funny notion about you. I don't know, just do me a big favor."

"Go."

"Don't miss. Golly, please don't miss."

Doctor Leighton looked away, and Captain knew that she was imagining what Trench would do to him if given a second chance.

"Why is he so cruel? Tell me now. Is he sick?" he asked.

"Is he sick?" She laughed. "Does the bear poop in the woods? Yes, he is sick, Captain, because he has no penis. He was born deformed in many ways, but the most terrible is that his urinary tract ends in a stub of a thing the size of a thimble. He pees out of that. His testicles are the size of peas. I suppose you'd be cruel too."

"Goddamn, that is too bad," Captain said, feeling truly sorry for the deformed creature. Little wonder, he thought, that the man is jealous.

"Did he watch us when we had sex?"

"Probably."

"Then he saw my big cock."

Doctor Leighton laughed. "Yes, Captain, he probably saw your big cock."

They both laughed and had a drink on that one. Captain spun around and looked into the mirror. "A little chewed up but not bad. Shit—lucky," he said.

"Yes," she said, "but don't forget the tetanus shot." They looked into each others' eyes in a solemn way, and an unspoken consideration was in the tiny bathroom. If you make it, if you're alive tomorrow.

"Where are my clothes?"

"Oh, those I do have. I was ordered to incinerate them."

Captain trusted her to go and bring his things, which he got into quickly. He was particularly comforted to feel the sneakers on his feet.

"So Trench hates people but loves the horses, right? Or is that just cover? You never told me."

"Jack loves the horses, Captain, really loves them as much as he can love anything. You see, he watches them make love. He helps the stallions into the mares and stands close and watches. Sometimes he even holds on."

"So you and Trench have really got a lot in common, don't you?"

"In that way we do, yes." She laughed and Captain did too. "Why would you see him dead? Why not do it yourself?"

Doctor Leighton smiled, her bruised eye closed, and she said, "Because I get Jinx. And besides, I could never do it myself. I've never killed anything that wasn't already half-dead. Jack is much more clever and way ahead of me in that area. Besides, I just don't have the nerve.''

"But God wants him dead, I'm sure of it.''

She laughed. "Oh you are, are you? Well, I'd say God is the one who's dead.''

Captain said, "Oh, no, He isn't,'' and Doctor Leighton said, "Oh, yes, He is. He has to have laughed Himself to death.''

After a moment he laughed with her and told her that she was quite a card. He had a last shot of vodka and didn't chase it.

Turning the light off, he paused and then gently kissed the blonde doctor. She put her arms around him and standing there in the dark, unable to see her, he felt a surge of love for the woman.

"I could make you come,'' he whispered.

"No, you couldn't, but it would be fun to let you try.''

They hugged and Captain asked, "Where is he?''

She broke away, ran to look at a clock and returned to say, "In the barn, the big barn, at the end of the big barn—that end.'' She touched his shoulder and gestured toward Algonquin Road. "He's probably alone with Jinx. It's a good time, really.''

"Thank you, Doctor.'' He squeezed her hand.

"All right, Captain. Goodby.'' They kissed again softly, and Captain broke away to leave.

"Captain?''

"Yes?''

"Please, don't miss.''

Doctor Leighton walked Captain to her front door and made certain he understood which barn she made reference to. She patted him on the bottom as he left. Like a mother, Captain thought, smiling, sending her son off to school.

The Flight

With the Winchester carbine close against his right thigh and leg as he walked, Captain moved briskly and stayed out of the floodlights. Two men sat on the fence smoking at the compound's far end. No one else was in sight. He watched the experimental rodent station across the compound while he walked and saw nothing that he considered unusual. He envisioned Squeak reduced to a skeleton and shuddered.

The large white barn was not locked. Captain stepped quickly into the place without hesitation. The ground down the center of the barn was hard-packed dirt or clay. Box stalls ran neatly up and down both sides of the high, arch-ceilinged building. A box stall stood open at the barn's far end.

Surprised and aware of each other both at the same moment were Captain and a man to his right who jumped up from a rocking chair for a confrontation. The sentry wore a six gun,

Western style, at his side but never got it out of the holster. Captain drove the steel butt of the carbine into his forehead, and the man crumpled where he stood. Captain took the Colt .45 from the downed man and tucked it into his own belt. Hugging the stalls to the left, he ran the length of the barn to the opened box stall at the end.

Jinx saw Captain before Trench did. With his ears back, he looked frightened and shied away toward the back of the stall. Trench stood on a stool, his hunched back to Captain, working Jinx's black coat with a curry comb. Reacting from Jinx, Trench quickly turned around. His black eyes seemed to bulge at the sight of Captain. Then he glared in a hateful way and didn't speak.

"Step away from the animal, heroin man," Captain said, cocking the hammer of the carbine.

Jinx backed into the corner of the stall. When the horse moved, Trench moved with him. Jumping off the stool, he ducked his small, misshapen body underneath the big horse's belly to stand on Jinx's far side, in the corner.

Holding the stall door open wide, Captain yelled, "Get out, Jinx. Get out or I'll take you with him."

The big black stallion got a crazy bloodshot look in his wide eyes. He shied and danced. Captain stepped away from the front of the stall.

"Come, boy, now. Come, Jinx."

The stallion curved his beautiful black neck, pawed the ground once with his front hoof, glanced toward Captain, snorted and made for the stall's opened door. Captain saw Trench's tiny fingers come through the horse's mane from the other side and grab hold there. Captain jumped across in front of Jinx to be with Trench.

The stallion galloped, and Trench rode with him, hanging onto his side. Captain grabbed Trench by his full head of thick black hair and dislodged him from the horse as Jinx burst by. Trench tried to jump to his feet, but Captain stood on the small of his back.

Jinx stopped moving up near the far end of the barn. He looked back over his shoulder at Captain and Trench and then turned away to stand perfectly still. The sentry lay where he had fallen, unmoving. Trench lay spread-eagled beneath Captain, his face into the hard ground, and did not move a muscle. The horse did not so much as twitch. The guard lay there. Nothing moved.

He looked at them all again without moving his head and felt suddenly paralyzed, frozen in the moment as though locked in a time warp. He let some time pass and then some more, until he wasn't sure how much time had elapsed. He understood that he was standing perfectly still. The movement of a limb seemed impossible; the impulse wouldn't send. Weird, he thought, not sure what to do. What should I do, he asked himself, and he heard Brad's voice loud and clear, "Kill him, kill him."

Without aiming much, he made a real conscious effort to squeeze his trigger finger. A gunshot roared in the stillness. The sound echoed and echoed and echoed. Moving in slow motion at first, things began to move and then to quicken until Captain felt part of an accelerating, blurred, silent movie gone wild. Jinx appeared to jump a foot from the sound of the explosion and began to run around awkwardly in circles. Captain watched him and felt dizzy, then faint. He put his hand to his forehead.

Trench writhed under Captain's foot. The sentry did something too, and Captain moved the carbine to his shoulder. When the sentry paused for the time needed to squeeze out of the barn's main door, Captain fired and dropped him. The shot echoed with a *boom boom* off of the barn's arched interior, and Jinx began to rear and whinny loudly.

Demonstrating considerable strength and agility, Trench knocked Captain off his feet. Captain let himself fall, while he moved the sights of the carbine carefully along Trench and fired. The blast caught Trench above the right ear and blew much of his curly black hair and the top of his head off. Trench's body dropped to the hard earth, a dead weight.

Captain sat there on the ground next to him. After a moment, in what seemed to Captain a pathetic involuntary gesture, Trench's little hands flew to the top of his head. Then they fell away to twitch and become still. ·

"Tenacious little fucker, aren't you," Captain said.

The front of the barn opened, and several people appeared. Jinx bolted for the open air. The people scattered, and Captain ran out of the barn's rear door.

Heaving the rifle out into a field, Captain ran as fast as he could in the direction of the hangar and the airstrip. There was a considerable amount of commotion back at the main barn. Captain passed Doctor Leighton running in that direction. She stopped when she saw that it had been Captain who she passed and yelled, "Well—?"

Captain turned and yelled back, "Go get your horse."

He heard her scream, "Yahoo." Her voice mingled with his footsteps and heavy breathing to trail off behind him.

The front of the hangar was open and well lit. Three aircraft sat pointed toward the lighted runway. He saw that they were two propeller-driven planes and a small jet.

Breathing heavily, Captain walked to the hangar office where three men sat playing pinochle, drinking coffee and smoking cigarettes. Walking directly to the closest man, he put the Colt .45 against his head, cocked the hammer and said, "Who is the best pilot here, and is the jet ready to go?"

The man under the gun put his cards down carefully.

"Answer fast," Captain said. "Is the jet ready? How long to get into the air? Come on, pal, there's no second chance at this stage of the game."

"I'm—I'm a pilot, yes. So's Bill. Randy's only a mechanic. The Lear could fly in about six minutes, don't you think, Bill?"

Bill shook his head. "Yeah, about ten minutes."

The man with the gun against his head began to shake. "Easy, son. Easy with that gun, son." And then he broke down. "Shit, Bill, you promised no guns. It ain't worth the money to get yourself killed."

Bill said, "Shut up, Dwayne, you chicken shit. He won't use it. Just sit tight. Jack has gotta be close, and we ain't going—"

Captain swung the Colt from Dwayne's head and blew Bill off his chair. A good amount of powder and flash came from the loud gun. Dwayne screamed and put his hand over his ear. The mechanic dove under the table.

Captain could hear his own panic. "Dwayne, move your ass and bring the keys. Don't forget anything. I want to be in the air right now."

Trembling, Dwayne turned to Captain and with his eyes jerking back and forth, said, "Well, well, we could get off faster in the Cessna. It's just settin', ready to roll."

"Will it make—" Captain leaned over and whispered into Dwayne's ear, "Will it make Los Angeles?"

Dwayne shook his head up and down in an absolutely positively yes gesture.

"Well, let's go. Get the key."

"The keys are in it."

Captain and Dwayne ran to the waiting, red-and-white-colored, single-engine airplane. Fuselage lettering indicated that the aircraft was a Cessna Model 182. The plane's engine started on the second try.

"Don't talk—just go. Take off," Captain urged.

Captain thought that they were creeping as the Cessna moved out onto the runway. "Come on, come on," he yelled.

Suddenly the window closest to Dwayne popped a bullet hole, as did the windshield in front of Captain. Dwayne turned the plane's interior lights off. The instrument panel glowed in green fluorescence. Another slug twanged through the cockpit behind them, and there came the whining sound of a ricochet off of the speeding propeller blade.

Captain looked to see people running alongside the runway shooting at them. Reaching past Dwayne, Captain pushed the window flap open and fired four times in the direction of the flashing guns. The silhouettes seemed to fall to the ground, to duck and scatter.

Captain thought that Dwayne seemed like a nice enough guy and told him that everything was going to be all right when the man expressed his fear by uttering *"Geeeeee"* between clenched teeth.

And then, just as it seemed they would leave the ground, a pair of headlights pulled onto the runway ahead of them. A hail of gunfire poured into the plane's cockpit, and Captain held his breath. Then they were airborne.

"Climb, Dwayne, climb."

They did, and the tingling sensation inside of Captain's rectum began to subside. He slowly let out his breath. There was the sound of a crisp metallic ricochet in the cockpit, and Dwayne said "Ow," in an irritated, whiney fashion, like a child when you begin to tousle him too severely. "Ow," and Dwayne slumped onto the Cessna's steering wheel with all of his weight.

The plane nose-dived instantaneously. Gravitational pull made it impossible to get Dwayne off of the wheel and back into his seat. The plane's engine roared, and they screamed toward earth.

Captain envisioned a Japanese kamikaze plane on black and white film plowing into an Allied aircraft carrier. In desperation, Captain pulled Dwayne sideways off of the steering apparatus and onto his own lap.

Captain jerked *his* steering wheel up against his own chest as far as it would go, closed his eyes and held his breath. When the plane's nose came back up, the wheels or undercarriage, or both, clipped something in the darkness beneath them. There was a loud, shattering sound. The plane stalled and seemed to want to come apart, but it lurched forward and went into a radical climb.

Captain yelled, "Dwayne—Dwayne—Good God, man, come on."

There was no response. Captain eased the stick gently back and pushed Dwayne into his own seat.

"Fuck," Captain said. The Cessna seemed to make a remarkable recovery. Captain found a plunger-shaped stick on the dash, which turned out to be the throttle, and he reduced the straining engine's speed. The RPM indicator on the dashboard settled quickly away from its red zone. There was an instrument on the dash, an air bubble, moving back and forth in a horizontal tube full of fluid. It appeared to be an indicator of level flight. Practicing, he was able to keep the bubble in the middle of the tube. The plane seemed to fly along smoothly, effortlessly, properly.

"Holy shit," he said. "I'm flying it."

Moving the wheel back toward himself, he decided to continue to climb. Shit, he figured, the air will get thin, or I'll get goofy if I get too high. The compass was lit and sat atop the dash. Captain turned and headed west.

Dwayne's body reflected no pulse. "Dead as a fucking doornail. Shit, goddamn—shit." He thought that he might cry. The tears came but he said, "All right, all right, settle down." He cleared both nostrils by blowing through them hard like a street bum, first one then the other. "Fuck this shit," he said cockily. "I'll fly it myself, but I don't need you, Dwayne old boy." Reaching over, he undid Dwayne's door and after nearly going into another nose dive, managed to push the dead pilot out. The Cessna zoomed upward fast in what seemed a direct vertical path as Dwayne's weight fell away. Captain leveled the plane out, threw the Colt .45 out into the blackness behind Dwayne and fastened the door. "Sorry, Dwayne. Sorry, God, about him."

Trying to figure out all of the dials and gauges that were before him at once, Captain sought to concentrate on slowing his thought processes down. "You are alive and well," he said. "Don't think about anything else. Yes, be grateful. I am grateful, yes. So fly it, man. Knock off the bullshit and fly it home."

There was a gauge that showed him to be flying at 4,200 feet and climbing. The compass read due west, and his air speed was holding at between 145 and 150 miles per hour. Unable to find a clock, Captain could only guess that the hour was about midnight.

"You're doing a good job, kid," he told himself. "Especially for being in a light plane only once before, as a passenger. Jesus Christ, what a consideration. Never mind, fly it. I am, I am. I'm doing good. Shit, it's easy."

Over the city of Tucson he sensed that he was flying too low and took the Cessna upward to reach 8,000 feet. The air at that altitude seemed fine and he determined that his thinking was not muddled. Tilting the plane over a bit, he was able to look down on the array of city lights beneath him. "Wow," he said, thinking that the sight was spectacular.

Maybe, he thought, I should drop it in Phoenix or in whatever airport that I come across that is lit. The thought of trying to land the aircraft made him cringe and immediately perspire under his arms. Then there are the police. It's a cinch, he figured, that

Trench's people will know who took him out, as will their police contacts anywhere in the country, if they want them to.

I just don't feel, he thought, that this is going to be a problem. The entire thing was done in the middle of what must be one of the largest narcotic hotbeds in the country. The kingpin is gone, so the next guy steps in. "Oh, no, you don't, Brad. Don't get any ideas. I'm going to Montecito and get down with Iris. I'm done taking chances. I got him for you, and I hope that it makes you happy. Yeah, Brad, it's done. The guy that kills the kids is dead. The King is dead."

Captain laughed, being careful not to rock the plane. "Maybe he's someplace where you can get your hands on him yourself, Brad. Yeah, I'll bet Brad is duking it out with Jack Trench right now. Sure he is." With a vision of a cheerful Brad punching it out with Trench and with Penny standing there cheering her daddy on, Captain felt a nice warm glow come over himself. "Yeah, Brad, he's all yours now. Have at him."

Breathing deeply, Captain gazed up and around at the star-studded blackness. "God, it's beautiful. Goddamn, I feel wonderful." He felt happy and full of goodness in some new special way that he hoped would last. "Eight thousand feet away from anyone," he said, relaxing. Naw, he thought, the Meadowbrook people won't call the police. What would the investigation expose? One hell of a lot more than me. Nope, no way. "I'll bet that they've got him down at the mortuary right now, for cremation. Next case, right? Right." He found the plane's heater and made himself comfortable. "God, I won't want to come down," he laughed.

The special feeling of freedom and exhilaration lasted. How about the rented car? he wondered. I'll call them when I get back and tell them where I left it. Let Hertz worry about it. They like to worry. He had a hunch that Doctor Leighton would look after everything. "Margarette—Cry, will handle things back there. Of course, she will. I'm sure of it."

The drone of the Cessna's engine, the slight vibration, the monotony brought solace to Captain. He flew into a cloud that looked like white cotton candy. He watched in awe as it evanesced around him. Back into the clear night a feeling came to him that he didn't think he had ever experienced before. It was a sense of peace and calm. It was a spiritual feeling. It was the absence of the question Is that all there is? All of his life there had been that disappointment. After Christmas he had wondered, Is that all there is? After the circus, winning at athletics, helping a friend, sex, the feeling was always there: Is that all there is? But right then, in the black, star-filled, clean night sky, that disappointed, anxiety-filled question, Is that all there is? was gone. He stared into the darkness and considered it a friend. He looked at the stars and at the clear cut of the quarter moon and understood that that was all there really was. But he understood too, with a tingling sensation in his spine, that that was enough and he said, "All right," like a Hollywood hippy. "I am satisfied," he said, and a wonderful feeling of contentment came over him.

"Wait a minute," he said, sitting up straight in fear. "There are mountains between me and the ocean. Holy Toledo, wait a minute." Panic set in and Captain pulled the wheel and climbed. "Now wait just a fucking minute," he whispered to himself, thinking. "There is Lake Arrowhead and Big Bear, San Gorgonio—that entire range. Jesus, how high is it—10,000 feet, 12,000? Shit, I don't remember, but high—too high, and black as the ace of spades. Shit." And he remembered that Sinatra's mom had died against that mountain, "Being flown by a pro yet—Shit, fuck."

Then Captain made a decision and turned the plane north. He brought the plane back down to 7,000 feet and watched the ground carefully for what must have been the better part of an hour. When he felt confident that he had found Route 66, he gained altitude again, and with the huge interstate diesel trucks pulling westward beneath him, Captain prided himself on his good idea and headed for California and home.

Feeling good again, he began to sing, "Off we go, into the wild blue yonder, Sailing high, into the sky." He pretended to be a fighter pilot and, pressing his thumbs into the steering wheel, made the sound of a machine gun firing. "Take that—and that, you dirty Jap." He felt embarrassed that he'd said that and laughing, said, "You asshole." He sang, "You get your kicks on Route 66," and adjusted his air speed to 160.

He guessed at the cities as he passed over them: Flagstaff, Needles, Palm Springs, San Bernardino. He tried to take it easy, to relax. He whistled a tune. And then he was into the lights of Los Angeles. "What a spectacle," he marveled. "What a fucking city."

The city was quiet, the traffic light as he followed the Hollywood Freeway west. He tilted the Cessna and looked down at where he knew the Silverlake region to be, where Los Angeles visitors see the big, green freeway sign for the first time. He thought about the first time that he'd seen it. He remembered the feeling of excitement that it brought. The big green freeway sign that seemed to somehow say it all: 'Hollywood Next Eight Exits."

"Exit there," Captain said, "and you'll exit for good." He laughed and thought about Dolly Parton and his favorite saying of hers, "Show business, it's a big money-making joke, and I've always liked telling jokes." Captain laughed and thought that he'd give almost anything to see her bare naked without her wig. "Goddamn," he said.

Both gas gauges showed a quarter of a tank, and he still didn't know what to do. When he flew past the end of Sunset Boulevard, out over the ocean, he quickly dropped the idea that he had been conjuring about ditching the Cessna in the water. He didn't have to get too low to see that the Pacific Ocean was rough. It appeared extremely treacherous and black. "No, thank you," he said and flew up the coast toward Malibu to see if he could find Iris's house.

He thought about her secret and murmured, "I hope that she's all right." Soon he distinguished her beach lights and a lit room in the house. He felt lonesome and wished like crazy to be down there with her. The beach appeared damp and firm, good for running, and he wondered aloud if he would ever run that beach again.

"I'm so close," he said, "yet so fucking far."

The thought scared him and he said, "Don't talk like that."

He decided that it would have to be Santa Monica Airport, and the more he thought about it, the more approval he gave the idea. "I've always liked the place," he said. "I'll get down there. I'll go for it. If I'm going to get down, that's where it will be."

Unable to suppress the deep feeling of fear that was steadily rising within him, Captain tried deep breaths and singing a nutty made-up tune. He fastened his seat belt and shoulder straps for the first time.

The main runway at Santa Monica Airport was well lit and appeared huge. It also looked, Captain thought, like very, very hard, light gray-colored, concrete. Reducing the Cessna's air speed to ninety miles per hour and using the backward and forward motion of the wheel in front of him, he eased the small plane down close enough to have a look at things. The control tower was dark and had a large blinking neon sign hung off of the roof that was tilted skyward; it read: "Tower Closes 10 P.M.— NO JETS." "That's just fine with me," he said.

He flew over the runway time and again and met no other air traffic. He flew back out to the ocean and then back to the Santa Monica Airport. He made the approach several times. "It scares the shit out of me," he said to himself. He constantly had to wipe the perspiration from his hands onto his trouser legs to grip the wheel firmly.

The airport itself seemed to be built high on a sort of plateau, with no surrounding trees or mountains. Captain knew that with the clear approach to the place and the long, wide, well-lit runway, landing would be a piece of cake to anyone with the knowledge of how to do such a thing. The flaps, he wondered. Are they part of it or can I do it without?

Suddenly Captain was brought out of himself by the sight of another small, single-engine aircraft flying ahead of him and off to his left. The plane was going in. With a roaring, ill-thought burst of speed, Captain flew to approximately 100 yards of the small, yellow-colored craft. He tried to fly in what he knew to be the blind spot, behind the other plane and slightly to the right, where the Highway Patrol knows to hang when following an automobile. "Behind you and to the right, out of sight. I don't want to scare the shit out of you, pal, but I'm going in with you."

Whatever the other plane in front of him did, Captain tried to do. He refused to look at the ground, just the plane, stay with the plane. Total concentration. Together they slowed and dropped, slowed and dropped, until Captain's heart was pounding in his neck. His eyeballs felt dry and swollen from too much blood pressure. He clenched his teeth. Lighted buildings, the city of Santa Monica, came up around him.

Without being able to hear to make sure, it appeared that the plane in front touched down, bounced and was touching again. Captain felt as though they were both still going very fast and glanced to read eighty miles per hour air speed. "Shit," he blurted.

384

Captain's Cessna touched the concrete with a squeaking crunch of the tires. He slowed the engine and eased the wheel forward. "Lower away, baby—easy, but lower away."

The Cessna made a *boom boom* sound that chattered the plane's superstructure, but Captain clenched his jaw and eased the wheel forward. The next thing that he knew, he was down; both wheels were rolling and he was on the very, very hard, gray concrete runway, taxiing. "Goddamn," he shouted.

He taxied away from and off of the brightly lit runway, over into the shadows next to a row of tied-up light planes. He saw a place to park just ahead of him between two other similar, single-engine aircraft. With a roar he pulled ahead into the spot. "Just like a pro," he said, turning the engine off. "Just like a fucking pro." He let out a deep sigh and said, "Thank you, father."

When the safety harnesses were off, Captain sat very still. His ears were ringing and he began to giggle. He put his hands over his face. He sat in the darkness of the Cessna's creaking cockpit and cried out loud. "Shit," he sobbed. "I can't believe it. I just can't believe it. It's a hard one to believe."

A good deal of pain shot up from Captain's feet when he jumped down onto the cement runway. He stood there dancing on them for a moment to wake them, and after checking the best he could to make sure that the coast was clear, he ran for the end of the runway.

Captain not so easily scaled the cyclone fence that surrounded the airport, only to look back and see an automobile drive out through an open gate. "Stupid fucker," he said to himself.

Not exactly sure what to do, he walked north past Ocean Park and decided he'd take a chance on Sparrow's Reef, a close beer bar run by his friend Sparrow Cinzani, a known bookie, gambler and well-thought-of Santa Monica character. "She's always glad to see me."

385

The street was quiet. Not one vehicle passed him as he walked. The homes along the street were closed up, dark and looked cozy. The air was damp.

Finally the beer bar came into view. It was dark, but he took a chance. As usual, the back kitchen door was open, and he walked in to find four men dressed in paint clothes sitting laughing and talking with the bar maid while they sat huddled together at the bar. Sparrow was gone for the night, but a five-dollar tip to start bought Captain two iced brown bottles of Budweiser. The clock said 3:30. It was with an enormous amount of relief that he drank the two bottles of beer in rapid succession. After buying another round, Captain offered any one of the painters twenty dollars for a ride home.

The painters were all together in one truck and agreed to take him only if he would accompany them or wait in the truck when they stopped at the Kinchu Massage Parlor along the way.

Captain said, "Sure, either way," and paid them in advance after buying another round.

When he got inside the paint truck, which was a panel truck without windows in the rear, and when he lay back onto the painters' stiff canvas tarp, he moaned, smiled, belched beer and said, "Oh, Jesus, this is total comfort. You guys go get massaged; I'll wait right here."

When they stopped at the Kinchu on Olympic Boulevard, Captain stayed in the truck's dark rear compartment, drank beer and dozed. They startled him when they returned and made him chuckle all the way to the apartment when they compared the hand jobs that they had just gotten and argued about whose had been best.

It was ten minutes after four o'clock in the morning when Captain felt the driver make the last turn and the familiar hill roll out underneath them that led from Fountain Avenue to the front steps of his apartment building.

"Okay, friend, twenty bucks worth to the front door. How's about that for service?"

When the painters pulled away, Captain stood out in front of the building. He stretched and yawned and inhaled the damp morning air deep into his lungs. He thought that he could smell his garden and was anxious to play in it the next day. Boy, he thought, it's good to be home.

The Champion

Aset of headlights blinked quickly on and off from across the street and up the hill a bit. This was followed by another blink from a set of lights down the street below the building. Captain thought that he heard a radio or walkie-talkie squawk, and when his eyes became adjusted, he was sure that the first set of blinking headlights belonged to Pepper's unmarked police Plymouth. The headlights below him looked to come from a black and white police car.

"Oh, my," he sighed, as he moved quickly into the building. Stopping, he kept his foot in the front door when it closed to watch up the street.

Pepper came across the street with another plainclothesman. They held snub-nosed police specials in their hands. "Shit, that was fast," Captain said, trying to figure it. He thought for an instant about taking the elevator to the garage and going to his storeroom for a gun but didn't like the idea. Shoot one of those assholes, he thought, and end up in a corner against a SWAT team. There's no winning.

He thought about meeting them and talking, but they didn't look like they wanted to talk. Kill me and say I was trying to run, that's probably what would happen. And going to his apartment was out. "I'd be trapped."

He wondered if Pepper was coming on police business or if it was a pay back for Trench. Trench, he thought, it's a cinch. They're going to pay me back for Trench. "Time, I need some time. Get the hell out of here and let John handle it, that's the best idea. Get a good lawyer out in front of me. John will cut those boys a new asshole. There's no proof. Besides, if they don't get me now, they may never try again. I need time. Ruthie—That's it, Ruthie."

Sure, he thought, get your ass up to Ruthie's. Let her hide you until they go away. Running up the stairs, he thought, they'll think I went out the back way or climbed down from the roof. He ran quietly down the third floor hall to stand in front of Mrs. Pearlstein's door. Who'll question her? he asked himself. Nobody. She'll put on a good show, and that will be that.

Catching his breath, he pounded lightly on her door. He heard the front door of the apartment building open, and after a beat he heard the rear door. Those fuckers, he thought.

"Yes, who is it, please?" Mrs. Pearlstein asked from behind her door.

"It's me, Captain. Open up, hurry," he said in a harsh whisper.

Captain could hear muffled voices inside of her apartment, but no one touched the locks. He heard the front stairs creak.

"Goddamn it, Ruthie, open it or I'll come through it. Right now, by the count of three: One—two—"

The door unlocked and opened approximately two inches.

"What do you want?" Mrs. Pearlstein asked, not sounding herself.

Captain pushed at the door, and when she stepped back away from it, he let himself it and shut the door quietly behind himself. The apartment was completely dark and smelled of stale tobacco.

"Do not turn on the lights," Captain said softly.

"What do you want?" she asked in a frightened tone.

"What is it, Captain?" came Henry Aldrich's voice sternly.

"What the fuck difference does it make what I want? You guys are my friends, aren't you? I need a favor. I don't ask many."

"Don't ask us to go along with you, Captain," Henry Aldrich said, lighting a cigarette. The match showed him sitting on the side of the bed. Mrs. Pearlstein stood leaning against her desk, her hands folded into her crotch. She was dressed in a nightgown.

"I don't get it. Aren't we friends?" Captain asked sincerely.

"No, I should say not," she said, sounding disgusted.

"Be careful, Ruth. You don't know if he—" Henry's voice trailed off.

"If he what? If I what, Aldrich?" Captain asked in an angry tone, but inside he felt suddenly weak and exhausted.

"Will you please leave," Mrs. Pearlstein said.

Starting to speak, Captain heard his voice stammer. He wanted to figure it out but couldn't think. Henry Aldrich's cigarette glowed red. He lit another cigarette off of his and handed it to Mrs. Pearlstein. Embarrassed and confused, Captain shuffled around awkwardly in the dark. He said, "But—" and gestured out into the black room with both hands, "but—" He felt helpless and didn't know what to do with his hands, so he let them fall and hang at his sides. Then he felt angry.

"Why? Speak to me, Ruthie. Why all of this bullshit? What's wrong between us?"

Henry Aldrich said, "Look here—ah, Captain—"

"Shut up, Henry, I don't know you. And you wouldn't be here in her bed if it weren't for me. You'd still be here alone, Ruthie, pissing the sheets with worry. Ruthie, what the fuck—?"

Mrs. Pearlstein crossed the room. "We know about you." The glow from their cigarettes showed them sitting together on the side of the bed.

"Know about me? What about me?"

"About—" She spoke hesitantly. "About Mister Bloom. You're the one who did it to him."

Captain had to laugh. "Reno Bloom? Suppose that I did. That asshole was screwing people—old people, old poor people—out of their last money. And he got off behind it, Ruthie. He got his kicks being unjust. He was a bad person, Ruthie. Besides, who said I did it?"

"The police have been here asking questions and waiting around. You can't just kill someone for being dishonest. You can't just murder them in that terrible way." She began to sob and said, "You burned him."

Captain laughed and felt better talking about it. "But he burned you, didn't he? And, Ruthie, is there a crime worse than dishonesty? Why do you think our beautiful country is fucked?"

"But there are laws," Henry Aldrich said, scolding.

"Made by people to suit themselves. Was it against the law for Reno Bloom to sell defective merchandise to old folks and get rich? Is it against the law to fix our air and water so that it gives us cancer? Is it against the law to sell sugar to children or cigarettes to adults? Those cigarettes will kill you, you know, kill you. Is it against the law? Henry, you mean, is it against the dollar? Come on, you guys, God's laws are the only laws. And I don't mean the shit that Jesus or any man laid down, either. And besides, folks,

391

there's no proof that I did anything like that, no proof. They may want to talk to me, but they've done that before. Believe me, there is no proof that I—"

Captain was interrupted by a loud knock on the door.

"Police, Mrs. Pearlstein. Open up."

Captain felt his stomach sink. "Answer it Ruthie, but stick up for me. Smile and tell them you haven't seen me."

The door resounded again.

"Coming," she said.

When Mrs. Pearlstein crossed in front of Captain, he reached out and held her for a moment by the upper arm. He put the back of his hand softly against her cheek. "Remember, Ruthie—friends, they save our lives. I've cared. I've been your friend." Taking his hands away, he kissed her gently on the cheek and let her go.

Captain tiptoed across the small room and crouched at the far side of the bed, ready to crawl under if necessary.

Captain heard the apartment door open. The bright overhead light splashed on, and Captain listened to Mrs. Pearlstein's desperate voice. "He's here. He's in there, right in there." At the same moment the bed springs squeaked loudly, and the bed bounced as Henry Aldrich ran out into the hall to join them.

Henry said, "He's not armed. I didn't see a weapon."

Captain squeezed his eyelids shut in reaction to the terrible stomach pain that wracked him into a ball. He heard himself whine and then Pepper's voice: "Step aside. Step aside. He's in here, Bert. Bert, he's right in here. We got him."

In one powerful move, using all of his muscle, Captain sprang from where he sat curled and with his fists outstretched, dove through the middle section of Mrs. Pearlstein's apartment window. He heard gunshots behind him.

Falling through the blackness, Captain tried to get his feet

392

under himself and prepare for the concrete that he knew to be coming up. Cocksuckers, he thought. He thought that he heard music. The concrete was there fast. He hit with one foot, then the other, in an awkward way that broke at least one of the bones in his lower left leg with a loud, agonizing snap.

He went down in a heap and tried at once to get back up but couldn't. He crawled toward the end of the narrow alley. He heard rock and roll music and heard the commotion above him. Flashlight beams from overhead searched him out and found him. The damp early morning air echoed with the loud explosion of police specials. Slugs ripped and twanged off the concrete around him. A searing pain shot through his hip. He fell down but dragged himself back up to crawl. People from the surrounding apartments yelled and slammed around in rudely awakened panic. Police bullets ricocheted. Carly Simon sang "The Spy Who Loved Me." Captain dragged himself to the alley's end.

Two bicycles bearing newspaper sacks over the handlebars and a blaring portable radio sat parked into the mouth of the alley at the street. On his hands and knees, Captain pushed the closest bike over. The bicycle fell, spilling the newspapers onto the sidewalk and down into the garage. The radio on the other bike played on.

Captain shook the newspaper sack off of the downed bike's handlebars and crawled over next to it to put the corner of the building between himself and the gunfire. Using the bicycle for leverage, he forced himself to his feet. Pulling the bike up, he screamed out when he sat, but he managed to get onto it. The two paper boys came out of the building next door.

"Hey, man, that's my bike. Get off of my bike," yelled the biggest boy, sounding aggressive and capable.

Captain wanted to explain his predicament to the boy. He knew that the boy would understand. Any kid, he thought, who peddles papers at five o'clock in the morning has got to have something going, a strong character. Captain thought that he liked the outspoken newsboy, but there was nothing to say, no time.

Captain felt woozy but thought he said, "Sorry, man," to the kid before he pushed off with his good leg to coast down into the open dark street.

"Goddamnit, you turkey. He's stealing my bike," came from the newsboy behind him who could scream really loud.

Not quite to the corner, Captain could hear the police radios squawking and the police scrambling for the chase. The sound of rock and roll music seemed to be coming close, and Captain realized that the aggressive newsboy was chasing him too, on his friend's bike. He was yelling, "Stop, you turkey, stop," over a Peter Frampton hit record.

At the alley to his right, just before Santa Monica Boulevard, Captain turned the bicycle in, stopped it and let it fall. He went down with the bike and after recovering from the possibility that he might pass out from pain, managed to get up and drag himself into the well-lit alley.

Taking stock, feeling himself as he stumbled along and glancing, he said, "Jesus Christ, I'm soaked with blood. I'll bet that I'm hurt, really hurt."

It scared him, and he continued to struggle on halfway into the alley. His legs seemed to weigh a ton. A sensation of extreme nausea overcame him, and he stopped to throw up. After doing it once, he was able to contain the feeling with a deep breath. He thought that he tasted blood. He said, "Fuck," just as a pair of bright headlights swung onto him from the far end of the alley. The lights were accompanied by a loud roaring engine. "Garbage—garbage man," Captain said, trying to think.

Gritting his teeth from the pain, Captain struggled into the garbage alcove behind Chow Inn, a Chinese restaurant that he liked. It took all of the strength that he could muster to get into the large, green metal trash container in the restaurant's alcove.

He let the iron lid down and lay down into what he expected might be putrified food, but the container had a delicious smell about it. Like being in the Chow Inn's kitchen, he thought. He breathed the pleasant odor in deeply, and a tremendous pain shot through his chest, leaving him perfectly still, concentrating on hanging onto consciousness.

Then the lid came away and in came the alley's floodlights. A large, dark silhouette of a man stood above Captain holding the lid and peering in. The garbage truck roared outside.

"Hey, Cap, is that you? It's Hays, man. What are you doin'? Oh, man." His voice changed. "Oh, man. You—you're all covered with—"

"Get me out of here, Hays. I'm shot up bad. Scoop me up and toss me into your truck. Help me, friend."

Captain heard a police radio. The lid dropped with a loud crash. He heard the rock and roll radio. He heard voices in the alley. Hays was trying to send them away. Captain's heart was pounding. Then the garbage truck was closer. The engine roared. Captain felt the garbage receptable begin to move under him.

Hays yelled to answer someone. "No, man. Nope, I ain't seen a soul. Are you a cop? Yeah, well, no, sir, I ain't seen a soul."

Pepper was outside. He yelled to Hays to get out of there and to do it now, but Hays said, "Aw, man," in his falsetto voice and argued that this was his last stop of the morning. One more can and he could leave. Otherwise he'd have to come all the way back from Compton, and the residence run would get all messed up.

"One more can," he said, and the container began to move again.

Pepper yelled at the newsboy to get out of the area, and he said something else to Hays that Captain couldn't hear.

And then Pepper yelled, "Hold it. Hold it right there. Let me have a look in that thing. Hold it."

A cold chill came over Captain. He tried to dig into the garbage; he raked at the stuff. He screamed through clenched teeth and shook all over.

Lighting and fresh air entered the steel bin, and Captain saw the silhouette of Pepper's paunchy upper body.

Pepper yelled, "Holy shit," and dropped the lid. "Bert—Bert, come here. We got him. He's in here."

The next thing Captain knew, the metal lid was thrown back with a loud bang, and two men stood above him. He saw the black, shining pistols in their hands. Captain smiled and reached out to them.

Pepper fired first. It was that first gunshot that hurt the worst and made the iron can ring loudly to pain Captain's eardrums. He cried out and threw his hands over his ears. Hays was screaming, "Stop, stop, murderers. He ain't got no gun."

The pistols made bright picturesque flashes when they exploded. Captain was positive that he felt himself splash onto the cold metal walls that surrounded him. Pepper's cold voice echoed into the container, "Like shooting fish—"

The guns stopped when Officer Bert yelled, "No, get away from there. Get out of that car, mister. Jesus Christ, don't—"

There was a crazy blend of noise from outside of the iron canister. The rock and roll was there and the shouting, but Captain envisioned the pistons racing up and down in the garbage truck's engine. They produced a distant beat that sounded like his own heart throbbing hot, sticky and wet in his ears. His mouth tasted full of blood. He opened it and let it spill. The sounds from the outside came loud then soft with an echo.

"Look out, Bert. The nigger—the shotgun—No, out of the car—"

"Murder—rers—murder—rers," Hays's voice echoed.

Gunfire roared outside of the iron container, and Captain watched bullet holes appear in the wall of the garbage can in front of him.

"Get him. Get him. No, no—Christ, no. You shot the kid."

"Murder—rers. Murder—rers—"

The guns roared again for a long moment and then stopped. Jerry Lee Lewis sang "A Whole Lot of Shakin' Goin' On." The garbage truck screamed.

There was no feeling in his lower body. He tried his legs but couldn't move. Digging through the garbage to reach under himself, Captain moaned, "Oh, God, no," when his hand touched what felt to be his shattered backbone. "Oh, God," and all kinds of thoughts ran through his mind about athletics and sex and children and Iris.

There came a clawing sound against the outside of the garbage container. Hays's head finally appeared, then his shoulders, in silhouette. He stood there staring and began to sob. "They killed you, cocksucker pigs."

"I'm still here, Hays, my friend," Captain interrupted.

"You are? Oh, thank the Lord. How bad are you? They killed the kid, the news kid, blasting away. Pigs, Come on, we'll take you to my brother. You remember, the doc?"

"Shit, I'll be his first patient since he's out of stir, Hays. Can we trust him not to take all of my pain medicine himself?" Captain smiled but didn't dare laugh. He knew that Hays was grinning that toothless purple grin of his.

Hays said, "What do we give a shit? Let's go."

"No, Hays, I can't make it. How about the newsboy?"

"Dead. No help for him. Shot him right in the face, fucking pigs. Here, I'm coming in to get you out of there. We'll get you to my brother."

Captain watched Hays struggle to get himself into position to climb in. "Are you hurt?" Captain asked.

"Yeah. No, not bad. I'm shot in the ass, the fucking ass, but I'll come in. I've got to step on this fucking pig's face here to—Ooops, broke his fucking nose. I'm coming."

A feeling of joy came over Captain while he watched Hays go through the trouble to put himself out for him. Hays finally pulled himself over the metal side and fell into the garbage can with Captain.

"Oooh, shit, man, that smarts," Hays said, sweating profusely and smelling of body odor. He tried to adjust himself.

"What did you do out there?" Captain asked.

Hays snuggled in alongside Captain, getting himself into position to do some lifting. Hays's wet face reflected the light. "What did I do out there? I got ahold of that riot gun and had me a riot, hee hee. Fuck it, man—I mean, I've had it. They knew you didn't have no gun. Just blast away, chicken shit pigs. They shoot my people like that every day. Fucking country, it ain't right. It ain't right, I tell ya. Them that's got keeps on getting more. Me? I got nothing. Work hard all my time for what? To get my ass shot off helping my friend."

Hays laughed and said, "What the fuck are we doing sitting here? We must be nuts. Gotta get movin'. Here, man, let me get ahold of—Oh, fuck. Oh, fucking man alive—Oh—You're all shot to shit. Oh, man—No."

Hays began to cry. He put his big bearish paw and strong arm around Captain's shoulders. He held him tight and rocked him. Captain thought that Hays smelled good.

"Hays, get out of here. I can't make it."

"No way, man," he said indignantly. "You'd stay with me. I know you would, wouldn't you?"

"Yes," Captain said, admitting the truth.

"Are you hurting, Cap. God, you must be hurting."

"I can take it. Hays, say 'motherfucker' for me, like you do when you're with your people, like you say in Watts."

"Huh?"

"Motherfucker—like when you're with your black buddies and you're jiving, the secret way—"

Hays tried to laugh. "Ain't no secret way, Cap. Just mother-fucker, that's all, motherfucker."

"Motherfucker," Captain said. "Motherfucker. How's that?"

"Yeah, it's a motherfucker, all right, but come on, Cap, don't die on me. Don't fade. Who'll I drink with on those hot after-noons?"

"Hays, hand me a motherfucking egg roll."

Hays said, "Huh?" but then went scrounging around in the garbage. "Here, Cap. Here's a real good motherfucker."

Captain smelled it but couldn't taste. He tried to chew it, but his teeth felt broken. He swallowed it anyway. A sharp pain in his chest made him cry out, and Hays rocked him.

Outside, the alley lights clicked off, and the early morning sun was there. The garbage truck roared, and a new song began to play on the dead newsboy's bicycle radio. It was a pretty, mod-ern song that Captain liked:

"I've paid my dues
Time after time.
I've done my sentence
But committed no crime.
And bad mistakes,
I've made a few.
I've had my share of sand
Kicked in my face,
But I've come through.

399

We are the champions, my friends,
And we'll keep on fighting till the end.
We are the champions,
We are the champions.
No time for losers,
'Cause we are the champions of the world."

"God, that's a good one," Captain said, and Hays agreed.

"Want to hear a secret, Hays? Promise not to tell?"

"Sure, Cap, I promise."

"Iris is pregnant. I'm going to have a son, I think. No, I'm sure—It'll be a boy."

"Oh, that's swell, Cap. That's just swell."

"Yeah, I guess. They've got it cut out for them, don't they."

"Who, the kids?" Hays wanted to know.

"Yeah, the kids. I guess that they are the champions. This is their music, don't you think?"

"Yeah. They could be champs, but they don't seem to get it. They're fuck-ups. You're a champion, Captain."

"No, no I'm not. It's my son—It's the kids—But they've got such an impossible chore."

"Yeah."

"Yeah, bless them," Captain said.

And Hays said, "Yeah, bless them."

The hazy Los Angeles sun began to break over the lip of the garbage container. Captain thought about Iris some more and how beautiful she was going to look pregnant. He pictured her with her belly big, shiny and good smelling from cocoa butter, under the wonderful Montecito sun that he'd loved so much and that he knew now he would probably never see again.

The noises outside began to fade. The pain was gone, and somehow things seemed the way they should be. A long way away Hays was saying, "I think that you are the champion, Captain."

Then the most horrendous chill ever passed through him. Trying hard, he thought that he could manage a smile and said, "Thank you, Hays, for saying it. But, no, I'm not, I'm no champion. I'm just a—a motherfucker." He laughed lightly, and an awful pain came. Captain grabbed Hays's strong arm, and everything stopped.